THE KINGDOM WE KNOW

The Kingdom We Know

HALLE CLARK

IngramSpark

This book is dedicated to all of those who have guided me along the way. Thank you for your support and inspiration.

Map of the Continent

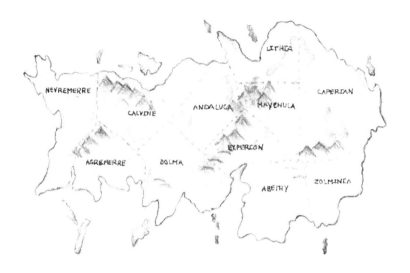

Map of Nevremerre

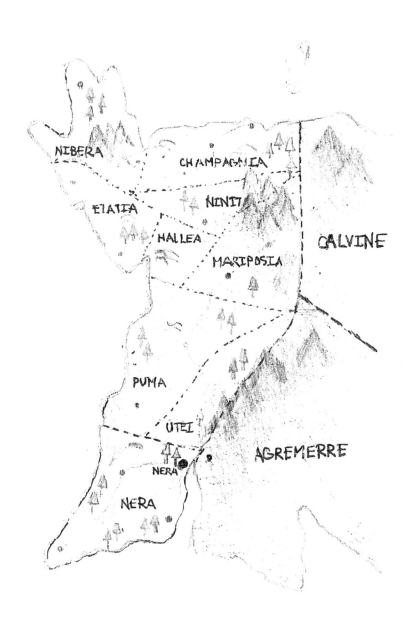

Nevremerre Royal Family

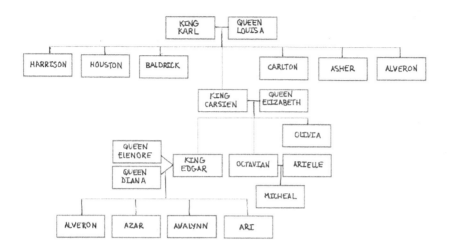

Contents

1

PART ONE

Chapter 1

The King's Gift

If you had to ask me where my story began, I'm not sure I could give you a specific time or date or even season because, the truth of the matter is, there isn't a single moment of my life that was unimportant to this story. Of course, writing down every moment in one's life would be rather difficult, so I've managed to narrow it down to a few key events. In that sense, I suppose we should begin at the beginning. I'm told it's a very good place to start.

I have no knowledge of when I was born. We have never celebrated my birthday, instead we celebrated my "found" day - the day my father declares the Gods gave him the ultimate gift. If you listen to him tell the story, he and his knights had been wandering along the grassy plains of Nevremerre, our kingdom, for days before they came upon a small stretch of beach along the western shore. Eager for some rest and a chance to play, they left their horses and armor and ran onto the sandy shores, racing to the ocean despite the early spring chill and the overcast sky that overcame them that day. On his way towards the crashing gray waves, my father spied a lone boat on the shore. Curious, my father approached the boat while everyone else kept pushing toward the sea. Inside the wooden vessel, Father found me, a tiny baby girl wrapped tightly in a blanket with only my olive toned face peeking out. I was fast asleep, and my father reached towards me. As soon as he touched me, my eyes opened and our emerald eyes met each other. Staring into my eyes, Father knew that I would be his daughter. He called out to his knights that he had been blessed by the Gods with another child and introduced me as Princess Avalynn of Nevremerre.

Of course, this whole story was entirely incorrect, as my mother pointed out at every retelling with a roll of her eyes and a slight smile. I was found in the boat by knight Yakobv while the King, my Father, was splashing around in the ocean with his knights. They spent two hours looking for any biological parents before the King declared I would be his daughter. Furthermore, the whole journey took less than one afternoon and not, as my father claimed, several days.

"It's not Kingly to lie to your subjects, Edgar," Mother would laugh.

"It's not a lie, Elenore! Just a more dramatic retelling!" Father would cry, his arms flailing in exaggerated offense.

"Well, if you want a dramatic story, it's far more interesting to tell the story of how Elenore and I discovered we had gained a daughter! I mean you were only out for a few hours! You claimed you were going out to check on the region, and then you came back with a child! At least three people fainted, and Nanny Lilian was screaming for two whole days that we didn't have enough baby clothes," Mama would butt in, her red hair flying in every direction as she grandiosely mimed every word.

Her dramatic response caused my brothers and me to burst out into fits of giggles.

"Diana!" Mother would exclaim, laughing at Mama, "Honestly, what am I to do with you both?"

"I'm afraid the only thing you can do is love us, my dear, as there is no known cure for a love of theatrics," Mama would say before giving Mother a kiss.

This scene was replayed every year on my found day with various levels of dramatization, much to the delight of my brothers and me. However, no matter what level of theatrics were involved, the end result was always the same: I was brought home as the third child of my father and his two wives, the Princess Avalynn.

My father was a jubilant and hard working man. Tall, broad, and very strong, he had short red hair and a scruffy beard that shook every time he laughed. He had light green eyes that could shine with either laughter or ferocity, depending upon what situation you encountered him. Nevremerre was a land of warriors and Father was a master of the sword. Arguably his greatest qualification, however, was his compassion. Father cared deeply about the people of Nevremerre, and the Nevremerre court was largely nomadic. According to Father, this allowed us to go wherever we were needed the most. As soon as we could walk, my brothers and I were brought into the tent that served as Father's office. Here, he would explain to us the problems of the people and the role and responsibility we had as leaders. We would sit in as he met with townsfolk, nomads, farmers, and all those who chose to call Nevremerre home. Once Father had spoken with the people, he would consult with his two Queens and the counsel to find solutions to the problems he had just heard. Father always reminded us that we had a duty to the people, to help them in any way we could and to allow our country to grow. This constant mantra meant that even in my earliest memories, I was aware I was a Princess.

Although we spent many hours as children with Father, learning what it meant to rule, at five years old we would start spending even more time with Mother. Mother was brilliant. She would often tell us that as a child, she was too frail to take up the sword, a bow, knives, or fight in hand-to-hand combat, but that did not mean that she was weak and defenseless. Mother had her mind, and with that, she said, she could fight anything. When she fell in love with Father at just 18, she began to focus more on military strategies. When she married Father at 24, she was the top general in the country. After she and Father met, and they subsequently fell in love with Mama, who is a skilled warrior, Mother switched her studies towards agricultural experimentation to improve our crops. This led to studies on weather, healing, textiles, economics, and a large variety of topics Mother thought would be both useful and interesting. As such, there was no better tutor for my brothers and me. We often found ourselves crowded by a plant or inside a factory or a shop aiding Mother in her experiments, as excitement practically radiated off of her midnight skin. Her dark eyes beaming with curiosity, her voice practically bubbling in the air, and her black hair was meticulously and painstakingly pulled back into a dark bun that would never dare to come undone.

In everything she did, Mother was the very picture of elegance and grace. She had a quiet voice that rang with authority. When Mother would speak at an event, the room would fall deathly silent, and that quiet voice would take over the whole space, resounding against the walls in a way that made it impossible not to hear. Everyone would be locked into the mesmerizing cadence of her words. In arguments, her voice would become sharper than any sword our knights brought into battle and twice as deadly. However, my favorite voice of hers was the one she saved just for us, the gentle hum as she sang us to sleep and the rumbling warmth of her chest as she whispered of her undying love for our family.

When we were seven, we would start training with Mama. She was slightly taller than Father and trained in all forms of combat. As children we learned the basics in all forms of fighting, but it wasn't long before we each began to specialize in one or two weapons. We would have specialists teach us in our chosen weapons, but Mama stuck with our fighting training throughout. She was a fighter through and through, and there weren't many who could best her in a sparring pit. However, outside of a fight, Mama was truly a gentle soul. She was loud, gave large, all consuming hugs, and could never manage to keep her red hair in place. On more than one occasion she declared she was done trying to tame her hair and chopped it all off with her sword. Eventually it would grow back out again, and the cycle would start once more. Her hands were rough from sword use, and her body was littered with scars that would take over her skin. Her muscles were tight and hard, and, somehow, her hugs felt softer and more comfortable than any bed I had ever laid on. She would pick us up and throw us in the air, and we would land back in her strong arms, safe and warm. Mama lived a life of passion, but her dark blue eyes sparkled brightest when it was just Mother, Father, and us children. Mama would do anything for our family.

When I was brought back to my mothers on my found day, I already had two older brothers. Alveron was the oldest at just four years old. He had black curly hair like Mother that he always kept short, but he looked to have obtained Father's broad stature, something that would only become more and more obvious over time. Just two years younger was Azar who, even as a child, was the spitting image of Father, just with sky-blue eyes instead of green. Five years after I came home, I got one final sibling. A younger brother called Ari, whose bright red hair and freckled face contrasted dramatically with the gentle, blue green that filled his eyes.

The final family member that traveled with us as we moved around the kingdom was Nana. She was my Father's mother, and, technically, the Dowager Queen, although the title was rarely spoken aloud. Nana never complained as we bounced from place to place, living in tents and providing aid to the people. Unlike my parents who aided Nevremerre in more labor intensive physical ways, Nana helped our people spiritually and emotionally. Nana said she could talk with the heavens and bring change and positive energy into any person, place, or thing. For some, Nana's presence in a place was more revered than even my father's. She had short white hair, and a thin body frame that seemed to float from place to place as she moved. Her voice, however, was grounded and strong, pulling you back down to the Earth, as she connected your energy towards the heavens. With Nana, my family felt complete, and my story was ready to begin.

Chapter 2

The Crown's Competition

Alveron's laughter shook the trees as he sat on the branches above us. "You're never going to catch me," he squealed, climbing higher up the branches, "I'll be king of the world."

"Nuh uh," cried Azar as he scrambled up the tree, his face furrowed in concentration, the harsh lines of his skin only deepening with every shout of laughter from above.

Azar's frustrations, however, were not nearly as great as my own. No matter how high I jumped, no matter how much I ran, I couldn't even get close to the very first branch. At five years old I was still remarkably small next to my two older brothers, and was dwarfed completely by my parents. Tears of frustration welled up in my eyes. And a white hot rage flared through my body. Why couldn't I climb the tree?! If I could just get started I knew I could get as high as Alveron and go faster than both my brothers, but the stupid tree wasn't even letting me up to the first branch. I screamed all my frustrations out, banging my fists into the bark. "Stupid tree! Just let me climb! I want to climb," I yelled, tears spilling down my cheeks.

"Ava, Ava don't cry," said Al poking his head down from the branches above.

"I want to climb the tree," I wailed, still pounding my fists into the bark despite the radiating pain that was creeping into my palms. I couldn't stop, a point needed to be made, and my fists seemed the only way to make it. I thought as I continued my assault of the tree. I just needed to climb it. I just needed to make it up to that first branch.

"Al, I am going to beat you!" screamed Azar from somewhere above.

"Not now, dummy. Ava's crying. We can't compete when Ava's crying, so it doesn't count!" responded Al.

"Well stop crying then!" Azar called down, glaring at me through the branches.

"No!" I yelled back with a white hot fire fueled by my frustration and the pain in my palms pushing me forward, "I want to climb too! It's no fair if I can't climb too!"

"I think you'll find, little miss, that none of you should be climbing that old tree," a cool voice said from behind me. Whipping around, I found myself gaping at the image of my Nana, wily smiling at the three of us.

"But Nana," Azar called out, already scurrying down the branches, "Al said whoever got to the top of the tree would be King, and I was going to win!"

"No you weren't! I told you it doesn't count because Ava was crying," Al responded indignantly.

"No! It doesn't count because I couldn't even get in the tree, so it's not fair!" I cried, tears filling my eyes once more.

"Now, now little one," Nana said, cradling me in her arms. "We will have none of that, and Azar, no matter what your brother says, the next ruler of our country will not be determined by who climbs a tree faster. The next ruler will be decided by the council and the current King and Queens, your parents, based on who they feel will best lead the country into more times of peace and prosperity. The official decision will happen the day after your youngest sibling's 21st birthday, unless we go to war or your Father gets an untimely illness. Since Ari is not even six months old, there is still a very long time before anyone gets selected to be the next ruler."

"But then I will have no hope!" yelled Azar. "Al is ahead of me in school and is already specializing in the sword! He has a two year advantage! How will I ever catch up?"

"Just accept it Azar. I'm always going to win," replied Al with a smug smile.

"No! You -"

"Enough of that!" Injected Nana as Azar squatted, poised to jump on Al. "Little lion," Nana called out to Azar, "The reason that the selection doesn't take place until the youngest child is 21 is so that everyone has the opportunity to finish their education as well as have the opportunity to decide if they would like to take themselves out of consideration for the throne."

"Who wouldn't want to be King?" Azar questioned.

Nana just laughed, "Quite a lot of people, actually. It is a very complex and challenging job. Your Aunt Olivia, for example, took herself out as a potential ruler and declared she wanted to run a bakery. Now she owns quite a wonderful cake shop, and the cupcakes she makes are just to die for. Ruling is just not some people's passion. That's why at 21 any Prince or Princess can remove themselves from consideration for the throne. Generally, the council does accept it when a Prince or Princess removes themselves from ruling consideration. Although, nearly 150 years ago your great-great-great-grandmother Estelle took herself out of the running for Queen, but the people and council believed that she would be such a strong leader that they begged her to become Queen anyways. She did, eventually, accept the role, and her reign was a time of great prosperity. Living your passion is the most important thing after all, and you kids can have any career you desire."

"Well, I don't care about those other careers! I want to be King!" declared Azar, confidently, "I am going to be the King and a hero, and ride around saving people and being praised wherever I go!"

"That only happens in your dreams, Azar. You'll never beat me," responded Al.

"I will! I will beat you Alveron, and I will never let you be King! Absolutely never!" Azar said definitively before turning his back on Al and racing back to the campsite.

"Get back here! I'll make you accept me! I will be King!" Al chased after him through the grass.

I sat back with Nana. I had never seen Al and Azar so mad as I listened to their shrieks fade into the distance. To my surprise, however, Nana just laughed. Interpreting my curious gaze, she explained, "I remember a very similar fight between your father and your Uncle Octavian when they were about this age. Octavian swore he would become stronger than your father and be the next King. Your father said that he was the oldest and would be guaranteed to win. Now look at them," Nana laughed, "your uncle is Edgar's most loyal supporter. Something similar will happen here, just you wait and see, little one."

"So does that mean Al will be King just like Father?" I questioned.

"Now that I don't know. Besides, they are not the only candidates! You or your younger brother both have the potential to become the ruler and lead us all one day! What do you say to that, my dear?" Nana asked as she stood up and took my hand, "Would you like to be Queen?"

I thought upon her question for a moment, as we made our way back to camp, a crisp autumn breeze swaying the tall grasses. "No," I decided. "I want to climb that tree and sing and fly with the birds!"

Nana let out a roaring laugh that bounced along the wind, carrying her voice through the meadow towards the pale blue sky. "Then fly you shall, my little songbird, for I am convinced there's nothing that you can not do."

Despite Nana's assurances that Al and Azar would get along, they seemed to fight worse than they ever had before. They raced to be the smartest, the fastest, the tallest, the best fighter, the one to hand out the most blankets in the winter, the one to plant the most seeds in the spring, the one to pick the most crops in the fall, any and every task was a competition for the crown. Before I knew it, six years had passed and Ari and I were struggling just to keep up.

But, all that was their fight, I had my own goals to accomplish and challenges to overcome. My challenge stood perched before me, a sword in her hand, ferocity in her eyes, and red hair flying every direction.

"Again," Mama called, "you are small, but strong Ava. Do whatever you have to in order to get an advantage." I retrieved my own sword. When I first started weapons training, defeating anyone seemed nearly impossible. I was shorter than most of the other children, and my endurance was practically nonexistent. Although we were trained to use a variety of weapons, no one believed I would fight well with any of them. I could see the apprehension in their eyes each time I reached for a weapon. My brothers were too wrapped up in their own war to pay any attention to my struggle.

"Just give up," Azar told me, rather unhelpfully, the first time I asked for his advice. Al informed me that I didn't need to be good at fighting to help our country. "Just look at Mother, she doesn't fight, but we'd all be lost without her." This was kinder than Azar's response, but as someone who was still looking to fight, it was just as unhelpful. They both couldn't understand why I was so desperate to be a good fighter. Why I would try so hard to do something I simply wasn't made for, or why I would choose the weapon I did. I could, perhaps, have better luck as an archer, but I couldn't shake the looks I received every time I went to grab a sword. It was a look of sympathy, pity, and/or disapproval that I would even decide to try to fight with a weapon dominated by the tall and strong. Those eyes fuel me. I couldn't stop training with the sword because I just had to prove all those eyes wrong.

It was Nana who gave me my solution. About a year after I began my weapons training, she came across me throwing my sword onto the short grasses of an empty field. I was yelling at the inanimate object to do better, strike faster, and to work for me! It was she who gave me the advice I so desperately needed. "You are not as tall, you are not as physically strong, and you lack the natural abilities of those who fight here," she told me her deep voice and white hair rustling on the back of a gentle breeze, "but, that does not mean you cannot fight and it certainly doesn't mean you cannot win. You are not like those here, so you cannot fight the way they can. However, you are quick, energetic, and smart my little songbird. Do not fight like something you are not, instead you must create your own style in battle. You must fight your own way." With Nana's words, we worked to create my own brand of sword fighting. We trained and researched our way through. And, five years later, I was close to wiping the doubt off of everyone's face.

"Come on Ava. Let's show them what you've got," Mama smiled briefly as the crowd grew around us. With those final words of encouragement, she swung her sword and brought it crashing down against my own. I pulled back, moving to the side as she attempted to battle me once more. I learned over the years that each failed swing of my opponents cost them more energy than if I met their strikes head on. With this in mind, I twisted and twirled around Mama's heavy blows looking for a weakness I could exploit. Mama, however, was no novice, and soon her sword was inescapable.

Forced into a head on battle I reverted to my next tactic: causing her to fall. It wasn't long into my training that I realized that, being much smaller, I was far more mobile and less likely to be hurt after a fall than my larger opponents. By tripping or forcing an overbalanced foe to the ground, I could easily gain the upper hand. To do this, I needed to counter the weight Mama threw into one of her swings, and then quickly move away. Hopefully resulting in Mama falling forward. With heavy effort, I threw myself into my next swing, connecting with Mama's sword then dropping to the ground. Mama's face of concentration flashed quickly into one of surprise as I moved away. However, ever the warrior, her moment of imbalance turned into a rather neat roll, and she was far too quickly back into a fighting stance. It was not much longer after that when I found myself flat on my back with a sword at my throat.

My breathing heavy and my mind furiously trying to come up with a new strategy to win, I almost didn't hear the clapping behind me. When I did, I quickly rose to find the smiling face of my father behind me. "Well done Avalynn! Even some of my knights can't stay up longer than a minute fighting Diana. And, here you lasted nearly five! We will make a warrior out of you yet my darling girl." Father beamed as he scooped me up into a large hug. I squeezed him tightly, looking around at the impressed faces of Father's knights. I had done it! I had accomplished my goal! The knights could no longer doubt my ability, and my heart soared at this victory. A large smile took over my face as I laughed into Father's hug. I continued to gaze triumphantly at the awed faces of the knights. However, my elation was brought sharply to a halt as I caught the eyes of my brothers. Al and Azar's faces were twisted into frowns, and Azar was even openly glaring at me from across the designated training pitch. It was then when I realized the unintended con-sequences of accomplishing my goal. By proving myself a warrior I was now just as viable a candidate for the crown as my two older brothers. Like it or not, I was now actively their competition.

Chapter 3

The Job of the King

I was in the weapons tent cleaning my sword when my brothers found me. Azar came barreling up to me first. At just thirteen, he towered over me. His broad shoulders shadowed me from the yellow light surrounding the tent.

"You're not better than me," he claimed.

I was taken aback by his confusing statement. "What?" I replied, "I mean you are bigger than me, but you specialize with the mace and the hammer. It's been years since you've picked up a sword. I think, at the very least, it would be a good match." I was trying my best to be objective, but I was feeling deeply offended that he had already decided he could best me, especially when I had just proven that I was a talented fighter! "Plus, the hammer uses completely different moves. I think I could beat you in a sword fight." I pushed on in a further attempt to defend my fighting skills.

"No Ava," Azar sighed, aggressively slamming his palm onto his head, "I mean you're not better than me overall, so you won't be chosen as Queen."

"Being King or Queen doesn't mean you are the best overall, it just means you're the best suited for being the ruler of Nevremerre," Al piped up from his place at the opening of the tent.

"Whatever, the point is I am going to be the best, so I will be King!" exclaimed Azar, who promptly turned and stormed out of the tent.

Al sighed as he watched Azar's departure, "When will that kid ever learn?" he mumbled. Turning towards me he smiled. "You did a good job today Ava. I am very impressed with how far you've come. Mama, Mother, and Father must be proud of you too." I smiled, feeling the joy of my success once more. Al pulled up a stool and sat by my side. He was broad like Father, but his presence was soft and calm compared to Azar's earlier temper. He gently took my sword and polish and placed them on a nearby table. Then he took my hands. "Avalynn," he said, his obsidian eyes boring into mine, "Abdicate the throne."

"What?" I recoiled, snatching my hands back from his dark calloused palms, "Why would I do that?"

"I know you can't do it now, but when you turn twenty-one, you must abdicate," Al continued just as calmly.

"I don't understand. Why would I do that? Why are you asking me? Do - Do you think I am not good enough?" My eyes welled up as I fought against tears. Unlike Azar, whose aggressive and loud personality never stopped him from fighting with me, Al had always been kind to me. He encouraged me with my studies, broke up fights between Azar and I, and would always help dry my tears whenever he could see them. I could not understand what I had done to make him think so little of me. Despite my best efforts, I could not stop the few tears that rolled down my cheeks.

"No, Ava!" Jumped Al, panic showing in his voice and shining in his eyes. He quickly stood up and pulled me into his arms, knocking down the stool he was sitting on in the process. "Of course I don't think that! The reason I am telling you this is because I think you are capable. Azar's temper will rule him out as a good candidate for King, he is a dedicated fighter, and our little "competition" has pushed him forward in his academic studies, but he's quick to anger and often acts rashly. These are not the traits of a good King, but you, Ava, are compassionate and wise beyond your years. Probably because you spend all your time with Nana," he added almost as an afterthought. Al paused a moment as if in thought, and then continued. "You've done well in our classes with Mother, and, now that you've proven your combat proficiency, you have all the makings of a great Queen."

"So why are you asking me to abdicate," I replied angrily, still feeling hurt and growing more and more confused. "Is it because I am your competition? Am I your enemy now?" I felt rage boil into my heart at the thought. So much for compassionate and wise, I thought as I tried to push myself out of his hug.

"No!" Al cried, still holding me against his chest, "Just sit still Ava, please. I'm - I'm not explaining this right," he gave an exasperated sigh, and, as I wiggled my way to look up at his face, I saw a deep sadness permeating through his dark eyes. My anger washed away as quickly as it came, but a bitter wariness still clung to my heart. I just couldn't think of any other reasons for him to ask me to abdicate. I couldn't understand why he was asking this of me.

"Alright, please explain it better then." I said as I stopped my struggle against him.

"Okay," Al replied, loosening his grip on me even more. A moment of relief passed through his eyes, "Ava, you've got to understand, being King is terrible."

"Okay..." I replied, blinking in confusion.

"Once you're King your life is no longer your own anymore. Everything you do must be done for the betterment of your people. There are no breaks, no down time, just constantly working for others. What kind of a life is that?" Al responded, his ferocity increasing with each word.

"Father does it," I said, despite his impassioned response I was still deeply confused by the direction this conversation had taken. A King worked for his people. This was an obvious fact. We had been told and shown this nearly everyday of our lives. How could Al think I would not know this?

"Yes. Father took on the burden of being King to help his siblings as well. Plus he has Mother and Mama to help him af-ter Grandpa died. But, don't you see Ava, being King or Queen takes over your life. You won't get to live your passion, and even your spouse or spouses must work for the good of the realm."

"But what if your passion was helping the realm? What if being the King or Queen made you happy?"

"Is ruling your passion Ava?"

I thought about Al's question for a moment. Was ruling my passion? I didn't know. I'd never actually tried ruling. I was only eleven after all, no one was asking me to make policy decisions for my kingdom. "I don't know," I finally replied.

"It won't be," Al said confidently. "Of course, you can enjoy helping people, but helping them at the expense of your own health, passion, and desires all the time is exhausting work. The people who say they would love to be king are people who either do not know what they are talking about or intend to use the power of the king for only themselves. I want you and Azar and Ari to live a life you can enjoy. I don't want you to have to take on this burden, so abdicate. Live your passion doing something else. Let me take care of all of you."

"Al, being King isn't your passion though. If you think being King is a burden, you shouldn't have to do it either," I said, covering the hand he had resting on my shoulder with my own.

"Someone has to, Ava. Let me be the one who helps all of you."

"I -" I didn't know what to do. How could I let Al take a job he clearly would not enjoy? Could I really be Queen in his place? I had never given much thought to being Queen. It was strange really, but even though I knew I was a Princess, and technically had a chance to be on the throne, it always seemed like Al or Azar's race. As such, I knew only the parts of ruling I'd watched my father do. There was a lot of sacrifice. Father had spent hours poring over reports of the land, then he would spend even longer listening to the problems of the people. While some of these were petty complaints over minor disagreements, sometimes there would be people coming to court with tragic tales of losing everything. For these people, Father was their only hope. Father was also responsible for training his knights, meeting with the council (although none of us were allowed to be present during council meetings, so I still didn't know what really happened there), and, on several occasions, Father was called on to race out in the middle of the night to deal with some urgent problem in various regions of the country. On those nights, we knew that the whole court would spend the next day preparing to move to wherever Father had raced off to.

Al was right, it was not an easy job, but Father had always looked happy to me. Perhaps Al was wrong about it being a job no one could love. The real question was could I love it? Would it be better to do as Al said, to move on and find some other passion? At the very least, I was pretty sure I could love the job more than Al, but I suddenly found myself feeling very unsure. "I will think about it," I replied at last. Yes, I nodded to myself. This was the best plan. I could get more information, and come back with a better and more prepared answer.

Al frowned at my response, but did finally release me from his grasp. "Alright, Avalynn. Just don't keep me waiting too long," with that Al stood up and walked towards the tent flap, leaving me standing on the dirt floor next to two fallen stools and a mind full of questions I had never thought to ask.

What do you do when the direction of your whole life just completely shifts? Perhaps that question is a little too dramatic, especially when considering the events that occur later in my life, but, for eleven year-old me, this was huge! It sounds silly now, after all I was one of the King's children. My name had been down on the list of potential rulers since my found day, and I knew I was a Princess. My Father had instilled in all of us the responsibility we had to care for the people, but despite all of that, my child's brain had never even considered that I would become Queen. I had no desire to enter in the kicking match that was Al and Azar's race to the throne. Especially not when it so often led to one or both of them being broken or bruised. I had always just assumed that either Al or Azar would be King, and Ari and I would end up somewhere in the court, supporting them in whatever way we could. And yet, here I was being told by someone I loved and respected, someone I admired and looked up to that I not only was in the race, I had somehow become the greatest competition. Simultaneously, I was being told that the grand prize in this competition was being trapped in an ornate, but painful cage for the rest of my life. It didn't matter that this was knowledge I should have already had, my eleven year old world was shattering.

I am lucky, I suppose, to have had my Mother as a tutor. Without her classes and warnings that we should never listen to just one source when debating a topic, I probably would have just taken Al's word on what being King was really like. Instead, I sought out the only primary source I knew to ease my troubled thoughts. I walked down to Father's office. A light breeze blew through my hair as I passed the rows of tents, the colorful flags representing the hopes and dreams of Nevremerre fluttering in the air. Father's office was a tent right in the center of our camp, next to the large red tent used for council meetings. I walked towards the slightly smaller blue tent where Lauren and Meano stood guard.

"Afternoon, Princess!" called Lauren, "Your Father's free, so you can go right on in." I thanked her and pushed aside the entrance. Father sat on a wooden chair behind a large oak table. Papers were scattered all over the desk, and his quill was dangling between his teeth. Books lay haphazardly strewn across a shorter table near the tent's entrance with blue cushions on either side of the table for more comfortable seating.

"Avalynn, my gift, you're just what I needed," Father called when he saw me. The chewed on quill falling from his lips as he bustled towards me, picking me up in the air and bringing me back to his chair. I leaned into his large chest and breathed in the smell of ink and sword polish that cloaked him.

"Hello, Father," I sighed into his chest.

"How can I help my favorite daughter today?"

"Father, I'm your only daughter," I laughed, sinking further into his arms. Father's laugh rippled through his chest and bounced my head as I laid against it.

"That's how we can be sure you are my favorite, my gift." Father said, his chest expanding with pride. "I saw your work today in training. You're an excellent swordswoman! I know how hard you must have worked to move like you did. I couldn't be prouder, Ava."

"Thank you, Father," I smiled.

"Now tell me, my gift, what brings you here on this wonderful afternoon?" I sighed recalling the events that led me to his office. Pushing myself out of his embrace I moved to jump on top of his desk carefully brushing the documents out of my way. I'd learned early on that ink from Father's papers would quite easily stain the dresses or trousers I wore. Looking back at my Father's emerald eyes I asked my question.

"Father, does being King make you happy?" Father's eyes widened slightly, but he gave no other indications of being shocked by my question. He stared at me for a moment before letting out a large sigh. The bright twinkle in his eyes just moments before faded, making his eyes appear more grassy than emerald.

"I won't ask what brought this on. I imagine Alveron and Azar spoke with you after your fight today. It's true that your performance this morning demonstrates what many have already suspected, you have the potential to be an excellent Queen. You-"

"Wait, 'already suspected'? People were looking at me to be Queen before the fight?" I exclaimed.

Father gave a small chuckle. "Mhm, yes they were. Although it might be wise to learn to stop interrupting people if you decide you want the crown." My face grew hot as I tried to push my embarrassment down. "Although your brothers have yet to believe me when I say it," Father continued, "Nevremerre does not require its rulers to master any weapons. A knowledge of war and weaponry, yes, but practical knowledge is not required. You have always worked hard in your studies, both academic and physical. Your dedication and willingness to try are far more important skills than winning a sword fight. Although, becoming more adept at the sword does better your chances."

"Because I can now fight for Nevremerre," I nodded.

Father laughed once more, "No, my gift, because it shows you are able to overcome obstacles in your path with new and creative solutions. You were shorter and weaker than all the others, but you found a way to use that to your advantage. If you become Queen, you will face many obstacles, the ability to adapt and overcome them is crucial. But, my gift," Father said, holding my face in his large calloused hand and bringing his eyes to mine, "know this, you do not have to be Queen if you do not want to. Life is all about choice. Just because you potentially could be a good Queen does not mean you have to take the position."

"But somebody has to," I indignantly replied, recalling Al's words from earlier.

"Yes, but it does not have to be you, if you don't want to. In fact, none of my kids have to be the ruler. If you all chose not to lead the council I would just pick someone else, maybe your cousin Micheal, maybe someone entirely unrelated to us. The point is, whoever rules will rule because they choose to, and because the people choose not to overthrow them."

"Alright," I replied, feeling oddly more secure in my new position, "but you never answered my question Father. Are you happy being King?"

Father paused for a moment, his hand leaving my face as he studied my expression. Finally, he sat back and replied, "I will not lie to you Avalynn, being King is not an easy job. I am responsible for the lives and well being of nearly two million people, or so says our latest census reports," he said gesturing to the table I was currently sitting on. "I must make sure every citizen has food, clean water, and shelter when they need it, and some years our resources can't support our population. If we go to war, it's my job to lead our troops into battle, and, at times, it has been my job to order knights on dangerous missions. Each person that does not come home from those missions, each soldier that draws their last breath in an attack, and for every civilian that starves, freezes, or dehydrates because I could not provide them with the supplies they need to survive, is another death on my conscience. A death that I must take the responsibility for because it was decisions I made that led to their demise. The choices I make affect more than just me. I have been King for 16 years. There have been many deaths on my hands. The only way for me to keep going is to constantly learn and grow from my mistakes. I must do my best to ensure they never happen again.

I have to constantly listen to the problems of the people and take them on as my own, for the problems of the people are the problems of their King. It's emotionally draining. I have had to place my people equal to and sometimes above my own family, and often above my own desires. Did you know you almost had another Father? Your Mother and I met him a few months after our marriage. He was a cake designer at a local bakery. Your Mother and I were completely smitten. He was handsome, charming, and made a wonderful sheet cake, but one day we came over to the bakery to surprise him. As we approached the back door of the bakery, we found him talking with someone else about us. He was telling a coworker that his plan was to get close to us going well, and that soon he would have all the power and wealth of a Prince of Nevremerre. Your Mother, smart as she is, was shocked by his words, but I was all too aware of what was going on. We've kept you kids relatively isolated from those who would try and con you. This is partially just a by-product of us moving around so often, but your mothers and I have made a concerted effort to travel with a council and court of people who we know we can trust. However, even we know that we can not protect you indefinitely. As a Princess, you will meet people who want to control you for your power. This only gets worse as a King. I have missed Azar's birth, Ari's first steps, your 2nd and 8th found day celebrations, and Al's 10th and 12th birthdays because of crises related to this country.

Being King requires sacrifice, hard decisions, and brings a lot of pain, and yet, I would not have any other career." I stared at him in shock. He had just described a life of grief and suffering. How could he still want his job? "For me, there is no greater joy than seeing my people, my family, and this land thrive. It is my greatest privilege to lead this country to prosperity. I would not trade that privilege for the world.

However, my gift," Father said smiling at me, "this is not a problem or a decision you have to face now. You are all just children for heaven's sake! You still have 15 more years before the crown selection begins, and, trust me, a lot can change as people grow up. Now have I answered your question to your satisfaction?"

"Yes, Father."

"Then off you trot. The kingdom won't run itself," smiled Father as he lifted me up off the desk giving me a small wink. "I love you Avalynn."

"I love you too, Father!" I said throwing my arms around him before running out of the tent.

Chapter 4

The Quest to Be Queen

I kept running as I left Father's Office, past the tents of the court, past the designated training grounds, and past the edge of our campsite. I kept running until I hit the edge of the forest that bordered the town we were staying in. Heading towards the nearest tree I began to climb going from branch to branch, as if by going higher I could fly away from all that I had learned. Despite what my Father said, I knew my choice was more urgent than just 15 years. Al would not wait for long for an answer, he would continue to push himself to be the King. If I did nothing I was sure to be left behind, so, if I did nothing, by the time I would need to make a decision, Al would be so far ahead I would have no chance of catching up. Al had not been wrong when he said being King was a struggle, Father had confirmed that and more. Yet, Father said he loved his job, and it satisfied him. Could I live a life like my father? Could I be King like him?

"Have you learned to fly yet, my little Songbird?"

"Nana!" I peered down through the branches trying to spot her, "How did you find me? I can't even see you!"

Nana's breathy laugh filtered through the branches, "I could see your energy swirling from half a mile away! Unless you've already learned how to fly, come down here so I can help ground you back to Earth."

"Yes Nana," I smiled as I lowered myself down the branches. As I dropped further down the tree, Nana slowly came into sight. Moving onto the lower branches I pushed myself out of the tree, rolling rather clumsily out of my leap to the ground below. "I'm getting better at flying now, Nana." I laughed as I brushed the dirt off my clothes.

"Yes, you have, my Songbird. I have no doubt you'll soon be soaring through the skies," Nana cooed as she brushed the dirt off my back, " You should be more careful in your practice though. You've got a couple of scrapes right here" she said pressing her finger along my lower back. "I've got some water here to clean it up for you, as I do, perhaps you'll tell me what's got your energy spinning so fast. What's got you so scared, my Songbird?"

I sighed playing with the end of my braids, "It's this whole business of becoming Queen. I know it's silly, but I've just realized I'm part of the competition, and Al wants me to abdicate because he says it's a horrible job, and Father says it's - AHH" I jumped feeling the wet cloth against my back, "- Father says it's a difficult job and a burden, but you can love it. And, I know I should be deciding whether I want to be Queen now in order to have a chance of beating Al, And, I just don't know what to do about it all." I said feeling the tears building up behind my eyes once more.

"Oh, is that all," replied Nana nonchalantly.

"What do you mean "is that all"?!" I cried spinning around to face her. Her short white hair lay flat on her head and her blue eyes sparkled serenely as she folded the damp cloth and placed it back in her bag.

"Come sit with me, Songbird," she called, planting herself against the tree and spreading her legs so I could crawl right into her open arms. I leaned with my back against her chest, and she wrapped her arms and red shawl around me. "What have I told you, Songbird," her voice chimed in my ear, the smell of sage and lavender washing over me, "you cannot live the life of others and you cannot fight your battles like they do. Edgar is a great King, but he blames himself for more than he should. He forgets that people make their own choices, and he cannot be blamed for all the choices they make. Those who rule do accept a lot of responsibility, but they are never solely responsible for all the kingdom's weaknesses nor all the kingdom's strengths. Furthermore, ruling a country has always been a task that can bring someone great joy and that they can love. Edgar is not the only person who can love ruling. You have no experience ruling, so you cannot be expected to know whether you enjoy it. Now, ignoring all Edgar and Alveron said about ruling, you must ask yourself if you think you'd want to be Queen."

"Yes. Yes I do," I responded after a long pause.

"Why?"

"Because I enjoy helping people, and I want to be in a position where I can do that more effectively."

I could feel Nana smile behind me, "Then why, Songbird, are you letting other people's thoughts, perceptions, and opinions get in your way? You will never be able to rule in an identical manner to your father, even if you tried. Your perception of being Queen will always be different from his. If you think you could be happy being Queen, why are you letting Alveron's opinion on who should lead or thoughts on what being King means trouble you?"

"I... I guess I thought they mattered."

"In questions about your life and your future, it is only your opinion that matters." As she spoke my heart settled and the new weight I had started to carry lifted from my shoulders. Nana was right, this was my life, and I wanted to live it my way.

"Good--now breathe for me. Big deep breaths, in and out. Most any sort of problem can be solved with a few deep breaths." said Nana as I felt the air fill up my lungs, and I pushed it back out again. I lay there breathing, I felt more relaxed than I've ever been. "That's better, but remember you don't have to be Queen to help people. I don't know what will happen in the future, but, Queen or not, I know you will have the ability to live a happy and fulfilling life. Now my little Songbird, let your Nana hear that lovely voice of yours."

I opened my mouth and I sang. I sang a song of love and contentment as I was wrapped in my Nana's arms, and we watched the sky turn into a burning orange. I sang for her as orange turned to streaks of pink, and I sang until inky black cascaded over where the sun had just shown. As the first twinkles of starlight graced the sky and as my song came to a close, I embraced the knowledge that, whatever may come, as long as

I could still see the sunset or even just feel the vibrations of a melody, everything would be alright.

Nana and I walked back to Camp hand-in-hand. The night air taking on an ever-growing chill as the half moon leapt higher into the sky. It was in the dim stream of moonlight where I spotted Al, already in his night clothes, leaning on a barrel of water. I bade Nana goodnight and cautiously approached him. I stopped about a foot away from him. His hands gripping the water barrel tightened, the only signal he acknowledged my presence. The rest of his body was still, his head down staring at his reflection below.

"I won't abdicate, Al," my voice was quiet but sure. "I want to do my best, to learn as much as possible in weaponry and war, as well as in governing. I want to help people, and, if my actions make me Queen, I will not regret the steps that I've taken." Al sighed bringing his hand up to his head he rubbed his eyes. He breathed in once more and dropped his hand back to the barrel.

"You don't know what you're taking on," Al said, his head determinedly looking down at the water.

"Neither do you," I determinedly pressed on, my hand gesturing in his direction, "No one can truly know what ruling is like until we are given that position, if we are given that position."

There was a long silence between us, the rustling of leaves and the noises of those knights and courtiers working late were muffled by the distance. "Perhaps you're right," Al finally responded, "but, I won't just watch you give up your life on such an uncertainty."

"Does that make me your enemy now?" I quietly asked. For the first time since this conversation started, I felt uncertain.

Al's head snapped up, "No, you will never be my enemy," Al said walking towards me. He put a hand on my shoulder, looking down at me. Then I watched his posture stiffen as his eyes moved from my face to behind me, "but now you are my competition." Once again Al walked off. This time, however, I was not left behind questioning and uncertain. I knew what I wanted to do, and I knew, whatever the outcome, I would thrive. With one more deep breath, I, too, walked back to my tent ready for what was to come next, at least, so I thought.

Chapter 5

The Palace of Nera

The next eight years passed largely without incident. My skills and swordsmanship, accounting, agriculture, strategy, and Nevremerre law all improved as I worked towards becoming the best option to rule. Alveron and Azar still fought like dogs, but a surprise came when our youngest brother, Ari, at just 12 proposed a new taxation system that led to an increase in the Royal budget without too much strain on the people. He called it a luxury-tax, and the idea was praised all throughout the council. I saw a dejected, but determined Al leaving Ari's tent the night he suggested the luxury-tax on jewels and fine fabrics, confirming what I already suspected, the crown was now anyone's game. I now knew we were all fighting to win.

Our routine stayed the same as we moved to where we were needed, we studied in the mornings and trained in the afternoons. We celebrated all the traditions, birthdays, the summer and winter solstice, the fall and spring Harvest. Both Al and Azar became knights of the court just after their 21st birthdays. Yet, despite everything looking the same, we had all changed. Despite what Father had told me about it not being time to choose a ruler, I was now painfully aware that every action we took was being watched and evaluated to see our ruling potential. This only grew as we aged, and now, with Ari's 21st birthday only seven years away, even our parents seemed determined to test us. We would often find them posing a "what-if" question at dinner. This was all presented as a fun way to bond with each other, but we all noticed that these "what if" questions all began the same way. "What if you were crowned and...". Oddly, I became more and more grateful for Azar, even though he now openly considered all his siblings as enemies, he still treated us all in the same loud, rash, and competitive manner he had before we were obstacles to his crowning.

And so, eight years of increasingly obvious competition passed, and I think that's where the problem occurred. You see, Ari, with his analytical brain, was too busy calculating his odds on receiving the crown. Azar was barreling forward, his only focus on winning. Al was patiently watching us, finding our flaws, and making them his own strengths in an attempt to save us from a threat only he saw. I, too, got swept up in the madness of our race to the throne. Over eight years, and I had forgotten what Nana had said. I had forgotten that my personal goal could be completed with or without a crown. We were so wrapped up in our fight we didn't see what was going on around us. And, when the inevitable came, there wasn't a single one of those fighting for the throne who was prepared.

It was early summer, we had just celebrated the summer solstice four days previous, and the whole Court was now packed up and lined into a parade of horses, carriages and wagons that were filled to the brim with tents and other camping supplies. The sun beat down, and an uncomfortable heat clouded our whole party. Still, laughter bounced through our whole massive congregation. After 10 months of roaming through the country and living in tents we were finally headed back to the official Royal Palace. Back to Nera, the capital city. For the next two months or so we would be working in an actual building, having constant running water, and sleeping on beds with sheets of the finest silk. After so much time traveling, the time we spent at the Royal Palace was a much needed respite. The palace did have its drawbacks, though. While traveling the court was made up of only council members and the most trusted knights, when we entered the palace our world would become political as nobles from every corner of Nevremerre would gather, each with their own agenda. As possible future leaders, my brothers and I were often swarmed by those wishing to integrate themselves with us. Needless to say, despite the comforts of the palace, my immediate family was always happy when the harvest began and we left to help the country's farmers.

There was one other reason for me to dislike the palace, and, as Nera came into view, my family pulled out of the caravan to face this yearly challenge.

"Do you have to go Nana?" I whined in a rather undignified manner for a 19 year-old Princess, pulling my black stallion, Kolasi, to a halt.

"You're technically The Dowager Queen, so you should really be coming to the palace with us," said Ari in a haughty tone that fooled no one into believing his comment was only about propriety.

"Oh my darlings," Nana laughed, her white hair shaking. Her hair, impressively, matched her trousers, shirt, and her horse, making her look like some kind of ethereal goddess. "I must go where I'm most needed, and that snake's pit most certainly does not need me," she snorted. "Oh come now, no need to look so down. You've all managed every year before now. It'll all be just fine, and I will see you again in the fall. Now, Edgar, give my love to your siblings for me and be sure to tell Olivia to write to me more often. Honestly, I don't know how she calls what she writes letters. They're barely three sentences! Tell Octavian I will be there for a visit once the harvest ends."

"We'll be sure to tell them, Elizabeth," Mother said, "but we will miss you terribly."

"Yes, well you should! It's good to miss those you love from time to time, it makes you appreciate them more," Nana grinned.

"I don't need you to leave to appreciate you!" Azar shouted, looking put out.

"Of course you don't, my lion," Nana said, giving Azar a wink, "now your court is anxious to push forward." It was true, the whole court had stopped, waiting for us to say our good-byes. I could feel the piercing stares of the knights, workers, and council members who hoped their stares would make us move faster. None of them quite realized the extent of the maze of rats we royals were going into and how our figure of wisdom and inner peace was leaving us before we'd even en-tered.

Father sighed and nodded, "Take care of yourself, Mom. Connor, Lilly, Asher, her safety is in your hands". Father's eyes were dark, and his face was hard as he looked into the eyes of each of Nana's knights. He was showing them exactly what fate would await them should Nana be harmed.

"Goodbye my loves. Good luck in the capital, I will see you all soon," and with that, Nana and Gaia, Nana's horse, turned and sprinted off into the distance. Her knights stumbling to follow her. Father turned towards Nera and signaled for us all to move forward once more.

We stopped only once more before we entered Nera's main gates. The whole party halted and my family rode out into the lead. "Crowns on," called Mother, giving her usual speech as we all reached into our saddle bags. "Remember appearances are just as important as how you rule. Sit up straight, chins up, and wave to the people. Oh, and Ari, do remember to smile."

"Yes, Mother," Ari frowned before pulling out his thin silver crown and placing it on his head. In Nevremerre, Kings and Queens wore large gold crowns coated in sparkling gems. The Crown Prince or Princess wore a thin gold crown. All other Princes and Princesses wore crowns of silver. Once we turned ten we were able to design our own crown. For my crown, I had chosen a metal weaving that appeared like two branches twisting around each other. Ari, on the other hand, had never asked for anything more than a plain silver band. Azar had stuck with the same design since he was ten; a circular row of a hammer and a mace on either side of a gladiolus flower adorned his crown. Al went through crown designs most frequently. His latest design was made up of three braided rows of silver. Ready to go, I gently placed my crown on top of my hair, which had been braided down the side of my head earlier that morning. I pat down the errant wisps of my dark brown hair, and carefully brushed the dirt off of my clothes ensuring that my look was presentable. Mother gave us all a final glance before she declared us fit to proceed. Soon the whole party was riding through the purely decorative main gates of Nera.

Father led, his purple vest and gold cape fluttering as he rode forward. His outfit very clearly resembled the Nevremerre flag. Even without the ostentatious golden crown on his head, one would have been left in no doubt over who the leader of our country was. Mother and Mama entered next in tunics of green and blue respectively. Then my brothers and I entered, all in matching white tunics, black trousers, and short gold capes hooked over our right shoulders; our silver crowns were glaringly obvious against the cloak's shimmering gold.

As we rode through the city, we were greeted with the cheers and applause from the citizens of Nera. Nera was, by far, the country's largest city, and it always seemed like every resident came out to welcome us. At the edge of the city sat the Royal Palace. The castle sat protectively at the top of the city near the edge of the Dormian cliff. Only 200 yards away from the Dormian cliff sat the Serrian cliff. However, the Serrian cliff was not a part of Nevremerre's territory, rather it was guarded and cared for by the neighbouring country of Agremerre.

Nevremerre bordered only two countries. Up north was Calvine, which, other than to renegotiate peace and trade treaties, we mainly avoided. Agremerre, on the other hand, not only shared our longest border, but also was our closest ally. Queen Anora was even a close friend of my family as had been true of Nevremerrian and Agremerrian rulers for millenia. Right before the harvest there would be a celebration of our two country's shared history: the Unajo festival. It would start with a meal with each country on its own cliff side. The tables would be arranged so that all those attending faced the opposite cliff. Then a big dance would occur on the connecting land between the two countries. Then, for a whole week, various other joint activities were planned along the entire border. The celebration was always one of my favorite times of the year.

The palace gates opened and we were greeted by the smiling face of my uncle, aunt, and cousin. "Octavian!" My Father boomed, leaping from his horse and pulling his brother into a hug. Uncle Octavian's official role was the Duke of the South, so he wasn't actually meant to use the royal palace. However, as a Prince and my Father's brother, he was given leave to run the palace in Father's absence. I dismounted Kolasi and walked over to where Father and Uncle Octavian were laughing happily. They looked like twins as they stood together. Practically identical if it weren't for Octavian's misty blue eyes. Mother and Mama went to great Octavian's wife, my Aunt Arielle. Aunt Arielle was only a few inches taller than I. If one were to encounter the image before me on the streets, one could be forgiven for thinking that Mother and Mama were bullying Arielle as they towered over her to give their greetings. Micheal, my cousin, was being pulled into a large hug by Azar, and I, too, moved over towards him to say hello. Soon enough we were all shepherded into the main hall exchanging kisses and hugs along the way.

"I am always glad to see you Octavian, but I think we could all use some rest," Father said, throwing his arm back towards the council and knights who had entered behind us. "My family will retire to our chambers. I have asked Prince Octavian and Duchess Arielle to find rooms for all of you. My loves," Father finished, stretching his hands towards Mother and Mama. As they turned towards their rooms, I took my cue to escape to my own bed chamber. Even though we did not live here permanently, my family all had permanent rooms in the castle. Mine was on the second floor of the west wing. I moved through the halls, excited for a chance to bathe and rest after being out all day. When I made it to my room I was greeted by two maids.

"Good afternoon, Princess Avalynn," They bowed.

"My name is Ana. I will be in charge of your wardrobe," said the shorter maid. She had short platinum blonde hair that fell neatly around her face, cream colored skin, and startling ice blue eyes that screamed confidence as they met my own.

"And my name is Charlotte. I will be in charge of your hair. We both will be taking care of your room. We are very happy to serve you, Princess," Charlotte smiled. Well over a head taller than Ana, Charlotte had light skin and long raven black hair that she had somehow managed to intricately weave into a braided bun on the back of her head. Clearly she was perfect for the job she had been assigned. Her almond shaped eyes sparkled as she looked at my hair.

I smiled at them both. In the past I had always felt a little young around my maids. However, both Charlotte and Ana looked to be only slightly older than me. I felt a small bubble of hope fill me that I could actually become friends with my maids this summer. "I'm so pleased to meet you," I beamed at them. "Ana, we will need to choose a dress for tonight's welcoming ball. For now though, I think a bath would be welcomed."

"Of course, Princess," they both replied.

I thanked them once more, and Ana started removing my clothes as Charlotte moved to the bathroom, filling the tub with water. Sinking into the hot water, I let the steam surround my face and I breathed in the thick air, letting my head roll back against the porcelain. Feeling the water wash away the stress and grime of the morning ride. The lavender soap filled my nostrils, and I was certain that suffering all the nobles was worth it if I could always have baths like this. My brain moved on to the night's dance, and an exuberant smile made its way onto my face. Every year we start our stay at the palace with a welcome feast followed by a big dance in the town center for all to attend. There was nothing more wonderful than the breathless joy that filled my body after I danced.

"Shall we choose your outfit for the Welcome party, Princess?" Ana bounced with enthusiasm as I got out of the tub.

"Oh yes!" I exclaimed as I was wrapped in a lavender robe. I sat on the ottoman at the foot of my bed as Charlotte sat beside me brushing out my long hair. "Are you both going to the dance?"

"Of course! Ana had her dress picked out over a month ago," Charlotte claimed, laughing as Ana gave her a small pout before diving into the closet that contained my palace wardrobe. Even though we were here for only two months, the closet was surprisingly full. Probably because every year Mother and Mama dragged us all out to get the newest styles and clothes to wear for the rest of the summer.

"What she doesn't tell you," called Ana, her voice slightly muffled by the years of clothing she was currently wading through. "Is that she wore the pants suit she bought for the party for two hours last night trying to figure out what hairstyle would look best." Ana and I both giggled at Charlotte's blush.

"Would you like to wear pants or a skirt, Princess?" Ana asked, pulling out pieces of clothing. We spent the next three hours choosing an outfit, doing my hair, and swapping stories. We learned Charlotte's frantic preparations were to attempt to impress a knight.

"You should see her, Princess. She's got these massive biceps, and her smile could just knock you out," Charlotte mooned, dramatically flopping on the bed.

"Charlotte, you're going to mess up the sheets!" Ana scolded with a smile, as I giggled at Charlotte's antics. Ana, we learned, had big dreams that left no time for romance, at least for now.

"I am being trained by Katernia now, and, if I work hard, it won't be long before I become head maid. From there it's a straight shot up to housekeeper. I'll be running this house in no time!" Ana claimed, a fire lit up her eyes. "I'll be the best, and youngest, housekeeper in the history of the royal palace." The determination that she held in her voice left me with no doubt that her claim would be correct.

At the end of it all, I stood in front of a full length mirror in an emerald green halter top which cut off across my midriff. Paired with a long cream skirt with a high slit that ran up my thigh. A cream shawl hung at my elbows, embroidered with leaves and wild flowers. The outfit was completed with a pair of silver flats that matched the silver arm band, and silver crown. My hair spilled down towards the middle of my back in light waves.

"You look beautiful, Princess," Ana concluded as she gave me an examining gaze. "That top matches your eyes perfectly." She gave a self satisfied smile before turning away.

"Thank you both," I said before dismissing them to begin their own preparations for the dance. "Stay out as long as you wish tonight. I can get myself ready for bed. I also will tend to myself in the morning as well, so you can sleep in too. Oh! And be sure to save me a dance!"

"Of course, Princess!" Charlotte laughed as she and Ana exited the room.

Only a few moments later a knock came at my door. I pushed it open to find Mother and Mama. Pulling the door open wider, I let them come into my room. "Oh Ava, you look gorgeous," Mama gushed. She grabbed my hand and led me into a twirl that caused my skirt to fly up around me.

Laughing, I smiled back at her, "Thank you! You both look phenomenal as well!" It was a remarkably true statement. Mama's outfit was similar to mine, but in a sapphire blue top with sleeves that fell off her shoulder. Her abs were highlighted by the cut of the top, while also revealing a plethora of little pink scars from her various battles. She wore matching blue trousers and shoes. Her red hair was still relatively short, having cut it all off just a few weeks prior. Mother looked just as stunning in a bright yellow dress that popped against her dark skin. It had thin straps, and a deep V-neck that dipped down to the middle of her chest. The rest of the dress flowed down to the floor. Her braids were pulled into a knot just below her crown.

Stepping back to look at us both, Mama gave a happy sigh. "Girls are just so pretty!"

Mother gave a sly smile as she looked Mama up and down. "Yes," she said, grabbing Mama's chin and pulling her into a kiss. "Yes they are." I rolled my eyes, but my mock irritation was betrayed by the smile that had never left my face.

"Where's Father?" I asked as we left my room and headed towards the banquet hall.

"Oh you know men," Mama replied, "They take ages to get ready."

Mother smiled before actually answering my question. "He said something about his beard needing to be just right as we were leaving. I'm sure he's just trying to take our breath away when he makes his entrance tonight."

"And I'm sure he will succeed," Mama replied, "After all, he's managed it every year so far."

Chapter 6

The Son of Count Rosin

"Her majesties, Queen Elenore and Queen Diana, and, her highness, Princess Avalynn," a herald called out as we entered. The hall paused and dipped into a deep curtsy. I spotted Ari in the left corner, looking like he was wearing the same outfit we rode in with. Mother gave an exasperated sigh, and I knew she had spotted the same thing. Al and Azar had yet to appear, so I headed towards Ari as nobles swarmed to greet my mothers. Before I could reach him, however, another figure walked into my path. I paused, now faced with a blue tunic covered chest.

"Good evening, Princess Avalynn," the chest spoke, bowing down to reveal a head of brown hair. My eyes followed the hair as it rose to expose a pale face with dark brown eyes. "I am Nicholas, son of Count Rosin of the Armon province in Elatia."

"It's a pleasure to meet you, Lord Nicholas. I'm sure it must have been a long journey to come from our northernmost region, especially now that you must endure the southern heat." I nodded politely as I moved to step by him.

"Actually, it has been a warm summer even in the north, but, even if it had been cooler in Elatia, seeing a face as beautiful as yours would have made all the travel and the heat worthwhile." He grabbed my hand and kissed it, raising his head afterwards to give me a full smile. My eyes roamed his face and his charming smile, which felt just a little forced, and I made a decision. A gentle smile graced my own face, and I reveled briefly in the sparkle his eyes made at the sight. I leaned towards him and whispered, "Lord Nicholas, you aren't nearly attractive enough for me to justify you touching me. Do it again and the palace guards will escort you out of the palace permanently," my voice was icy and I relished the shock in his eyes as I snatched my hand back. Smile still planted on my face, I switched back to a pleasant tone as I loudly said, "It is lovely to see you, Lord Nicholas. Please enjoy your time in Nera."

I smirked at my minor victory as I walked past him. Why some people believed they could sway any of us with a few kind words was beyond me. I didn't grow up as a Princess to not see when a person's smile didn't reach their eyes or notice when a compliment was faked.

"Did that Lord talk to you, too?" I started at Ari's comment. I hadn't registered that I had managed to walk next to him. "I don't know what he wants." Ari continued, oblivious to my brief moment of shock. His face was wrinkled in concentration as his gaze fell on Lord Nicholas' back as he spoke with Lady Milfred, the council's treasurer. His charms were apparently more successful than they had been on us, as Milfred's long gray braid was thrown back as her body shook with laughter. "He told me I had stunning eyes, and asked me for a dance this evening." I turned to Ari, my eyebrows shooting up. "But I don't think dancing or my pretty eyes were actually what he wanted. When I said that, he just said he spotted someone he knew and excused himself. It was all rather odd."

I nodded, "Well at least he gave you the courtesy of specifying which part of you he found beautiful," I said feeling oddly annoyed. "He just said I had facial beauty in general. He didn't even bother to try and find a part of me he found stunning." I frowned, placing my hands on my hips.

"What do you think he actually wanted?"

"Well-"

"Announcing his highnesses, Prince Alveron and Prince Azar," the herald interrupted my thought. Once again the majority of the room paused to bow as Al and Azar walked in. Azar stood tall in a cool blue suit with pink flowers embroidered all over it. Al, on the other hand, simply wore a pair of plain black trousers that looked suspiciously like his riding pants, and a bright pink tunic. A glance at Mother's frown told me that just changing his shirt did not meet her appearance standard. Despite Mother's insistence that appearance was an important part of ruling, only Azar and I really got the message.

I turned back to Ari, "Now that Al and Azar are here, we best make the rounds."

Ari nodded back, "Until later then," he said as we both moved across the room. As I smiled and talked with the nobles in the room, I noticed Lord Nicholas talking to both Al and Azar individually. Azar laughed and patted him on the back, but Al's talk lasted until the herald finally announced Father.

As predicted by Mother and Mama, Father's entrance was indeed grand. He wore golden trousers and a shiny emerald shirt embroidered with gold and with an open V that hit almost as low as Mother's. His beard looked perfectly trimmed, I noted with a smile.

"I hope I did not keep you waiting long," Father smiled, "but, if I have, I won't keep you waiting any longer. It is my pleasure to welcome all of you to the Royal Palace, please join me in the dining room as we celebrate this joyful time." Father then signaled to the staff and the side doors opened to reveal the dining room. The large room was filled with one long table covered in white tablecloths and plates of porcelain. On top of that lay a spread of meats, pastas, dumplings, vegetables, and fruits.

"I could have sworn we had more meat last year," Azar said. As I was, once again, shocked by the presence of one of my brothers so near. Azar stood at my right, his gaze inspecting the food as if it would give him some answers as the rest of the court moved around us to take their seats.

"It's more cost efficient to have less food at banquets," Ari's voice commented from my left. I jumped again and then resolved to do more periphery training tomorrow. My thumping heart was not ready for all these surprises.

"So this is your doing!" Azar almost roared, tuning towards Ari and glaring, "I'll have you know that I ate that food!"

"Peace, Azar," I jumped in as Ari opened his mouth to reply, "I'm sure that you will not be lacking in food while we are here." I grabbed both of their hands, "Now, let's go and eat! I'm starving!" I laughed as I pulled them both into the dining room. I maneuvered us to the head of the table where we always sat for the welcome feast, ready to eat and debrief with the rest of our family. When everyone was in their assigned place, Father sat down, and the banquet began.

"Ari," Mother began, "Why are you wearing the same outfit we rode in with?" Azar and I shared a smile from across the table. The banquet started this way nearly every year. The end result was always the same, after a lengthy debate, Mother would decide that Al and Ari couldn't be trusted to pick out their own clothes.

"Mother, not this again," Al responded, "It makes no difference what we wear, it's our actions that matter most."

"Boys," Father interrupted, disrupting the usual flow of this conversation, "Your Mother is absolutely correct. Not everyone who sees us will get to speak with us, or will see all the actions we take. They will not know the exact state of our country, but, if they see us looking neat and polished with outfits to spare, they will believe our country is safe and prospering, which is exactly what they should believe. In a room like this, more formal attire shows our power, and makes those who wish to take the throne out of greed think twice. The same is true with diplomats from other nations, of which two are in this very room. You must not let them believe we are weak, or we may end up in an unnecessary war. Both of you are old enough to know better. You both wish to be King, yes? Well, if you do not learn the importance of public appearances you will never see the throne." Father growled, leaving our section of the table in a quiet shock. Father's voice only got this low when we were seriously in trouble. Like when Al and Azar were fighting indoors as children and Azar pushed Al so hard they both would have fallen down the stairs had one of the knights not been there to grab them. Besides that, Father never brought up our internal fight for the throne. He said he was determined to remain neutral.

Bringing myself out of my shock, I looked up to see Azar sitting up straighter in his chair, smirking at Al. It struck me then that Father's words had just declared Azar and I were more fit to rule. A spark of pride shot through me as I sat with the thought. Starting on my plate of food, I forced my pride and excitement back down. We still had seven more years before a decision had to be made after all. We sat, silently eating for a while longer before Father looked back at us all, a more jovial expression taking over his face. "Now, who's excited for the dance tonight?" he said, pushing the conversation forward. The night rolled on without any further comment, but I did catch Al occasionally glaring at his tunic and trousers.

"Oh, I'd been meaning to ask," I said as desserts were being presented, "Al, Azar what did Lord Nicholas want with the two of you?"

"Lord Nicholas?" Mama asked, "Who's he?"

"The eldest son of Count Rosin," Ari chimed in thoughtfully, "He came up to Ava and me earlier this evening. I didn't realize he spoke to you guys too." Ari nodded his head towards Al and Azar.

"Oh yes! I remember him," Azar jumped in, loudly. "He told me I looked handsome in my suit and asked me to dance this evening. Unfortunately, I had to tell him that I was not attracted to men, but I promised him that he could still have a dance if he wanted one! Poor guy, I mean who could blame him for falling for me. He must be absolutely devastated right now." Azar mused, and I had to bring my hand over my mouth to stop the laughter that had bubbled up inside of me. "But what did he want with the rest of you?" Azar continued.

"He told me that I have pretty eyes." Ari replied, apparently unaffected by Azar's rejection of the man.

"He told me that I was beautiful," I chimed in.

"He said he was mesmerized by me," Al finished. Azar's fork dropped, clinging down onto his plate.

"Do you mean he was flirting with all of us?" Azar exclaimed, his mouth hanging open, "The nerve!"

"But Al," I said, suppressing a smile at Azar's antics, "I think the rest of us only spoke to him briefly, but you were talking with him until Father came in."

"Well, he was clearly only looking for a throne, but you never know when someone might turn out to be useful." Al replied easily.

"Hmph" I huffed, or dangerous, I thought to myself.

"You seem to be particularly interested in him, Avalynn," Mother gave Mama a smile I couldn't interpret as she spoke to me.

"I just can't believe the gall of some people. I mean did he think that just because we were all competing for the same position we wouldn't talk to each other? I mean we'd be bound to find out he was flirting with all of us. Not to mention, he was pretty obvious in his fake interest."

"Hey! I'm a catch," Azar insisted. "His compliment to me was probably genuine."

I felt my eyes roll. "Well regardless, I have no desire to get involved with someone so disingenuous."

"I see," said Mama, smiling at Mother again. This time though, Father caught on and was looking between the two of them curiously, so at least I wasn't alone in my confusion.

"Well then," Father finally decided, "now that we've established that, I think it's time we head down to the town square." Father stiffly turned and spoke towards the court, "My lords and ladies, Thank you for a wonderful meal, I hope you will all join me now for the Welcoming dance!" There was a round of applause and then people moved out of the hall and into carriages heading for the town. I shared the ride with my brothers, and soon we stopped in the already packed square. Fire lit up the square, and a band was sitting on a raised stage in the middle of the crowd. As we exited the carriages, the people parted so my family and I could move towards the center stage. Father soon stepped out in front, holding Mother and Mama's hands.

"Citizens of Nevremerre. I thank you for your warm welcome! I would like to start this dance by thanking each and every one of you for all the work you do for this country. Every job we do serves an important role in creating this wonderful country and city. I promise I will continue to serve this country to the best of my ability, and I will work harder than anyone to ensure our continued success. May the honor of Nevremerre be everlasting!" The cheer from the crowd was thunderous as they roared back, "May Nevremerre prosper evermore! Good health to King and country." After a few moments of continued applause, Father raised his hand and spoke once more

"Now please join me in grabbing your partners for 'The Dashing White Sergeant'."

There was a flurry of movement as people gathered into groups of three. This had been the starting dance every year after Mother and Father met Mama, or so I was told. Al and Azar would dance with Uncle Octavian as their third partner, and start facing our parents, while Ari, Aunt Arielle, and I danced across from some random pair. The crowd settled into a circular formation, and the music began. Twisting people spun around weaving between their partners, and flying under other groups. The crowd that wasn't dancing clapped loudly along to the beat, and soon the shrieks of laughter pierced the midnight blue sky, twinkling with stars. For just a moment time stood still as the music created it's own little pocket of the world that nothing could touch. Everyone inside breathless, dizzy, and exuberant. Drunk on the air we breathed and the deafening sounds of the crowd. Faces hurting from smiles that could not fall and throats sore from laughter we could not stop, as we danced in our perfect moment.

Our little bubble popped when the music came to a close, but the cheers from the crowd thanked the bubble for existing anyways.

"Find your partners for 'The Gay Gordons'." The band leader called, and I turned around excited for the next dance. My excitement was dashed as I turned to see the face before me.

"Princess," bowed Lord Nicholas, "since we are out of the palace, I trust I won't get into too much trouble if I ask you for the next dance."

My eyebrows shot up, "What a kind offer, but I'd hate to prevent you from dancing with somebody else."

"I assure you, Princess, there is no one I'd rather dance with," Lord Nicholas replied. A perfect smile was plastered on his face as he held out his hand.

"Oh," I said with a slight smile, "Not even my brothers?" A shiver of satisfaction rose through me as I watched his smile falter.

"Of course, Princess," he recovered quickly, "I can assure you I would much rather dance with you than them."

"I'm sure," I muttered trying not to glare at him. Forcing my own smile, I said "They'll be most disappointed to hear that, you know. And, I'm afraid that I'll have to disappoint you too, you see my next dance is already taken. Excuse me." I swiftly left walking towards where I had just, thankfully, spotted Ana in the crowd.

I spent the next few dances bouncing from partner to partner. Dancing with Ana, then Charlotte, then some other citizens, and a few members of my family. It was late in the evening when I came across Lord Nicholas again. Though young children had now been shepherded to bed, and the crowd had dwindled somewhat, energy levels were still high, and I knew there'd be many people dancing until sunrise.

"Princess, how fortuitous," I turned from the table where water and other drinks had been laid out to see Lord Nicholas walking towards me. "I'm sure by now you've danced with all whom you've promised. May I once again ask to be your partner?" he smiled, charmingly at me, and I felt a swirl of disgust in my stomach.

I sighed, "Lord Nicholas, I have no desire to dance with you, so please do not bother me again," I said firmly.

"As you wish, Princess," he replied, his smile falling. "It would see that it is of no use trying to become close to you." Lord Nicholas' previous light tone fell away, and his voice was washed in an icy cadence as he gave me a calculating stare. I returned his gaze with one of my own, realizing I was finally looking at the real Lord Nicholas.

"I'm not sure what exactly you want, although, I could hazard a few guesses," I stared at him unflinchingly as I made my address. "But, unless you can give me a written report with clear arguments and evidence on why you should have it, you will not get what you want from me. And, even if I do get a written report, I make no guarantees."

Lord Nicholas smirked as I finished. "I'll bid you goodnight then," he said calmly. I released a breath I didn't realize I'd been holding as Lord Nicholas walked away. For just a minute, the fire light and dancing looked oddly uninviting. I shook my head and put back on a smile. No, I thought to myself, I love to dance, and I love this celebration, and nothing or no one would change that for me. I gave myself a quick nod before turning around in search of my next dance partner.

I danced until about two in the morning, when Ari and I took the carriage back, leaving Al and Azar still dancing, our parents having left a few hours earlier. Despite this late night, I still work up promptly at eight o'clock in the morning. Breakfast would not be until ten, due to the dance, and I had no wish to disturb my maids, both of whom were still dancing when I'd left last night. I got up and put on a pair of brown trousers and a blue tunic. Slipping on my boots, I planned to spend the next hour riding Kolasi, and then maybe get some sword training in before I needed to change for breakfast.

I was sure most nobles would still be sleeping, so I was positively giddy at the thought of a morning ride. Leading Kolasi out towards the woods that bordered Agremerre, I was startled to find someone riding in my direction.

"Princess," said Lord Nicholas cooly. There were no residual traces of the warm smiles and pleasing tones he'd used just hours ago.

"Lord Nicholas, and here I thought I'd get to stop seeing you," I replied, a small bite in my tone as I thought again about the solitude I should have had.

"I assure you, Princess, I had no intention of meeting you here," Lord Nicholas frowned. "You don't like me," he added calmly.

"Oh? How did you figure it out?" I gasped, in false shock. Lord Nicholas ignored my theatrics.

"Why?" He queried.

"I should've thought that would be obvious."

"Tell me anyway."

I sighed, "There are many things I value in this world, but I think perhaps the most important traits to me are honesty and respect. You start off our acquaintance by lying to me in an attempt to manipulate my behavior, and, had I been more receptive to you, you would've continued to do so. So yes, I do not like you, and, as of right now, I have no reason to put up with your falsehoods."

"I must ask one more thing," Lord Nicholas stopped me as I moved to ride on, "Why the qualifiers? 'As of right now, I have no reason to put up with you' and 'unless I write a report on what I want.' Why do you say that?"

"Lord Nicholas, if you had approached me in the manner you did because you wanted something you genuinely believed would help Armon, then I would listen and consider your request no matter your attitude. If at some point in the future you have a request for the Armon province, or even any other area of Nevremerre, that you believe would help our people then I would consider it fairly and without any bias caused by this incident. However, as you did not greet me today with a proposal, and as you've yet to speak with the King or Queens, and because you turned away from me so coolly last night, I'm inclined to believe that what you want has more to do with your own personal greed and not the good of the country. Am I wrong?"

"Perhaps not," Lord Nicholas replied, pulling his horse closer to mine, "but perhaps what will satisfy my "personal greed" would also benefit the country."

"I wouldn't place any money on it," I replied, simply. Lord Nicholas smirked as he began to trot away.

"Oh, but Princess," he called as his horse moved, "there is one thing I didn't lie about," he turned his head around to look at me. "You are very beautiful." I scowled as I turned away and put Kolasi into a gallop across the forest trail, And, if I hit the training dummy harder than usual during my morning practice, it certainly wasn't because I was still irritated by him.

Chapter 7

The Hospital of Nera

When I walked into breakfast a couple of hours later I was astonished to find the whole family already seated at the table. Usually the night after the welcoming celebration Al, Azar, and occasionally, Mama, would skip this first breakfast in an attempt to reclaim the sleep that they would've lost last night. Indeed, as I walked towards the table both Al and Azar looked like they were going to pass out.

"Oh there you are Avalynn!" My Father called. "Your maids said you were going out this morning so I was hoping I'd see you at breakfast. You always have been an early riser," Father's face was as jovial as always as I took my seat. One look at Mama's face, however, told me not all was being said. Mama lacked Father's early king training and Mother's cool demeanor, which led to them both being effortlessly able to conceal their emotions. Although she tried her best, in times of crisis, it was her face that told the true story. Today her brow was creased with worry.

"Now that Ava's here can you please tell us why we had to be up so early?" Azar practically whined into the palm of his hand.

"It's nearly 10 in the morning, Azar, that's hardly early," Mother began.

"Oh, hush, Elenore, we both know it counts as early the day after the Welcoming Celebration," Mama admonished before turning to us. "We have a good reason for doing so today though, so listen to your father."

"Yes. You are all now old enough to start playing an active part in helping our country. Today it is vital to begin this task. At noon today you will leave for Nera, each of you will be given an area to look into and help with any task they have for you. You will do this every third day while we are here. There will be someone supervising your work. Listen to them and work your hardest. Your crowns must be worn at all times, you must always be polite, and you must never complain about any of the tasks you were given. Have I made myself clear," Father's instructions ended in an unusually strict tone that caused even Azar to snap up to attention. I shared a knowing glance between all of my brothers. I could tell we had come to the same conclusion: this was a test for the throne. Mama's frown made more sense to me now as she had always disapproved of the competition among us.

Al was the first to respond to Father, his earlier exhaustion seemed to fade away. "Of course, Father. Where will we be positioned?"

Father nodded as he took in our serious expressions, "Your placements may change as the summer continues, but for now, Ari you will be working at the docks with my cousin Austin. Azar you'll be working with construction workers outside of Nera. Alveron, you'll be working with infrastructure repair crews inside the city. Avalynn, you'll be working under a healer at the hospital. The carriages will take you at noon. Your Mother will be picking out outfits for all of you. You will all be working with citizens of our country, so remember whether or not you want or will be on the throne, right now you all represent the crown. Make me proud."

"Yes, Father," we all dutifully responded.

"Good! I know you will all do your best." Father smiled, his eyes bright. "Your mothers and I need to start our day, but remember to be outside and ready for the carriages at noon, lunch will be packed for you there. I love you all." Father called as he got up to leave.

My brothers and I watched as our parents left the table, as soon as they were out of sight we all turned to each other conspiratorially.

"This is a test for the crown," Azar stated.

"Clearly," responded Al condescendingly.

"I wonder why Father chose the tasks he did?" Ari queried.

"Probably to show us what different lives in Nevremerre are like. I wouldn't be surprised if this is also meant to teach us about what life is like for our citizens as well as our ability to lead," Azar responded, unusually insightful.

"Do you think I'm at a disadvantage because Duke Austin is supervising me?" Ari said, looking down.

"I doubt it, it's probably just because you're still pretty young and Father's cousin can be trusted to keep an eye on you. You may even have an advantage because he can help you mingle better. We have no idea if our supervisors will be any good," I said in an attempt to be reassuring. It seemed to work because Ari smiled at me.

"Well, I better try and get some sleep before work begins," said Azar getting up.

"Ava, Ari," Al began as Azar left, "I think there's another reason why we got assigned the jobs that we did. It's a chance for us to find another career outside of ruling." I barely stopped an eye roll. This was clearly another attempt from Al to get us to abdicate. However, my irritation was poorly concealed as Al hurriedly added, "Just look at the jobs you got. Avalynn, you've been learning about herbs and basic healing from Nana for years." I couldn't deny that, but I often saw my healing studies as more of a hobby than something I actually wanted to do. "And, Ari, Duke Austin is a successful businessman. You have already shown an interest in money management. I'm sure that will be a part of what you learn." Ari seemed unimpressed by Al's declaration. Recognizing defeat, Al sighed and concluded, "Just think about it, okay?" Before walking out of the room.

"What do you think of Al's theory?" I asked Ari, grabbing more toast.

"It's not useful to speculate on what we will be doing until we get there," Ari replied sagely, "but also, if Father were pointing at us towards options for careers, I doubt Al and Azar would find construction very interesting."

I snorted into my toast, "I don't know. They could surprise us," I said with a wink. Whether or not this was meant to find us other career paths, I was feeling excited about the task to come.

Not long afterwards, I practically bound down the halls, bursting to go on this new task and prove my value as a Queen. Mother had laid out black trousers with a purple shirt and instructed Charlotte to pull my hair back into two braided buns at the nape of my neck, each tied with gold ribbons, once again making the silver of my crown painfully obvious. However, it seems like I was not the only person to clash today, as, when I entered the main hall, I found my brothers wearing the same outfit. Azar, too, had his long red hair pulled back with a golden ribbon, whereas Ari and Al had gold ribbons tied around their wrist. Clearly, we were all meant to look like the Nevremerre flag.

Slowing down to stand by my brothers, I noticed we were all standing impossibly tall. Azar had his chest puffed out and appeared to be trying to fill the whole room. Al made this difficult, however, as it was obvious that he was attempting the same goal. Despite not being as broad as Al or Azar, Ari was standing with his head held high and a fire in his eyes. I would have to be on the top of my game today. Fortunately, I had an advantage. Today I would be working with healers. I had already learned to treat minor cuts and wounds, not to mention I'd learned the medical properties of plants from all over Nevremerre, due to Nana's guiding hand. I was sure I could impress everyone with my work while we were here, after all, I already knew most of what I was doing!

The carriage arrived and we all got in, heads held high, booming with confidence, and completely and utterly unaware of how unfounded our confidence was. Two knights, Mateo and Carlos, were already in my carriage, however I was too caught up in my own thoughts to say much to either of them. Mateo had been a knight for several years, so he knew to let me have my silence. Fortunately, Carlos, who had only been knighted a few months ago, followed his lead. The carriage soon pulled up to a large brick building in the center of town. The crowd of people who were surrounding the building froze as my carriage stopped.

"Princess Avalynn," a stern voice called, as Carlos opened the door. I looked out to see a tall, stern looking woman bowing towards us. She was wearing a dark suit that covered all of her body despite the sweltering midday heat. The only nod to trying to be cool was seen in her black and silver hair, which was pulled back into a strict bun at the top of her head. She maintained perfect posture as she looked up at us. Meeting her gaze, I found her dark eyes giving me such a powerful stare that even though she was currently bowing down to me, I was left in no doubt that she was in charge.

"I am Matron Terrella. I am the healer in charge of Nera hospital. If you could please step inside, so the patients and their family members can continue to use the front entrance."

I looked around guiltily at the bowed heads of those surrounding this hospital. I was about to confirm my readiness to enter when Matron Terrella promptly turned and started forwards. Surprised, I somewhat ungracefully lurched forward to follow her, Carlos and Mateo following after me. We hurried past healers in their black and aqua uniforms, and the rooms full of patients lying on thin beds, up two floors to an office at the end of a large corridor.

"Sit," Matron Terrella said, her rough, brown hand gestured towards a set of wooden seats with fuzzy, aqua cushions that matched the staff's outfits. Still in a state of shock at the speed of our earlier departure, and a bit out of breath from the walk to her office, I promptly did as Matron Terrella asked.

"You are here to help Nera hospital, one of the nation's greatest hospitals, and internationally renowned for our teaching, research, and quality of care," Matron Terrella began with obvious pride. "Even though you are a Princess, your role here is to be of aid to the staff in any way possible, whether we ask you to support and gather supplies, or treat patients. His Majesty assures me that you will work with a smile and treat our patients with the same quality and care our regular staff would."

"Of course Matron Terrella. I'm happy to help." I smiled after a pointed stare from the Matron.

She nodded, apparently satisfied with my answer. "Just call me Matron, Princess, everyone else does. Now, I understand you have knowledge of herbal remedies and properties of plants?"

"Yes Matron, and I can do basic injury care." I added, keen to seem useful.

"People do not come to the hospital for basic injuries," Matron admonished, causing any pride I had in my knowledge to promptly disintegrate. "However, it is good you have knowl-

edge of herbs. At least then we won't have to teach you everything.

We will start today with a tour of the hospital. We will
have you watch a few treatments, and observe a few doctors
to see how the hospital runs. This will prepare you for what
you might be doing here. At the end of today, we will stop
by the research lab and I will give you books on basic human
anatomy and steps for simple procedures. You are to learn as
much as you can from these books before you return in two
days time. And, you will continue to learn more for every subsequent time you return to work with us this summer."

I nodded, but, as if my task hadn't seemed daunting
enough, the Matron continued with, "For the rest of your time
here you will arrive promptly at 8 a.m. Your carriage should
drop you off down the road so it does not block the entrance.
You will then work until 6 PM. You will get an hour off for
lunch each day, but there is no set time for your lunch break.
You are encouraged to bring your own or buy lunch from a
restaurant around the hospital as there will not be enough time
to go back to the palace. At some point, you will be assigned
a Healer whom you will work immediately under, but who you
work with won't be decided until I assess your performance
over the next week or so. Do you understand your duties?"

"Yes Matron." I responded feeling rather intimidated by the
Matron's speech.

"Good. Now about your knights-"

"Forgive me," I interrupted with the start, "I did not introduce my knights. This is Sir Mateo and Sir Carlos of the Nevremerre royal guard." I had been so flustered by the Matron's

tasks and overall mannerisms that I had completely forgotten the proper etiquette. I smiled, trying to put back on a more regal face of grace, calmness, and understanding, even though my heart was sinking. Less than 10 minutes in, and I was acting more like a scared schoolgirl than a potential future Queen.

Matron gave me a slight frown at my interruption, confirming my fears that I was indeed failing my first test. "Yes well, I've asked His Majesty that your guards stay the same while you are here so that I only have to say this once," she turned her fierce gaze to Carlos and Mateo, "While you are here you will stay out of the way of the healers and the staff. You will remain outside of the patient rooms unless they have given their express permission for you to enter, even if the Princess is treating a patient. I have assured His Majesty that no patients in this hospital are in any condition to cause any real damage to the Princess, so this won't be a problem." Mateo made a sound of protest, but Matron quickly shut him down by adding "My rules have already been approved by the head of the royal guard, as I'm sure you've already been told." I turn my head to see Mateo and Carlos nod. I was comforted to know that I was not the only one frightened by the Matron.

"Finally, and this goes for all of you," Matron said looking at me before once again addressing the three of us, "You may experience a lot of gross, strange, or unsettling things during your time here. It is vital that you do not react to these things. Neutral faces and smiles only, understood?"

"Yes Matron," we all replied in unison, and I dreaded to think about what lay in store for us if we couldn't keep our composure. I forced myself to try and smile once again.

"Good. Now then, are you ready for your tour?" Matron said with a smile I had not thought her capable of.

The next hour we spent being rushed through different rooms as I tried desperately to memorize the layout of the hospital. We were briefly introduced to healers as they passed by, and saw a number of storage areas filled with herbs, masks, sheets, and gloves. We passed rooms filled with patients, office rooms, rooms filled with glasses and fire as doctors mixed combinations of herbs before we finally entered a massive library. Books filled the shelves that stretched toward the ceiling, and rows upon rows of bookcases filled the space. The only gaps were where long wooden tables rested, a handful of healers taking up the seats. Some doctors were hidden by large piles of books, whereas others sat calmly flicking through just one or two. Looking at the books themselves, I noticed that many appeared to be sheets of paper tied together with brown string with small paper tags hanging from one side.

"Oh, Murphy!" Matron called out suddenly.

"Yes Matron," responded a brown-haired man as he wheeled up to us in a wooden chair.

"This is Princess Avalynn, she'll be working with us while the King is in Nera. Please explain to her the library system and fetch one of the copies of 'Anatomy of the Humans' and 'Medical Basics'. The man nodded at the Matron's words, but his eyes were fixed on me. Their clear blue made me feel like I was some sort of specimen to be dissected. "Princess Avalynn," he acknowledged, bowing his head.

"Murphy is one of our student researchers here at the hospital. It's likely that you all will work together often. Now, I'm going to see if there are any procedures you can observe today while Murphy explains the library," the Matron said, already rushing off in the opposite direction.

"It's a pleasure to meet you, Murphy. Thank you for taking the time to help me," I smiled. I needed to impress everyone here to improve my chances of becoming Queen.

"Follow me while I get your books, I can explain it as we go." Murphy replied nonchalantly as he began to maneuver around the shelves and tables. "On the front half of your right hand side are all medical texts. These contain practically all of our knowledge on human anatomy and treatment. There are at least two copies of everything, and it's likely you will be asked to scribe something while you're here, as all the new data we collect gets recorded here as well. Here's your copy of the 'Anatomy of the Humans'. We have 15 copies of that one," Murphy said, handing me a thick book in a red binding with a silky gold print on the front. "And here is 'Medical Basics'," Murphy continued, moving to another shelf before passing me a blue book only slightly thinner than the last one. "If we keep going down I'll explain the rest of the library." Murphy wheeled further into the room, leaving us to scurry behind him.

"Let me take those for you, Princess," Mateo whispered gently into my ear before scooping the books out of my hands. I smiled at him gratefully as we followed Murphy through the shelves.

"In the back half of the right hand side we have records of everyone who has ever died in the hospital and their cause of death. These are grouped by reported cause of death. The causes are labeled above." Murphy pointed upwards and, sure enough, my eyes moved up to find a shiny gold plaque on the shelf with black letters saying "chicken pox". Only two shelves down, another plaque was placed with the word "childbirth" on it.

Following my gaze, Murphy commented, "That and unknown infections are the biggest sections." He didn't seem too perturbed by this though as he promptly turned around and rolled through the bookshelves across the room. "Here, on the left hand side, we have the records of every single still living patient at Nera hospital. If someone was ever a patient here we have their records. As you can see," Murphy said gesturing to the back half of the room, "the back shelves are empty so we have the room to add more patient records. These are all organized alphabetically." Moving back to the entrance, Murphy concluded his tour by clarifying that you could borrow any books from the medical resource section, but all other files were never to leave the hospital as there was only one copy.

"I suppose you'll just have to wait here until the Matron gets back, then," Murphy said casually.

"Well yes, I suppose so." I opened my mouth to ask him what we should do when Murphy promptly rolled out of the library.

"You know, I was under the impression that healers were supposed to be nicer," Carlos commented from behind me.

"I'm sure they must all just be very busy," I replied, cognizant that my every move here was likely being judged, but, privately, I agreed with his assessment.

"Perhaps we should sit, and wait for the Matron?" Mateo suggested, still carrying my books.

"I'd rather not get called up for sitting around not doing anything. It's probably best if we stayed on our feet." I had to force myself to keep from sighing. This afternoon was not going to plan.

Fortunately, only a few minutes later the Matron came bustling back in. "Good, you're done. I have two procedures you and your knights have been invited to watch. Come quickly," the Matron strode purposely out of the library, my knights and I hot on her heels.

"The first procedure you will watch is a gory one, but we need you all to get used to some nasty sights. It's unlikely that you'll ever have to assist on a procedure like this one again, but you never know." We stopped in front of a wooden door. "Put these on," the Matron handed us each a pair of gloves from her pocket, "We have three different glove sizes, I gave you a small, Princess, and you Sirs, received larges. Be sure to tell me after we finish if you believe you require a different size." I slipped on the white cotton gloves, ready to go in. I watched Mateo and Carlos do the same. Mateo had some difficulty as he attempted to do so while still carrying the books from earlier, but he refused any assistance from Carlos or me. Once we were all wearing gloves, the Matron gave us one final warning not to display any emotion as we entered before pulling open the door.

It was at this moment I realized that the Matron did not like me, or, at the very least, enjoyed torturing people because inside the room was an unconscious man lying on the bed with half of his shin bone protruding out of his skin. If you like someone, you would probably at least tell them what they were about to see. My stomach lurched uncomfortably, my palms started sweating, and I could practically feel the blood leaving my face. I kept my composure, however, and did not express my shock and horror even though the man with the broken leg was clearly unconscious and I did not have to do so. I knew that the Matron was watching us all closely. I refuse to fail even at an unnecessary task.

Satisfied we would not express any emotion, Matron ushered us over toward the table where the two healers were working on the broken bone. "You will likely encounter many broken bones during your time here. The key is trying to match the break, so the bone can heal in the correct position. Then we must hold the leg in place with a cast until the bone seems fully healed. This usually takes a few weeks, but with a break like this it would likely take the rest of the summer."

We watched as one of the healers carefully pushed the exposed bone down through the muscle. The bone made a strange squishing noise as she maneuvered it back into the leg. Once again my stomach rebelled against me, and I had to remind myself to breathe and keep calm. The other healer, however, was standing by the man's head holding a cork vial and wearing a mask.

"What is he doing?" I asked the Matron, gesturing towards the man.

"Excellent question! In painful operations such as this one, patients often pass out due to pain, or the sight of their own blood or bone. However, this is often a good thing as patients can potentially increase the damage done if they are awake and moving. What Healer Aldric has is a combination of valerian root and a type of seaweed found on the northern coast that when combined create a powerful aroma that puts a person to sleep. Healers are trained to quickly allow the patient to inhale the gas before capping the vial once more, so that no one else in the room will be put to sleep.

Ah look, now Healer Karaway has set the bone, she will now suture the wound. You can learn how to suture with Murphy, It's relatively simple and used often in the hospital. Now, Healer Karaway will clean the wound with water and alcohol, this -". The Matron's, rather in-depth, descriptions of the procedure lasted for the rest of the operation. I wondered if her throat ever got tired, as she had been talking with us almost constantly since we got here. Not to mention, she somehow managed to keep up her intensity throughout. The only good part was she managed to distract me from the surgery, although, the longer I watched, the easier it was to handle the blood in the trauma of the injury.

Once the operation had finished we were quickly rushed out of the room, and up the stairs to the second floor, as we went, the Matron addressed what I had initially believed to be proof of her distaste towards us. "I apologize for not warning you about what exactly you would face in that room, Princess and Sirs." Her words were kind, but her face and tone lacked any sincerity, "However, I need to know how you would react to the possibly gruesome events you might encounter during your time here. You all did very well," Matron conceded with a slight smile. "Next you'll be assisting with a birth. Clarrissa has already been in labor for 14 hours, so we are hoping the baby will arrive soon. However, labor can be a long process, and you may not be able to stay for the whole birth. Remember neutral faces," the Matron lectured before opening another wooden door. However, this time we were greeted with the long scream of a person in pain.

"You're doing amazing Clarrissa. Just keep breathing," said a male voice.

"I am breathing!" yelled the heavily pregnant Clarrissa as we stepped into the room.

"Oh Princess Avalynn!" the man practically bounded up to me, quickly bowing. "It's such an honor to have you here at the birth of our child! We were so excited when Matron Terrella asked if you could be a witness to the birth for your training! I'm Tahoe and this is my wife Clarrissa."

"It's a pleasure to meet you. I am honored to be here." I said with a smile.

"Hello Princess Avalynn," gasped a tired-looking Clarrissa before another scream of pain filled the air.

"Sit down, Clarrissa," a healer called. We spent an extremely uncomfortable hour listening to Clarrissa's screams and Tahoe's babbling, when, suddenly, the birth really got started. I will spare you the details of the birth itself, but the following series of events was perhaps the most chaotic I've experienced. It began with Tahoe running to try and watch his child be born, and then, upon gazing at the blood, fluids, and other discharge that accompany a birth, promptly fainting. This in turn caused Mateo to loudly drop the books he was holding to try and catch him. Fearing the same fate for Carlos, the Matron had quickly rushed him outside where I was later told, he immediately threw up in a nearby bucket. All this time the healers and Clarrissa were shouting as she tried to give birth. Carlos then returned and was given the task of holding Clarrissa's hand as Tahoe was still out cold.

It was then we learned that the baby had not flipped, which was apparently not a good thing as I was soon brought into the actual delivery process. I had to press down on Clarissa's stomach in certain places while the healer physically turned the baby. There was a lot of screaming. Tahoe then briefly woke up, just to faint once more, although this time he was still safely being held in Mateo's arms. Matron told Mateo to just take him out of the room after that. Two hours after the chaotic birth had begun, Tahoe and Clarissa had a healthy baby boy, and Mateo and Tahoe were allowed back in the room.

Picking up my books, Matron ushered us out of the room as we said our congratulations. Looking at the sundial at the end of the hall, Matron announced we were done for the day. "Study those books, Princess. You may just be useful to me yet," said Matron with a pleased nod, "but don't get cocky. Read up and impress me when we next meet. If you don't work hard, I can assure you that you will not enjoy your time here," the Matron finished, her severe face returning.

"Yes Matron, I promise I will work hard!" I responded immediately.

"Then you're done for the day," the Matron nodded, "I will see you in two days' time." Not even waiting for our response, she turned quickly to march down the hall.

Chapter 8

The Nobles of Nevremerre

My knights and I were silent as we exited the hospital in search of the carriage. The instant the carriage door closed each one of us slumped into our seats with a communal sigh. "She's even scarier than knights training!" Carlos cried, running a light brown hand through his curly brown hair. Mateo nodded his agreement, his black ponytail flopping behind him. "I don't know how you're going to manage, Princess. So many people give birth!" Carlos continued, "Oh no. How am I going to manage?"

I laughed a little at his antics. "I will manage because I have to. It's a lot of work, but it's a task I've been assigned in order to help the people. We all made it through today, and we'll all make it through the next time as well, and the time after that, and so on. Plus now I have materials," I said holding up the books. "I will read and become more prepared!" While the events of today absolutely shattered my confidence that I would do well on this test for the crown. It also presented a unique and interesting challenge, and I love a challenge. I was more determined than ever to help the hospital and to surpass Matron Terrella's expectations in every way. Focusing back on Carlos and Mateo I added, "I can share these with you too if you want, we can all try to become more prepared."

Carlos opened his mouth to respond, but was quickly cut off by Mateo, "Thank you, Princess. I believe that would help all of us." Carlos looked like he wanted to cry.

"I wish I could have gone with Azar," he moaned before snapping back up and quickly saying, "Not that it's not good to be with you too, Princess!" I laughed. Azar and Carlos have been friends since they were younger. Carlos' father, Lord Jesu, was the council member of foreign relations and his mother, Dame Helena, a knight in the guard, so they had all traveled with us growing up. Carlos and Azar had both been knighted just after their 21st birthdays earlier this year. Although I had never spent much time with Carlos, I could understand Carlos' desire to be with his friend right now. Plus, I felt sure Azar's task had to be easier than what we were going through.

"I don't mind, Carlos. Although I am surprised it was the birth you had trouble with. I felt more sick looking at the broken leg." I shuddered at the memory.

"We're knights, Princess. We've seen gruesome injuries before. The birth, however, was something new," Mateo frowned.

"I don't know how women can do that," Carlos agreed, his face going pale once more. "Did you hear how much she screamed?" he paused in horror. "Princess, I've decided, I don't think you should have kids. It's not worth it. I mean did you see it! It wasn't even cute! You shouldn't have to go through so much pain for something so ugly!" Mateo and I both laughed at this one.

"I'll keep that in mind, thank you," I said between giggles.

"I'm being serious!" Carlos cried, as Mateo and I laughed once more.

"I wonder how your brothers fared," Mateo thought out loud as we approached the palace, and saw other royal carriages pull into view. The thought made my heart drop. I was in for a difficult task ahead if I was to impress the Matron and pass this test, and I knew my brothers were just as determined as I was. I was sure that they had done better than I had on our first day. Which likely meant I was behind. I tried to turn my melancholy at my failure into something positive-- determination--while our carriage pulled up to the Royal Palace, but as I opened the door my heart was pounding.

The first thing I noticed as I stepped out of the carriage was a wet Ari making a beeline for Al's carriage. Sufficiently intrigued, I followed him to where Al was stepping out of his own carriage with white bandages on his hands that definitely had not been there earlier. Ari marched right up to Al, leaving a trail of wet boot prints behind him. "I did not learn about business!" he practically hissed at Al before storming off into the palace.

"What do you think that was about?" I asked Al who was still gaping at the entrance hall Ari had just gone into.

"I...I don't know," sighed Al.

"Are you alright?" I queried, gesturing towards his hands and noticing the exhaustion in his eyes.

"Oh just shut up," Al snapped back before he too stomped off into the entrance hall. Stunned, I just stood there a moment before I was joined by an excited and, for some reason, shirtless Azar.

"Ava!" he smiled. "What's got Al in such a fuss?"

"I have no idea," I replied, "Where is your shirt?"

"Ah, that, well it was so hot outside that me and the construction team couldn't stand to keep them on. I kept the crown on though, so I still followed Father's rules. But, honestly Ava, I swear it was hotter today than it was all of last summer."

"Are you sure that's not just because you were working outside?"

"Well, maybe," Azar laughed, "But, the construction team agreed with me!"

"At least it sounds like you had a good time at your placement," I said as we walked into the Hall.

"Absolutely! It was so much fun working and building things. Plus everyone there was so friendly. I've got to wash up, but I'll tell you more about it over dinner," Azar called as he bounded up the stairs. I too was eagerly awaiting a pre-dinner bath, so I hurried up the stairs. I was stopped only briefly by Mateo who gave me the two study books which I left in the carriage.

Dinner was an oddly quiet affair. Father was engrossed in some report, and Al and Ari refused to say more than a few words about their placements. We did, however, learn that Ari's drenched appearance from earlier was the result of falling into the harbor, a feat he apparently managed more than once. Any questions I may have wanted to ask Al were halted by him falling asleep. It would have been funny to see him repeatedly starting awake as his head slipped from his palm, if I hadn't felt so bone dead tired myself.

I had spent years training with a sword, moving around the country aiding people, and harvesting crops, and yet none of that had left me feeling the aching exhaustion that had come from just a half day moving around the hospital. I couldn't explain it. It felt as if my life before had moved slowly, as if time was nothing more than a word used to explain the sun's jaunt across the sky. However once I stepped into the hospital it was like being engaged in a fierce battle where I had to demand for every second to be longer. Fighting for every millisecond to matter, to give me the time I desperately needed. I couldn't understand why I was even struggling. I sat with that thought for a moment before I was suddenly reminded of the man with the broken leg, and Clarrissa with her new son. My duel with time, I realized, was not for me, but for them. In the hospital, I had to fight for time, so that when people left they could enjoy the seemingly time-free life I experienced outside of the hospital.

My silent musing was abruptly paused by Ari's head falling onto the table. The rest of us jumped at the noise, even Father jerked up from his report. Completely unaware of the scare he just caused, Ari was laying on the table, fast asleep. "Perhaps we should all just get an early night," Father whispered, still looking a bit shocked.

"It's a shame he's too big to carry up to bed," Mama smiled wistfully.

"We're just lucky we didn't have a formal gathering tonight," Mother frowned, looking between Ari, and a sheepish looking Al. "These placements are important, but do remember that some nights you will be required to entertain noble guests afterwards." Despite her stern words, her voice was gentle as she rose to stroke Ari's back and wake him up.

"Huh," Ari roused, looking confused.

"Time for bed, for all of you," Mother said, looking at the four of us. I was quick to leave the table. Kissing my parents, I bid them good night as I practically dragged myself up the stairs to my room. For the first time I was frustrated with the size of the palace. Ana and Charlotte were waiting for me once I got inside my room. I was quickly undressed and changed into soft blue cotton shorts and a thin camisole before sitting down for Charlotte to undo my hair.

"With all that's happened, we never got to ask you if you enjoyed the dance, Princess," Charlotte spoke, her fingers adeptly running through my hair.

"Oh! the dance! I completely forgot that it was just last night. It feels like it happened weeks ago!" I sighed, closing my eyes and relaxing into Charlotte's hands. "Well, I always enjoy dancing. I almost wish we could have a dance every night." My heart felt warm as I thought about the previous midnight and the yellow glow of the evening. Between the movement of Charlotte's hands, and the joy I recalled from last night, I felt the tension and stress from this afternoon fade away, and I felt a small smile push itself onto my face.

"How about the two of you, did you enjoy the dance? You both look wonderful."

"Thank you, Princess. It was nice to have an evening off, and the dance was absolutely stunning this year. The staff really outdid themselves," Ana nodded.

"I had an amazing time!" Charlotte exclaimed, "I got to dance with so many pretty girls, including you, Princess," Charlotte winked. My laughter could not be stopped and with it, it took away the residual heaviness I felt since entering the hospital. In that moment, I was so grateful to these two women, who somehow managed to recognize and relieve my emotional aches with just a few simple comments. They soon left me to sleep.

Despite my previous tiredness, I was determined to start studying. My revelation from earlier motivating me even further to learn, not just win the crown, but to help my subjects live their lives unaware of the ravages of time. I opened "Anatomy of the Humans" and began to read. Sadly, despite my early enthusiasm, I woke up the next day with my head still on page two.

The next morning passed quietly. I rode out early, and, thankfully, did not run into Lord Nicholas this time. I trained both before and after breakfast, and then spent the afternoon trying to learn as much about medicine as I could. I held Ana and Charlotte from their usual tasks by having them quiz me on each new page. By the time I had to get ready for dinner, I felt as if my brain was going to explode and I somehow felt that despite my previous hours of work, I had learned absolutely nothing. I was almost glad that we had to entertain the nobles tonight, as it allowed me to take a break from those grueling books.

"You think they could make medicine sound more exciting," complained Charlotte as she weaved together my long hair into an intricate braid. "My sister is a healer up a Ninita, and I never really appreciated what she had to go through. Of course, she learned after several years of training. Gods, I would hate to be a healer." My heart bubbled at her tirade, a weary smile making its way upon my face. I marveled at the energy she had. I felt like I needed to shut off my whole head for years in order to properly recover from the studying I'd done today.

"Are you looking forward to your meeting with the nobles?" Ana queried, likely searching for a way to stop talking about medicine.

"Not particularly. It's rather tiresome to deal with the whims of people who all want something from you, and, sometimes, they try to manipulate you in order to get it!" I huffed.

"I'm sure it won't be all bad," Ana commented as she began to take out tonight's jewelry. "I saw Lord Elijah's son on the way in. He's absolutely breathtaking!"

"Oh I remember him," I laughed. "He is pretty, dull as paint, but very nice to look at."

"Lord Nicholas is pretty handsome too," Ana noted.

"Oh, I know him!" Charlotte called out. "Yes, he helped me when I tripped up the stairs yesterday. He was very nice about it, and even helped me pick up the spilled laundry."

"What was he doing in the palace?" I jumped in, suspicion creeping its way into my chest. As I whipped around to face her.

"Well, I think he said something about meeting with the council," Charlotte said, her eyes flicking down as she tried to recall the details.

"Hmm," I responded noncommittally, turning forward once more.

"You seem very interested in him, Princess," Ana smiled.

"Oh no, we just had a rather curious conversation once, that's all." Yet, I was unsettled by this news. Lord Nicholas clearly wanted something, and had now turned to the council to get it. I had a sinking feeling that whatever he wanted would not be good.

"You're all finished now, Princess," Charlotte declared as she proudly placed my crown on my head.

"Thank you both for your work today. I'll take care of myself this evening, so get some rest."

"Thank you, Princess," they both called while exiting the room.

Even though I wasn't late, the Great Hall was already filled with people, and a bit of panic filled my chest at the sight of the large crowd in the room. I had to work to control my facial expressions as the page called my name and all eyes in the room turned my way. Raising my head, I meandered through the crowded room speaking with all the various nobles. The conversation was largely centered on the new jobs my brother and I had taken on. It seems everyone was eager to see how this challenge would play out. They all apparently agreed with my brothers and my assessment that this was a battle for the crown. I also discovered that there was really no need for me to have been quizzed on my medical journals by Ana and Charlotte earlier, as no less than five different nobles sprung medical questions at me. I'm not entirely sure why these people thought that determining my medical knowledge was the key to deciding who would get the throne, but I ran under the assumption that they believed the more knowledgeable I was about the subject, the better I'd do.

The highlight of the pre-dinner soiree, however, was when Lord Bushbee asked me if I thought my being given a medical job when already having medical knowledge was a result of the council's already given support for me on the throne. This question perhaps wouldn't have been too bad under normal circumstances. At the very least, I believed myself capable of answering the question gracefully. However, Lord Bushbee apparently believed that the best time to ask me this question was right in front of Al.

"I'm sure we were all just given positions His Majesty and the council believed we were suited for," replied Al curtly.

"No need to get snippy, Your Highness," Lord Bushbee replied, his gray mustache shaking as he hurried his response. "It could just as easily be that they thought the Princess needed the most help!" I had to hold back laughter at Al's glare. He was never fond of Lord Bushbee, whose blunt nature tended to rub Al the wrong way. I, however, found him to be a refreshing change of pace. After all, Lord Bushbee managed the entire Ninita region remarkably well. Plus, he never seemed to realize when he'd said something to make another mad, or, if he did, and never stopped him from being honest once more. As if reacting to my thoughts, Lord Bushbee finished by adding, "You really shouldn't be so standoffish, Prince Alveron, it's not an attractive quality in a future King."

"Of course, Lord Bushbee. Now if you'll excuse me," Al said, abruptly turning around leaving me covering my mouth to hide my amusement.

"Good lad," Lord Bushbee remarked, "I do hope he takes my advice." I snorted and then quickly tried to hide it with a series of dainty coughs.

"Well then, Princess Avalynn, do you think you have an advantage?" Lord Bushbee turned to me.

"Sadly no," I replied honestly, "Hospital work is proving far more difficult than my previous herbal knowledge can keep up with it presently. I'm afraid I've been tasked with a great deal more studying to do before I can be of any real help to the hospital."

"Ah, well perhaps I should put my money on another horse," said Lord Bushbee thoughtfully. "Although, I'm not sure I'm ready to count you out just yet."

"I should certainly hope not!" I smiled as we both moved to greet others. Not long after that we were all called in to dinner. A long table filled the dining hall, unlike the welcome dinner, I wouldn't be sitting at the end with my family, rather we would all be split throughout the table. Only my Father's seat remained the same. He sat proud and tall at the head of the table. I found myself at the lower half of the table next to the Marchioness of Utei, the region just north of Nera, and General Growsmith. I spotted Al and Azar further up the table both eagerly speaking with the nobles besides them. Ari was further down the table, and appeared to be staring right through the poor Lord across from him. I froze when I spotted Lord Nicholas though, he was engrossed in a conversation with Lord Arthur, the recently elected commoner representative for the council. What on Earth could Lord Nicholas want with him?

I was shaking from my deliberations by Marchioness Eliza, "I hear you've taken an assignment at the Nera hospital."

"Oh yes," I smiled politely, "it should be very interesting."

"How exciting! Have you learned your tea recipes yet? They can be very useful before and after procedures, and for more common ailments. Do you remember the time it takes for the leaves to be boiled? And you remember whether it's meant to be drunk with or without milk?" The rapid-fire of her questions gave me a brief sensation of being back at the hospital. Honestly, what was with these pop quizzes? I was beginning to suspect that the nobles who quizzed me were Matron Terrella in disguise.

"I'm afraid I haven't completely memorized the uses of different herbs, but I believe I know most of them. Herbs should be boiled for three minutes for the best results in medical teas, and milk can negate some of the effects of herbs, so it's best not to add it," I answered, trying to remain lively.

"Good," Marchioness Eliza nodded, "You really are doing well. Jeremiah just had the hardest time memorizing everything. He says the practical portions are a lot easier, even if they are nerve-racking."

"I... what?" I responded dumbly not expecting her response. "I mean, excuse me, I'm not sure I understand," I hastily corrected.

The Marchioness gave me a small smile, "You probably don't know, of course. My eldest son, Jeremiah, became a healer."

"Really? I had no idea. How interesting!"

"Yes, he's always loved it."

"I apologize if I sounded rude earlier. I really had no idea your son was a healer," I replied a little bashful.

The Marchioness laughed at this, "It's perfectly all right. Surprisingly, there are not many noble children who do pursue careers as healers. Many instead try to work in business or take over their parents' title. There's a small collection of us with healer children, though." The Marchioness then pointed out six nobles who had a child or sibling become a healer, this included all of the nobles who had previously quizzed me. "That's why I asked about the teas, Jeremiah always struggled with them. I used to stay up with him for hours as he listed off different herbal remedies." she smiled fondly.

I found shame building inside of me. I had assumed these nobles had quizzed me in an attempt to see if I would win the crown. I found them suspicious and irritating, but it was likely they were just trying to help me like the Marchioness. I never even gave them the benefit of the doubt. I resolved to try and do better in the future. "If it's at all possible, I'd love to hear more about your son's experience. I felt a little overwhelmed by all the work it takes to be a healer," I admitted.

The Marchioness looked thrilled, "I'm not surprised. Jeremiah said the hospital was like a whole other world where everything moved 10 times faster." I gave her a relieved smile, glad I was not alone in my panic at the hospital's quick pace. The Marchioness and I talked for most of the rest of the dinner as she explained her son's experience and helped me ease my fears. It ended up being one of the best noble dinners I've ever been to, and I ended the evening with a genuine smile on my face.

Chapter 9

The Work of a Healer

One day later I found myself bleary-eyed outside of the palace at 7:30 in the morning next to two, only slightly more alert guards as we waited for the carriage to take us to the hospital. I was carrying my two medical journals, as I had convinced myself that I would study on the way, but, as the three of us crawled into the carriage it was all I could do not to simply fall asleep on Carlos' shoulder. In the end, Mateo took the responsibility of keeping us awake for the journey.

"Carlos, you are a knight now. You cannot fall asleep on the Princess," Mateo scolded, as Carlos jerked up next to me.

"Yes sir!" Carlos practically yelled, causing Mateo and me to wince. "Sorry, why do we have to go so early?" he continued in a quieter tone. "I mean your brothers probably aren't even up yet."

"That's not true. Prince Azar left an hour before us, apparently it's better to work early to avoid the midday heat. He'll have an extra long lunch break compared to the rest of us though," I corrected.

"That bastard! He swore he wouldn't have to get up 'til 10 when we were training yesterday. He lied!" Carlos exclaimed, suddenly bursting with energy. "When I get my hands on him -".

"Carlos. You are a knight. You cannot threaten a Prince, nor can you call him a bastard and a liar, especially not in front of the Princess," Mateo sighed, as I tried to hide my laughter.

"But what if he is?" Carlos responded, and I swear I felt Mateo's soul leave his body as he sighed once more.

"That's something you discuss with the Prince in private."

"Being a knight means following so many rules," said Carlos with his own sigh.

"There are rules associated with any job," I chimed in. "I mean just consider the rules we have to follow in the hospital."

"However, not threatening the royal family is a rule for everyone in the Kingdom. And, it is a rule that most people should have learned in childhood." Mateo added with a smirk, causing Carlos' face to heat up.

"Even with all the rules, being a knight is still better than being a healer. I'm dreading going back to that hospital, and all we had to do was stand there! Plus the Matron is scary," Carlos shuttered, and even Mateo nodded his head in agreement.

"What about you, Princess? How are you feeling?" Mateo asked. If I really wanted to be honest, I could tell him that I felt exhausted just thinking about it. That despite spending most of the past two days trying to memorize these two books, I felt completely unprepared for what's to come. Not to mention whether or not I got my dream job was likely highly dependent on my performance, and, even more importantly, people's lives depended on me doing this job well. So, I was extremely stressed, anxious, and nervous. I couldn't tell Mateo and Carlos that, though. Even though my own negative thoughts were pushing their way into my head and demanding attention. I knew I was also responsible for these two men who had just expressed similar concerns. I couldn't lead us into the hospital with only fear, doubt, and apprehension. I thought back to my conversation with Marchioness Eliza two nights ago, and responded.

"I, too, am nervous about what is to come; however, I do know that whatever happens we will get through it. I also know that the longer we keep doing this, the more we will learn, and the easier these hospital visits will get."

"Well said, Princess," Mateo smiled.

"Alright! We can do this!" Carlos exclaimed. It wasn't long after that when the carriage stopped, and we all got out and made our way to the hospital. As we walked down the block, I had to remind myself to smile and to keep breathing, even though I felt the disturbing sensations of fear and panic try to crawl their way up into my chest.

"Good morning, Princess. You're right on time." Matron Terrella nodded as we walked through the door. "This is Healer Autumn. They will be your mentor for the day. Follow them, and do what they say. Come to my office before lunch and I will review your performance."

"Yes, Matron. Thank you," turning to Healer Autumn, I said, "Thank you for working with me today. I will do my best to learn and to be of use." Matron nodded once more before she turned on her heel and walked away, leaving us with Healer Autumn.

"We will start today by checking in on the patients who are staying at the hospital," they began as they started to walk towards the ramps, "then we will head down to the emergency room, and work with the incoming patients. I'll be quizzing you throughout the day, and, if you do well, I may even let you do a few basic procedures," Healer Autumn finished with a smile. It was clear by their tone that I should have been thrilled at the idea of doing procedures, and, admittedly, it did sound more fun than just watching in the corner. However, I couldn't shake the feeling that I was woefully unprepared to do anything of the sort. Not to mention that these were real people with real lives at stake!

We continued walking up to the third floor. "Today we will be working in treatment room F, and with patients in rooms P26 through P32," Healer Autumn said, pausing in front of a long hallway. "Did Matron show you a treatment room yesterday?"

"Yes, she did."

"Good. They're all designed the same way. Herbs are on the right hand side, the workbench is near the back, and water, food, and the stove are on the left hand side. Plates and cups will be in the cabinets above the stove."

"Thank you for the reminder," I smiled.

"I will introduce you to the patients as we go in, so follow my lead. Be sure to keep up a smile and be friendly."

"Of course."

"Alright," Healer Autumn smiled, "let's begin."

Healer Autumn moved to the first door with a wooden sign next to it labeled P26. They knocked on the door, and called "This is the healer, may I come in?"

"Yes of course!" A feminine voice called from inside. Healer Autumn opened the door and we walked in to find a slim woman with long brown hair and blue eyes sitting on the bed holding the hand of a tall and very concerned looking dark-haired man.

"I am Healer Autumn, and this is Princess Avalynn. She's training at the hospital at the request of His Majesty the King so that she may help better serve the kingdom of Nevremerre." I smiled politely at the couple.

"Oh, Princess!" The woman exclaimed, "It's an honor to meet you!"

"Do we - should I -" The already concerned man panicked and nearly fell over as he moved into a deep bow.

"Please rise," I inwardly startled at the man's frantic movements. "I am here to aid the healers and to help the people of Nevremerre who come to this hospital, so please be at ease."

"As she said, today, the Princess is just a student, so there is no need for any formalities. However, with that being said, is it alright for the Princess' two guards to join us. They have all taken vows of secrecy regarding any patient information," Healer Autumn smiled. The couple shared a quick glance before the woman smiled and consented. Mateo and Carlos soon came in. Carlos stood seriously by the door, and Mateo partially hovered by my side.

"I will also be quizzing the Princess about proper treatments to aid in her learning. Will this be alright, or would you prefer I test her away from you?"

"No, of course it's alright," the woman smiled, "I am happy to help the Princess learn. Although, I must ask, Princess, does this mean you are no longer a candidate for Queen?" My heart lurched. Could this placement lead the public to believe that I'd chosen another career? Could that affect their confidence in me if I were to actually take the crown?

"Not at all," I hurriedly replied, "I am still a candidate for the throne. All my siblings and I have been placed by the King on a job in Nera to help the people, and, presumably, become better rulers in the process."

"Oh, how exciting," the woman clapped, a warm smile on her face.

"Shall we get on with your appointment then?" questioned Healer Autumn, "I believe the doctor's aide downstairs would have given you a file on your way in."

"Yes, here you are," said the woman, handing Healer Autumn a few sheets of parchment bound with twine. On the outside was a tag, which Healer Autumn consulted first. "Thank you very much Ms. Arabella."

Turning towards me, Healer Autumn explained, "These are Ms. Arabella's patient records. The doctor's aides bring them up when a patient checks in. It is our job to update them and return them to the library, sorted alphabetically then by birthdate, when the patient checks out." Turning back to Arabella, Healer Autumn continued the appointment. "Now, what brings you in today?"

"I've been getting really sick in the mornings. I learned in my last appointment that we are pregnant," Arabella smiled, grabbing the man's hand. I shot a discreet look at Carlos, and was amused by the look of utter terror he was now giving Arabella before he carefully restored his face to a neutral expression. "This is my first pregnancy," Arabella continued, still focused on Healer Autumn and me, "so we just want to make sure everything is okay."

"The baby's fine, right?" The man suddenly jumped in, his brows furrowed and a frantic look in his eyes, "They are both alright, right?"

"Calm yourself, Mr.?" Healer Autumn replied.

"Oh, I'm Taylor," the man responded.

"Well Mr. Taylor, and Ms. Arabella, there is absolutely no need to be concerned. Sickness in the morning is a perfectly normal part of the pregnancy, and is often a sign that the baby is healthy," Mr. Taylor released a huge sigh of relief at this news. "We can of course help with the nausea, Princess Ava-lynn, what would you prescribe?" Healer Autumn asked, turning towards me.

I felt my body seize up and my brain go numb as I tried to recall all I had learned in the past two days. It took what felt like forever for me to remember what treatments were made with what herbs, but I finally landed on a solid answer. I smiled, "I would prescribe a tea brew of ginger once a day."

"Nicely done," Healer Autumn nodded, and I felt myself swell with pride at her praise. "Now, Mr. Taylor, I notice that you have a bit of anxiety, would you like something to help you keep you more calm during this time?"

"I -" Mr. Taylor began his face twisting through several emotions before he breathed and continued, "Something to keep me calm would probably be for the best."

"Of course. Please understand that we can only treat the symptom, and not the underlying causes of your anxiety. However, since your stress seems mostly related to Ms. Arabella's pregnancy, I believe it is only temporary. If you continue to feel anxious or would like to seek further treatment, the hospital can introduce you to a variety of transitioners who are fully qualified to deal with mental health. There are also several hospital groups for new parents where you can discuss your fears with other new parents and hear from people who have already had their children. When we finish today you can return to the front desk if you wish to be connected to one of these groups. I will also be prescribing you a mild anxiety reliever."

"Thank you, Healer," Mr. Taylor nodded.

"Now, Princess, what would you prescribe for Mr. Taylor?"

I was quicker to respond this time, as Al occasionally suffered from bouts of anxiety and had a similar prescription. "A tincture of lavender and camomile applied to the temples should do the trick."

"Right again, Princess," Healer Autumn smiled. "Now, Mr. Taylor, I don't have your file on me, but do you know if you have an allergy to either of these herbs?"

"No, Healer."

"Good. We will go prepare both of your prescriptions now. We should return in about 10 to 20 minutes." Arabella and Mr. Taylor both thanked us as we left the room. I then followed Healer Autumn down towards the end of the hall. We entered a large room on the right hand side. I was immediately taken back by the room's brightness. Unlike room P26 which was an interior room lit by lanterns, the treatment room had three large windows letting the natural light illuminate the room.

"Princess, please measure out 21 teaspoons of ginger for Ms. Arabella. Morning sickness typically lasts about six weeks, but we'll have her come in again about three weeks from now to do her next check up. We can reevaluate her morning sickness then. I also need you to get me one camomile flower and two sprigs of lavender. We are running low on anxiety tinctures, so we should start steeping the flowers while we are here. The herbs will be in the closet over there, out of the sunlight." Healer Autumn then moved to the stove where she began grabbing bottles of what I assumed were vinegar and alcohol. I did what I was told, and soon a pungent aroma of herbs filled the room. Fortunately, the smell was not unpleasant. I was then asked to brew some ginger tea for Arabella while Healer Autumn updated her file.

I was then asked to rush down to the library to find Mr. Taylor's file for Healer Autumn to update as well. However, upon my arrival to the library, I realized that there were close to a hundred Taylors that the hospital had treated, and I had to run back up to the 3rd floor to ask Mr. Taylor's birthday before I could go back and find the appropriate file. I was more than slightly out of breath by the time I got back to Healer Autumn, who cheerfully informed me that now, at least, I'd learned to get more information before going to get a patient's record from the library. Healer Autumn updated Taylor's file before they handed both files, a jar of ginger flakes, and an anxiety tincture to me as they moved back towards room P26.

"I apologize for any delay," Healer Autumn smiled, "Here are your ginger flakes. Add one teaspoon to boiling water for three minutes every morning. Be sure to never have more than one cup of ginger tea a day to avoid any negative side effects. And, Mr. Taylor, here is your lavender and chamomile tincture. You may use this as often as necessary. Just apply to the temples, or wrists as needed. Ms. Arabella, please come back in three weeks so we can check on your status."

"Will do. Thank you very much!" Ms. Arabella replied, and Healer Autumn, Mateo, Carlos, and I gracefully ducked out of the room.

"Well done so far," Healer Autumn said cheerfully, "Now run those files down to the library and return them back to their correct positions. Then meet me back in the treatment room, and we'll go to our next patient. Be as quick as you can! We don't want to keep anyone waiting."

The next three hours were filled with the same basic pattern: 5 to 10 minutes spent leisurely discussing the patient's condition, followed by 10 to 20 minutes of frantically preparing the treatment, and returning the patient records back to the library. Then the process would start all over again. It was a little after 11:30 when we exited room P32 and Healer Autumn declared that we had finished with all the patients in this sector. I heard Carlos give a relieved sigh at Healer Autumn's words.

"We will now go discuss your performance with the Matron," Healer Autumn said brightly, and the sigh Carlos had just released was brought back in with his quick intake of breath. It was nice to know that even if I couldn't outwardly express my emotions, Carlos would do it for me. We followed Healer Autumn to the end of the hall, where they knocked on the corner office we were in just two days ago.

"Enter," came the Matron's voice from inside, and we all pushed inside the room. The Matron was sitting at her desk, her face was scrutinizing a series of documents, and her fierce gaze did not fade as she looked up to see us. "Healer Autumn, Princess, and the knights, please sit and give me your report," Matron Terella said, gesturing to the two chairs in front of her with her dark hand. Healer Autumn and I took our seats, and Mateo and Carlos took their place standing behind me. My stomach twisted and flipped as I waited for Healer Autumn's report.

"Overall, the Princess did very well," Healer Autumn started, and I couldn't help the relieved smile that came onto my face. "She was polite and kind to the patients. She has an excellent grasp of herbal properties. However, she does struggle with whether some of the treatments are best used as tinctures or infusions, but that is something that can be learned with more time. She works quickly and effectively without any complaints, so far. She did not do any diagnosing work today, however, with proper training, I believe she could work in any of the treatment rooms with scheduled patients quite effectively. She could stand to be a little faster, as we were about 5 to 10 minutes behind schedule. Speed can naturally increase with greater familiarity, though," Healer Autumn finished. Their report made my chest feel lighter, although I did seriously doubt I could speed up my work without sprinting through the hospital, something I'm sure the Matron would not be a fan of. Despite my good report, I was holding my breath as I waited for the Matron's response. To my astonishment, the Matron smiled. To say I was shocked would be a dramatic understatement. I was flummoxed, flabbergasted, astounded, and absolutely baffled that the Matron was smiling at all, even more so that she was smiling at me.

"Excellent," Matron said, "It's good to know she can be useful somewhere." If I wasn't still reeling from the Matron's continued smile, I'm sure I would have been offended by that statement. "How were her knights?"

"Not in the way at all." If possible, the Matron's smile grew even wider.

"Absolutely wonderful," the Matron exclaimed before her smile quickly vanished, "Now, Princess, you will get an hour off for lunch, be sure to return back to the hospital on time. You'll be working in the ER next. You will primarily be observing, although there may be times when you and your knights may be asked for assistance. If not expressly asked, stay out of the way. The ER can be very hectic. That being said, I will see you back in this office in exactly one hour." I thanked the Matron, and Mateo, Carlos, and I made a quick retreat out of the hospital.

"What time is it now?" I asked Mateo as we walked out onto the sunlit street. A hot breeze hit the back of my neck, and I realized, for the first time, how cold the inside of the hospital was.

"It's a quarter before 12, Princess," Mateo answered.

I nodded, "We should try to be back by 12:40, to ensure we aren't late," I said, not even wanting to imagine Matron's reaction should we be tardy. "Now what should we have to eat?" In the end we settled on some meat pies from a nearby butcher. We ate by a fountain in the Town Square after hastily hiding my crown in the butcher's bag our pies came in so we would be less likely to be disturbed. Mateo quizzed me on more medical facts from my textbooks, while Carlos kept track of time. Even with the hot sun beating down upon us, my lunch with Carlos and Mateo was the most relaxed I'd felt all day. It seemed like all too soon I was putting my crown back on and we were hurrying back to the hospital.

Despite my brief respite, and good review from earlier, I still felt nervous as we approached the brownish-red brick hospital building. I knew the Matron wasn't one for exaggeration, and her words surrounding the ER scared me. I couldn't help but remember the man with the broken leg, and my stomach gave a lurch in revolt. I had no idea what to expect as we made our way back to the Matron's office.

"Good, you're on time," Matron called as we entered her office. "Healer Autumn should be here any moment. While you wait, I shall remind you all once more to not show any reactions as you greet your patients. There's a variety of reasons people come to the ER, some are more mundane and easier to work with, but some can be gruesome. However bad an injury might be, you need to stay calm. The patient and the person who brought in the patient will likely be extremely anxious and concerned. By staying calm you give them the greatest assurance that you are capable, responsible, and will do everything in your power to help the patient. Easing their fears will be one of the best ways you can start to treat someone. Just don't tell any lies. If a patient's friend or family is overly concerned, just inform them that this is the premier hospital in Nevremerre, the doctors here are some of the most highly trained individuals in the nation, and that we will be doing our absolute best to treat the patient. Can you handle that?" Matron looked sternly at the three of us.

"Yes Matron," we all hurriedly replied. The Matron just nodded in response, returning her attention to sign some document before her. Mateo, Carlos, and I stood in the stiff silence for a while longer before Healer Autumn entered the room. I don't think I've ever been more relieved to see anyone in my life.

"Oh, you're here," they smiled warmly, "Let's get going then. Anything else, Matron?"

"No," the Matron replied, waving us off. We were quick to leave the room. We followed Healer Autumn down to the first floor where we stopped in front of a supply closet. As we entered, we were each given a pair of cotton gloves and a mask. They were to prevent any strange bodily fluids from getting on us, Healer Autumn explained. "Having other people's blood coating your skin is an uncomfortable experience," they added with a self-assured nod that could only have come from personal experience, "The mask is because occasionally things fly onto your face, it covers most of your face without blocking your vision," Doctor Autumn continued brightly. With gloves and masks on, we were ready to enter the ER. I held my breath as Doctor Autumn pushed open two wooden cream-colored doors, and we entered a large room full of bustling people.

The shift was instantaneous. Everyone here moved with a purpose. People called out for supplies. There was a heavily pregnant woman screaming as someone who appeared to be her wife failed to calm her. A mother was loudly yelling at her son, who was looking rather miserable with a gash on his arm. And, there was a man in the far corner sitting on a bed with a bucket looking distinctly pale and queasy. Healer Autumn went to a desk of healer aides, picked up a file, and our ER shift began.

A little over five hours later I found myself sitting on a bench on the first floor of the hospital next to a dazed looking Mateo and an exhausted looking Carlos, who was cradling his head in his hands. All of our clothes were spattered with blood, courtesy of an irate man who insisted on gesticulating wildly with his open arm wound. A case of food poisoning resulted in my nose still feeling clogged by the uncomfortable odors of herbs, blood, and vomit. My feet ached from running back and forth from patients, to supply closets, to treatment rooms, then to new patients again. Despite the hustle of the hospital still surrounding us, I felt like the world around me had slowed, dragging my energy with it. And yet, I couldn't help but think about the relieved smile of the mother who was told her son's broken arm would heal, the laughter of the man whose boyfriend had accidentally cut him while preparing dinner, at said boyfriend's panicked apologizes, and the sweet kisses shared between the two new mothers as they held their new-born daughter.

Healer Autumn was as cheerful as ever as they bid us good-bye, informing us that we did very well today, and that they would likely see us in two days' time. As we silently trudged out of the hospital and down the street to the carriage, I was greeted with the sight of a group of children screaming and laughing as they chased their way down the street. Their laughter rippled through the orange and pink sky, their smiles illuminated by the soft light of the street lanterns as the workers began to light them for the evening. It's for them, I thought, the ache in my feet still ever present. These smiles, these laughs, and these moments of joy and love, that's why I work until my feet ache. They're why I push myself to stand tall even if my back has tension and is in pain. It's so I can keep their smiles present, their laughter free and easy, and give them as many moments of joy as I possibly can. That's why I fight to be Queen, that's why I will keep trying my hardest to heal those who come to the hospital. It's all for the people of Nevremerre, my people.

Chapter 10

The New Competitor

The carriage ride back was a mostly silent affair. Largely due to Carlos falling asleep on Mateo's shoulder. I occupied myself by looking out the window, and I watched as the burnt orange of the sun was slowly consumed by the inky blue of the night. The carriage was rocking around me as we moved over the cobblestone streets, lulling me into a gentle peace. I savored the quiet stillness that I had not had since this morning. The exhausted quiet that we had created in the carriage was shockingly permeated by my Mother who was waiting for us as the carriage pulled up to the palace.

"You're late," she called as Mateo opened the carriage door, "and why are you covered in blood?" Mother frowned. This was a bit of an exaggeration, in my opinion. The blood splatters were pretty thin, and largely invisible against my purple tunic. I opened my mouth to explain, but was promptly cut off. "It's not important, just go upstairs and change for dinner," Mother all but pushed me towards the castle.

"Mother, dinner doesn't even start till 7:30, it's not even 7:00 yet, I don't understand what the issue is."

"Don't argue. Just get cleaned up. Your Father's got an announcement for you all. I've laid out something for you to wear. Just don't be late."

"I... alright, I'll get going then," I eyed her curiously, but I switched to a more active pace to get to my room, although my feet gave pained protests. Ana and Charlotte were already waiting for me when I entered the room. Ana immediately grabbed a wet towel, and began to wipe down my body, while Charlotte grabbed a stool and began redoing my hair.

"What's with everyone? We're not expecting guests this evening, are we?" I asked, a little dismayed at the mad dash my maids were going through to get me dressed. I was also slightly disappointed by the feeling that I was going right back into the rushed hospital pace rather than getting my highly desired leisurely rest.

"It's the Queen's orders, Princess. We don't know exactly what's happening, but it's best we prepare you to look as regal as possible," Ana replied swiftly. I stood there quietly as I was quickly changed into an oddly formal blue dress with silk straps lightly falling off my shoulders. It cinched at my waist, but flowed down at the bottom. My crown, which had been taken off to adjust my hair, was wiped down and placed back on my head, adding an uncomfortable pressure to my skull. My hair was now loose, and fell in light curls down my back. A silver necklace and bracelet were added, and my swollen feet were stuffed into a pair of stiff blue flats that pinched uncomfortably into my skin.

"You best hurry down now, Princess," Ana said, giving me a final once-over. I held back my comment that I still had

10 minutes until dinner, and thanked them before leaving the room. I felt curiosity and anxiety well up inside my chest. What could father possibly have to tell us that would warrant this kind of frenzy? In my heart, I knew it had something to do with the succession to the throne, but I refused to consider the possibilities. Worst-case scenarios of me being cast out of succession were already trying to force their way into the forefront of my mind, and my exhausted mental faculties struggled to hold them off.

Despite being early into the dining room, my whole family was already sitting there. I noticed a curious extra seat to Ari's left, but I made my way towards the table without comment. There was a tense atmosphere in the room. Mama was fidgeting with her hands, and Mother was sitting up straighter than usual, if such a thing were even possible. Even Father had a small frown as he watched me take my seat. My brothers looked just as confused as I was, and Ari's eyes kept flickering to the extra seat beside him. I also noted that everyone in the room was more finely dressed than usual.

"Ehem," Father cleared his throat, "Now that you're all here, there have been some developments we should discuss." Father paused looking at my brothers and me. A heavy and anxious silence filled the room, as our undivided attention focused on Father. "It seems that a Lord has expressed interest in becoming King. He met with the council today, and explained why he should, at least, be given the opportunity. The topic was given much deliberation, but it was eventually decided that he should be considered for the position." My stomach dropped. What on Earth was going on?

"What?!" Azar cried, speaking my thoughts aloud. Al and Ari wore matching expressions of shock. Al opened his mouth, pushing himself forward as if to argue with Father. His arguments, however, never saw the light of day as Father raised his hand to stop him.

"Silence! I understand your feelings," Father insisted. How can you possibly understand? You only had to fight with your brother for the throne, I thought bitterly. For some reason I felt my eyes prick with tears that I had to hold back. "There will be much stricter rules for his candidacy than any of yours. For starters, he can be eliminated at any time. Unlike any of you who can only be eliminated as an option once Ari turns 21. In the meantime, however, he will join us living in the palace, and, when we tour the country again in the fall, he will join us. He will learn a ruler's trade as you do until he's either eliminated from consideration or until the final decision is made the day after Ari's 21st birthday." Father continued on.

"But on that day, whoever this Lord is could be King? If not eliminated previously that is," Al asked.

"If not eliminated previously, then yes, he could be King," Father replied. Silence loomed over the room once more, this time a shocked and contemplative one.

"And, just who is this noble? " I asked, finding my voice once more.

"Ah, yes, August and Lydia, if you would tell him to come in," Father nodded at the two guards by the door. They opened the door, and a white-hot anger roared inside of me. "I believe you all know Lord Nicholas," Father said, as Lord Nicholas swept into a bow. His brown eyes were gleaming as he stood up.

With an easy smile he said, "Your Majesties, Your Highnesses, it's a pleasure to be here."

"Please sit, Lord Nicholas," Mother said with a polite smile," King Edgar will briefly go over your schedule while you are here."

"Yes," Father nodded as Lord Nicholas sat down. "As you are twenty-one, and no longer require a formal education, your schedule will closely align with that of my three elder children. However, since you are not a knight, and I believe you said you do not train with a weapon you will have some more freedom."

"I may not train with a weapon, but I do like to study strategy and battle planning, like Her Majesty Queen Elenore," Lord Nicholas interjected.

"That's good. Since my two eldest children are knights, your schedule will mirror Princess Avalynn's, while we are at the royal palace." At that moment I recognized how very grateful I was that the Matron had been training me not to outwardly show in a reaction. Without her training I believe I would have recoiled in outrage and disgust at the idea of sharing a schedule with this man. Instead, I kept a graceful smile on my face as I began to eat my dinner.

"Your mornings will be free, and afternoons will be spent learning and observing the generals during soldier training. Evenings will usually be gatherings with the nobles, as you have already experienced. Finally, every two days you will go out on assignment with one of my children. You'll spend the next two weeks with Prince Alveron working on Nera's infrastructure, then two weeks with Prince Azar working on landscaping and construction, then two weeks with Princess

Avalynn at the hospital, and, finally, two weeks with Prince Ari at the docks. I should warn all of you the council is debating making you work at these assignments every other day, so be prepared."

"Yes, Your Majesty," We all chimed in, cognizant of Lord Nicholas' presence. I found myself wondering if I would ever again have a normal, relaxed dinner with just my family. I internally shook my head. No, of course I would. Lord Nicholas didn't have the power to change everything in my life, I quietly seethed.

"Princess Avalynn," Mother called, "How was your placement today? You came back with blood all over your shirt," she said. I immediately understood that this was her attempt to allow friendly, not awkward conversation at the table.

"A hazard of working at a hospital," I smiled going along with her plan. I went on to describe my day at the hospital, and, if I embellished my role in helping people slightly, you could hardly blame me while Lord Nicholas was there trying to weasel his way onto the throne. Dinner progressed remarkably calmly, for an event where at least four participants were actively plotting the downfall of another person at the table, and soon it was time to say good night. To my horror, it seemed Lord Nicholas' temporary room was near my own, and he walked with me down the halls of the castle.

"So, how did you like my little surprise?" he smiled.

"Is that what you call it? Well, if you consider becoming King just a little change in your life then your surprise is no matter to me, as you won't be here very long," I replied quickly.

Lord Nicholas just chuckled, however, and replied, "How very like you, Princess, but I think you'll find that I'll be here for a while."

"I'll believe it when I see it," I snorted.

"Oh, now tell me Princess, why won't you even consider the idea of me being King." I stopped walking, and turned to face him, my emerald eyes meeting his brown. Speaking slowly and deliberately, I laid out my point of view so there could be no misunderstandings.

"Lord Nicholas, you would make a terrible King because everything you do is done out of selfish desire for power, nothing more. If you were King you would inevitably make decisions that put your own goals above what is best for the people, and the King cannot rule like that." Lord Nicolas looked briefly taken aback.

"How could you possibly know what my motives for becoming King are?"

"Well, to begin with, it seems clear now that your first plan was to seduce my brothers and/or myself to get on the throne," Lord Nicholas at least had the decency to look a little bit ashamed at this, so I pressed forward, "Then there's your timing. We still have seven years before the official decision, and all my brothers and I have been working tirelessly to become the best rulers we can be. It's not like there is a lack of good candidates," I declared, trying to keep the hurt and anger out of my voice. "We will have grown even more in seven years. You can't say that you thought we would have been bad rulers because even if you were right at this point in time, we still have seven years to change that. Father is still healthy, so it's not like he needs an immediate replacement. So, you coming forward now can't be anything more than personal greed. Know this, Lord Nicholas, there's no way I will allow someone as greedy as you to become the caretaker of Nevremerre. For that's all a ruler is really, a caretaker of the land and its people. Our people deserve more than you," I finished my tirade.

I felt myself panting slightly as I finished speaking, letting me know that I let out more of my anger than I intended to. However instead of calming me, I felt my anger continue to grow. "I'll say good night, Lord Nicholas," I turned and walked away so no more of my anger could leak out. It was only when I made it back to my room that I realized he had not followed me despite his room being in the same direction.

Ana and Charlotte were as efficient as ever in getting me ready for bed. Father had informed us before dinner had ended that it was best to keep Lord Nicholas' candidacy for the throne a secret for now, so I didn't bother to tell them about my evening. Fortunately, they were kind enough to let me be alone with my thoughts and did not press the issue. Once they had left for the evening I flopped onto my bed and stared at the red canopy above me with a sigh. Weren't my brothers and I qualified to rule? Why did the council just let some Lord become an option for King? Despite my passionate declaration to Lord Nicholas earlier, I couldn't help but wonder if this all happened because of some failing of mine. Was I not a good enough candidate for Queen? I had studied for this job for eight years. What could I be lacking?

Whatever the reason, I thought, I meant it when I said I would never allow Lord Nicholas to become King. I would just have to work harder, I decided. I'd become a better strategist and General. I would befriend and gain the trust of more nobles. Above all, I would work harder than anybody else during this placement. I would work hard for my people to become the best Queen they could have. I would make it so no one could have any doubts about my abilities to be Queen. With my goal in mind, I soon fell asleep, ready to work hard for Nevremerre the next day, and all the days after that.

2

PART TWO

Chapter 11

The Rumors About Lord Nicholas

Two weeks had passed since Father's fateful announce-ment, and my days had only gotten busier. As Father sug-gested, we did end up working every other day at our respective jobs. I spent hours in the hospital learning how to treat patients, identify illnesses, and assist in medical re-search. All my days not in the hospital were spent in the library, reading whatever I could about Nevremerre. I was re-ed-ucating myself on our history, our economy, our trade deals, our taxation policies. Basically, I was reading whatever I could to make myself Nevremerre's perfect Queen.

At least for the first week into his candidacy, I was being almost constantly followed by Lord Nicholas; who, unfortu-nately, turned out to be reasonably smart, fairly decent at gen-eral strategy, and infuriatingly charming. Although his position as a possible future King was being kept quiet, he had some-how managed to befriend most of the knights. Many of whom were spending their training laughing with Lord Nicholas, in-stead of actually practicing their fighting techniques. Even beyond the knights, Lord Nicholas seemed to have the impossible ability of making every single noble like him. In my darker moments, I was forced to recognize that his charisma, along with his knowledge and ability, would make him a great King. The ability to make people cooperate and listen to you, to have them feel safe and respected around you, these were vital aspects of ruling.

I could not let Lord Nicholas ascend to the throne, however. Deep from my core, one truth radiated through my bones, and even though he never had officially said it, I knew the truth – Lord Nicholas's quest for the throne was nothing more than a desire for personal power. So, I studied. At noble events, I made a greater effort to speak to each noble, to learn the names of their kids, their hobbies, and other mundane trivia that might help me connect with these people. I worked to show them that they could trust me and that I wanted to help them and Nevremerre grow. Every night I would return to my room exhausted and each day it would feel that sleep just barely helped me recover. Even though I was there to study, the silence of the library became a refuge. There was an indescribable pleasure of knowing that nobody would try to talk to me if I was hidden away in the corner reading.

I was, of course, not the only one who ramped up their education and hopes of ruling. Al was in the library almost every time I entered, and more than once, we had whispered arguments over a book we both reached for at the same time. Ari was spending more time than ever on the training ground and it looked like his lanky beanpole shape was finally starting to broaden. Oddly, the only person who did not attempt to ramp up their King training was Azar. Despite his outburst at dinner the night we were told of Lord Nicholas' candidacy, Azar had not changed his behavior at all. When I asked him one afternoon why Lord Nicholas' candidacy didn't worry him, he simply replied, "because he will never be chosen." I was taken aback by the certainty of his answer. I was even more astonished when he followed it up with, "I could learn something from how he interacts with people though." I stared at him, my mouth gaping open. Had Azar grown and become wise at some point? Would I actually have to start listening to him now? "Hey, do you think I could beat a bear in a fistfight?" Nope, he was still my favorite bonehead.

With that, two more weeks passed, and I found myself sitting in the hospital's library next to Murphy. The uncomfortable foreknowledge that Lord Nicholas would soon be spending two weeks working here, loomed over my head. As a late-stage apprentice, Murphy was still stuck doing basic patient rounds, despite his obvious disdain for having to talk to people. Thus Healer Autumn had often taken us both along on her rounds. Soon, however, Murphy and I were allowed to go on rounds sans supervisor. It was here, after a few arguments with some rather startled patients that it was agreed that I should take over the speaking part of an examination. Despite his... direct approach to talking with patients, it was clear that Murphy was going to be a brilliant healer. He was well-versed in various illnesses and their treatments and he was able to discover the source of an illness almost as soon as he began an examination. However, where his brilliance really showed was in his research.

About twice a week, my afternoons at the hospital were spent in the research library or in a lab trying to find new and better cures for the diseases we encountered. During my first few weeks at the hospital, it was clear that Murphy only grudgingly allowed Mateo, Carlos, and me to be with him as he worked. However, as we proved to not be wholly incompetent, our presence became more tolerated. It didn't take long after that for our presence to be welcomed, as Murphy's obvious enthusiasm spilled over and Mateo and I began giving our own suggestions on how we could improve medicine. After several ideas that were immediately dismissed as utterly idiotic, we finally landed on one that was deemed "not impossible" and "could be worth a try". From then on, Mateo and I were eagerly included in Murphy's work, and it quickly became one of my favorite parts of the week. Carlos, it seemed, never quite got the hang of medicine, nor was he in any way interested to learn anything more than the absolute basics. As such, he spent his time trying to find the weirdest diseases he could or practice his sword drills. One memorable afternoon, he elected to try to practice stealth and observation. This was quickly shut down after the Matron, whom he had been following, suddenly turned around and yelled at him for "practicing stalker-like behavior unbefitting of a gentleman". Suitably chastised, Carlos never did try to hone his stealth skills again, much to Mateo's and my disappointment. It was, after all, very entertaining.

So, when the Matron walked into the library two days before Lord Nicholas was meant to start his two week stint at the hospital, she saw nothing out of the ordinary as she walked over to our table. Mateo, Murphy, and I were discussing the benefits and drawbacks of using garlic versus thyme in preventing strokes, and Carlos was leaning back in his chair tossing an apple.

"Feet off the table," the Matron said sternly, interrupting Mateo's assertion that daily walks could do more for preventing strokes than either thyme or garlic. Her voice caused Carlos to fall backwards. He was only just able to catch himself, and his chair, on the table behind him. The apple did not have the same luck, however, and it hit the floor with a smack. Carlos looked sheepishly at the Matron, who only raised an eyebrow in response. Although, I could have sworn I saw a slight smile on her lips.

"I'm here to give you these," she said, handing me a stack of books that looked suspiciously like the original stack of beginners medicine books that I had received. "His Majesty informs me that there will be another royal volunteer coming for the next two weeks."

"He's not a royal," I blurted out, irritation flashing within me at the thought of Lord Nicholas joining us.

"Excuse me?" the Matron queried, raising her eyebrow at me this time.

"He's the son of a Count," I replied. I felt more than a little foolish at having insisted on the clarification, but I carried on anyway, "Therefore, he's not technically a member of the royal family."

"Nevertheless," the Matron continued, curiously glancing over at me, "See to it that he receives these, and inform him that I expect him to be well prepared for our work here."

"Of course," I nodded. Satisfied, the Matron turned and walked away.

"So, who is he?" Murphy asked, staring quizzically at the books the Matron had just left. "I wasn't aware that any other roy- erhm - nobles were coming. What is he like?" I opened my mouth to respond, but Carlos beat me to it.

"He's a selfish bastard."

"Carlos!" I admonished, shocked.

"What? It's true!" Carlos grumbled.

"Well, I must admit you are the first to say such a thing to me. Most people find him charming," I said, desperately trying to keep the contempt out of my voice. Judging by Carlos's smirk after my words, I was not wholly successful.

"It's true that most people he's acquainted with speak highly of him," Mateo added helpfully.

"Well that's just because most people don't know that –"

"Sir Carlos" I interjected, quickly, realizing where this was likely going, "Whatever Prince Azar told you, I am quite confident it was meant to be kept a secret." Carlos lowered his head, and I saw a tinge of red for his cheeks.

"I apologize, Princess. I forgot myself momentarily."

"It's alright Carlos," I replied, but mentally I was kicking Azar for running his mouth so easily. Not that I would begrudge him having a friend and confident. Plus, I was 98% certain that Carlos would never betray Azar's faith. However, there was no doubt that Carlos could, at times, be a little careless with his words. If word got out that another person was added to the competition for the crown, it would likely inspire other greedy and power-hungry men and women to try their hand at claiming the throne. My musings were banished from my head as Carlos spoke once more.

"There's all kinds of rumors about him at the palace," I frowned at Carlos, who apparently only needed a moment to forget his earlier shame. However, I found myself responding anyway.

"I wasn't aware he was the subject of such gossip," I prompted, my curiosity getting the better of me.

"Oh yes! It's not gone unnoticed that he appears to be getting special attention from the royal family. They say he's taking lessons from the first Queen, and he's been fighting on the training grounds with the second Queen. Now, I can't verify the first one, but we have seen them on the training grounds, haven't we Mateo? Although, I've never actually seen him spar with the second Queen." I glanced at Mateo, who was looking at Carlos exasperatedly. Apparently he was not thrilled at the thought of being pulled into Carlos's gossip. In no way fazed by Mateo's lack of response, Carlos plunged recklessly forward with his tale, "There are three main theories for his presence with the Princes and the Princess. The first states that he is being considered for a council position and needs to learn the ropes and become close with whomever becomes the next ruler. The second theory is that he is betrothed to one of the Princes or the Princess. He's been seen reportedly flirting with all of them, so it's anyone's guess who he might marry."

"Ari is only 14! How could anyone possibly think he's engaged?" I interrupted.

Carlo sent me an irritated glance, which I returned with a raised eyebrow of my own. "Stranger things have happened," Carlos argued. Although, as I sustained my incredulous look he conceded, "Well, most agree it's likely not the third Prince."

"Plus, with the Princess' obvious disbelief at the notion, I think we can safely disregard the idea that the Third Prince is marrying this mysterious noble," added Murphy, helpfully.

"All right, fine, but it's a much better story to say he was flirting with all of them," Carlos grumbled. I didn't feel the need to mention that technically that part of the story was true.

"And so what's theory number three?" I encouraged.

"Oh yes, theory three is that the King and Queens found him charming and are trying to set him up with one of the Princes or the Princess!" Carlos finished excitedly. Murphy looked back at the books thoughtfully, and Mateo's face relaxed ever-so-slightly, a sign they both had accepted the three presented theories. However, I wasn't quite so easily sated. None of these theories were even correct after all, although the first one wasn't too far off.

"Is that really all there is? No one has any other theories?" I asked Carlos.

"None that anyone believes," he replied with a knowing nod in my direction. It appears that no one even thought his increased appearances had anything to do with a desire for the crown.

"I had no idea court life held so much gossip," Murphy said idly, his research seemingly forgotten for the moment.

"Well, I'd never heard any of these rumors before, so it's not that bad," I said, feeling the need to defend the palace life.

"That would be because usually people have the tact not to mention the baseless rumors to the person those rumors are about," Mateo said, looking accusingly at Carlos, who at least had the presence of mind to look ashamed.

"Still, it may be helpful for me to know what kinds of rumors are spreading around the palace," I said thoughtfully.

"I wouldn't worry about it Princess, I doubt His Majesty pays any attention to rumors," Mateo assured me.

"Perhaps, but it's a poor choice to underestimate word of mouth," I maintained.

"Well, either way, I hope this mysterious noble can keep up," said Murphy, turning back to his research. I noted however, that his eyes stayed on the same page for the rest of our time in the library. The rest of the afternoon was spent in silent study. It wasn't long before Mateo, Carlos, and I were heading back to the palace.

Chapter 12

The Transitioner's Arrival

As I walked into the main entrance of the palace, I had a mad thought to just not give Lord Nicholas the books and watch him struggle on his first day at the hospital. I quickly dismissed this idea as insane; however, and I forced myself to remember that this would really only hurt the patients and myself in the long run. I steeled my nerves and moved through the west wing towards where Lord Nicolas was staying. I felt almost awkward walking through the palace halls. As I approached Lord Nicholas' room I had the curious sensation that I wasn't quite welcome in this part of the palace. I also felt the eyes of the passing servants linger upon me. I wondered if my brothers had ever come this way before or if I was just adding fuel to the wedding rumors Carlos had spoken of. Finally, I reached Lord Nicholas' door. I realized, suddenly, as I raised my hand to knock, that he may not even be in right now. I might just be able to leave the books by the door and not see Lord Nicholas at all! For a glorious moment a bubble of hope filled my body as I tapped on the door.

"Just a moment," a voice called out, and my bubble of hope popped, leaving only a twinge of disappointment, and a large spike of annoyance in its wake. True to his word, Lord Nicholas opened the door a moment later. "Avalynn," he gasped, looking more than a little shocked.

"The correct way to address me is 'Princess Avalynn', Lord Nicholas. You must be aware that the use of one's title is a matter of common decency between people," I replied haughtily, my annoyance growing inside me.

Lord Nicholas recovered from his shock with a quick smile, "Does that mean you find me decent, Princess Avalynn?" he said, brazenly leaning on the open door frame.

"I treat all people with decency, Lord Nicholas, as it is only basic courtesy to do so. However, I must admit, in your case you do make it rather difficult," I frowned. I felt my face twitching in irritation as the bastard had the nerve to smile even wider at my statement. "These are for you," I thrust the medical books into his hand before he had the chance to say something else to anger me. "The Matron at the hospital expects you to have read them before you go to the hospital in two days time. They will allow you to assist in treatment and care of the patients, so be sure to read them thoroughly," I finished, turning to leave.

"You can't mean we're actually treating the patients?" Lord Nicholas exclaimed, and I turned to see the shocked look was back on his face.

"Of course. What else would we be doing?"

"I don't know, hospital management or something? Stocking cupboards maybe?" Lord Nicholas said, running a hand through his brown hair.

"Hospital management? Lord Nicholas, we are not healers, we have no medical knowledge or training, what could we possibly know about hospital management?" I asked incredulously.

"What do we know of treating patients? Surely, a person training to run a kingdom has some management skills."

"It's not like we're asked to treat patients unsupervised, and I've just given you the basic information on treating patients. While it's true we do get educated on accounting, resource allocation, and supply management, we are not aware of the specific needs of the hospital. Thus, we would have a hard time managing a medical facility. Not to mention, the Matron, and all those who manage the hospital, are highly capable. They most certainly do not need us coming in and making a mess of things. Besides, most of the medical work we are asked to do is to make tinctures, balms, and teas that are used to treat people. Surely even you can boil tea!" I snapped.

"They could just as easily teach us management as they could teach us how to boil tea. How does it teach us anything about ruling to just be subpar healers?" Lord Nicholas persisted.

I took a deep breath, as fury filled my veins. "Lord Nicholas, the purpose of a good ruler is to help the people, and whichever way they may need it. We are to be healer's assistants because a good healer's assistant increases a healer's efficiency by 13%," I responded remembering the fact the Matron told me during my second week of hospital work. I was assuming this was meant to be a compliment that she had said it with a slight smile, and I kept my job as a healer's assistant. "The more efficient the healers are, the more patients we can treat, and the more people we can help. Not to mention the healthier our people are, the more people can work, spend, and help our economy grow. Keeping our people happy and healthy benefits everyone in Nevremerre. So, I suggest that you take your books, read them, and turn yourself into the best healer you can be in the next two weeks, so that we can help the people of Nevremerre," I finished, storming away.

My blood rushed to my head as my anger roared inside of me. How dare he! The purpose of a monarch was to help the people. The purpose of the tasks Father had given us was to help the people. If we were all meant to learn hospital management, we would have all been sent to the hospital! Or, more likely, someone would have come to tutor us. The Matron specifically put us where she thought we would have the most impact and be the most helpful, and here Lord Nicholas was only worried about how this might help him be King. I stormed through the palace in such a rage, I didn't even notice another person until I landed rather ungracefully on my butt looking up at a tall figure.

"Best be careful now, Princess," a dark hand reached out to help me up, "We can hardly have you running into everyone you meet, you might end up with a nasty bruise on your rear." I blushed as I looked up to apologize to the man I'd run into. He had dark skin and a flat nose. White locks were tied behind his head, and he had wrinkles around his eyes and mouth. Despite my running into him, his dark eyes shined, looking more amused than disturbed or annoyed.

"I apologize, Sir, for running into you," I said with as much dignity as someone who had fallen just a minute ago could muster.

The man just chuckled lightly, his deep voice reverberating with a calm joy as he responded, "It's no matter; she said I might find you all in a rather anxious state. Clearly, she was not wrong."

"She?" I inquired.

"Oh, allow me to introduce myself, Princess. I am Sir Abel, a good friend of the Dowager Queen Elizabeth. She sent me your way about a month ago, asking me to help support you, your siblings, and your parents. She sensed you might all be in some distress, and, as per usual, Betty appears to have been correct. I'm only sorry business kept me from coming sooner."

"Nana sent you?" I queried processing his words.

"Indeed she did," Sir Abel smiled, "I just introduced myself to His Majesty, and gave him the letter of introduction the Dowager Queen gave to me. It appears I will be staying with you until the Harvest. I believe I will enjoy the chance to get to know you, Princess."

"And I you, Sir Abel," I responded curiously. As I moved around him to head back to my room, I was astonished to find the fury I held onto on the way here had all but vanished. In all of my 19 years, Nana had never sent someone to visit us in the palace, and yet here was Sir Abel. I couldn't deny that if he could calm my inner turmoil like Nana, he would be a welcomed asset right now.

Sir Abel was already at the table when I came down for dinner an hour later. It seemed that he, along with Lord Nicholas, would be joining us for family meals. I had to admit, that despite his jovial attitude and calming demeanor, I regretted his intrusion in our family meals. It seemed like these days I hardly ever got a chance to speak with my brothers or even my parents without someone being pulled away to some other task. In the past, no matter how much we were all fighting for the crown or how busy we were, we would always try to make the time to sit and to eat together, just the seven of us, and sometimes Nana. Now that each meal had the addition of Sir Nicholas, they felt more like a formal dinner party than a quiet night with my family. It seemed like Sir Abel, too, would be joining our mix.

"Hello there, Princess," Sir Abel called out, "I hope I am not sitting in your usual seat." I looked around to notice that he was, in fact, sitting in my seat, two seats over from where Mother already sat at the end of the table.

"It's no matter, Sir Abel," I said sincerely as I took Ari's usual seat across from him. In truth I was grateful for the ability to switch sides of the table as, for the past fortnight, I had been forced to endure Lord Nicholas seated to my right. The seat change was a result of Ari nearly yelling at Lord Nicholas two weeks earlier after he accidentally drank from Ari's water glass.

When Ari entered, slightly after Mama, he shot me a confused glance and stated, "You're in my seat."

"Yes, our guest, Sir Abel is occupying the seat I normally use. Why don't you sit next to me?" I offered, selfishly blocking myself from Lord Nicholas at all sides.

"Alright," Ari shrugged, taking the seat to my left, "but be careful of Azar, he pinches."

"He what?" I countered, but I never received an answer because Father opened the door, almost dragging Al and Azar with him as Lord Nicholas followed gleefully behind.

"Found them fighting on the staircase again," Father said by way of greeting, "Hardly the behavior of two fully grown men, and two official knights to boot!"

"They didn't break anything again, did they?" Mother asked, exasperation evident in her tone.

"No, I believed I arrived before a physical fight broke out," Father replied.

"It was not a fight," Al insisted, "merely a spirited debate of views." No one seemed to believe this, and Mama even snorted at his words.

"Well sit down then, all of you," Father said, "I believe it's time to eat, and for me to introduce our new guest," be finished gesturing to Sir Abel. Al and Azar exchanged similar glances of shock, as they both noticed Sir Abel's presence for the first time. Lord Nicholas's face, however, expressed a quick frown before it morphed once more into a clearly fake smile and he slipped into a small bow.

"A pleasure to meet you Sir, I Am Lord Nicholas."

"Yes, this is Sir Abel everyone," Father explained as Lord Nicholas took his seat, "The Dowager Queen has sent him here to assist with all of our mental well-being. I know this has been a stressful time for everyone here, and it is vital that we all take care of our minds, bodies, and souls. For our own benefit, and for the Kingdom's. As such, Sir Abel will join us for dinner each evening, and I wish each of you, including you, Lord Nicholas, to spend an hour with him on the days you are not working at your jobs. He's well aware of Lord Nicholas' position, so there is no need to hold anything back," Father finished with a smile.

"Thank you for the welcome, King Edgar," Sir Abel said sincerely, "I have been granted the use of the green sitting room on the first floor for meetings. I prefer to work when people need me, so please come and visit at any point in the day. However, if I am in the middle of a meeting with another one of you, I will put a ribbon on the door handle. If you come by and a ribbon is present, please come again at a different time. I greatly look forward to meeting and getting to know all of you," Sir Abel finished, smiling.

"And you as well, Sir Abel," Al responded quickly, as the rest of us followed up with polite nods. As we all settled into our dinner I wondered what exactly my sessions with Sir Abel would include. Father had suggested that we could talk to Sir Abel about Lord Nicholas' recent intrusion on the competition to the throne, but at the same time, who knows what Sir Abel's role would be in determining who became King or Queen.

As if reading my mind, Mother piped-in and said, "I should like to clarify that Sir Abel is not a member of the council, and will not be included in the decision on who will rule. He also insisted that any private conversations we have be completely confidential, so please feel free to speak with him however you wish." Sir Abel nodded, agreeing with Mother's words.

"How interesting," Lord Nicholas commented. "I'm sure this will be a very helpful exercise in order for us to learn how to lead," he smiled at Sir Abel. "I'm sure your work must be fascinating please do tell me more about it, and yourself, Sir." I fought the instinct to roll my eyes, as I watched Lord Nicholas' rather blatant attempt at flattery. His treacly sweet voice was just a pitch or two higher than normal. It made my stomach want to revolt, and left a bitter taste in my mouth.

Sir Abel, however, did not share my disgust, and he was still smiling as he responded to Lord Nicholas' question, "I usually work in the town of Atla, where I spend my working time as a transitioner."

"A transitioner?" Lord Nicholas jumped in, "What's that?"

"Have you never worked with a transitioner before?" I asked, genuinely shocked by his question.

"No, I can't say that I have," Lord Nicholas responded cautiously. He still kept up his fake smile, but his eyes were flicking between everyone else at the table, probably attempting to determine if this admission would damage his prospects in any way.

"Then you, my Lord, are very lucky," Sir Abel responded smoothly. "A transitioner," he continued, "is one of the five kinds of spiritual workers. Transitioners have three main jobs: help people transition from one stage of life to another (this mostly includes helping people find and change careers or helping people shift into retirement, marriage, or parenthood), help people overcome grief and heartbreak (this mostly entails helping people work through the loss of a loved one), and, finally, to help departed souls transition from life to the universe beyond."

"Al and I both spoke with the transitioner before joining the knights," Azar commented, "it's a requirement for all knights to ensure they are healthy and mentally prepared to take a knight's role. It was actually a very interesting experience. She asked me a lot of questions that I never thought about, but, at the end of it all, I was even more confident in my decision to be a knight. I had this interesting sense of clarity that I really wanted to do this, and that I wanted to become a knight for my own sake instead of to please anyone else. Being a knight is a choice made by me, for me, and I am very proud and delighted to serve."

"I had a similar experience with my Knighthood transitioner," Mama smiled, "but, they don't always end up like that. The Dowager Queen was the transitioner for Queen Elenore and me when we both married King Edgar. She needed to transition us to what life would be like as the wife of the Crown Prince and the duties we'd be taking on as Princesses and later Queens. Personally, when I went through that transition, I came out rather more subdued than I had walked in. I now knew the extent to which I could and would affect the kingdom and all who lived in it. It was a daunting task, but the transitioning also assured me that I was well equipped to handle it. And, I knew that I would not be alone in doing so."

"Yes, the Dowager Queen is an excellent transitioner, and, as the only known master of all five spiritual professions, it must have been a wonderful experience to work with her. She and I study transition work together, at the Eastern Temple. She is quite the gifted spiritualist," Sir Abel added.

"So," Lord Nicholas said, turning towards Ari and me, "When did you two go through transitioning?"

"If I remember correctly, the Princess has an aptitude for transition work, and even aided in the aftermath of the Merino fires this past winter," Sir Abel said before I could respond.

"Really?" Lord Nicholas exclaimed, showing his first genuine emotion of the evening. "You're a spiritualist?"

"Everybody has a spiritual aptitude," I responded curtly. "But, yes, my grandmother... the Dowager Queen, that is," I hastily corrected, "has taught me the basics of transition work so I could help people in the city of Merino who were affected by the fires. I must admit, however, to never having had a transitioning myself. Neither has Ari. Unless someone dies that you are close to, people usually won't have a transitioning until well into adulthood."

"Not that we would discourage younger people to come talk to us. Transitioners are available to anyone at any age," Sir Abel smiled at Ari and me.

"How fascinating. I must admit to never even considering working with the transitioner," Lord Nicholas responded.

"Are you not a very spiritual man?" Sir Abel smiled.

"I find myself more focused on my present state of being rather than what comes beyond it," Lord Nicholas responded genially, "but of course I understand how spirituality is very beneficial and important to some." Lord Nicholas rushed to add on.

"There is indeed a benefit to focusing on your present, my Lord, however, I would caution you about thinking too much of your own self," Sir Abel finished thoughtfully. For just a brief moment I thought I saw Lord Nicholas' features twist into a dark scowl, but just as quickly, Lord Nicholas' face morphed once again back into the polite smile that endlessly marred his features.

"How were everyone's days?" Father asked, turning towards the rest of us. Conversation flowed smoothly then, as each of my brothers rambled on about their days. Azar finished his tale with a story about him misplacing one of the bricks he was working with, then spending 15 minutes looking for it, only to promptly trip over it and land face-first in a pile of dirt. True to form, Azar punctuated his story with wild hand gestures, and the reenactment of his fall that had us all in stitches. For just a moment it felt like my family was my family again. A loud dining table, laughter bursting at every crevice of the room, and a warm feeling that filled every inch of my body. A feeling that ran through my bones and screamed, "you're home, you're safe", and, "your joy will last forever". There was no fight for a crown, no unwanted dinner guests. Just my family, and the love we shared. This moment of peace and joy filled the room, and, just as quickly as it came, the moment slipped away.

"Lord Nicholas!" Father exclaimed. "Are you excited for your work at the hospital? No doubt it will be a change of pace from your repair and construction work you've been doing with Al and Azar until now."

"Certainly, Your Majesty. I am quite eager to help the people in whichever way they need," Lord Nicholas smiled, and I found myself staring at him incredulously as he brazenly re-peated my words from our argument earlier. Honestly, the nerve of this man! I clenched my fist into the napkin in my lap as I fought the inexplicable urge to punch something, preferably Lord Nicholas's smug, pale face.

"Although, I do wonder why we are handling the treatment of patients?" Lord Nicholas continued clearly blind to my current efforts not to vault over the table and pummel him. "Surely it would be more beneficial for us to be working in hospital management. I must confess to knowing very little of medical care." Lord Nicholas finished, flashing my father a, frankly, ridiculously charming smile.

Fortunately, Father seemed unaffected by his display. "Not to worry, Lord Nicholas. The hospital Matron has undoubtedly placed you where you are needed most. Any treatment information you need I'm sure will either be taught or provided to you," Father smiled. I, too, found a smile greet my face as I saw Lord Nicholas's smile fall at the instant dismissal Father gave him. There would be no possible way to weasel out of this one, I thought with no small measure of glee. Never in my life have I been so excited about someone having to learn anatomy. I had no doubt that Lord Nicholas would have to spend the next 24 hours or so studying if he wanted to be at all prepared for working in the hospital. The, rather mean spirited, joy I felt at the thought of Lord Nicholas having to pour through medical textbooks all tonight and tomorrow carried me through dinner, and towards a comfortable sleep that evening.

Chapter 13

The Day's Work

I woke up early the next morning, still smiling at the turn of events last night, so, instead of making my way down to the training grounds, as I had done for the past month since Lord Nicholas's arrival at the palace, I found myself heading to the stables for a morning ride. I felt almost giddy as the scent of dust, sweat, and horses hit my nose. Somehow, in the past month, I had forgotten how much I loved to ride, and the feeling of freedom that came with having a moment completely and utterly away from all other people. I found myself picking up my pace as I entered the stables. "Hello Princess," a voice broke through my revelry.

"Sir Abel," I smiled, "good morning."

"Indeed, and please call me Abel, Princess. While I understand why there is a need for such titles, I often find them rather superfluous when there is already a clear level of familiarity and understanding between two people."

"Of course. Please call me Avalynn as well," I responded, a little flustered by the compliment I believe he had just given me.

"Are you going out riding this morning?" Abel queried.

"Yes, and you?" I asked, and belatedly realized that he was quite obviously saddling his horse as we spoke. I felt heat rise to my cheeks.

"Indeed, I am," Abel replied calmly, as if it was perfectly normal to ask someone if they were doing the task they were obviously doing. "Might I suggest, Avalynn, that we ride together? I believe you are to have a session with me today, so, if you are amiable, we can have our first session on horseback this morning."

"I..." I stuttered, thinking about my earlier dreams of riding completely alone.

"Of course, you are always welcome to ride on your own, or even with me, but without a transitioning session," Abel smiled.

"No, I think your first idea was the best one, Abel. Let's have my first transitioning session on horseback," I finally decided, a little surprised by the sincerity in my decision. I suddenly found that a transitioning session sounded all the more appealing than solitude. Abel waited patiently as I saddled up my own horse. He looked rather striking in an emerald green flowing top and black trousers. His deep brown skin contrasted with the richness of the shirt. His white locks were pulled back in a loose ponytail. In the right light, you could call Abel intimidating, with his perfect posture and impressive height.

However, this imposing figure was softened by the crow's feet wrinkles sitting by his eyes, and the lines near his mouth that suggested a life of joy and laughter. His deep brown eyes showed only kindness, and his soft words created a sense of ease. As I hurried to try and saddle my own horse faster, Abel smiled with a quiet satisfaction as he watched the trees around us. It was as if he had all the time in the world. As if I could have spent all day saddling my horse, yet to him, I would still be right on time.

It was perhaps because of Abel's serene demeanor that I found a strange nervousness come upon me as we began our ride. I realized with a start that despite all of our conversations the night before and my previous work as a transitioner, I had no idea what to say or do next. Our horses marched on in a comfortable silence that contrasted with the jumbled feelings that rolled around in my stomach. "Er–" I cleared my throat and started again, "I'm afraid that I'm not quite sure what to do next."

Abel laughed gently, "You were a transitioner, Avalynn, what would you say to your client?"

I wanted to argue that I wasn't really a transitioner. I had only trained briefly with Nana to help at a one-time event, or, to point out that most of the work I did was helping people with deceased loved ones, and whatever this was felt entirely different. But, instead, I thought about what I would have said to one of the people I worked with. I felt a laugh of my own flow through me as I landed on my answer. "I would have said that next, we talk about anything or nothing at all. There's nothing we have to say, and I have all the time in the world."

"My dear Avalynn, you took the words right out of my mouth," Abel smiles. My earlier tension easing out of me. We rode along in silence for a little while longer before I spoke again.

"I don't like Lord Nicholas," I blurted. The words almost felt forced out of me as they rapidly tumbled out of my mouth.

"I must say, I did get that impression last night," said Abel. "Why don't you like him?"

"Because he's infuriating," I ranted, letting all the feelings Lord Nicholas brought up within me rise to the surface. "He's arrogant, fake, and doesn't give a damn about anyone other than himself," I fumed.

"Alright then, let's start from the beginning, why don't we. First of all, please tell me why you find him arrogant."

"Because he's so convinced that he is the best thing for this country, and he is so sure that he's going to be King!"

"And this hurt you because?"

"It hurts me because what if he isn't? His arrogance that he must always be right, and that his choices are always the best could be deadly as a King. He could hurt people and this country! And, how can he think that he is always right? I've been training for this job, to rule, for eight years, and I doubt 90% of my decisions! I'm constantly finding errors in my work or weaknesses in my leadership style. Some errors I'm not even sure I could fix. How can he possibly know that he lacks error in his thoughts and actions?" I finished, nearly crying.

"Wait, how did you know that it hurt me?" I added as I finally processed all that I had said.

"Anger comes from one of only two places, Avalynn, fear or hurt. I doubt Lord Nicholas' arrogance scares you, although I can see why it might in regard to your view of his ruling the kingdom. However, I think it's clear that your most immediate issue is how his arrogance makes you personally feel."

"I –" I began, a little offended. I wondered first and foremost why my feelings were so "clearly" the main problem. "Well... it's just... I," I tried to continue, not really sure what to say.

"Take your time to think of an answer. Transitioning is not a conversation. It's not required that you think of an answer immediately," Abel said softly. I felt my mouth closed as I pondered my previous words. I found myself being drawn to something I had said earlier, how could Lord Nicholas be so certain in his ability when I have so much doubt in my own. I felt my conclusion hit my body, there was a wave of certainty that crashed over me, and a swelling aftermath of embarrassment at my own perceived weakness. "I..." I opened my mouth to answer Abel, and my newfound embarrassment hooked onto my throat making it hard to say my flaw out loud. I took a deep breath and pushed on anyway.

"I'm insecure," I finally pushed out. "I find that I'm constantly doubting my ability to be Queen. All I have ever wanted to do was help people, and I do believe being Queen would be the best way to do it. However, there's so much involved in the task, and I want to be sure that I am the best possible option because I want the people to have the best ruler. And, so, I find myself constantly seeing flaws in my way of thinking, my mannerisms, and my actions. I watch my brothers, and I wonder if they could do a better job. I try to push past my doubts, to work harder, to try to correct my errors, and, for the most part, I do. I move forward, work on a new area, expand my thought process and keep going. But, then Lord Nicholas came in, and he was just so sure that he was the best thing for this country, even though his values and thought processes are so entirely contradictory to my own. He's so annoyingly confident that he's right. He has no doubts about it at all, and I... I think I'm envious of it. I'm envious of his ability to just know he's right. I still do not believe that the inability to question your own judgment is a good trait for a ruler, but I do wonder what it's like to live with that much certainty," I finished, staring off into the trees.

A small laugh brought me back to Abel, and I saw him unsuccessfully trying to hide his mirth. "Forgive me, Avalynn," Abel said, clearly stopping his attempt to hide his laughter, "it's just that, although I've yet to meet with his lordship, I rather suspect he would say the same thing about you."

"Me?"

Abel chuckled, "Yes, Avalynn. While it does seem that you could use a hand improving your personal self-trust, when it comes to your convictions and beliefs, I have a hard time coming up with anyone more unshakeable. This is neither a good nor a bad thing; it just simply is. You have the same confidence and determination as Lord Nicholas. You simply choose to exhibit this trait around your beliefs and your ideology whereas Lord Nicholas uses his confidence for his personality and goals. Having confidence in your beliefs and yourself, can be very beneficial, especially if that confidence is layered in with the courage and wisdom to do self-reflection and admit when you are wrong. Now, let's talk about how you can improve your own self-confidence, and then, next time, I would like to discuss why you find Lord Nicholas "fake".

The conversation flowed on, as Abel gave me some mantras and sage advice on self trust and its connection to self-love. Abel's advice seemed easy enough, and, by the time we rode back into the stables, I was feeling calmer and more confident than I had in a while. I also felt a strange sense of determination to implement all the tools Abel had given me. Abel announced that our session had concluded as we dismounted, but he informed me that he would enjoy conversing with me as a friend until our next session. So, as we brushed down our horses we changed the conversation to lighter topics, our horses' personalities, the purpose of having animals and plants in one's life, and so on. By the time we walked into the dining room for breakfast, we were in the middle of a thrilling conversation about the process of reincarnation.

"Of course there are many different theories as to the exact method of reincarnation," Abel explained as I unthinkingly sat beside him at the breakfast table. "For some, the concept of karma is thoroughly ingrained, so the actions you choose to take in this life, affect the flow of your next life. In this model, there is no way to change the level of ease or difficulty you will face in this life as it was already determined by your last. Others believe that your soul determines the circumstances of your next life based on where your soul can experience the most growth. You'll still experience karma from past lives in this model, but the difficulty in your life is determined by how quickly you learn your lessons. There's also a theory that states that your next life is chosen simply by your soul's curiosity to try something new or where your soul can do the most good. Some spiritualists combine-"

"Ava, you're in the wrong seat," Ari's hard voice pierced through Abel's lesson. His sudden appearance caused me to jump as my heart skyrocketed out of my chest. "You moved yesterday to my side because of Sir Abel. You can't just switch back now," Ari continued frowning above us.

"You're right of course," I smiled at him, rubbing my chest to soothe my thumping heart. I stood up and moved around the table to the seat I'd occupied the previous evening. I patted Ari gently on the shoulder as I walked past him, "I just got lost in a discussion. Thank you for reminding me." Ari nodded, seemingly satisfied with my response, and took his own seat. As I pulled out my own chair, I felt a hot prickling at the back of my neck. I turned to see Lord Nicholas watching our interaction from the doorway, a curious look in his eye and a small smirk at his mouth. He caught my eye, and his smirk turned into a rather obvious leer, as he smoothly sauntered in, taking the seat I'd just previously occupied.

Interestingly, I was not met with my usual annoyance at his presence, perhaps due to my session with Abel earlier, however, I was filled with a deep sense of unease. I wasn't sure what about this scene pleased him so much, but I was certain I would not like it. I sat contemplatively as the rest of the breakfast table filled in. Soon, however, my family's usual merriment drew me in, and I put Lord Nicholas' curious behaviors to the back of my mind. Breakfast was a lively affair, as Azar and Al began arguing over the best training techniques for the longsword. Mama would occasionally jump in occasionally to egg on my brothers by supporting or refuting one of their claims. All the while she was sending flirtatious winks at Mother, whose attempts at a disapproving glare were betrayed by her thick lips turning up into a smile. Breakfast was finished with an uneasy truce declaring that, perhaps, different training styles work better with different people. Father reminded us all to meet with Abel at some point today before returning his attention to some documents in front of him. I felt a rather childish sense of smugness as Abel announced that I had already spoken with him. And, I must admit, I enjoyed the identical looks of shock and annoyance that graced my brothers' and Lord Nicholas' faces as Father smiled and said "Good work, my gift." I had to remind myself that meeting with Abel this morning wasn't even my idea in order to keep the smirk off my face.

I spent the rest of my morning sparring with Carlos, Mateo, and Elise, Charlotte's now girlfriend. Azar sat around the training squires, and loudly griped that his best friend chose to hang out with me instead. Carlos dramatically declared that he could never leave his friend before Mateo knocked him on the back side of his head. Mateo then lectured him on how he needed to improve his fighting skills against different styles and informed him that it was more than a little embarrassing if the person he was supposed to be guarding could beat him in a fight in under 10 minutes. Elise, the squires, and I were all holding back laughter, with varying degrees of success at the scene. Azar, however, still managed to look like a kicked puppy as Mateo apologized for the ruckus and dragged Carlos away. Azar passionately announced that he would come back for Carlos one day before he finally collapsed in his own fit of giggles.

The afternoon was spent reviewing medical text with Charlotte, Ana, Mateo, Carlos, and Elise. Elise claimed she was there to study for basic combat first aid, but as she, Carlos, and Charlotte spent most of the time trying to find the oddest diseases or picking out random books off the library shelves, I suspected that that wasn't actually true. I didn't mind, however. These afternoons spent in the library together created an easy atmosphere that I could never seem to find on the road. Before now, I didn't have a specific set of knights, nor was able to be close to the maids I had at the palace. Just a few years ago they were far older than I. Now, these were my friends and time around them felt easy and fun. It was like a hole I never knew I had, had been filled.

Dinner was loud around me, but I found myself in quiet conversation with Ari, who'd been both confused and enthralled with his own transitioning session. We entered our own little space and time as we shared insights into our subconscious that were brought to the surface through transitioning, and what they might mean for our future.

"I want to be King," said Ari, "but, I think I would be happy if we could just all live in peace and contentment. I mean, that's the role of the King right? Making sure his people have all the tools necessary to live in peace, so in that sense, it doesn't really matter who becomes King, as long as the rest of the country has the best chance for peace and happiness." I felt a rush of affection for my younger brother, who at just 14 seemed so wise and caring. I placed my hand on his shoulder, "You're right. Of course," I smiled. "At the end of the day whoever wins the crown is not important as long as they can help the people."

"Mhmm," Ari nodded, looking between Al and Azar and giving a slight sigh. I giggled, Ari and I had always bonded over Al and Azar's rather overbearing rivalry.

"While it may be rather loud and just a little obnoxious for us, you can't deny that it's made them both stronger and smarter people. You're too young to remember, but Mother

used to yell at Azar all the time because he'd never go to class,"
I giggled. "Plus, their silly war makes us work harder too, and
you know it. With the amount of work all four of us have put
in, provided one of us becomes King or Queen, I have to assume we'd be the most well-trained monarch in Nevremerre
history." Ari mumbled his agreements, and the evening flowed
on.

The dry heat of the summer evening took over my room
as Ana and Charlotte got me ready for bed. We lazily chatted
about Charlotte's upcoming dates with Elise. Ana's work with
the housekeeper for the upcoming tournament, and how it
might help her get the housekeeper's job in the future. I regaled them with Carlos and Azar's dramatic scene from this
morning. The conversation was then flipped to Lord Nicholas'
stint at the hospital, which would start tomorrow.

"Do you think he'll be okay at the hospital? What if he
faints like Carlos did?" Charlotte wondered kindly. Neither Ana
nor Charlotte were aware of Lord Nicholas's bid for the throne.

"Carlos didn't faint. He just threw up," I defended. A darker
part of me thought that I might enjoy seeing Lord Nicholas
faint before I suppressed that instinct. "You might be right
about him being shocked, though. Unlike Carlos and Mateo, I
doubt Lord Nicholas has seen much blood."

"It'd be quite funny if he did faint though."

"Ana, what a terrible thing to say!" Charlotte cried out.

"You didn't have to move all of his furniture around three
times once he started living in the palace," Ana said, looking
not in the least bit sorry.

"That was nearly a month ago; surely you've forgiven him by now," Charlotte exclaimed, pausing her work brushing my hair.

"Well, I probably would have," Ana admitted, "if Tavian, you know the footman, hadn't told me he was still rudely ordering around his new attendants."

"Tavi loves to gossip and complain. There's no way of knowing if what he says is true," Charlotte admonished.

"While it's true he exaggerates, he rarely tells a story that's not at least based in fact. I don't like him," Ana announced. "And, we still don't know why he's at the palace. Not to imply anything, Princess, we know you're not allowed to tell us."

"Hmm, well I still think it's best not to judge when we don't even know the man," Charlotte finished turning back to my hair. I couldn't help but think that Charlotte was a far better person than I. "Either way, will you be able to tell us how he gets on, Princess?"

I smiled at them both. "I'm not sure what tasks the Matron will assign Lord Nicholas, but if there are any stories to tell, I'll be sure to share them." That seemed to satisfy them, and we all sat around chatting for a little while longer before Ana and Charlotte left me to sleep. After a peaceful day, I was excited to work at the hospital and see how Lord Nicholas would handle it. A part of me hoped he found his first day just as hectic and nerve-wracking as I had found my own. At the same time, however, I was comforted by the knowledge that he would likely find a rhythm at the hospital as well. Perhaps he would find a love for medicine that could take him out of my hair, but, at the very least, the number of people who were able to be seen by a healer each day would increase. I found myself once again smiling as I fell asleep.

Chapter 14

The Choice of Lord Nicholas

I did not see Lord Nicholas at my early breakfast the next morning, and for a brief moment I worried he would make me late for the hospital. My fears seemed ridiculous 15 minutes later when he strode out towards the carriage at precisely 7:30, and I remembered he was far too preoccupied with stealing the throne to ever be late to something like this.

"Good morning, Princess," Lord Nicholas said, stepping into the coach. He gave polite nods to Mateo and Carlos. Mateo nodded back, but Carlos sent Lord Nicholas a glare before he returned the nod and moved to stare out the window.

"Good morning, Lord Nicholas," I replied as the carriage lurched forward, "Why have you brought those?" I asked, pointing to the medical books in his lap. "You won't need them, and they are going to be useful for studying back at the palace."

"Oh no, I plan on returning them," Lord Nicholas replied confidently.

"You can't have already memorized them?" I said, shocked. Suddenly feeling the need to pull up Abel's mantras about trusting myself, and reminding myself that it's pointless to compare oneself to others as we all have our own strengths and weaknesses.

"Oh no, that is far too much to memorize in one day," Lord Nicholas replied.

"Then why are you returning them?"

"Because I will not be needing them."

"How- how could you possibly know that? Have you managed to just suddenly acquire medical knowledge?" I sputtered.

"No. I'm just confident that whoever's in charge will realize the benefit of putting me in a managerial position instead."

"What?"

"Oh yes. This happened with the work Prince Alveron and Prince Azar were doing as well. In both cases, I was able to clearly explain the benefits of me as a manager, and I was, happily, exempted from doing any hard labor," Lord Nicholas explained confidently.

I looked at him incredulously before looking at Carlos and Mateo. Mateo looked just as bewildered as I was, but Carlos didn't seem surprised. He most likely had heard this story from Azar, and I was now determined to hear what Azar had told him. Turning back to Lord Nicholas I queried, "Did you even read the textbooks?"

"No," replied Lord Nicholas, "it will not be necessary."

I sat there in shock for a while, unsure of how to respond, until I eventually came to the conclusion that I wouldn't have to; if we got to the hospital and he remained unprepared, Matron Terrella would probably kill him. So, I just shrugged it off and turned my gaze towards the carriage window. As the carriage pulled over at the end of the street, I actually felt a bit of apprehension on Lord Nicholas' behalf. I, personally, would rather walk on hot coals than make the Matron mad. Of course I had no idea what the Matron's anger would look like, having never actually experienced it myself, but based on the Matron's overall demeanor, I would put money on it not being a pleasant experience.

"Why are we getting out here?" Lord Nicholas asked. "This definitely isn't the hospital," he said, pointing to the corner bakery.

"We always enter from down the street," Mateo answered for me, "so as not to crowd the front of the hospital in case of emergency." Lord Nicholas nodded as we continued to walk down the block. As we approached the hospital, I saw Matron Terrella standing outside waiting for us. I shared a nervous glance with Mateo, and then looked to see Carlos smirking from his place behind Lord Nicholas. Lord Nicholas, however, just pressed confidently forward, obviously completely unaware of the danger he was about to walk into.

"Ah- Princess," Matron said as she noticed us, "you are here right on time," she nodded approvingly. "You must be Lord

Nicholas. The King informed me of your arrival. Please follow me and I will tell you about the hospital. Princess, why don't you and Sirs Carlos and Mateo head upstairs and join Mr. Murphy on rounds." I heard Carlos make a rather disappointed sound behind me. I, however, was feeling a little relieved, and quickly replied, "Of course, Matron."

I moved to walk into the building when I heard the Matron say, "You might want to run those books back to the carriage. There will be no time for studying today, and, even if there were, we have several copies of these textbooks in the library." I felt Carlos slow down his walk beside me as he gave a gleeful smile.

"Ah, forgive me Madam," I heard Lord Nicholas say. "I actually intended on returning these. You see, while the Princess has had limited previous experience with medicine, I have not. So, I believe it would be in the best interest of the hospital if I aided in the management side of things, which, I can assure you, I'm very good at," Lord Nicholas concluded in his sickly sweet, fake voice.

"Then you can leave," Matron Terrella responded, and Mateo, Carlos, and I froze right in the middle of the hospital doorway.

"What?" Lord Nicholas responded.

"I said you can leave, right now. I don't need administrators. If I did, I would have sent the Princess home with books on hospital administration and health care law. I have administrators who do their jobs exceptionally well. What I need are healers. We are the only hospital for the entire city of Nera. We have so many patients that all my healers are fully booked for the next two weeks. They can all be put behind schedule at any given moment if a large accident were to occur that would require all hands in the ER. Beyond that we are still trying to be the best research hospital in all of Nevremerre because the more cures we can create, the more people we can save. So, no, I don't need administrators, I need healers and healer's assistants who can treat mild injuries and common ailments. I do not need people who are not going to take my words seriously or go against my instructions. So you, Lord Nicholas, can leave," Matron reprimanded.

"Excuse me," another healer pushed by us, reminding me that we were all still standing in the hospital doorway. I grabbed Carlos and Mateo by the arm, and pulled us through the door and up to the stairs.

"Oh Princess, why did you do that?" Carlos whined, "It was just getting good."

"We have work to do," I replied as we walked up the ramps leading to the third floor, "besides, we wouldn't want to have her turn on us after she's finished with Lord Nicholas."

"Very wise, Princess," Mateo agreed.

"Oh man, I wish I could have seen the look on his face," Carlos said grinning. "What do you think will happen? Will he have to go back to the palace? The King would not be happy with that."

"No, he most certainly would not," I replied, allowing myself a soft smile.

"You're late," Murphy said, bluntly, as we got to the third floor.

"Sorry, but it was for a great reason. I'll explain later," Carlos smiled.

"Let's just get to work. Maybe we can make up some of the time," I replied heading towards the first room.

We did indeed make up time as we breezed through the morning patients. Healer Autumn came in and joined us on a pregnancy check-up, and they taught me how to feel for the baby's body placement and the heartbeat. Healer Autumn announced that I would soon be ready to do maternity care all by myself, before they sent us off for lunch. Murphy suggested the pie cart down the road, so we all set out in the hot afternoon sun. I kept an eye out for Lord Nicholas as we left the hospital, but I had seen no trace of him since the Matron's smackdown earlier this morning. I wondered if he really did just go home, but Lord Nicholas wasn't the type to give up so easily. As we ate our pies by the main square's fountain, Carlos regaled Murphy with this morning's adventure.

"So he's an idiot," Murphy finally concluded.

"Well I wouldn't say that," I found myself defending.

"Yeah, it's more accurate to say he's a self-entitled asshat," Carlos interjected.

"Carlos!" Mateo explained, equal parts exasperated and scandalized, "You can't just say those things. No matter what you might think of him, he is still the current heir to the Armon province in Elatia."

"Count Rosin is picking him to inherit his title?" I asked, surprised.

"Yes. Apparently he beat out his brother and sister for the honor," Mateo confirmed.

"I always knew he was a greedy bastard," Carlos whispered in my ear.

"You do realize that, if he succeeds in his current goal, he will become your boss, and you will have to protect him," I whispered back, ignoring Murphy's curious stare.

"Yes, well inheritance claims can always be challenged," Carlos huffed.

"No one has challenged an inheritance claim in 32 years, and the King and council have to agree that the inheritor's unfit to hold public office," I shot back. "You don't have to like the man, Carlos, but you should be a little careful about what you say and to whom. Honestly, your father is the council member in charge of foreign relations and diplomacy, surely you've learned something from him?" I sighed.

"Yeah, yeah," Carlos waved off my concern, "but it doesn't matter here, right. I mean we're all friends here." I felt a warmth fill my body, and, hopefully, the blush that spread across my face could just be attributed to the dry heat.

"Yes," I smiled, "Yes, we are friends." I pulled myself together and asked what had been in the back of my mind. "Did Azar tell you something about what Lord Nicholas said earlier about doing management work at Al and Azar's placements?"

"Oh yeah. He just said that Lord Nicholas never ended up working with the construction crews. I said that it sounded like Lord Nicholas was skiving off, but you know Azar, he just said it was probably for the best. He was worried Lord Nicholas would break or something if he had to pick something up. The idiot."

"You're one to talk," I joked, "but honestly, everyone looks like they're about to break compared to Azar. Did you know he's half an inch taller than Father, I wouldn't even think that'd be possible."

"Well it might be impossible for you, Princess," Mateos smiled, causing Carlos to start cackling as he slapped Mateo on the back.

"Good one! I knew you'd get there eventually."

"Shall we head back?" Murphy asked, grinning. "Before you two insult any more nobles or royal family members that could take your jobs?" Carlos laughed, Mateo blushed and I smiled as we all pushed back to the hospital.

"Oh, Princess, good," Healer Autumn called as we walked in through the front doors. "Ms. Alexandria has gone into labor. She's carrying twins, so we need you and Sir Mateo to assist with the birth. Sir Carlos, perhaps it's best if you just continue onto afternoon rounds with Mr. Murphy." Carlos practically jumped at the reprieve Healer Autumn was offering him. Carlos never did recover from the first birth we've witnessed, and any subsequent births found him hiding in a hallway.

"Of course, Healer," he called and ran towards the ramp so quickly, he left Murphy behind.

"Wait for me you idiot," Murphy called out hurriedly rolling towards him.

"We best be on our way," Healer Autumn said, motioning us down the opposite hall. "Do you remember the breathing exercises? I don't know when her water will break, but check her cervix and send Mateo to grab me from the second floor when she's fully dilated. Until then, guide her through the breathing methods."

"Yes, Healer" Mateo and I confirmed. We opened the door to see Ms. Alexandria waddling across the room taking big exaggerated breaths as another woman paced with her, attempting to calm her down.

"You're doing great, Alexandria," a far slimmer, golden, brown-skinned woman comforted, holding Ms. Alexandria's hand.

"Oh shut it, Padma," Ms. Alexandria snapped, her deep black hair was pulled out of her face in a messy bun, and her dark almond-shaped eyes darted frantically across the room. "Where is Lee when you need him? Why can't he be here?"

"In Lee's defense, he's coming back from his business trip today and you weren't actually meant to go into labor for another 2 to 3 weeks," Padma supplied gently.

"Don't worry Ms. Alexandria, everything is going to be just fine," I chimed in. "I am Avalynn, and this is Mateo. We will be assisting you until you enter the second stage of labor. When that time comes, you will have Healer Autumn to assist you. I assure you, they are one of the best."

"Princess!" Padma gasped.

"No need for such formalities now," I smiled, "May I please examine your progress, Ms. Alexandria?"

"Yes of course, and just call me Alexandria," Alexandria said as she moved her way over to the bed. I put on my gloves, and began patting her uterus to find the position of the twins. Alexandra huffed and grunted as I moved through my preliminary examination. Mateo and I then guided Alexandria through some breathing exercises. The birth progressed quickly, and two hours later I sent Mateo out of the room to find Healer Autumn.

"What? I can't go into labor yet! It's too fast, and Lee's not here!" Alexandria cried.

"It's okay. Diego and Mitchell are at the public Stage Coach terminal waiting for him. They'll bring him as soon as he arrives." Padma soothed.

"But, it's too early! And too fast!" Alexandria cried out, her pale skin becoming blotchy and red.

"Alexandria!" I called out, "It's alright. Both of your babies have flipped, and 37 weeks is still considered a full-term pregnancy. You are very healthy, and you have some of the best healers in Nera taking care of you. We will all do everything in our power to make sure you and your babies are healthy," I said firmly. "Plus, your water hasn't even broken, we still have time for your husband to get here," I finished.

"Okay," Alexandria calmed, before her water actually did break and she screamed once more. I had a brief moment of utter shock before dragging myself back into the present.

"Alexandria, you are going into the next stage of labor, I'm going to need you to push now," I said. Alexandria screamed as the door behind me opened. I felt relief wash over me as Healer Autumn entered the room. I heard the sounds of others entering, but I focused on Alexandria.

Healer Autumn, pulled a stool next to me. "I am pushing!" Alexandria screamed, but she did as requested. Healer Autumn kept me near them as we watched the head of twin number one push through. Padma's hand was looking painfully white as Alexandria clenched it throughout the birth. Soon the first twin was born. Her umbilical cord was cut quickly by me while Healer Autumn held the baby and prepared Alexandria for the next twin. Baby one was thrust into my arms, and I heard a gentle voice behind me.

"Stand up, and bring the baby here dear," Matron's deep voice pierced behind me. She held a towel, and we took the baby to a corner where we cleaned it, causing its cries to mix with her mother's screams.

"Alexandria!" a male voice called out, bursting into the room, just as baby two had crowned.

"Lee!" Alexandria screamed.

"Please focus, Alexandria. We still need you to push," Healer Autumn called, as Lee moved to grab Alexandria's other hand.

"Where the hell were you?" Alexandria screamed as she pushed.

"I'm here now, love," Lee said, stroking her hair "You're doing great."

"I know that! I'm doing phenomenal! I'm a baby making Queen - Augh!"

"Almost there now, Alexandria! Just one more push!" Healer Autumn called.Soon, baby two was out.

"Just one more step, Alexandria. Princess Avalynn and Matron Terrella will check both of the babies' health while you push out the placenta. So, please, keep going a while longer."

"Ugh!" Alexandria said, letting her head flop back on the pillow before her screams filled the room once more. I brought baby two back to where Matron Terrella was with, a now clean, baby one.

"Two healthy baby girls," the Matron declared with a smile once all stages of the birth were complete.

"When did the second one come out?" Lee asked, looking a little shocked as he held out his arms.

"Right before you arrived, Lee. Do keep up," Alexandria taunted, but her eyes held nothing but a tired affection as I placed baby two on her chest. The Matron gently guided baby one into Lee's arms.

"She's perfect," Lee whispered in reverence, "they are per-fect," he said as his eyes moved towards baby two. "You're per-fect," he finished his teary gaze falling on his wife.

"They're wonderful, guys," Padma smiled.

"Well I should hope you think so, Padma, as their god-mother!" Alexandria smiled.

"Oh that's right! I left Diego and Mitchell in the reception area!" Lee jolted.

"We can go and get them," Healer Autumn said.

"Yes, now just for your knowledge, the baby in the green blanket is older. We will give you some space now, but some-one will be back later to update your chart, and write the chil-dren's birth certificates. We will want to keep all three of you in the hospital for three more days for observation," the Ma-tron said.

"Yes, thank you all," Alexandria smiled, as we walked out of the room. It was only then that I noticed Lord Nicholas walk-ing out with us. It seemed he was to work at the hospital af-ter all. We moved down towards the hospital lobby, and Healer Autumn threw their gloves in a wooden receptacle. Matron and I repeated her actions.

"Princess," the Matron said, "we should have a new collec-tion of herbs coming in today. Will you please take the boxes to storage, and then start restocking all the treatment rooms. If you could teach Lord Nicholas about our storage methods that would be much appreciated. No need to teach him what the herbs are, as he has assured me he'll be working on memorizing them as soon as he returns to the palace." The Matron looked sternly at Lord Nicholas, who gave an embarrassed nod.

"Of course I can, Matron," I replied.

"Good," she looked towards Lord Nicholas, "Come see me when you have finished." Matron then turned abruptly away from us, and hurried down the hall.

"You'd best follow me then," I said, waving Lord Nicholas down the hall towards the storage center.

"Princess," Mateo interjected as we moved down the hall, "should I go retrieve Carlos and bring him back down to storage?"

"Please do," I replied as Mateo nodded and moved in the opposite direction towards the stairs and ramps. I continued just a little further to a big door labeled storage. Outside was a man and a woman with two large crates.

"I'm here to accept the herb deliveries," I told them confidently.

"Princess!" The man jumped and stumbled into a sort of bow. The woman beside him followed suit with a puzzled expression on her face.

"Excuse me, but we were told we were delivering to healers for the hospital," the woman said as she stood back up.

"And delivering to the hospital you are," I said smiling. "I am assisting the hospital today."

"So the rumors were true!" the man jumped in, looking oddly vindicated.

"Yes, well then," the woman hurried on a bit sheepishly. "Can you please tell the Matron she's going to need to find some other suppliers for basil, coriander, and mint. We weren't able to grow enough of those right now. Hopefully we can get some more leaves to grow later. We still have the full stock of lavender and aloe vera though."

"Okay, thank you. I will let her know. How much of the normal supply did you bring?" I asked the woman, Diana, she told me. Embarrassed, she added that she was named after Mama. I just smiled, it was fairly common for people to be named after royalty. I had met more than my fair share of Avalynns when working with the children across Nevremerre. Father warned us that there would be even more if we actually became a King or Queen. So, I told Diana not to be embarrassed and assured her it was a very kind gesture, as I took the rest of the delivery details. Lord Nicholas and the man, Khan, brought in the rest of the boxes and soon the two farmers were on their way. Lord Nicholas and I then brought the boxes into the storage room. The large oak door slammed behind us, leaving us alone in the silent, windowless, storage room.

Chapter 15

The Tournament's Announcement

I quickly lit the lanterns around the spacious room, and turned back around to Lord Nicolas. He was still hovering by the door staring intensely back at me. "We need to prepare the herbs to be dried or extracted, in the case of aloe vera," I said. "Let me explain how the storage room works. The hospital receives a new herb delivery every three days. This is because most herbs require 72 hours to-"

"Why aren't you saying anything?" Lord Nicholas interrupted. I stared at him. I was fairly certain I had just been speaking. Although, I had a brief moment where I questioned whether I'd only started my introduction to the storage room in my head, but I quickly brushed that idea aside. "I mean about the hospital, and the work we are doing," Lord Nicholas continued in my silence. "You were right. You told me from the beginning that treating patients was the only way forward, and you were right. I didn't listen, and I know you heard what happened this morning. So, why aren't you saying anything?"

"Lord Nicholas, you are not one of my brothers, I'm not trying to compete with you," I lied, finding myself a little annoyed that he'd come to the completely correct conclusion that I would gloat in the face of his self-constructed failures. However, I knew this answer would not satisfy him, so I added, "Beyond the fact that we are working, right now our job is to prepare these herbs for medical use, and I am to explain the storage system to you. It's important that you learn this and get it right. In these boxes you have three leafy green plants that are going to be prepared in the same way, and look very similar when dry. It's vital that we organize them correctly. Mint, especially, can be dangerous if we misplace it. Mint can be harmful for pregnant women, but basil is often given to help morning sickness, if the patient doesn't like ginger or needs a stronger blend. If we were to mix up the two, there could be serious problems. Now, there are other systems in place to make sure that any mistakes are corrected, but it's better for everyone if we get it right the first time. The job and the people always come first," I finished. I left out the fact that if the first place I saw him after this morning was the carriage, it's very possible I would have gloated, just a little bit.

"Now, as I was saying-" I continued, explaining the storage system. I was just describing the two different methods for preparing the five herbs we had when Mateo and Carlos burst in looking a little out of breath. I stared at them waiting for an explanation or an order they may have been supposed to give, but none came. They did provide two extra pairs of hands though, so we all worked together to press and hang the basil, coriander, lavender, and mint, and I worked on extracting the insides of the aloe vera plants. Working together we were able to finish a little after six in the evening. Lord Nicholas then went back upstairs to meet with the Matron, and Carlos, Mateo, and I went to wait for him by the carriage.

"Man, I can't believe that guy!" Carlos grumbled as we walked out of the hospital. "I was sure he was going to be kicked out of the hospital for good, and now he's back and working with us! And, we're going to have to see him every other day!"

"Carlos," I whispered, "You can't keep saying those things. He could potentially be your future boss." However, even as I told him off, I couldn't help but wonder at his ability to just go out and say my innermost thoughts.

"Yeah, but that's not going to happen!" Carlos declared loudly. His total confidence was astounding, but it made me smile nonetheless.

"I wonder what he said to get back into the Matron's good graces?" Mateo said, and I tried not to stare as the straight laced Mateo suddenly seemed ready to gossip with us.

Carlos, however, was completely unfazed and just continued by saying, "Probably charmed her by making some false promises or something equally snake-like."

"I don't think the Matron is really one to fall for charms and false promises though," Mateo said instead of reprimanding Carlos as usual.

"True," Carlos continued, "Then maybe he begged! Man I would love to see that prideful man have to beg. Damn, we should have waited and listened more."

"We do have a job to do, Carlos, we can't just listen to drama... unfortunately," I murmured the last word, but I suspect Carlos heard me anyway because he gave me a disarmingly bright smile.

"Plus, our job is to follow the Princess and I will not allow you to slack off," the mature Mateo returned.

"I suppose we could always ask him how he did it," I said, switching the conversation back to Lord Nicholas.

"But then we'd actually have to talk to him!" Carlos exclaimed with disgust, and yet again, I wondered how he perfectly enunciated my inner monologue.

"Probably have to phrase the question a bit differently though," nodded Mateo.

"Do you think we should invite him to our study sessions? They could probably help him learn faster," I questioned aloud. Carlos and Mateo looked horrified at my suggestion.

"Princess!" Carlos exclaimed, "You can't!"

"Why not? I understand you don't like him, Carlos, but it's bound to help. Plus, there's no guarantee he'll accept," I shot back, a childlike impulse to never be told "no" pushing through me.

"We are so far ahead of him, Princess," Mateo chimed in, "Surely it's better for him to learn at his own pace, so we don't confuse him."

"We're not that advanced, Mateo," I responded incredulously. "Besides, it will give him the opportunity to ask questions if he's confused. I'll invite him," I decided.

Carlos and Mateo shared a glance I couldn't interpret before they both nodded and said, "Of course, Princess." The conversation then switched to what Carlos and Murphy got up to while we were assisting with the birth of the twins. We chatted amiably for about 30 minutes before I started to get impatient.

"Where, in the Gods' names, is he!" I finally burst. "He does know we have a noble banquet tonight, right? If he waits any longer, I will have no time to shower! That or my hair will still be soaking wet."

"I'm sure no one will notice, Princess," Mateo supplied helpfully. In my heart, I knew he was right. My hair takes ages to dry, so tonight was not the first time I would come to an event with wet hair. However, my patience was wearing thin, and I couldn't find it in me to be gracious in our delay.

"Even still," I continued, testily, "if he keeps this up we are going to be late. I know nobility has no expectations to arrive on time, but royalty does!"

"The King is the last to arrive at every event," Carlos pointed out.

"I thought that was on purpose," Mateo said.

"Nope," Carlo said, enunciating the P. "Azar says he just spends too much time trying to choose an outfit."

"Prince Azar," Mateo corrected.

"Yeah, him. So, don't worry about being late, Princess," Carlos finished with a smile. Carlos' information was correct, but I declined to comment in favor of my impatience.

"Yes, well I'd rather be on time," I huffed, plopping back into my seat.

"Well, fortunately, we won't have to wait much longer," Mateo said, gesturing out the window to where Lord Nicholas' figure could be seen meandering towards us.

"Finally!" I mumbled, sitting back up. Looking at the clock in the square, I realized I would only have 30 minutes to change after we arrived back at the palace. I spent most of the journey home mentally planning how I might get changed quicker, and silently willing Cassi, the coach driver, to go faster. I was so focused on my own plans I didn't even notice Lord Nicholas' vacant stares out the window or Carlos and Mateo's not-so-subtle glares at Lord Nicholas.

Fortunately, I did arrive at dinner at least somewhat on time, due to meeting Father as I rushed down the halls of the palace. He graciously escorted me into the main hall. You can't be late if you are escorted in by the King! At least, that's what everybody but my family would think. I could see Mother's slight eye roll as we walked in, very aware that the truth of the matter is we were both very late. But, Mother made no comment as Father invited us all into the dining room and dinner began.

Tonight, I found myself seated by Countess Serena of the Montania province in Ninita. Overall, Countess Serena was a delightful woman in her mid-30s who had been chosen to inherit her title from her father who retired just two years prior.

She had dark brown hair and golden brown skin, and a bright voice that carried along the table. She was kind, passionate, truly a wonderful person, however, I found myself sitting next to her nodding my head and not understanding a word that she was saying. To clarify, Countess Serena spoke clearly and purposely, so the words themselves made sense. However, she kept connecting those words to other words in a manner that was starting to make my head hurt. It was my own fault really. Early on in the conversation I aimed to impress the Countess by discussing Ninita's mountain exports, mainly marble and coal. I had, at the time, intentionally implied that I had greater knowledge of geology than I actually had. This, I soon discovered, was a grave mistake. Countess Serena, as it turns out, was a well-informed and passionate geologist. I'd even dare to say that she could be a scholar on the subject based on the number of phrases I simply failed to comprehend. It was clear to see why she had been chosen to be Countess, she definitely knew her province well.

I faltered, briefly, wondering if I would have to know this much detail about every province in Nevremerre in order to be Queen. I felt my stomach drop in horror at the thought. I could probably make do with the provinces that dealt primarily in agriculture. I often found myself in long discussions with Marquis Graeme of Mariposia, whose entire region dealt primarily with agriculture. All the provinces in the Mariposia region were filled with extremely fertile soil. Over the years, I have spent many a noble banquet seated near the Marquis debating various new methods of decreasing pests or increasing pollinators. We debated wildlife buffers, a push and pull method of farming, the benefit of crop rotation, selective plant breeding, and even using various liquid mixtures to prevent pests. The Marquis was nothing, if not an innovator of new agricultural techniques.

I could definitely go in-depth about agriculture. I enjoyed agriculture. While it was always nice to see someone talk about something they were passionate about, Countess Serena's speech was not only incredibly technical, but also incredibly boring. Geology, it seemed, was not my passion. Although, it did cross my mind that it might only be boring because I had no idea what she was saying.

"The lack of snow this winter provided a wonderful opportunity to see the different layers of rock on the Ritwidge Mountain Range," Countess Serena's lecture broke through my train of thought, and I grasped onto a sentence I could understand. I wracked my brain for some way to provide an insightful comment without giving away that I had been steadily falling into a greater and greater confusion for the last 20 minutes.

"And were you able to discover anything new about the mountain range with the lack of snowfall?" I finally settled on a question, internally cursing myself for extending this topic of conversation and asking what, even to my own ears, sounded like a rather stupid question. My faith in my intelligence had taken a steep plunge since the start of this conversation. Maybe, I should just stop thinking all together. Azar seemed to be doing it with some success, so perhaps I should just follow his lead.

"Now that the snow has melted from the alpine zone, we've been able to see aspects of the mountains we couldn't before. For instance, the glacial moraines running down the valleys and possess some rock samples with strange colors or minerals that we haven't yet documented. Their luminescence is not unlike fluorite, though apatite is also quite similar. They have a far higher sheen than apatite, however. Glaciers still sit atop and cover some of the Arêtes, so there may be some secrets up there but the lithology we can see is predominantly a mixture of foliated metamorphic outcrops alongside a larger igneous complex, which is the main component of the mountain range. It's really a pluton that metamorphosed the existing country rock. We've even seen some carbonatite diatremes though haven't tested them yet either," the Countess continued once again, destroying my hopes at any sort of mutual understanding. I had resigned myself to confusedly bumbling along to the countess's own brand of genius for the rest of the evening when Father stood up and the packed room fell to a hush.

"My fellow noble men, women, and people, as always it is a pleasure to welcome you into the palace, but tonight it is an even greater pleasure. For tonight I have the honor of announcing that in two weeks time we will host the annual Warriors Tournament." Cheers went up through the banquet hall, the loudest of which occurred at the end of the room where the knights usually sat. "Yes, it's a wonderful affair," Father smiled, "As always, we will begin with the Introductory Tournament, where you will see all the new knights compete and show us the new talent our armies have acquired. Then we will have the Open Tournament where anyone who is currently a knight or who has at one point held the title of knight," Father turned and smiled at Mama, "can compete for the grand prize. Sign-ups are with General Clara in the war ministers office. After the final day's matches, I hope you will all join me for a ball held here in the palace to honor those who fight, defend, and help build up our country in times of peace and war." Cheers once again filled the room, and Father had to raise a hand before he finished. "I look forward to seeing all those who compete. Now please, enjoy the rest of your meal." Applause filled the room once more before it was replaced with an excited buzz of chatting voices.

"Isn't Prince Azar competing in the Introductory Tournament this year, Princess?" Countess Serena asked. I found an immense rush of gratitude for the change of topic, and I resolved to learn at least a little more about geology in the library tomorrow.

"Yes he is, so is my knight, Sir Carlos, who has been guarding me while I assist in the hospital. Prince Azar turned 21 this spring and was able to take the knight's test. He was quite eager and took it the day after his birthday," I smiled at the memory. "He passed on his first attempt, and has been a knight for the past two months."

"How exciting! It'll be fun to watch them both compete. I believe this is the first year Prince Alveron is eligible for the Open Tournament after having won the Introductory Tournament last year. Do you think he will choose to compete in the Open Tournament? It would be interesting to see him fight Queen Diana, if she chooses to compete again, of course." I smiled at the mention of Mama, although she was less than a year away from being 50, she had fought in every open tournament since she was 22. By her own admission, she wasn't quite as strong as she once was, but her matches were still a sight to behold. Not to mention she always ranked at least in the top ten, even the time she was four months pregnant with Ari!

"Now that would be an exciting match!" Count Davin said from my right, causing me to jump a little. He had been studiously avoiding our conversation since it turned to rocks earlier, but apparently now he felt safe enough to rejoin. "Although I must say, I do find it odd that we haven't seen

Prince Alveron in the Open Tournament before. I always think of Prince Alveron as two years older than Prince Azar, but I suppose with a fall birthday, Prince Alveron's still wouldn't have been eligible to compete two years ago."

"Count Davin, your eldest wanted to be a knight, correct? Is he in the Introductory Tournament this year?"

"No, Countess, it's my middle child, Marcus, who hopes to become a knight, but he still has a year to go before he can even take the test. Roderick, my eldest, wants to become an artist of all things. Although, I'm told he's rather good, he recently has been granted an apprenticeship with Master Chen!"

"How exciting! So, does that mean your youngest will inherit, or will your title go to someone outside the family?"

"Well my two youngest are still too young to decide, but they have both expressed interest in the title. I think they both will make a fine Count or Countess, so I'll leave the decision up to Lady Guienever. As the Lady of the Hallea region she will surely know what's best. I think Marcus would be happy just leading our county. I must confess, I think my youngest, Elizabeth, has some interest in becoming the lady of Hallea, as Lady Guienever has no children. I rather think Elizabeth would be suited to that role too, but I may have some bias as her father. Still we have three more years before she reaches the age of maturity, and, as I said before, Marcus is still one year away from the age of maturity, so who knows what will change in the meantime."

"It will be wonderful to see what happens to them all," Countess Serena smiled. "Now what kind of art does your eldest do?" the countess asked innocently. This proved to be an exceptionally bad move. Count Davin was a very devoted parent as it turned out. This, I'm sure was a most wonderful thing for his family, but it was rather unfortunate for the rest of us, as Count Davin immediately launched into a long spiel about various forms of art that his son partook in. Throughout the conversation I came to the conclusion that, just like geology, I knew absolutely nothing about art. I was once again trying desperately to follow along to a conversation where I understood less and less. However, I did feel as though, this time, I had two saving graces: the confusion was not entirely of my own making, as Countess Serena had asked the question, and Countess Serena was looking as lost as I felt, so at least this time I wasn't alone. I resolved to pick up and read two books from the library tomorrow, one on geology, and one on whatever impressionism was. I somehow managed to meander my way through an evening of confusion, and practically fell on my bed, falling asleep before Ana and Charlotte could even take down my hair.

Chapter 16

The Failings of Lord Nicholas

I woke up, still dressed from the night before with a blanket placed over me. A gentle note from Ana was on my desk, explaining that they didn't want to wake me up to change. A more abrupt note from Charlotte detailing how I should brush and style my hair for the morning ride so it wouldn't be "all knotty" by the time she gets to it was added to the end. Both messages put me in a good mood as I changed and followed Charlotte's hair care regime before heading outside to the stables.

I once again met Sir Abel, as I went to saddle up Kolasi. This time, however, I was ready for another transitioning session, and, despite Abel guiding me to acknowledge some unfavorable qualities in myself, I found I left the session feeling lighter and more motivated for my days to come. I did find myself overcome with curiosity for what my brothers and Lord Nicholas would be talking about in their sessions, but I held back under the assumption that it was not an appropriate question. I, in all likelihood, wouldn't be too thrilled if Sir Abel divulged my conversations with him. So, it was probably best to afford my brothers and Lord Nicholas the same courtesy. Even if I were dying to know.

Breakfast was an oddly quiet affair, minus a small chat in which both Mama and Al confirmed that they were going to fight in the Open Tournament. Mama was her usual exuberant self, and playfully told Al she hoped they would oppose each other in the tournament. Mama cheerfully continued on about who else she might fight, and Al's dark skin took on a slightly paler shade as he stared at his half-eaten breakfast. It was only as I rose to head to the training grounds that I remembered my words to Mateo and Carlos the day before.

"Lord Nicholas," I said, quickly turning towards him before I lost my nerve, "my knights and I go to the library in the afternoons when we are not working at the hospital to review medical texts, and continue to prepare ourselves for our roles at the hospital. You are very welcome to join us if you'd like," I said, throwing what I hoped was a polite smile at the end.

"Thank you, Princess, but no doubt I would be far behind the rest of you," Lord Nicholas replied stiffly. I stared at him, before blinking to my senses and trying again.

"We've only been learning medicine for about a month longer than you, Lord Nicholas. We are not all that advanced yet, and, even if we were, reviewing the basics is helpful in any subject. It's a great opportunity to voice questions or confusions that you might have that someone else might be able to answer," I finished.

"Given your admission of your novelty in the study of medicine, I must confess that it sounds like voicing any questions

I may have would be akin to the blind leading the blind," Lord Nicholas replied, "No, Princess, I find it's better to study on my own." I gaped at him. Was this man, who had already been chastised by the Matron and nearly kicked out of the hospital for not following my advice just two days ago really going to turn down my help? My help--which both my knights had argued against giving. Was this man really going to pretend he could do this all on his own when his last idea landed him in so much trouble?

"Was there anything else, Princess?" Lord Nicholas said with a tilt of his head and a clearly fake smile.

"No," I fake smiled back, "of course you must do what you feel is best. I just wanted to inform you that you had other options," I bit out, trying my best to keep the derision from leaking out of my voice. Judging by the look Al gave me, however, I most likely wasn't completely successful. I couldn't find it in me to care about my anger seeping through, so I simply turned and said, "Now if you'll excuse me," before exiting the breakfast room. What I needed now was to hit something. Fortunately, I had a sword and training dummies were easily replaceable.

Hitting things turned out to be less than effective at ridding me of my anger. In fact, the only thing it really seemed to do was deplete my energy. After only two hours of training, I found myself crashed on my bed, debating how likely Ana would be to kill me if I wrinkled another outfit by sleeping in it. As if summoned by my thoughts, Ana and Charlotte entered the room. Ana was holding a large basket full of clothes, and Charlotte was carrying a rag and duster. "You're back early, Princess," Ana said, giving me a slight raised eyebrow before moving to hang up my clothes.

"Yes, you usually don't come back here until it's time to change for dinner," Charlotte smiled, her dark eyes suddenly taking a mischievous gleam. "Although, now that you're here, it would be a perfect time to do the deep skin care treatment!" she explained.

"Yes and we can take the time to try on the new outfits Queen Eleanor had made for you for the tournament," Ana agreed, eyeing me carefully. Despite the fact that everything that they were saying sounded lovely, Ana and Charlotte both had identical predatory smiles that made me feel a bit terrified. Still feeling as though I was missing a piece of information, I hesitantly agreed to their plan. Almost instantly I was whisked into a bath, and Charlotte whipped a paste of some sort of over my face to sit while she and Ana fussed over my hair and nails. Then I was popped out and dressed in a variety of different outfits while Charlotte and Ana sat on my bed providing color commentary. All in all, it was a bit like being a walking doll, but my skin felt smooth and my spirits were lifted by the laughter of my two maids. I still felt a little tired though as lunch finished and I made my way to the library where everyone else was already waiting.

"Princess!" Carlos exclaimed upon my arrival, "You've changed!"

"I change clothes every day, Carlos. Sometimes multiple times a day if we have a noble banquet, which you've gone to since you were fifteen," I said dryly as his face went a little pink.

"Yeah, but it's not like the knights get to see the royal family close up at banquets," Carlos grumbled, and I supposed that

Carlos and Mateo would have seen me mostly in pants and training gear.

"The point of noble banquets is for the nobles to interact with the royal family and help inform them about the state of affairs in their region. Most knights see the royal family all year round, it's not like we really need a banquet to talk to them," Elise said smiling, "I love this dress, Princess. Charlotte and Ana chose well!" Elise complimented, smiling at me, and kissing Charlotte on the cheek.

"Of course we did!" Charlotte beamed, "You don't become an exclusive maid to the Princess of Nevremerre without having a little talent!"

"Or a lot," Ana agreed, proudly. We all managed to gather around a large mahogany table near one of the library's windows. The table already held a smattering of books that Ana and Charlotte had brought down, as well as a few medical texts Mateo and Carlos had found in the Royal Library.

"Should we be waiting for Lord Nicholas?" Mateo asked as we sat down.

A pang of irritation flashed through me before I managed to calmly reply, "No, Lord Nicholas believes his studies would be more effective on his own.

"Good riddance, I say," said Carlos leaning back in his chair happily.

"That seems like a very unwise choice for someone whose first day went so poorly," Mateo frowned.

"I find that I agree with you, Mateo," I sighed.

"What do you mean?" Charlotte jumped in, "What happened on Lord Nicholas's first day?"

"So you haven't told them either?" Carlos looked at me accusingly. When I did nothing but stare back at him, Carlos clarified, "I told Azar what happened at the hospital during training today. I felt sure you would have told your family what happened! But, you haven't even told your maids! Why not?" Carlos explain passionately.

"I haven't told Ana and Charlotte because we've been busy," I studiously avoided mentioning that our business was mostly me falling asleep. "But, as for my family, what exactly were you expecting me to do? It's not my job to report on the actions of Lord Nicholas. Did you expect me to go up to His Majesty, who is so busy that he often brings work to mealtimes just to inform him that Lord Nicholas almost got kicked out of the hospital? I really don't think that warrants his attention," I finished as Carlos sighed.

"Azar said something similar, so I guess you're right," Carlos said, looking a little put out.

"Prince Azar," Mateo corrected automatically.

"Yes, him," Carlos nodded.

"Wait, wait, I still don't know what happened with Lord Nicholas in the hospital," Elise said, staring between the three of us expectantly. I let Carlos tell the tale, counting on Mateo to jump in, if Carlos was ever too excessive in his hyperbole. As Carlos began, flailing his hands around as if he was trying to mime a verbal conversation, I started going through the medical text once more. I also went and grabbed a basic geology and art history book as well. By the time I got back the rest of the group was ready to study, although there was the occasional interruption, from Carlos or Charlotte speculating what Lord Nicholas did to get back in the Matron's good graces. Each guess was more ridiculous than the last, until Mateo put his foot down and shouted that "Lord Nicholas did not seduce the Matron into letting him stay!" This seemed to pull the matter to a close. Although I could have sworn I heard Carlos murmur, "He's tried it before," under his breath. With another noble banquet this evening, we wrapped up our study session a bit early.

"Elise, Mateo, will you be entering the Open Tournament?" Ana asked as we were cleaning up the table.

"All knights get three full days off if we aren't competing," said Mateo. "I usually take the time to visit my parents in Casia instead of competing," he pointed in a vaguely Northwards direction where the town of Casia was located between the border of the Nera and Utei regions. "It's only about a three-hour journey on horseback, so I'll be back before the ball on Sunday."

"I think I'll try to compete," said Elise. "I did alright in my Introductory Tournament two years ago, but the Open Tournament is a much higher caliber of fighting. I think I improved a lot this year, though. So, I reckon I'm going to try my hand in the Open."

"It will be exciting to watch you fight! I wish you the best of luck," I said excitedly.

"Hey!" Carlos jumped in, turning to Mateo, "That means you won't watch me fight in the Introductory Tournament!"

Mateo looked at him kindly and said, "It's not like you need me there to do well. You are a very strong fighter."

"I am!" Carlos smiled, pushing forward and out of the library.

It was only then Mateo leaned forward and whispered in my ear, "Besides, we all know Prince Azar will win anyways." I couldn't hold back the snort of laughter that rang through me. It was very true, Azar was a phenomenal knight, and had the advantage of being trained by Mama since childhood. Still, I thought it was going to be a very fun event.

That evening's banquet went by painlessly as everyone was still excited about the tournament. Although still a fortnight away, the excitement in the room was palpable. Many nobles were former knights before releasing their knighthood for their title. It was a common practice from my great-grandfather's time when Nevremerre was still at war with Calvine, and all nobles were encouraged to fight. In the decade it took for Nevremerre to win the war, nearly every noble and their children became knights. While Nevremerre had always placed a high value on knights and warfare, this surge of noble knights rebirthed an old tradition of nobles becoming knights before inheriting their title. It also sparked a tradition of commoner knights being more likely than other commoners to take a title that had no inheritors. While being a knight did not legally have any effect on who received a title, it was still a prominent tradition. Needless to say, there were many nobles and knights alike who had a vested interest in the tournament.

Beyond that, the tournament weekend was also very popular for the general public and thousands would come from all over Nevremerre to watch the knights. Thus, the whole royal family had their hands full organizing food vendors, preparing the knights' tents, ensuring the tournament grounds were safe and clean, preparing medical tents and supplies, and so on. Every year since we turned fifteen, Father would give us each a list of tasks we would need to accomplish before the tournament. He'd given me my list in passing this afternoon. I was pleased to note that my to-do list was shorter than last year, although it was likely due to the fact Lord Nicholas would help out this year as Ari was still a year too young to receive official duties.

A boisterous evening passed, filled with talks of past duels and fights to come. In the excitement, I was able to slip away early for some much-needed sleep before heading to the hospital the next morning. It was still a little bit of a shock to have Lord Nicholas riding in the carriage with me on the way to the hospital and it seemed that, despite his previous track record, he was in a rather cheerful mood. Lord Nicholas spent the whole carriage ride asking Carlos and Mateo questions about the upcoming tournaments. Obviously not in the same chipper mood, both my knights only deigned to answer him in monosyllables. It was, frankly, impressive that Lord Nicholas managed to continue a one-sided conversation for the whole 30-minute carriage ride to the hospital and still come out with a smile. Although, around minute 15, I did start to question his sanity.

Matron Terrella was waiting for us outside the hospital once more and quickly urged Carlos, Mateo, and me towards Murphy and the patients as she took Lord Nicholas aside. Unlike last time, we weren't in a position to covertly eavesdrop on their conversation and instead found ourselves pushing through the oddly busy hospital floor towards the stairs and ramps. Murphy greeted us on the landing with a smirk, "Happy birthing season! Did you like having to push through the crowds? It'll only get worse, you know."

"What?" Carlos asked, staring at him.

"Oh, that's right. You've all never worked in the hospital before. Every year there are two blocks of time where a large number of births occur, typically about nine months after each solstice," Murphy supplied as he rolled down the hall. "The next birthing block is technically still a little over a month away, but as the due date approaches parents start to get a little anxious, especially if it's their first child. So, they will come into the hospital more frequently. This causes an influx of people in the hospital. You saw the beginnings of it this morning."

"How awful," said Carlos, looking pale.

"I hope, for your sake, that you don't want kids," I commented with a small smile.

"Nonsense," Carlos brightened once more, "Tahoe fainted twice, but the baby still made it out. Plus, I could always adopt!" All of which were valid points, so I simply nodded my head in agreement. Although, I was fairly certain that Tahoe and Clarissa's child birth was not the standard one would want to emulate.

"I'm more concerned with how much more crowded the hospital is going to get. It may be a problem if we need to evacuate for the Princess's safety," Mateo said, his amber eyes staring at me intensely.

"That's what you're worried about?" I asked in disbelief, "What kind of evacuation emergencies are you expecting to happen at the hospital?"

"We need to be prepared for anything, Princess," Mateo said, seriously.

"It does get pretty crowded, but not all the time. Plus we still have two to three weeks before we start reaching the peak of things. Makes it a hell of a lot harder to get around in this," Murphy said, gesturing to his wheelchair. "But, I perfected my shout last year. One loud 'wheelchair coming through', and any crowd will part like a ship through water. Now, are you all ready for our first patient?"

Our first patient was easy enough, but I was surprised to find Lord Nicholas in the treatment room when I went to grab a tincture of lavender for our second patient. We briefly stared at each other as I paused on my way into the room. Shaking myself out of my shock, I moved to grab a small vial of lavender tincture. Lord Nicholas appeared to be waiting on some water to boil. I wondered if he needed help. He'd likely only been studying for a day, and while making tea wasn't exactly hard, there may be some complications for the patient if something went wrong. I quickly banished the thought. I was positive my offer of assistance would not be well received. I paused once more. On the other hand, I probably shouldn't let my own pride get in the way of patient treatment. Taking a deep breath, I asked, "Do you need help with anything?"

Lord Nicholas practically snarled in response, "If I needed help, don't you think I would have asked for it?"

I was dying to reply "No! I know nothing about you, every time we meet all we do is argue, and whenever you're at dinner, it always feels like you're lying about everything!" But, instead, I simply said "Alright then," before turning and heading out the door. I did have my own patients to attend to after all.

Chapter 17

The Tournament Begins

And, so flew by the two weeks of Lord Nicholas' hospital work. Lord Nicholas worked with Healer Autumn while Murphy, my knights, and I took on our own cases. With the exception of the carriage rides to and from the palace, I hardly saw Lord Nicholas at all during hospital days. Talking with Al and Azar, I learned that the same held true when Lord Nicholas worked with them, although that was primarily because Lord Nicholas was working with management while they were working with laborers. Azar, oddly enough, seemed to have spent the most time with Lord Nicholas. Al and I agreed that Azar's "conversations" with Lord Nicholas probably consisted of Azar talking Lord Nicholas' ear off. "Poor guy, probably couldn't get a single word in edgewise," Al commented about Lord Nicholas. Causing me to giggle while Azar let out a disgruntled, "Hey!"

Just as Murphy said, there was an increase of pregnant women coming in and Matron started filling my schedule with prenatal care. She also put three heavy tomes in my arms about dealing with pregnancy. She said she was determined to make me an independently functioning midwife in two weeks time. She sternly told Carlos he was going to have to get used to childbirth, which caused him to go into a very long rant during our next study session about the horrors of pregnancy. This was cut off by Charlotte mentioning that she'd happily go through childbirth, if it meant that she could have a uterus. Charlotte's trial of being born in the wrong body shut Carlos up quickly. And, oddly, he never complained about helping with childbirth again. Although, he still got very pale and quiet whenever we assisted in a delivery.

My off days soon became filled with planning for the tournament. My tasks this year dealt with trash collection and crowd control, so, instead of training, my mornings were spent finding the best places and times for trash collection, painting barrels green for excess food waste we could use to fertilize our soil, and scheduling knights to make sure there were limited numbers of people in each area. Two days before the tournament, my siblings and Lord Nicholas all got excused from our work placements to help set up for the tournament. The team of servants I recruited helped me place marked trash receptacles and signs indicating what the colors meant. I also spent a lot of time with Al, who was in charge of food stalls this year to help set up roped-off lines for each stall. My oldest brother pointed out all of the stalls that held my favorite foods. Al also made a point to inform me of the stalls that serve foods I was allergic to so I could avoid them. When I pointed out that my allergies weren't actually deadly and I could probably try those foods on their menu, I was firmly told not to even risk it. I found a deep gratitude fill me as I thought about how much my brother cared for me. As he turned to point out other stalls I might enjoy, a joyful smile made its way onto my face.

The afternoon before the tournament started, my whole family made our way through the bustling food stand section to a large stand with a big purple and blue sign saying "Princess Cupcakes" in big curly letters. A smaller sign was hung up underneath saying, "For a taste that is royally good!" In front of the stall was a large, heavy set, woman with curly, dark blonde hair confidently directing workers on what to do. "Aunt Olivia!" I called when she was in sight. I threw decorum to the wind and ran towards her, jumping into her outstretched arms. Although I was far smaller than any of my relatives, I never once minded for this exact reason: I fit absolutely perfectly into all of their bear hugs. Aunt Olivia pulled my feet up off the ground, and squeezed me tightly leaving me feeling safe and warm.

"Hi-ya shortstack!" Aunt Olivia beamed, gently putting me back on the ground, "how-ya been?"

"Good!" I replied happily.

"And there's the rest of them! How is the royal family doing on this fine day?"

"All the better for seeing you, Liv," Father said, pulling Aunt Olivia into a hug.

"If I make your life so much better, you think you would visit more," Aunt Olivia teased.

"You are the one who refuses to come up for dinner while the nobles are here," Uncle Octavian grumbled, "Usually, I see you once a week!"

"The point of being a baker instead of a Princess is that I never have to attend those events again!"

"You're still technically a Princess, Aunt Olivia," Ari said diligently. "All children of a King gain their titles for life unless they can improve upon it, and you still use your title for marketing purposes," he finished pointing up at the sign.

"Right you are, Ari my boy. And, a great marketing job it's doing, too. I make the best damn cupcakes in Nera, but you need a few things to draw in the new customers. There aren't many Princesses who became world-class bakers out there. Everybody's going to be curious; I might as well use that curiosity to make a profit. Now, to make up for the fact that none of you are visiting me as often as you should, you're all going to be taste testers for my latest creations!"

Father and Uncle Octavian blanched. "What exactly did you have in mind?" Father asked cautiously. Uncle Octavian, on the other hand, shouted, "This better not be any more of those sea themed cupcakes you made me try last time! Whatever you do, fish does not belong in cake!"

"Now, now, don't worry too much, all these new ones have already been approved by my staff. These are tournament specials! Although, I do have some new ideas for those ocean-flavored cupcakes, and you'll be relieved to hear that I'm staying away from fish. I'll have you try some once I begin experimenting after the tournament." Uncle Octavian did not look relieved by this news. In fact, he looked rather horrified as he let his younger sister drag him up to her stall. It was always a guessing game as to whether Aunt Olivia was genuinely experimenting or if she was just trying to torture her brothers. Azar believed it was both and she was just adept at killing two birds with one stone.

Aunt Olivia started us all off with her savory cupcakes line, which, I assure you, tasted a lot better than they sounded. My cousin, Micheal, my brothers, and I sat at a high table around Aunt Olivia's stand, while our parents sat at an identical table across from us. Large stalls were only allowed two tables to keep the food area from becoming too congested. Guests were encouraged to go to their seats, or to the other tables set outside the three arenas. Azar and I were handed meatloaf and mashed potato cupcakes, while Ari, Al, and Micheal munched greedily on buffalo chicken cupcakes. Despite the initial oddity, we all gave Aunt Olivia rave reviews as she brought out her dessert cupcakes.

Aunt Olivia then came out with a mango chili cupcake, a pineapple coconut cupcake, and a lemon lime cupcake that all tasted divine. Ari didn't like the mango chili one, so Aunt Olivia brought him his favorite double chocolate cupcake. It was the most relaxed I'd seen my family in over a month, I thought as I grabbed a second lemon lime cupcake, which was quickly becoming a new favorite. My father was laughing at some joke his brother made, his face beaming in the hot afternoon sun. His shoulders bounced up and down freely, a looseness in his arms that flew up and down wildly as he spoke with his hands. His tension, which I really only subconsciously registered with me these past few weeks, eased away and in turn, released a tension in my brothers and me that I had not realized we were holding. Al was laughing in the exact same way Father was. Azar's smile mirrored the one Mama was wearing. Ari's slow dissection of his cupcake matched Mother's careful inspection of each cupcake's design. It felt like home. Like at this moment there was nothing else in the whole world other than enjoying these cupcakes in each other. Perfect moment in time.

Then it ended. A messenger came up to Father, and his back straightened, with his shoulders set back and tight. His voice became serious, and his eyes focused. He said hasty good-byes to his family and rushed back towards the palace. Never frantic, but always pushing forward, his pace as a King always moved quickly. My brothers and I had seen this behavior before. We'd watched this exact scene play out hundreds of times before in various different places, but each time I think we were all struck with the understanding of the cost of this job we all coveted. As usual, there was a beat of silence after Father left before conversation flowed once more. However, we were never fully able to recover the freedom that we had when Father was here.

Mama called Azar and Al away first to begin a special pre-tournament preparation ritual that Ari and I had yet to experience. Uncle Octavian, Aunt Arielle, and cousin Micheal slipped away next. Until just Ari, Mother, Aunt Olivia, and I sat together at one table discussing new cupcake ideas, Aunt Olivia's experimentation process, and sharing stories of Father's youth that we'd all heard before but never grown weary of. We talked until the sky began to darken, with Aunt Olivia occasionally jumping out to direct nearby workers. Happy and filled with sugar, Ari and I walked hand-in-hand with Mother back to the palace, excited for tomorrow's adventures.

I woke up early once again, although today there would be no time for a ride. No, today when I woke up, I rang for Ana and Charlotte to help me get dressed. The Introductory Tournament would begin at exactly ten in the morning, but due to the large crowd size, there was often a line to the arena starting as early as eight-thirty. My maids speculated lines would begin at eight because Azar would be competing this year. I looked out my window as I waited for Ana and Charlotte to arrive, and saw that they were correct. At only a little past eight, I could see tiny figures lined up by the arena's entrance.

"Good morning, Princess," Charlotte called as she entered the room, drawing me away from the window.

Ana came in swiftly behind her holding a tray of food. "There won't be any time for a formal breakfast today, Princess," Ana said, "So I brought some fruit and a sausage sandwich." I felt my stomach growl at the words and I moved predatorily towards the tray.

"No!" Charlotte moved in front of me, "It has to wait until after I've washed your hair." Charlotte grabbed my hand and maneuvered me towards the bathroom. I was quickly washed and my hair dried, to the best of the poor towel's ability, before I was finally able to eat my breakfast as Ana pulled out the outfit we agreed on the night before. My hair was still not quite dry, so I was put into my dress first. Ana efficiently laced me into a thin amethyst gown with a corseted waist. There were silver flowers embroidered on the gown's waistline. A rush of gratitude filled me as I realized that I would not be required to mesh gold and silver tones today.

Finally dressed, I sat down at the vanity where Charlotte began doing my makeup while we casually chatted about today's matchups. Carlos, Azar, Al, and Elise would all fight today. I would likely not be able to see Elise's first fight, as it was happening at the same time as the Introductory Tournament finals. I was in a cheerful mood by the time my hair was finally dry enough to style into a braided updo that Charlotte made look easy, but I was sure was actually fairly complicated. Charlotte was just finishing up the final touches on my hair when Mother walked in.

In a long gown of deep purple with a high halter neck top and an intricate gold embroidery falling down the length of her dress, Mother looked stunning. Her black hair was braided into a tall bun on her head framed by her golden crown. As she turned and looked at me she said, "Just perfect, Avalynn. I knew it was the right move to go to your brother first. Gods above, that boy needs all the help in the world just to get properly dressed. Let me help you finish," Mother said, as she grabbed my laid-out jewelry and started to put it on me. After daintily slipping on my silver bracelet and necklace, she placed my silver crown on top of my head. She then put her palms on my cheek before tilting my eyes up to hers. My green eyes met her deep brown ones and she gave me a gentle smile. "How lovely you look, my daughter," she said, kissing me softly on the forehead. Taking my arm in hers she guided me towards the door. "Great work this morning, ladies," she nodded towards Ana and Charlotte. "I hope you two have a wonderful time at the tournament today!"

"Thank you, Your Majesty." Ana and Charlotte called before we left the room. We walked down the hall towards Ari's room. When we entered the room after a short knock, we found him standing alone fidgeting in the mirror. He was dressed in a thin white shirt covered by a purple vest with silver embroidery and purple trousers with a silver stripe down the side. His crown was a thin strip of silver with ridges all around.

"You look wonderful, Ari," Mother said gently.

"It's very busy," Ari commented, wrinkling his nose.

"Yes, but it projects stability, and allows us to support clothing manufacturers all over Nevremerre," Mother insisted.

"I suppose," Ari said, but he stopped fidgeting and turned to join us as we exited the room and headed down to the tournament grounds.

There was a loud bustle of people walking around the tournament grounds. Large crowds gathered at the entrance of each of the three stadiums. I was pleased to note that each queue appeared orderly and controlled. The roped-off barriers that created the lines were working perfectly, and I congratulated myself on a job well done. Traditionally, the Kings and Queens opened the tournaments in the Grand Arena, while Princes and Princesses, or another high-ranking noble, opened the tournament in the two lower arenas. As Al and Azar were both competing today, it was up to Ari and me to make the welcome speech in the lower Arenas.

I had been responsible for opening the Small Arena the year before. I remember practicing the four sentences needed to open the tournament under my breath for the whole day before the actual event. The rising nausea and my clammy hands remained for two hours after I made my speech. I looked over at Ari, who was intently staring at the road in front of us. Although his face looked as impassive as ever, his knuckles were turning white as he'd grab Mother's hand. Mother seemed not to mind, fortunately, and I knew she was doing her best to support Ari before his first welcome speech.

"Alright, my dears," Mother said gently, her honeyed voice sliding around us. "I will see you both at the Small Arena in an hour to watch Azar's first match. Raise your heads high, you both make our country and me proud." She gave our hands a quick squeeze and a kind smile filled her face. Then she raised her head and walked confidently towards the Grand Arena. I gave Ari a smile of my own before saying a quick "good luck" as we both went off to our respective arenas.

I walked off towards the back entrance of the Middle Arena to get to the royal box, smiling at the people bowing at either side of me. Galileo, a knight fighting in tomorrow's tournament, walked behind me in full knight's armor, adding a clanking sound to accompany my movements. It took only about 10 minutes to reach the royal box, where a row of wooden chairs lined with purple cushions were set around a singular raised chair with a gold inlay on the back. With a deep breath, I stepped on the raised platform and took a seat on the chair.

With about another 30 minutes until the tournament was set to begin, I settled in and watched the stadium around me begin to fill up, as Galileo stood dutifully behind me. The Introductory Tournament was divided into three groups determined by age. The Grand Arena held matches of the eldest age group, who are generally thought to be the strongest; as such, it usually attracts the largest number of spectators. This is likely aided by Father opening the tournament in that Arena as well. The next biggest group goes to the Middle Arena, where the next oldest group of knights would fight. Usually, the smallest crowd is in the Small Arena, where the youngest knights fight. However, this year, there would likely be a larger crowd there as Azar was a part of the youngest group. Nevertheless, there was a large crowd filing into the rows of the Middle Arena. I spotted the occasional noble and knight walk in with the crowd, likely to watch a friend or relative compete.

Ten minutes later and my box was still empty. I felt a little awkward, next to 12 empty chairs. I shifted slightly trying to keep my back straight. Obviously, I wouldn't be alone this whole time, at least one member of the council would have to come to judge my performance. However, it seemed like there might only be one who would come. As a sign of honor, the highest ranking royal always entered the royal box first. However, based on previous experience, the box usually filled faster than this. Admittedly, this was only the second time I had the right to go in the box first. I tried to soothe myself, desperately trying not to fidget in my seat. It took another five minutes before a clear voice broke through the emptiness of my box.

"Good morning, Princess," Sir Abel bowed, followed by Lord Martin and Lord Heathcliff. I greeted them all with a smile and indicated that they should sit on either side of me.

"I must say, I am surprised to see you, Sir Abel" I said smiling as the three of them sat down beside me. The royal box was, usually, only permitted to members of the council and those with the title of Prince, Princess, or above.

"His Majesty has considered Sir Abel an exception, as his work this summer has been aiding the council," Lord Heathcliff smiled, his silver hair glinting in the morning sun.

"Yes, I'm very grateful for the honor," Sir Abel responded. "I must confess I first tried to go to the small Arena to support the Third Prince in his speech, but I found the box already quite full." I laughed at his feigned shock.

"Yes, I can imagine! I believe Prince Octavian and Princess Arielle will be there, and six seats will have to be saved for the rest of the royal family. That only leaves four open seats!" Lord Martin laughed.

"Yes, and Princess Olivia just came," called the disappointed voice of Lady Milfred who just walked in. "That damned Lady

Rosewell managed to get there before me, so I had to give up my seat. Damn young people and their spry hips!"

"Lady Rosewell is 43," Lord Martin laughed.

"Just you two wait," Lord Heathcliff said, raising an eyebrow at Lord Martin and me, "one day you both will get to be Lady Milfred's and my age, may the Gods allow it, and then you'll see that 43 is quite young in deed." Lord Martin and I shared a smiling glance.

"Well I'm just glad my youngest sister was old enough to be in the second bracket," Lord Martin smiled.

"Oh come now, if your sister were competing in the third bracket, then even Lady Rosewell would have to move!" Lady Milfred admonished playfully.

"Princess, my Lords and Ladies, and Sir, the starting gong will ring in a minute's time," a servant called from the box entryway.

"Are you ready, Princess?" Lord Heathcliff asked.

"Most definitely," I responded honestly. "I must admit I was quite nervous last year, but now that I've done it once before, I feel very prepared to do it again. Plus, I'm rather excited for the tournament."

"Yes, experience makes most things easier," Lady Milfred said sagely. Not long after, a loud gong rang out, and silence fell over the crowd. I stood and walked over to the edge of the box.

"Citizens of Nevremerre," I called out, projecting my voice like Mother had taught us, "Thank you for attending today's events. Today I have the pleasure of introducing you to eight new knights of Nevremerre as they compete to win this bracket. I am honored to be served by the wonderful knights you will see fight today. Best of luck to the competitors, and let the tournament begin!" Cheers rose up from the crowd as I moved to sit back down.

"The first match is between Sir Austin," a cheer went up as a knight with a blue tassel on his longsword came out, "and Sir Rajesh," another cheer followed by a knight walking out with a red tassel on his long sword.

"Two longswords! How fun!" Lord Martin called out while the two opponents got into place.

"What will your sister fight with?" I asked, as the official called for the match to begin.

"She's a dual sword wheeler," Lord Martin responded. A clanging rang out as Sir Austin attacked first. I watched the match with interest, but not too much investment. I entertained myself by trying to decide how I would win against the two opponents below. Both knights were fairly slow in their movements, I quickly realized. Heavy in their motions, and easily stopped if you could manage to trip them. Which, I recognized, I could probably do. It was clear to see that these two, while on par with each other, would not go far in the tournament overall. After about half-an-hour of back and forth, Sir Rajesh knocked Sir Austin off-guard and dealt a decisive blow that knocked him to his knees. Cheers went up from the crowd once more as Sir Rajesh was given the victory. On a large board Sir Rajesh's name was moved up to the next round.

"The next match will begin in 26 minutes," the announcer called. Audience members began to shuffle around, so I, too, headed out of the arena. Saying my goodbyes to those in my box, Galileo and I began to walk towards the Small Arena, where Azar would fight next. The stadium was packed with people watching the two knights down below, and the royal box felt very squished compared to my previous location. Father was already sitting in the raised chair, indicating the match in the Grand Arena had also come to a conclusion. I moved to the only empty seat next to Mother, hurrying by Al, Mama, and Father all of whom were decked out in full armor, avidly watching the match down below.

"How's it going?" I asked Mother as I sat down.

"Poorly," she replied just distastefully, "While both knights are fairly strong, I believe both of them to be idiots. The short sword has failed to realize that the dual sword wielder is left-hand dominant, and keeps directing her attacks to the left side. Meanwhile, the dual sword wielder fails to follow up on attacks. Neither of them are thinking as they fight. Take heed, Avalynn, no matter how much strength you have, if you cannot also back it up with wisdom, you are doomed to fail." I nodded, smiling at her. "Ah look, the dual sword wielder has started to slow his pace. Short sword's stamina remains. Short sword will win in about seven minutes. What a boring match," Mother sighed. Seven minutes later the dual swords went flying, and the short sword wielder won. Mother just shook her head as cheers went up in the crowd.

"Ten minutes until the next match," an announcer said.

"Azar is up next!" Mama squealed with excitement.

"Did he seem nervous when you saw him this morning?" I asked.

"Hm, I don't know about being nervous, Azar has always been confident in his own ability. However, he was very quiet. You know the way he gets when he's seriously thinking about something," Mama replied.

"Good!" Father jumped in, "No matter how strong you may be, you must take every fight seriously. You never know who may surprise you with their skills. Not to mention it's a sign that you respect the opponent in front of you!" Mama and Al agreed instantly, but Mother just gave a pursed lipped nod. We continued to chat for the next 10 minutes, joined by my aunts and uncle as well, until it was time for Azar's match to begin.

"The next match is between Sir Indiga," a pause as cheers filled the stadium and a night with the short sword came out, "and second Prince Azar." The screams that filled the stadium were deafening as Azar walked out. His presence felt like it loomed over the stadium. His body towering in glistening silver armor, and a large hammer occupying his hands. The two opponents took their places in the arena, and the match began. With the level of excitement radiating off the crowd, you might have thought this match was between two experts in their field. However, it was very clear that this impression was false, when, not even 10 minutes later, Azar claimed victory. Fortunately, this decisive victory did nothing to dampen the crowd's spirit, as their cheers and shouts echoed through the stadium. Even more so in our box.

"That's my boy!" Father cheered. Mama, Al, and I jumped up with applause. Mother and Ari were more reserved in their movements, but both had wide smiles on their faces. Although as the applause wore on, Ari occasionally winced from the noise.

"He is really using intimidation techniques to his advantage," Mother smiled as the crowd calmed down. "Sir Indiga looked ready to give up as soon as Azar walked out and word of this quick victory will certainly reach his next opponent making his intimidation even greater. It is far easier to defeat someone who's already given up."

"Yes, well these two sons of mine certainly look tough!" Father grinned, reaching over to clap Al on the shoulder. I felt a pang of jealousy ring through me. Many things may be said about my appearance, but I had neither the height nor the width to appear intimidating. I also had the tendency to smile far too often and any attempt at an intimidating glare often fell flat. Once, when I was 9, an 11 year-old Azar had stepped on, and promptly ruined, my brand new dress. Furious, I turned to yell at him only to be met by laughter. Azar said that I "looked just like an angry puppy". This did, in no way, quell my fury, but it also, sadly, reinforced my "puppy-like" expression. Azar did keep trying to apologize, but it lacked any effect since he couldn't stop laughing.

Ari seemed to be mirroring my thoughts as he was looking at his twig-like arms questioningly. "Don't worry my dears," Mother called out to us, "There are ways to be intimidating without having height or an imposing size. There's a wonder to be held in merely being inordinately confident in any environment that will strike fear and doubt into your opponent's heart. That being said, there's also a value in being underestimated as well. It's all about when and how you use each tactic. For this event, and your brother's style of fighting, intimidation is a smart choice. It will easily weed out the weak-willed opponents and allow him more time to rest between matches. If he makes it to the finals, he will fight in five matches today, between that and the adrenaline surges, it has the potential to seriously drain him. Best to win swiftly and easily whenever possible."

"Well, he is certainly doing a fine job for now," Mama nodded, "We shall see if he can keep it up!"

Azar did manage to keep his skills up as he subsequently won his next two matches, setting him up nicely for the finals. I managed to see two of Carlos' fights as well. Overall, Carlos did well, just narrowly losing the final match in his bracket. And, after what seemed like no time at all, my family (minus Al, who had his first Open Match that evening) made our way to the Grand Arena to watch Azar compete in the final.

The Grand Arena was packed. There wasn't a single seat empty as far as the eye could see, and the same could be said of the royal box. The royal box in the Grand Arena was larger than the royal boxes in the two other Arenas. With three big thrones in the center and 14 seats on either side, it made quite an imposing structure on the top level of the stadium. My family filled in the middle seats as the entire council filled out the sides. The arena thrummed with excitement from the crowd. My own excitement buzzed with them, filling the space around me. At least it did, until I saw Lord Nicholas walk confidently towards me.

"What are you doing here?" I almost spat out as he calmly sat beside me.

"I do believe I'm fueling the rumors of our courtship or perhaps, a courtship between me and your brother," Lord Nicholas said with a mock curiosity. "Either way, I do have the permission of His Majesty." he nodded towards Father, who gave him a rather jerky nod in return, his lips pursed, before he turned back toward the stadium.

"How do you even know about those rumors?" I asked stupidly, grabbing the first thought that came to me in my shock.

"My dear Princess," Lord Nicholas said, leaning into my space with a sly smile, "if one is to become King, they must have a firm grasp on any rumors around them." I pushed myself away from him, which only caused Lord Nicholas to smile more. "I must say," he continued, leaning back once more, "I am rather happy with the rumor so far. I'm either someone so charming that a Prince or Princess fell for me at first sight, or I am a genius who might be the youngest council member ever at just 21. Now, those both sound like someone highly qualified to be King, wouldn't you say? And, now I'm sitting in the royal box at the finale for the Introductory Tournament. It won't be long until the whole country knows my name." Lord Nicholas gave a satisfied smile as he jerked his head towards the crowd below. Following his nod, it was clear to see that a large number of eyes and fingers had turned toward the royal box.

"The higher you soar, the harder you may fall," I responded simply. Although I felt a heat rising in my stomach desperately wanting to lash out.

"Do you really think I would ever allow myself to fall?"

"It is not always in our power to stop it. There will always be forces beyond our control."

"Are you quite sure about that, Princess?" Lord Nicholas said. His face took a dark turn as he looked at me, "This world was made by us. These buildings were made by us. This country was made by us. With enough strength and wisdom, of course we can control the world we created."

"You cannot control the rain, nor the skies, nor the fish in the sea. And you cannot control the hearts of people. You will never be able to control it all."

"Oh, no?" Lord Nicholas said as a gong rang out, silencing the crowd. Lord Nicholas moved closer towards me until his lips were next to my ear, "Just you wait, Princess, this world will spin exactly how I want it to." Perhaps it was the confidence in his voice, or perhaps it was simply the result of my varied emotions all day, but his words sent a lightning strike of terror through me that seemed to captivate my whole soul. I could barely hear Father's final announcements for the round-robin style battles that would be taking place below. It was all I could do to simply keep breathing with a smile on my face, as I forced myself to calm down.

My nerves were still on edge as we watched Azar fight his first match below. Although this match was far more interesting than the ones I had seen previously, I found it hard to keep my focus. I was finally jerked out of my reverie when Azar claimed victory and the cries of the crowd pierced the air. I pulled forward my previous conviction that no one could control everything and clung on to it for dear life as Azar prepared to fight once more. I used this belief to ground me as I focused on the next match. Forty-eight minutes later, Azar once again claimed victory, ensuring his title as the Introductory Tournament Champion even though his two previous opponents were set to fight one more match. My parents were all on their feet with applause, as Azar gracefully walked out of the Arena.

"So, it seems another one of your siblings has won the Introductory Tournament. That's some rather tough competition to follow should you attempt to become a knight," Lord Nicholas' voice grated through me, and a rather obvious attempt to bait me.

"Clearly, being a knight isn't everything, seeing as you haven't attempted to become one," I responded curtly as the last match began.

"True, true, but I am the charming genius invited to the royal box, don't you know. I don't need a knighthood to prove my worthiness." I briefly wondered what would happen to his "charming" reputation if I punched him in the face right here and now, but I decided against that in favor of folding my hands politely on my lap.

"You know Sir Abel is also in the royal box; your invitation is not as exciting as it seems," I responded, trying to keep my eyes focused on the fight below.

"You mean the man rumored to be the spiritual advisor to the King himself, and possibly an 11th member to the council. Yes, I can't say that really diminishes my prospects here." Lord Nicholas clicked his tongue at me, "Really Princess, you should pay much more attention to the rumors. I mean do you even know what the rumors say about you?"

A slight panic overtook me as I realized that I had no idea what rumors were currently said about me. "Since we're both aware of how false rumors can be, I'm quite sure I don't need to be paying attention to every little one," I tried to recover.

"I wouldn't be so sure. For some, rumors are the only way to get to know you. In a position such as yours, everything said about you is important." Intellectually, I was forced to acknowledge that he was probably right about this, but he said it in such a patronizing way that I'd be damned before I ever let him know that. I was saved trying to find a suitable retort by the match ending below us.

Father stood once more as he made his way down to the arena. He would present Azar with a championship medal, and then we would have a family celebration, which Lord Nicholas, thankfully, would not be invited to. As we waited for the awards, a sweaty, but happy looking Al walked in. "You won then," I guessed as all eyes in the room turned to him.

"I did," he responded with a proud smile. "I'll fight again tomorrow."

"Oh Al, I'm so proud of you!" called Mama, pulling him into a tight hug, their metal breastplates banging together. Mother, Ari, and I moved to congratulate him as well.

"I take it Prince Azar won as well," Al said, extracting himself from our hugs to look over at the arena below.

"He did," Mother replied proudly, "His Majesty will be presenting the award shortly, so let's all take our seats." She kissed Al on the cheek once more before heading back to her throne. With Al now returned, Lord Nicholas moved from the spot beside me as Al glared at him. I noted, with some irritation, that Lord Nicholas was entirely unfazed by Al's more intimidating expression, and simply gave Al a nod as he quietly changed seats. Finally, Father's figure appeared in the arena.

"Ladies, Lords, and citizens of Nevremerre," he projected. "I thank you all for coming to support our new knights as they demonstrate the skills and talents they will use and continue to develop to defend all of you. I congratulate all who participated in the tournament today and I look forward to continuing to train with you and to see you all grow into the best knights you can be. I extend a special congratulations to today's champion and my son, Prince Azar!" The crowd roared as Father took Azar's hand and lifted it into the air. Father gave Azar a hug before attaching a shiny metal to his armor. He then turned back to the crowd and raised a large hand. "I hope to see you all back here tomorrow, but until then I hope you will continue to enjoy the tournament's food, and the various shows we have prepared for you in each Arena. May the honor of Nevremerre be Everlasting!"

"May Nevremerre prosper evermore! Good health to King and Country," the crowd chanted back. My family and I said our goodbyes and we left the arena. We waved at the bowing masses as we walked back up to the palace. Along the way, we ran into Father and Azar. I ran up to congratulate him, and he picked me up into a crushing hug. I tried not to breathe in his sweat and grime. I informed him that I would have to apologize to Ana and Charlotte for the laundry he was making them do, but he just squeezed me harder until I was nothing but laughs.

For the first time since Lord Nicholas came, dinner was just my family and me. The table was filled with rambunctious laughter as Azar told us about his matches that we'd all just watched and Al told us about the match we had to miss. It was a loud peace as we talked the hours away before Mama shooed herself and Al up to bed for their matches tomorrow. A little while later, Azar's adrenaline caught up with him and a pink-cheeked Father practically dragged him up to bed. Mother then walked Ari and me to our own respective rooms, kissing us each on the head goodnight. Less than 30 minutes later, I was snuggled in bed, falling asleep to the echoes of the tournament celebrations down below.

The next day I woke up early once more. Today I was dressed in gold, and a tired, but happy looking Azar met me by the door. His dirtied armor was sparkling once more, and Azar assured me his footman, Calstin and Albert, would both be getting a day off soon. We walked to the arena with Mother and Ari, as we placed bets on how Mama and Al would do today. Based on their bracket positions, if they both won three matches they would face each other! We laughed as we discussed the possibilities. Soon we broke off to our respective arenas to open today's tournament with Azar not competing today. I was slated to open for the smallest arena. I wondered, briefly, if Lord Nicholas might show up, but fortunately, the morning saw him blissfully absent from my life. I cheered on Mama and Al in peace.

Although he made it to the top five, Al lost to Mama in an epic battle that threw him out of the finals. Mama too, missed out on the finals, but top four was an impressive feat for someone just shy of 50. The final match was of two seasoned knights, including Sir Galileo. It was such an intense and skillful battle, I hardly had a thought to spare towards Lord Nicholas, who had found himself seated beside me once more. It took nearly an hour before Sir Etian claimed victory, with thunderous applause overtaking the crowd below. Before the crowd had time to settle down, I was whisked away by Mother to prepare for the late-night ball.

Chapter 18

The Failings of the King's Children

The palace gardens sparkled in the moonlight, illuminated by rows and rows of strung up lanterns that painted everything in a pale orange. Tables of drinks and small food items lined the outskirts of the garden manned by footmen in flowing white shirts with the Nevremerre flag embroidered on the chest. A band gathered in an open amphitheatre on the far end, and the occasional notes of members tuning and warming up echoed over the nobles and knights who meandered nearby. The garden was still relatively empty as those who fought today were likely still bathing and changing, but there was a pleasant atmosphere of joy and excitement from the guests who had already arrived. I spotted Mateo at a drinks table. The silk fabric of my dark blue ball gown wafted pleasantly around my legs, as I walked over to him. "How was your family?" I asked as I stood behind him.

"Princess," Mateo bowed, looking not in the least bit startled by my sudden appearance. I was momentarily stunned as he looked back at me. He looked rather handsome in his pale blue tunic that stretched tight around his muscular arms and chest. His usually pulled-back hair fell loosely around his face, as he gave me a warm smile. "My family is doing quite well. They are a rather rambunctious lot, but it's always nice to see them."

"That's... that's wonderful," I blinked trying to get my heart rate back under control, "I'm glad you had the opportunity to see them. Did you just get back? No doubt Carlos will want to see you. He did quite well at the tournament after all."

"I suspected that he might," Mateos smiled, "Despite all his blustering, he is a good knight."

"Aw, I knew you liked me," a loud voice jumped in. I turned to see Carlos and Azar walking up from the left. Carlos pulled Mateo into a side hug, "It's good to see you! I've missed you!"

Mateo gave a long-suffering sigh, "Perhaps I spoke too soon."

"You sure did," said Azar as he wrapped his arm around each of them, "I did win after all, whereas this poor lad didn't even make it into the finals."

"Hey!" Carlos exclaimed, pushing himself out of Azar's grasp. Mateo just took another sip of his drink, apparently un-bothered by the fact that he was still being partially held by a Prince. "Anyways, Princess, who will be your first dance?" Car-los said, turning to me. He, I mused, also looked rather hand-some with his floppy curly hair and a red v-neck tunic. I forced myself to focus back on his question.

"I'm not quite sure, to be honest, whichever brother is free I suppose. Or, perhaps a dance with Queen Eleanor or Duke Micheal." It was traditional for royals to start the ball with a family member. With a start, I realized why Carlos had asked his question, and an evil mirth ran through me. "I may dance with anyone, anyone except Azar that is. His partner has already been decided." Carlos laughed.

"I don't see why you two are laughing. It's an honor to be the first dance partner of the King." Azar said with as much forced dignity as he could muster.

"Oh yes, it's quite the honor. Especially, the part where he loudly tells stories of the time you blew your diapers out during an important meeting or when you threw a tantrum on the palace steps in earshot of every noble in the country," Al replied, popping up seemingly out of nowhere with Ari by his side. His full lips pursed into a grimace, most likely recalling his dance with Father the previous year. He gave a visible shutter before grasping Azar firmly on the shoulder. "I wish you the best of luck, brother," Al said seriously, his dark eyes looking directly into Azar's.

"It can't be that bad," Azar said nervously.

"You called Al 'Prince Stinky Butt' for a whole two weeks, until Mother put a stop to it," I reminded him.

"Not your best insult," Carlos commented, as Azar's face slowly twisted into horror, "I'm sure Prince Al and I can come up with something better after your dance this evening." Al nodded his head In agreement.

"You know," Ari said, his monotone voice breaking through our crowd, "there's no guarantee that you won't also have to dance with Father, Al," all eyes in the circle turn to him. "After all," Ari continued, "it's possible that Father will want to dance with all of his family members that competed in the tournament, not just Azar."

Al's mouth gaped open. He stood still for a moment before pulling Ari close to him. "One day, it will be your turn for all of this, and I will make you regret all you've said today," Al threatened.

"By the time Ari is even eligible for any of this, you'll be nearly thirty, don't you think you'll be too old for such games?" I pointed out.

"Don't think you're safe either," Azar said, as both he and Al rounded on me. "You've only got two years left before this "honor" comes. Just you wait and see!" Azar finished gravely. I heard Carlos' stifled laughter from behind him. Motion from across the room caught my eye, and a cat-like grin came across my face.

"That may be so, but tonight, dear brother, it's your turn. Your dance partner awaits," I said as I gestured across the garden to where Mama, Mother, and Father had just walked in. Azar audibly groaned, and Carlos stopped bothering to hide his laughter. Even Ari and Mateo were grinning at Azar's expense.

Moments later, I found myself in Ari's arms as he skillfully maneuvered us close to Father and Azar. Though this was likely unnecessary as Father's voice seemed to carry the length of the garden, as he cried about how much Azar had grown. Throughout the waltz, Azar's face became steadily closer to the shade of his hair as Father recounted one embarrassing childhood story after another, no matter how much Azar attempted to stop him. Al looked positively gleeful as the music came to a close, this disappeared almost instantly, as a still teary-eyed Father asked Al for the next dance.

"Children shouldn't be allowed to do things," Azar said bitterly as he became my next partner. "They should simply be locked in a room until they grow up, and stop doing embarrassing things."

"I'm not sure that would work out the way you think it would," I responded.

"It has to! Children should not be allowed to speak," he whined.

"It's not that bad," I soothed.

"I told the entire army I loved them and wanted to marry them! Dammit, who even puts a five year old on the stage anyways!" his face, which had slowly become more pink, flushed scarlet once more. I didn't even bother to try and hide my laughter.

"I'm sure everyone found it very cute! Besides it looks like this is only a one-time deal," I said nodding to where Al and Father were quietly dancing.

"Thank the Gods," Azar agreed, as the dance finished.

"May I have this dance," Al asked Azar, "or do I have to wait for you to dance with your 5,987 army spouses first?"

"Damn it, Al!" Azar angrily grabbed his proffered hand as they set off for the next dance. I giggled at their exit and turned to find my own partner.

"It would appear all your family members are already taken, that being the case, may I have this next dance, Princess?" I stiffened as the overly saccharine voice of Lord Nicholas washed over me. Avoiding Lord Nicholas' eyes, I hastily looked around the room for a sign that he was incorrect in his assessment. Unfortunately, his statement turned out to be true as I spotted everyone from my family to my knights with another partner.

"I could simply not dance this round," I commented dryly. Finally, turning back towards Lord Nicholas, who was still standing in front of me with an upturned hand. He moved his gaze up to mine, and smirked, straightening up once more.

"And tell me, Princess," he responded, taking my unoffered hand and stepping into my space, "how would that look to the other nobles here? A Princess refusing a noble's offer to dance in favor of standing alone. How tongues would wag! Just imagine the rumors that would spread. We are no longer at a crowded dance, Princess," he whispered in my ear, "all eyes are on you here." With a sigh, I acknowledged the truth to his words, letting him guide me to a waltzing position.

"It's not very noble, is it, forcing a person to dance with you," I replied as the music began.

"You always had the option of saying no," Lord Nicholas sing-songed. I glared at him in response.

"You deliberately put me in a position where I had to dance with you or else face highly unfavorable personal consequences. It was manipulative and conniving," I snarled back.

"That's just how the game is played," and Lord Nicholas replied, twirling me around the garden's stone floor.

"People's lives aren't a game!"

"Oh, then what are you playing at? With your bleeding-heart trying to save the world. What kind of arrogance is that? Life has always been a game, at least when I play someone has a chance at winning." Any remnants of Lord Nicholas' charming personality had disappeared from his face. His jaw was clenched and his eyes burned with anger that I was sure mirrored my own. His hand on my waist was almost painfully tight as we robotically followed the dances motions.

"Winning?" I questioned, "Is that what you think you're doing by coming here? You're already the successor to a title, how much do you really think your life will change if you become King? I have never once believed that I had the power or that it was my responsibility to 'save the world', as you put it, but I do believe I have the power to make a difference, to enact real policies and to make decisions that will help the people of this country. That's what rulers have been doing in Nevremerre for centuries! If anyone's deluded here, it's you, who believes being King will give you anything other than more work."

"Money," Lord Nicholas shot back.

"I don't remember the Armon province lacking funds."

"Power," Lord Nicholas came back once more.

"Power to do what? What more power could you possibly need?"

"Perhaps I was just intrigued by how easy it was to get the position," Lord Nicholas smirked. I felt my whole body stiffening his arms causing Lord Nicholas to drag me through the next few steps.

"There is not a single member of my family who is not a worthy candidate for the throne," I hissed back. Lord Nicholas actually had the audacity to laugh.

"Really, Princess, how can you be so blind to the faults of those around you? I spent two weeks working with you and your older brothers, and each of your flaws are glaringly obvious. I'm sure your younger brother's fault will be just as easily exposed. Honestly, why do you think it was so easy for me to be considered as a candidate in the first place?"

I internally cursed Lord Nicholas' ability to poke at my insecurities every time we spoke. "Everyone has flaws, and, technically, everyone has the right to try to become King. Just because you've chosen this path does not guarantee you success," I fought back. Distantly, I registered the final slow beats of the song coming to a close.

"Some flaws are irredeemable," Lord Nicholas said as we came to a standstill. I eagerly began to push myself out of his arms, only to feel his hands tighten around me. "I'll tell you what, Princess, in two weeks time I will have worked with you and all your siblings. Since you're so clueless towards your family's flaws, come to my room, and I will tell you exactly why each one of you will be passed over for the throne, and my own ascension assured." Lord Nicholas finally released me, and his disarmingly fake smile returned once more.

I eagerly turned away, only to find Carlos behind me, his eyes like daggers pointed at Lord Nicholas, as he claimed to be my next dance partner. I gratefully let myself be swept away, and soon discovered that my friends had made some sort of Princess dance schedule, or something of that ilk as I had one or more of them asking me to dance for the rest of the evening. While they succeeded in raising my mood, I couldn't shake Lord Nicholas's parting offer from my mind. So, only a few hours later, I pulled away from Charlotte, who'd come as Elise's partner, and headed off to bed.

I couldn't decide whether the next two weeks passed agonizingly slowly, or far, far too quickly. I filled my days with hospital work and any sort of royal training I could think of. I spent time with my friends, and avoided Lord Nicholas like the plague. I met with Abel, and discussed my various woes. I didn't bring up my conversation with Lord Nicholas at the ball. I knew from the moment Lord Nicholas finished his offer that I would accept it, so I didn't see the point in telling Abel about it. Or, perhaps, I was just too scared to see what his reaction would be. Finally, preparations were being made for the Unajo festival with Agremerre marking the end of summer.

The afternoon of the festival, I had Ana and Charlotte finish dressing me early, carefully putting me into my two-piece yellow dress, and pulling my hair into an intricate knot. With over an hour to spare until the festival began, I made my way to Lord Nicholas' room. A curious mix of dread, excitement, and nervousness ran through me as I prepared myself to knock on his door. I was both desperate and terrified to know the "irredeemable" flaws he discovered in my family, and that he discovered in me. Taking a deep breath I knocked on his door. Lord Nicholas, too, was already dressed for the evening's event when he answered the door. His olive green shirt had copper leaves embroidered along the edges, and he wore a copper leaf pendant to match. "Ah, Princess," he said leaning across the door frame, "I was wondering if you'd come."

"Not when I'd come? And here I thought you had us all figured out." Lord Nicholas just smirked at me as he took in my appearance. "Are you going to invite me in?" I finally asked, "or are we going to have this conversation in the hall?"

"Come in," Lord Nicholas said, turning into his room. I followed closing the door behind me. Lord Nicholas was seated in his desk chair, and gestured for me to sit on the cushioned bench at the end of his bed. I did so, keeping my back straight and my head high as I gave him my whole undivided attention. "So," Lord Nicholas began, "you want to know why your family is unfit for the throne." Something in his words hit my gut like a sucker punch causing pain and anger to well up inside of me, but I forced myself to remain calm and simply nodded in response. I was rewarded by a small frown from Lord Nicholas at my non-response.

"Let's start from the top then, your brother Al," again I held off a response at his blatant disrespect for my brother, and waited for him to continue. "This one is a funny one for me because I have been on the receiving end of your very pointed lecture on why one should be a King for the people. Yet, only two days after I became a candidate for the throne I found myself on the receiving end of another very revealing lecture from Prince Alveron. He seemed to be attempting to inform me of the "trials" of being a King of a peaceful nation. However, what I really gained from his misguided attempt at manipulation, was that he thinks of himself as a martyr taking on the mantle of King to protect everyone else. What an egotistical ass he is. Thinking he has cornered the market on morality. Although, that might be a family trait," he said looking pointedly at me.

A fire filled my heart. How dare he speak of Al that way! I had a good idea of the kind of talk Al would have given Lord Nicholas, but I also knew my brother. While I couldn't argue that Al might have a bit of a martyr complex, I also know that he's never once thought of anything more sinister than wanting each of his siblings to find happiness. I also felt certain that Lord Nicholas only felt like Al was trying to manipulate him because, if the roles were reversed, manipulation would be the exact tactic he would use. "If he thinks that he's managed to keep his selfish desires under wraps, he's wrong. There are several council members that don't think his reasons for wanting to become King are good enough," Lord Nicholas continued.

"And what of your motives?" I finally snapped.

Lord Nicholas smirked, "Well, I'm just trying to do the best for the people. You taught me that one, Princess." Rage coursed through me. Fury filled my whole being and my hands shook with anger in my lap. I desperately tried to remember Abel's tips for staying calm, as I tried to control the urge to strangle the con artist in front of me.

"Shall we move on to Azar?" Lord Nicholas leered, looking at my shaking hands. I sent him a glare, but nodded anyway. "Ah, the impulsive, loud, idiot." My blood boiled, but Lord Nicholas just kept talking. "The man couldn't be diplomatic, if there were a sword at his throat, which there very well might be with his personality. How could a man who lacks so much tact ever hope to be King?"

"And then there's Prince Ari," Lord Nicholas continued, now on a tirade. "He's clearly the smartest of all of you, but the kid has the emotional intelligence of a lizard. I've watched him try to interact with people for the past six weeks, and he's so bad at it, it physically hurts me. Oh, and his speech at the tournament. He had an adoring and silent crowd in front of him, and he struggled to get his voice heard. A King has to talk to people, it's frankly a huge part of the job." I open my mouth, my anger finally boiling over. "Now, you're not going to argue before I even get to you?" Lord Nicholas jumped in, and my mouth shut automatically.

Part of me thought about just ignoring what Lord Nicholas wanted to say about me, and fighting back against what he slung against my family. However, I couldn't stop the morbid curiosity about what Lord Nicholas would find faulty in me. "To be honest, I can't stand your constant moral preachings, and your inability to accept that I might be right sometimes, but I can't say those things really affect your candidacy. In fact, you might be my only competition. Well, you would be, that is, if I don't manipulate the council. See, the thing is, as long as the council loves me, there's no way they'll pick anyone else. You have many talents, but manipulation will never be one of them. You're just too easy to read. No matter how hard you try, you can never really keep your feelings off your face. They show up, even when you're obviously trying to hide them. And, the best part about it is that I can tell you all this, and you'll never be able to tell anyone! You have no evidence, and I have enough support that others will have a hard time believing you." Lord Nicholas smiled brightly as he looked down on me. "Don't worry," he said, "if you really want to be Queen, you can always marry me."

I seethed with anger as I stood abruptly, glaring at Lord Nicholas, as if my gaze might cause him to burst into flames. I had to get out of his suddenly suffocating room, my hands trembling with just barely-there restraint, and despite it all, Lord Nicholas was still just sitting there, cool as could be, utterly unperturbed by my fury. I marched towards the door, lest I end up beating him up on his own bedroom floor. I paused only briefly, letting my "open" face fill completely with emotion before facing him fully once more. "You disgust me," I snarled before barreling out of the room.

3

PART THREE

Chapter 19

The Rules of Succession

Ever quiet in my anger, I was fuming as I walked down the stairs towards the noise of the Unajo festival down in the garden. How could he say such a thing, I seethed. He, who knew nothing more of ruling than to say a few sly words and present a stupidly charming smile. Who only wanted to rule for personal gain. How could he, so confidently, declare he would be a better King than my brothers. Better than Al, who has spent his whole life preparing to take the throne. He may not have the purest motives, but he cares about the people and he understands, possibly better than any of us, the responsibility he'd be taking on. Azar might be loud and brash, but he, out of all of my brothers, had shown the greatest ability to learn and grow, to be vulnerable and open to change. And, Ari! Ari is just 14. How could anyone expect him to be emotionally mature? He hasn't even finished growing physically! There is a reason why we don't choose a successor until all candidates are 21. And, even if empathy isn't his strong suit, at 21, Ari would still be a genius. He would find a logical and practical solution to the problems facing the country and he has proven he has the capacity to listen and accept other points of view that could ensure his plans would come with compassion. How dare somebody with no backbone, no moral compass, and someone fueled only by personal desire and selfish want say my brothers were unfit for the throne!

A threatening heat grew inside me. Bubbling and leaping, poised to erupt out of me at any moment. Devious voices in my head called out for me to just punch Lord Nicholas in the face next time I saw him. A calmer, but just as mischievous voice pointed out that I could easily shut him up with one good punch to the jaw. My fingertips itched, practically shaking with excitement at the thought of being used. A fierce tension filled my body, and, without even realizing it, I had made it down to the garden's entrance.

The hot breeze and loud chatter just beyond the open doors in front of me caused me to pause. This brief respite from my anger let rationality come through and enabled me to hear voices coming through the open doors. I quickly ducked behind a set of green curtains, and took a moment to compose myself. Lord Nicholas was just one man, one man blinded by greed, and he would never know or see what would make a great ruler because he was too busy trying to find faults in us that would justify his own agenda. I stood there, hidden by the curtains, taking big deep breaths and willing my heartbeat to slow down, waiting for the fire that filled my soul to die. Once my body temperature cooled, and my heart stopped racing, I stepped out from behind the curtain, ready to enjoy the festival.

"Ava, what were you doing behind the curtain?" A new kind of heat filled my finally cooled down body, this time rushing up towards my face. I turned, following Ari's curious voice back further into the palace. I quickly looked around, and let out a sigh of relief as I realized he was the only one who saw me.

"Just clearing my head," I called, walking towards him and lacing my arm through his.

"Oh, should I be doing that? Does it provide much benefit?" said Ari, making a move towards the curtain.

"No, no, you don't need to," I replied, practically dragging him out the garden doors as my blush grew. While the extra time in the curtain might have been helpful, I wasn't willing to explain my thought process to Ari.

Ari and I smiled and greeted nobles in the garden, stopping to make polite conversation every now and then. Ari seemed content to let me lead him around the gardens until I finally spotted my target. I hastily ended our current conversation with Countess Mierella, and practically dragged Ari to where Sir Abel was standing by a lone willow tree towards the edge of the garden. His silver locks had been pulled back into a half bun that held his hair away from his face. He wore a slim-fitting bright purple suit, which looked ever more vibrant against the green of the trees behind him.

"Abel!" I cried out as we approached him. I was practically running to him at this point.

"Princess, Prince," Abel smiled with a bow towards both of us.

"Don't start that now," I huffed, decorum promptly forgotten. "I couldn't do it. I was talking to Lord Nicholas, and all those tricks that you taught me, I couldn't remember them. I couldn't use them; so what do I do now?"

Oddly, Abel just smiled. Although, I suppose I should have been used to his eccentric calmness by now. "Avalynn," he said quietly, putting his hand on my shoulder and pulling me gently towards him, a spark of amusement was in his eyes. "You cannot change a person's mind just because you believe it should change, and you cannot force a person to grow. We are all responsible for our own growth, and we cannot make someone learn when they do not choose to. The only person in this universe we have the power to change is ourselves. So, with that being said," Abel pulled back slightly as his voice rose just a touch, "Why does all of this cause you so much pain?"

"Erm, should I leave?" Ari cut in.

"No, of course not," I huffed, trying to digest Abel's words.

"I can leave, you know. It's probably good for me to practice talking to more nobles on my own, and, well, this seems a little personal, Ava," Ari said, running his hand over the back of his neck.

"It's fine Ari. it's not personal," I insisted, perhaps a little too harshly if Ari's face was anything to go by. A pang of guilt wracked my body, and I turned to apologize to Ari, but before I could, Abel's cool and bright laugh interrupted me.

"Why don't you leave your sister with me, young Prince, and I'll see what I can do about the wildfire that occupies her mind," Abel chuckled, giving Ari a wink. I sent Abel a frown. Ari, however, brightened at Abel's words, and gave Abel a relieved smile before practically running back towards the crowd.

"He's a smart boy, your younger brother, but I suppose that could be said of any of you. Will you walk with me, my dear?" Abel lifted his arm out to me, and I tucked my hand into the crook of his elbow, following him into the quiet of the garden. "You remind me a lot of your grandmother, you know."

"Nana?" I replied a little befuddled. I was finding it hard to reconcile the serene and powerful Nana I knew with the angry and weak mess I felt in myself right now.

"Oh yes," Abel laughed, "Betty was very much like you. She worked hard to keep it under wraps, but when her temper exploded, even Kings would run away. It took her a very long time to address and heal her anger, but eventually she learned how to accept it, learn from it, and, when called for, use it in a productive manner. However, you, my dear, never cease to impress me, for even though you are still young, you are already working through your own anger and trauma much faster. Not to say healing is any sort of race, but it does take quite a lot of bravery to address your darkest fears and most intense pain so quickly. It's most definitely not the path for everyone, but it would seem you have things to accomplish in your life, Avalynn, that you cannot do without first healing yourself. It's with this in mind, dear one, that I'm going to ask you once again to go into the pain you feel and tell it to me, so I can help guide you to healing, if you choose to accept my help."

I sighed, leaning my head against Abel's arm I said, "Lord Nicholas is hurting people. His selfish attitude towards the throne will harm the people, and yet, he doesn't even seem to care," I cried, the heat of anger pulling me into its grip once more. "He won't give up! He's using underhanded tactics and relying on charm to make the rest of us look bad, and he still insists he's doing the right thing! And, now he's the new favorite for the throne. There's just no justice in it!"

"What a wonderfully complex line of thought you have, Avalynn," Abel said, "While I talk, my dear, why don't you just focus on breathing deeply. You'd be surprised how much can be solved by just continuing to breathe.

Let's begin with this: you are trying to control the future, and you're getting stuck there. You're in a competition where no one has explained the rules, and the only known requirement is your voluntary participation. This is the third crown selection process I have lived through, although I wasn't involved in the first, and I know this process has always been hard on its participants. However, the uncertain nature of the crown selection is a vital part of preparing the next ruler for the throne. Uncertainty comes in every life, but a ruler needs to have confidence, wisdom, and a calm demeanor when uncertainty arises in order to calm and lead the people.

For many people, the first response to uncertainty is to jump into the future. To try to plan every detail and try to see the unseeable. The truth of the matter is: every second that has not occurred yet is a black void, and when that second finally arrives the whole universe is instantly put together. The land stays together, the trees continue living, and the choices of every being on the planet come together to create one global painting of life for that second, and then the next second comes and it happens all over again. The future is never decided and set, and it is subject to great change at any given time.

So, what can we do with the future so variable and uncertain? The answer is simple, really; we breathe. We continue to breathe, and we sit in the knowledge that while the future will always be unknown, we have all the skills and tools we need to face whatever happens in the present. Then it's just a matter of choice. Choose the path that will lead you to the greatest amount of happiness, remembering you can always change your path, and choose to treat everyone with as much compassion and empathy as you can.

Lord Nicholas has not yet won the crown and even if he does, we do not yet know if he will harm the people. However, even if he does cause harm, then I already know, Avalynn, that you have all the capacity to lead a revolution. After all, ruling is nothing more or less than signing a contract with the people that you will act in their best interests to try to help them live peaceful, abundant lives. If you fail to do that one too many times, then the contract is void, and revolt is imminent. And, if you choose to, I think you could lead a wonderful revolution, my dear." Abel finished with a smile.

As Abel talked, I felt a warm bubble of comfort and security settle into my chest and spread through my limbs and soul. Abel was right after all, I could not control Lord Nicholas, or force him to change; but I would always be able to handle whatever challenges life presented me. I was a dedicated learner, a strong fighter both physically and mentally, and I handled everything I'd encountered before, so it was only natural that I would be able to handle everything that could possibly come next. Abel walked back with me through the green maze of the palace gardens. We laughed and talked of lighter nothings as we worked our way back towards the party. Soon we were back by the willow tree where I had first spotted Abel this evening. "So, my dear, what have you decided to do?"

"I will keep fighting," I replied with a hopeful certainty. "I will do everything in my power to try to be the best Queen I can be, and, if I can't be Queen, I will still do everything in my power to support and care for the people of this Kingdom," I gave Abel a smile, "and, that will make me very happy."

"There's my Queen," Abel smiled as he gave me a dramatic bow. "Now, go enjoy the party. Don't waste your exuberance on this old man," Abel finished with a wink.

"You're never a waste, Abel," I said, kissing him on the cheek before I followed his advice, and entering the crowd. My nerves soothed, and the weight on my shoulders suitably lifted, I made my way through the crowd, stopping to chat with Marchioness Eliza, Count Davin, and more of my favorite nobles. I was walking over to speak with Dame Nerys, when a silky voice called my name.

"Oh, Princess Avalynn, I was just talking to Lady Rosewell about my experience at the hospital. I was telling her of my idea to try to expand the building so we could add more treatment rooms. Having worked there all summer, I'm sure you'd have an inside view on the subject," Lord Nicholas' voice rang out. I turned to find him staring at me, with a frankly, infuriating smirk on his face. I chose to instead focus on Lady Rosewell. As the council member in charge of the national healthcare system, she was smiling at us both with apparent interest.

"Well, it's certainly an interesting suggestion. It's true that many people require treatment, and the hospital itself is increasingly busy. Not to mention with the growth in Nera's population, this is sure to get worse. However, I don't think adding more rooms to the hospital is the right solution." I responded, determinedly focusing on Lady Rosewell, "Nera is such a large city, and for many citizens the problem with the hospital is its distance from their homes. Many emergency patients aren't getting the timely care they need due to travel issues. Beyond that, expanding the current Hospital means either buying out the surrounding buildings which would be more expensive due to their location in the center of the city,"

"If it's for the benefit of the people, the King could just order the current owners to move," Lord Nicholas chimed in. I looked at him incredulously, and, apparently, Lady Rosewell shared my horror, as Lord Nicholas looked between us and hurriedly took back his sentiment. "Ah, I... erm... I just meant that," he cleared his throat, "I was just trying to think of the people's health. Obviously, I wouldn't want those people to have to give up their businesses."

"Nevertheless," I said coolly, "forcing people out of their livelihoods is not the best way to help the hospital. It would be better for us to open more, smaller hospitals with more locations around the city. This will increase the number of people we can treat, and give the citizens of Nera treatment options closer to them. There are already some doctors who have treatment centers outside of the hospital. If we incentivize them to work at some of these smaller hospitals, we can have more qualified staff working at all medical centers. This will also allow healers more time with patients, since we won't have only one hospital. More time with patients would also likely lead to fewer misdiagnoses. Plus, it will possibly open more time for researching new and different cures for various illnesses," I finished, a feeling of excitement rising in me as I thought of the possibilities.

"That is certainly a very promising idea, Princess," Lady Rosewell smiled at me. "I will put some more research and thought into the matter, but this could very well be the new way forward with Nevremerre's healthcare." I smiled brightly at her, barely managing to suppress sending a gloating smirk in Lord Nicholas's direction. Lord Nicholas had just opened his mouth to retort when the loud voice of a page broke through, "Dinner is now served on the cliff Dormian." I excused myself from Lord Nicholas and Lady Rosewell and made my way towards Ari, who was captivated by something Lady Milfred had said about the national budget. Both looked utterly engrossed in their conversation as they quoted percentages back at each other. I was almost loath to interrupt them, but decorum indicates that Ari and I, along with the rest of our family, lead the other nobles and knights through the windy garden path toward Dormian cliff. Once there, we would eat facing the opposing Serian cliff where the Agremerrian knights and nobles would dine "with" us.

Chapter 20

The Treaty with Agremerre

Ari and I chatted happily as we followed Al and Azar in front of us, with the din of chattering nobles behind us. Ari cautiously commented that he was glad I was feeling better, his turquoise eyes anxiously roaming my face in search of any residual anger. "Just keep Lord Nicholas away from me and that's sure to continue," I smiled back. I said it in jest, but Ari nodded seriously as a determined look passed over his face. I pushed the topic over to Ari's studies, and then to what to do for Al's 23rd birthday, which was just a month away. The conversation carried us through the gardens, into the forested path until we finally made it out to the large clearing on the cliff side. There we saw a long table covered in a white cloth with numerous platters of food set out. Big torches and candles lined the inside edge of the cliff face, waiting to be lit when the sun went down. Cushions were placed on the side of the table that was closest to us, facing out towards the edge of the cliff. In the distance, you could see the edges of the Serian cliff.

Flapping through the trees you could just make out a group of large yellow tents on the Agremerre and Nevremerre border. Later tonight and several times over the coming week, we would gather in these tents and meet with Queen Anora and Agremerre's High Judges to solidify our alliance with Agremerre. I was looking forward to it. Queen Anora was like another aunt to me and my siblings and the time we spent with her was always lively and fun. It was Queen Anora who taught Azar and me how to do various acrobatic tricks on a moving horse, while Al and Ari watched in horror. Queen Anora was also famous for challenging Father to an arm-wrestling match whenever she saw him. As Father got older, Queen Anora, who is nearly 15 years younger, started seeing more and more victories, which only served to make their meetings more and more rowdy. Usually, she would send us all letters throughout the year, although, I realize now, we hadn't received any this past summer. However, I remembered, the last letter we received had said she was pregnant, so perhaps the child or preparing for the child's birth was keeping her busy. Not to mention she did have a kingdom to run.

Around me nobles and knights moved to pick their places along the one-sided table. There would be no seating arrangements tonight, so I happily let Azar pull me and Ari along to where Carlos, Mateo, Elise, and some other knights were already sitting. Al, true to form, decided he would rather spend the time networking, and sat himself between General Clara and Marquis Dorian. I happily skipped over to Elise and her friend Dame Hortencia sitting toward the end of the table. I sat down with Ari following me on my left and Elise sitting on my right. I noticed Ari flash a satisfied smile when Lord Nicholas sat much further down the table. Father stood and called for silence. He moved over towards the end of the table on the far left side, a position that would be mirrored by Queen Anora on the Serian cliff.

"Today begins the Unajo festival," Father began, his voice carrying along the table. "It's a day where we celebrate our long-standing partnership with Agremerre, and tell the story of how our two countries began. Millenia ago two warrior siblings came to this land. They saw desolate people worked to the bone due to an unfeeling dictator. Angry at the dictator for leaving his people so impoverished, the siblings decided that they would fight back against the dictator. Together they fought and recruited the strongest warriors from across the land, and created their own elite army, the Unajo. Together, with the Unajo, the two siblings overthrew the dictator and his corrupt army. Together they took on the throne, but even though their fight had been won, they still faced a mountainous challenge: how should they rule this land? The corruption of the dictator was embedded in every corner of the government they could see.

The siblings debated for seven days and seven nights over how they could fix the problems and truly help the people. They each came upon a different solution. The brother, Dormian, believed that the root of the corruption lies with those in power using their positions for personal gain as opposed to a way to help those in their care. The sister, Serian, believed that the root of the problem lies in the lack of accountability and justice for those who committed crimes against the people, no matter how powerful. With these two different ideologies, the siblings decided to split the land in half, Dormian creating the merit-based monarchy of Nevremerre and Serian creating the judicial monarchy of Agremerre. However, they both promised that the kingdoms of Agremerre and Nevremerre would always have peace, open borders, and free trade with each other.

In the millennia since Dormian and Serian lived, each country has faced many trials and fought extreme corruption. However, each of our countries has come out strong. Each year, we celebrate the Unajo's takeover of the dictatorship, and the leadership decisions of Dormian and Serian by meeting with each other to support the betterment of both of our countries. Now we feast for the health of Nevremerre and Agremerre! May the honor of Nevremerre and Agremerre be everlasting!"

"May Nevremerre and Agremerre prosper evermore," we all chanted back, "Good health to King, Queen, and countries."

"Now please enjoy the feast." A cheer rose up as the food platters began to be passed up and down the table. Loud peals of laughter and a buzz of conversation floated around us. Ari was soon pulled into a conversation with Mateo on his left, and I turned to Elise and Hortencia. They gleefully made me the moderator and their debate on the best date spots in town. Which quickly devolved into a lively debate on what the best dessert is.

"But, you're related to Princess Olivia!" Hortencia cried, "How can you not think her cupcakes are the best? Her cherry chocolate cupcakes are one of the best parts of living!"

"I'm not saying they're not good," I said, swallowing a bite of chicken, "I'm just saying that she's yet to make something that can compete with the sheer artistry that is The Local Bake's apple pie with cream."

"You're both mad," Elise said as she piled more potatoes onto her plate, "clearly the best dessert in town is Frozen Tundra's maximum stuffed-". A loud clang cut off Elise's words, and a hush fell over the long table. I whipped my head down towards the head of the table. There stood a heavily pregnant Queen Anora, in partial armor followed by three fully armed knights. Queen Anora appeared to be holding out a bound scroll towards Father who was on his feet. The clanging appeared to have been Father's plate being knocked down in his rush to stand up. Even before I heard Father speak, I knew something was wrong. His body was tense, and his face red. His expression was too far away to read, but his energy felt tight and almost menacing.

"Dammit, Anora," he growled, "What is this?"

"As previously stated, it's a declaration of war." A chill went up my spine. The hush that had taken over the table turned to an icy silence as nobody dared to even breathe. Queen Anora's voice was calm and steady as she continued to speak, "We are in a drought, Edgar. We've asked you for aid, but you refused. We don't have enough supplies to feed our people, and we won't be able to produce enough this coming harvest. I don't want to fight you, but I cannot watch my people starve."

"Dammit, Anora," Father yelled, "We can't help you, even if you do fight us! Why do you think we refused your aid? We can't afford to help you! While we don't do agricultural inventory as quickly as you, we have been receiving reports for months that there hasn't been enough rain to support the food supply we need." Father ran a hand over his face before exasperatingly finishing, "Nevremerre is in a drought too." This broke the silence that had taken over the table as rushed whispers echoed all around me. I sat paralyzed, watching Father and Queen Anora stare at each other.

"It seems like this is something we need to discuss further," said Lord Jesu, Carlos' father and the council member in charge of foreign relations.

"Yes, I agree," said Father, while Queen Anora nodded.

"Lord Jesu, General Clara, and Duchess Amber - with me. Let us discuss solutions in the border tent," Father suggested, calling the council members of war and agriculture as well.

"Agreed," Queen Anora agreed, "Eustice, go get Kazi and Miraz and bring them to the tent. We have much to discuss." One of Queen Anora's knights ran off into the forest, while the rest of the group made their way towards the distant yellow tent. As soon as Duchess Amber, who was the last of their pack, was no longer visible, the table cried out in uproar.

"What do you mean there's a drought?" a voice rang out.

"What am I going to do about my territory?" called out another.

"Will we have to go to war?" The cries of the nobles and knights filled the early evening air, as people rose out of their seats to crowd my mothers. What was worse was the group of knights and nobles that surrounded me and my brothers as well.

"Will we starve?" a voice asked near me.

"What are we going to do?" cried out another. I sat staring back at them, completely unable to respond.

I didn't even know.

The words flashed through my mind, breaking through my mental fog, making themselves the only thing I could think about clearly.

I didn't even know.

The signs were all there, I realized. The endless bright, sunny days, the hospital needing to find more suppliers for some medical herbs, the decrease in banquet food. And, I didn't notice a single sign. Not one. I had spent all this time studying and training to be Queen, and I couldn't even notice when the people were in trouble. I was too caught up in my competition with my brothers and Lord Nicholas. I felt bile rise in the back of my throat as revulsion filled me. I didn't even know. There was a drought; people needed help and I didn't even know. Now, in front of me was a group of terrified and frightened people who needed to know that they were safe, that the royal family would protect them. I had nothing to give them, I realized. With no knowledge on the drought, I had nothing I could say, but here they were crying out with desperate eyes for something. I knew right there and then that I, at least, had to try.

"Everyone, please take a breath," I called out. My voice sounded shaky even in my own ears. I tried to will it to be still, as I continued, "It is difficult to give information if no one can hear it." I knew my voice failed to sound in any way commanding, but those around me did quiet down. Which allowed us to hear Mother's voice break through the cacophony of cries surrounding her and Mama.

"If everyone could please sit down, I will tell you what the crown and council have been doing to prepare and to answer all your questions to the best of my ability," Mother said. There was a minute of grumbling as everyone took their seats once more. I found myself taking a deep breath as nobles and knights removed themselves from my immediate area.

"In the spring, the crown received word that there was likely not enough rain to support the crops come fall harvest. It was at this point that the crown and council began to stockpile all non-perishable foods to be distributed equally among the people of Nevremerre. We also gave instructions to each of the four regional dukes and duchesses to do the same. As such, each of your regions will already have some stockpiled food.

At the beginning of summer, we learned the drought may be worse than we initially anticipated. We then began rolling out programs to fix any plumbing problems and infrastructure issues in all major cities. Prince Alveron and Prince Azar were even brought in to help with the construction and repair. This will help stop leaks from wasting valuable drinking water, and give citizens fewer worries during the drought. Princess Avalynn was sent to the hospital to help treat citizens, in order to keep citizens as healthy as possible before the consequences of the drought are upon us. Finally, we started investing more in our fishing industry, which Prince Ari assisted with. We have increased the number of fish caught this year, which will help offset the lack of food.

We deliberately chose to keep this from the public until after harvest time where we could see exactly how much food we had. We would then make an official statement with an official distribution plan. This was done to offset any panic from the general public that might lead to increasing the effects of the drought. If people panic and hoard food or water, there will be further shortages for others that could lead to death. Finally, as you've just seen, your King will be working with Queen Anora to find other solutions that will benefit all of Nevremerre. Droughts are scary and unavoidable natural phenomenon. However, we can get through this, and, with your cooperation, we can do so with minimal damage. Now, are there any further questions?"

A silence fell over the table. Mother's explanation was thorough and in-depth. Her calming voice washed over the anxious nobles like a soothing tonic. It did not, however, ease me. Perhaps it was because my worries were not solely about the drought. A sharp slice of guilt struck me as I realized that in the midst of a natural disaster affecting my people, I still managed to worry about myself. A self-deprecating voice inside me wondered if I was even qualified to be Queen, if I had missed such an important problem. I honestly didn't know anymore. I'd wanted to be Queen for so long. I wanted to help the people, but in the face of a real crisis, I didn't know what to do or that it was happening! Not to mention, the assignment that I was sure was just a way to test our abilities to rule was in fact an attempt to help the people. I felt shame and guilt grow in my chest. All this time I'd been insisting to Lord Nicholas that I could be Queen. How wrong I felt now.

"If there are no further questions, then please continue to eat and enjoy while we wait for His Majesty to report," Mother said before sitting back down. Around her, torches were being lit to fend off the darkening sky. The crowd began to rustle once more, the previous merriment was lost, however, as the table took on a disquietous murmur.

"Did you know?" Ari turned to me urgently, grabbing my arm as he whispered in my ear.

"No," I replied, honestly. "I had no idea."

"Me neither," Ari replied, loosening his grip on my arm, "I had no idea." My heart jumped into my chest at his reply, and I couldn't resist pulling him into a half hug across my chest.

"Ari, you are only fourteen. It's okay. It's not your job to know," I whispered to him.

"Yeah," his soft voice whispered back, "but I am a Prince. I should have known anyway." I couldn't find a response to his words, so I simply held him close for a moment longer. When he pushed himself out of my grasp a few minutes later, we slowly turned back to the conversations around us. It was Elise's conversation that drew me in first.

"Do you think we will go to war again?" she wondered.

"Probably not with Agremerre," Hortencia responded, "but perhaps with Calvine again. I mean, Agremerre thought war was a possible option, perhaps we will do the same."

"War will no doubt be our last option," I jumped in. This was, at least, one question I knew I could answer. "No matter how strong our armies, war has a high cost. We will never condone the loss of life if we have another option. We have the best minds of Nevremerre and Agremerre working on this problem. No doubt we will try other options first." Elise and

Hortencia nodded at my words, despite my uncertainty at my ability to rule, I felt a brief sense of pride that they had so much faith in my words. An hour later, the crowd started to get antsy. Sentences were punctuated by glances into the forest, and any rustling of trees was met by a table wide hush. Still, no one came. Had today been normal, it would have been about time to meet with Agremerre's high judges and nobles in the border tents. Yet, today, there was an unsettling knowledge that we would all be sitting here for a while.

A movement from the trees brought another bout of silence, but this time Lord Jesu moved out of the trees. He blinked momentarily at the sight of us all watching him. "Er, discussions are proceeding. We will likely bring news to you all shortly. In the meantime, however, I require Princess Avalynn." I straightened up in my shock as all eyes turned toward me. Ari gave me an inquiring look that Azar and Al matched from their seats further down the table. I had no answer for their stares as I tried to stand up as gracefully as possible. The table felt impossibly long as I walked towards Lord Jesu. I felt the eyes of everyone on me with each step, and I felt an odd desire to simply run away. After what felt like ages, I met Lord Jesu. He gently grabbed my arm and moved me towards the forest.

"Don't react, and keep walking," he whispered in my ear. "Queen Anora has gone into labor, When we get past the tree line you are going to need to run. We need you to deliver the baby."

Chapter 21

The Unexpected Delivery

Running through the darkened forest was, perhaps, a poor choice, even if we were in a hurry. The path towards the border tent was mostly flat and wide, but it was still a forest path. As such, both Lord Jesu and I found ourselves with various sticks jabbing at our legs and feet. Lord Jesu almost fell as he tripped over a fallen tree branch. Despite all this, we still blindly ran towards the border tent, the usual 20-minute walk cut in half. The murmur of people inside the tent wafted through the air as we pushed closer. Slightly out of breath, Lord Jesu and I pushed inside.

The tent was bright with large lanterns feeding every corner and several hung carefully above. Inside, Father and Duchess Amber were across from Queen Anora, who was pacing up and down the length of the tent with two of Agremerre's High Judges hovering on either side. General Clara was standing awkwardly with Queen Anora's knight, Eustice, if I remembered correctly, as they watched Queen Anora waddle determinedly around the tent.

"I can't possibly send you to Dolma alone!" Queen Anora said that she moved, "You don't know that place, Edgar, it's not - Aurgh -" she suddenly screamed out, her aides moving towards her before she quickly shooed them both back. Trying to get her breath back under control she spoke to Father once more, "It's not like any country you've ever been to. No, I must go! Eustice, go get the horses!"

"Like hell you will!" I cried out, any sort of decorum forgotten. "You're in labor. It's not safe for you or the baby to go anywhere, but to a hospital right now."

"Labor can take days!" Queen Anora huffed, but her dark skin was already beaded with sweat, and her hands were clenched and exertion.

"No. That's not going to happen," I said. "You can and should send people from Agremerre with Father to Dolma, then he won't be alone. You can give him any information he needs now while I examine you," I finished sternly. Spending time around Matron Terella must have helped because the entire room simply nodded their head in agreement.

"I can go with His Majesty, King Edgar," a judge next to Queen Anora spoke a little hesitantly, "No doubt they would be more willing to listen to both my words and his."

Queen Anora grunted. "No doubt," she said unhappily.

"I can also inform him of what to expect on the way over," the judge pressed on.

"Fine!" Queen Anora finally spat out, "Eustice, go to Agre-merre, tell them to send their fastest runner to Dolma to in-form them King Edgar of Nevremerre and High Judge Miraz of Agremerre will be coming to Dolma in three days' time. It will be a tight Journey," Queen Anora said, "but you will be able to make it to Dolma in that time." Miraz nodded, as Eustice moved to walk out.

"Wait," I jumped in. "You should also bring a healer," I told Eustice.

"No!" came the rezoning response of multiple voices.

"Avalynn, the contents of this discussion cannot be leaked to the public. Not until we have an official address to make. We cannot have the public go into a panic. The sudden call for a healer could cause just that. Eustice, go ahead," Father said gravely, waving off Eustice who ran off into the night. "From now on, Avalynn, you are the healer."

"I am the healer," I repeated vacantly before reality sunk in and I exclaimed, "I am the healer?!"

"Yes," Father nodded, "The report from Matron Terella said you have delivered babies, right?"

Not alone! I wanted to scream. Even if there wasn't always a qualified healer in the room, there was always one nearby I could go to for help. I am in no way prepared to deliver a baby in a tent for the Queen of another country! But, I couldn't say any of that here. There would be no other call for a healer. I was the only person who would be called, and even if I was under prepared and Queen Anora a strong woman, I could not give her a reason to worry. "That's right. I have been trained. I can do this," I said with fake confidence, as Lord Nicholas' comment about my face being read like an open book flitted across my brain.

"Augh!" Another scream from Queen Anora filled the tent.

"That was quick," I commented moving towards her. "How frequent are your contractions? And how long have you been experiencing them?"

"I don't know how frequent they are. I haven't had the time to count, but they started about three or four hours ago."

"You were having contractions when you declared war on us?" I deadpanned, looking at Queen Anora incredulously.

"Yes, well at that time they were much further apart! I didn't think declaring war would take this long!" she huffed.

"When this finishes, we are having a serious discussion about how to take care of your own personal needs," the other High Judge, probably Kazi, said sternly.

"You most certainly will be taking maternity leave!" Miraz nodded.

"There's no time for this now," Queen Anora snapped, "Edgar, we need to talk about Dolma."

"All right, but first I need to examine you, Queen Anora," I said.

"Just say Anora, child. We don't have time for social bullshit," Anora said.

"Okay, I need everyone except Anora on that side of the tent," I said pointing towards the side with the entrance. "I also need gloves, pillows, water, and some blankets if at all possible."

"Clara, Jesu, go see what you can find in the other tents. You can ask the servants back at the banquet for water if need be," Father directed. As he spoke Kazi and I helped Anora take off her armor leaving her in just her undershirt and flowing trousers. I then began probing her stomach in search of the baby's head. I mentally prayed to the universe that I would not have to manually flip the baby.

"You will need to bring at least six knights to Dolma, and two must stay with you at all times! The knights you select must be the gender they were assigned at birth and they must be heterosexual or possibly asexual," Anora began, and I breathed a sigh of relief upon discovering the baby had flipped.

"We've also heard reports of female knights being harassed. This has slowed in the years Queen Anora has ruled, but we suspect this might be a reaction to her being female, whereas her predecessor, King Orian, was male. It's probably best that you take only male knights," Miraz jumped in, "That's also why it's best I go instead of-" another scream from Anora drowned out Miraz's words.

"You – you need to be sure that all the knights you choose can hold their tongues. Dolma has all these ridiculous rules, and you can't have anyone disrespecting them while you are there - it won't go well," Anora said breathlessly. Behind her, Clara rushed back in with some blankets and pillows. I missed the next part of their talk as I laid out the blanket on the tent floor, and arranged the pillows so Anora would be facing the back of the tent. I quickly guided Anora to put her head on the pillows as I prepared to examine her. "It'll be so very different from what you know, Edgar, but the Agremerre knights will help out as much as possible, and so will Miraz," Anora said.

I felt my heart drop as I examined Anora. I took a deep breath to compose myself before saying, "Anora, you are fully dilated, your water hasn't broken yet, but you undoubtedly will give birth soon." Father and Miraz exchanged horrified looks.

"Okay, so, Edgar, you'll take Miraz, Knights Raymond, Alistair, and Oberon from Agremerre and Nevremerre knights..." Anora said quickly.

"Ricardo, Mateo, and Galileo," Father supplied, looking worried.

"Great! Then it's settled. Miraz will tell you more on the way, so if you'll excuse me, Mother fucker this hurts!" Anora screamed, another contraction coming upon her. It seemed that now the negotiations had been settled Anora no longer felt the need to control her pain. She let out a series of curse words as Miraz and General Clara went off to update the nobles and judges and get the requested knights. They would set off from the border tent as soon as possible, picking up any needed supplies in Agremerre along the way. During their mad rush out of the tent Lord Jesu returned.

"I found water, and stole a pair of gloves from the waiters table, so no one will even know we needed them," he declared triumphantly, just as Anora's water broke.

Earlier, I said that the birth of Clarrissa and Tahoe's son was the most chaotic event I've ever witnessed. That, I believe, still holds true, but Anora's delivery was a damned close second. Childbirth is said to be the worst kind of pain imaginable. Having spent the better half of this summer delivering babies and hearing the screams of their mothers, I believe this to be true. As such, I was prepared for the loud screams and curses of Anora. The poor knights who had just been drafted for a mysterious mission that set off from the border tent were not. Having clearly not been briefed on the current state of Agremerre's Queen, the tent was soon invaded by knights from both kingdoms with swords drawn ready to face whatever foe could cause the ear-shattering shrieks of Queen Anora. Unfortunately, said foe, was barely even crowning, and, thus, largely hard to fight. Later, I would recognize that I've been rather lucky not to have an Agremerrian sword pointed at my own throat as the only visible enemy near their Queen.

The confused knights just stood there as the half naked Queen screamed an almost impressive litany of insults, mostly, I think, aimed at the universe in general, but occasionally aimed at the gawking knights. Trying my hardest to focus on the delivery process it took me several moments to realize that the knights weren't leaving. It was at this point I think my day long stress broke. "That's it!" I roared over Anora's screams, "If you are not Anora, Kazi, or me then get the hell out of my tent!" I yelled at six fully armed knights, three members of the Nevremerre Royal Council, two High Judges of Agremerre, and one actual King. Conveniently forgetting that I had basically no power, and that it was not, in fact, my tent. Oddly, no one even questioned my command before every single one of them walked out of the tent.

From there, the birth went relatively smoothly, taking about another hour before the baby was delivered and the placenta pushed out. Despite the chaos that had preceded her birth, when she was safely placed in her exhausted mother's arms, the new baby was healthy and wonderfully quiet. The three of us who had remained in the tent embraced the encompassing silence of the night. My adrenaline high came crashing down and my limbs felt like lead weights falling against my body. Anora gazed lovingly at the little girl laying on her chest, "What shall we call her?" she whispered reverentially.

"Tiny?" Kazi joked, her hand still red from Anora's tight grip, "She sure is awfully small."

"How about Troublemaker?" Anora bantered back. "She certainly caused enough already," Anora finished, beaming.

"All good Princesses should cause at least a little trouble," I smiled, "but, a name like that might make diplomacy difficult."

"I'm not so sure. She'd already be an intimidating opponent," Anora laughed softly, "but if not Troublemaker or tiny, then what about Genevieve?"

"Princess Genevieve. It sounds just perfect," Kazi smiled.

"She is perfect," I agreed, "Hello, little Genevieve," I whispered to the sleeping baby. The three of us stared down at the, still somewhat bloody, baby between us.

"Do you think I could be carried back to Agremerre? I'm not sure I can walk back to the castle," Anora said, her exhausted voice betraying the sincerity behind her joking tone.

"As your healer, I would recommend that you don't walk for the next twenty-four hours or so. You need your rest, Anora, and I am not going to let you ignore your health like you did today," I said seriously. Having delivered Genevieve and been with Anora throughout the birth, I was not letting anything happen to them.

"I agree," Kazi said, "You've done all you can for Agremerre as of this moment. Now please take care of yourself, my Queen."

"I find I don't have the energy to fight you both on this matter tonight, but I make no promises about tomorrow." Anora looked at me, "Do we know if Edgar has left for Dolma yet? Is anyone left outside?" With the start I realized I practically forgotten about the men and women I'd unceremoniously kicked out of the tent. I quickly dragged myself up off the floor, and walked out of the tent to find Eustice, Lord Jesu, General Clara, and Duchess Amber sitting by the base of the nearby trees. General Clara was even laid out on the mulch, clearly fast asleep. As I moved up towards them Lord Jesu jumped-up, nudging General Clara with his foot. That movement also caused Eustice and Duchess Amber to rise. "How is Queen Anora? And the baby?" Lord Jesu asked.

"Both healthy," I eased. "Did my father get off all right?"

"Yes, he left shortly after you kicked us out of the tent," Lord Jesu responded a bit sheepishly as I blushed.

"Can we see the Queen?" asked Eustice.

"I'll ask her," I replied, turning back into the tent. Kazi and I wrapped Anora and Genevieve in an extra blanket, cleaning

Genevieve and covering Anora before inviting in Eustice and the council. They tiptoed their way across the tent towards Queen Anora. Despite their hesitancy, Anora simply smiled up at them and said, "Let me present to you Princess Genevieve of Agremerre."

"Life and health to the Princess," Eustice bowed and the Nevremerre council followed his lead.

"Thank you. Eustice, please make note that the Princess' godparents will be High Judge Kazi and Princess Avalynn of Nevremerre." My eyes flew open at Anora's statement, but Eustice just smiled and said, "Of course, Your Majesty." I stared in awe at Genevieve once more. The small being who'd made such a fuss coming into this world, yet whose life was already to be intimately intertwined with mine. Instantly, I felt my being filled with love for this tiny creature. She had so quickly found her way into my heart, and it was as if she was one of my family members. As I smiled back at Anora, I realized she was already a part of my family.

"What was done about the nobles and the judges?" Anora asked, and I picked my head up to hear the response.

"Both groups were informed that a mixed delegation of Agremerre and Nevremerre people went on a diplomatic mission to acquire more food. The delegation included King Edgar and Judge Miraz, while Queen Anora and the Nevremerre Queens would take care of food preservation until the party's return. We've already done this work, as you know, so there is nothing for you to do but rest," Eustice said sternly, echoing Kazi and my words from before. Anora rolled her eyes, but motioned for Eustice to keep talking. "We've informed them that we have high hopes for a positive outcome, but we will know more when King Edgar returns."

Anora nodded. "That should be good enough for now. It will not stop talk, but, really nothing but finding out a new source of food would. Now, my healer has ordered that I not walk, so can I kindly ask for help from everyone to get me back to Agremerre?"

We made a motley crew walking back towards Agremerre. Duchess Amber ran up ahead to tell the castle to get ready. Kazi came next, carrying a pilfered lantern from the tent. Next came Eustace who was carrying Anora bridal style. Then I followed, holding Genevieve close to my chest. The Nevremerre council trailed behind, carrying pieces of Anora's discarded armor. It took another 45 minutes to get to the Agremerrian castle. We all met with the rest of Agremerre's High Judges, their nobles having already gone to bed. It was decided Princess Genevieve would be announced to the rest of Agremerre tomorrow. With that all settled, the members of the Nevremerre council and I trudged back towards our own palace.

Our journey back was largely silent as we all focused on just trying to keep upright for the long march home. The silence was only briefly broken by Lord Jesu saying he would need us all to meet tomorrow at noon to debrief and to prepare a full report for the rest of the council. An hour and five minutes later we finally made it to where tonight's (or possibly last night's as I wasn't sure exactly if it was past midnight) dinner had been held. There, at the end of the table sat my brothers, Carlos, and Elise all sound asleep around a lone lantern. It was Azar who noticed our presence first, and he sat up, bleary-eyed for a moment before jumping up and shouting, "Ava, you're here!" This woke up the rest of the table who shot up at Azar's outburst.

"Ava, you're still here!" Al cried out.

"And you're covered in blood," Carlos noted, causing everyone else to swarm towards me. I looked down at my yellow dress to find the red and brown blood stains across my chest and skirt from delivering and holding baby Genevieve. My once yellow shoes were lined with dirt, and there were tears down the side. I noted with a vague disappointment that I would likely never be able to wear this outfit again.

"Are you hurt anywhere?" Al asked, grabbing my arm and looking me up and down. Azar did the same on my other side.

"She looks pale," Ari called, hovering nervously behind Al and Azar, "Should we get a healer?" I languidly tried to push myself out of their grasps.

"I'm fine. I'm fine," I said my throat felt scratchy as I spoke. "The blood is not mine," I slurred.

"You had to fight someone?" Elise exclaimed, "but you weren't even armed!"

"Who was it?" Al demanded, "and, why did you have to fight? You're not even a knight!"

"I didn't have to fight someone," I said indignantly. "I had to deliver a baby! What are you all doing here if you were all too tired to think straight?"

"Oh," replied Al, blinking at me, "that makes more sense."

"Was it Queen Anora's baby?" Carlos asked.

"That's it. Bedtime, all of you," Lord Jesu said in his best parenting tone, "That includes you, Your Highnesses. We can continue this conversation when all parties involved can think clearly. Come here Carlos, let your old man lean on you while we walk back, my feet are killing me." Carlos moved to his father's side as the council and Elise trudged ahead.

"Hop on, Ava," Al said, turning his back towards me. I pulled myself up onto his back and he carried me towards the palace, Ari and Azar close behind with the lantern.

"So was it Queen Anora's baby?" Ari whispered between us.

"Yeah," I replied, my head resting on Al's shoulder. "She's all red and wrinkly and she had this sort of smushed face, but she was kind of cute. She's called Princess Genevieve." I said, my voice muted slightly by Al's tunic. "I'm her godmother," I said proudly a moment later.

"That's great, Ava, but do you know what happened with the drought? Where did Father go?" Azar muttered back.

"I was there when they made the final decision..." I hesitated. "I... I don't know what I'm allowed to tell you about," I whispered back. "We couldn't even bring in a healer for Anora." I recalled Father's stern words when I'd suggested a healer and later, Lord Jesu's words about keeping a positive public story until we know more. I didn't think that my brother's counted as part of the general public, but then again no one had told us anything about the drought. My head suddenly shot up off of Al's shoulder. "Al, Azar did you know about the drought?"

There was a pause, where the only noise was our footsteps passing over the dirt and leaves, until Azar spoke. "No," he said, his voice low and broken, "No, we didn't know."

"We're supposed to be Princes," Al said bitterly, "We're supposed to do everything in our power to support the people. How could we have just not known? Why did we fail this time?" Al finished helplessly.

"I don't know how to fix this," Ari quietly spoke up from behind.

"I don't think we can 'fix it' this time," I said back. "I just wish I'd known about it earlier." My brothers all agreed. We walked in silence the rest of the way towards the palace. All three of them walked up to my room, Al still carrying me. The room was empty as we walked in.

"No doubt Mother and Mama sent your maids to bed," said Al. His hold on my legs stayed firm as he, Azar, and Ari filtered into my room. "No one knew when you'd come back, or even if you were coming back. As soon as Lord Jesu delivered the message that Father was going on a diplomatic mission for food, he left to go back to the tent; lots of people thought you might have gone with them as part of the Nevremerre delegation," Al explained.

"Then why were you all still waiting?" I asked.

"You hadn't come back yet," Azar said simply, "and we didn't know what else to do." A seeping warmth filled my chest as I held on tighter to Al. My heart rang out for my caring, but utterly ridiculous brothers, who may be the only people in the world who could understand the strange hollowness that filled me when I had heard about the drought. I had been able to push it aside when dealing with Genevieve's birth, but the feelings could be pushed away no longer. It was accompanied by a confusing swirl of thoughts that all stemmed from one all-encompassing question: how can I possibly think I could rule if I could miss such a big problem so completely? Standing in my bedroom, however, stood three other people who I knew were all obsessing over the exact same question.

I gently extracted myself from Al's grasp and stood back up on my own. "I have to change," I said making my way towards my closet, "but you can all stay here for a while. Just don't put any shoes on the bed." I grabbed some pajamas before walking past them towards my bathroom. I changed as quickly as I could, not bothering to move my stained dress or tattered shoes off the bathroom floor. However, my aching feet and drained body made any movement rather slow. No doubt this is why, when I left the bathroom in my pajamas with some bandages around my feet, I found all three of my brothers wrapped around each other sound asleep. Their tall bodies taking up most of the bed. I, thankfully, spotted a pile of large shoes by my doorway. Too tired to do anything else, I grabbed the blanket from my chair and curled up into the open space above Al and Ari's heads, strategically avoiding Azar's flung out arm, and quickly fell asleep.

Chapter 22

The Aftermath of Ignorance

Sunlight was lighting up the room when Ana and Charlotte woke me up the following morning. "Your Highnesses!" Charlotte jumped as she walked in. Her voice causing me to wake up as I raised my head. My eyes were still blurry from sleep, and there was an uncomfortable twinge in my neck.

"We're sorry, Your Highnesses," Ana jumped in, "but Princess Avalynn's presence has been requested by Her Majesties and the council." I briefly wondered why on Earth Ana was being so formal until a grunting around me brought back memories of last night. I briefly closed my eyes once more before sitting up to find Azar and Ari curled up on either side of Al, who seemed to be cradling each of their heads in his sleep. None of them seemed to be aware of what was going on, and Ari was openly drooling as his head rested on Al's chest. For a moment I was deeply disappointed that our parents weren't here to see this, but I thought with a smile and a glance towards Ana and Charlotte, I could simply just tell them about it. And, of course, I would have to tell Carlos, and the other knights, perhaps even the nobles, if they were interested. It was very cute after all, and I had the witnesses to prove it. I grinned.

"Princess?" Ana prompted, jerking me out of my plotting.

I nodded at her before clearing my voice and yelling, "Get up!" at my brothers. Azar jumped awake and stood up on the bed looking wildly around. Al, too, shot up, but he remained seated as he took in the room around him. Ari, somehow, stayed asleep. "I have to meet with the council, and you're scaring my maids," I said to them gently poking at Ari to wake him up.

"You didn't have to be so loud about it, Ava," Azar grumbled rubbing his ears as he jumped off my bed.

"Huh," Ari said sleepily as my nudging finally roused him from his slumber.

"We've got to leave, Ari," Al informed him, dragging Ari out of bed. "But Ava will find us after her council meeting, right Ava?" Al implored me.

"I'll let you know what I find out," I nodded as my brothers shuffled around for their shoes, each apologizing to my maids as they left. This included Ari, although he looked a little confused as to why, as he followed Al and Azar out.

"Sorry about that," I said to Ana and Charlotte, "They invited themselves over last night."

"I think it looked sweet," Charlotte smiled.

"Oh, it certainly did. Just think about what Carlos will say when we tell him," Ana smirked, causing Charlotte to laugh. I rested in their joy for just a moment before the serious nature of the day before me swept over me.

"Pick out something nice today. Something more serious to meet the council in," I informed Ana. "Oh, and don't mind the dress in the bathroom, there was a medical emergency last night, so just ignore the bloodstains." It was a testament to my maids incredible talent at their jobs that they did not even blink at my statement with Ana simply asking, "Are we going for a more regal look or more demure look?" before she moved to the closet.

"Regal," I responded as I moved to get ready.

Ana put me in a pair of emerald trousers with a sleek black top with thin straps. Charlotte pulled back my hair into a single long braid before grabbing me some toast to eat as I made my way to the council meeting room on the third floor. Even though I knew what the council would be asking me about, I still felt strangely nervous as I hurried up the stairs. When I entered the council room, I was met only by Lord Jesu, General Clara, and my mothers. "I thought we were meeting at noon," I said by way of greeting.

"That's our fault," Mama said, "We know you were out late last night, but we feel the council would benefit from hearing your report sooner, rather than later." As she spoke, Duchess Amber walked into the room, her blond hair flapping wildly behind her.

"We will leave you to create a concise, but informative summary of last night's events. The whole council will meet back here in an hour," Mother said formally before she and Mama walked out of the room, each giving my hand a tight squeeze on their way out. As soon as the door closed behind them, Duchess Amber slouched into the nearest chair.

"I hate early mornings," she sighed.

"There aren't many who'd call 9 a.m. "early", darling," General Clara joked. She seemed to be the only person in the room who was really awake and thus earned herself a glare from Duchess Amber. "Oh hush. Here, I'll do your hair while we talk," General Clara placated, taking the Duchess's tangled hair into her hands.

"I don't know why we have to get up this early," Duchess Amber hummed as General Clara ran her fingers through her hair before pulling it back into a low bun. "I mean even with a report it's not like there's anything we can do until King Edgar returns."

"You know they're just worried. Everyone is trying their best to find solutions, and even if there's nothing to be done, we all want to feel like we've at least tried something," Lord Jesu responded.

"I suppose so. Don't mind my grumbling; let's get on with this then," Duchess Amber said as General Clara finished her hair. They spent the next ten minutes summarizing the discussion that took place before I got there. Then they summarized the discussion that took place while I guided Anora through childbirth.

"What happened while we were out getting supplies for the birth?" General Clara asked, turning towards me, "I believe

Edgar was going to be briefed on what Dolma's like, what did they say?"

"Er- well she mostly gave restrictions about the kinds of knights we could bring. Apparently Dolma has rather strict rules about these things and it's very different from both Nevremerre and Agremerre," I responded.

"What were the restrictions? What kind of rules do they have? What did she mean different?" General Clara interrogated.

"I don't know," I said calmly.

"You don't know?" Lord Jesu repeated. "How could you not know?" His tone was more curious than derogatory, but I shot him a glare nonetheless.

"Well, partly because most of the information was to be relayed to His Majesty on the road, but mostly because I was delivering a baby!" I shot back.

Lord Jesu blushed and mumbled, "Oh, right," causing Duchess Amber to laugh in her chair.

"Okay, so we'll have to wait for the King's return to fill in all the gaps about Dolma's culture. It's a six day round trip, so we'll finish off our summary by saying we expect His Majesty to return anytime between seven and ten days from now. Then inform them that Queen Anora gave birth to Princess Genevieve and that Princess Avalynn is one of the two godmothers. Is that all?" Duchess Amber asked. We all nodded in response. "Good, we have twenty minutes before the council meeting which is just enough time to go to the kitchen for breakfast!"

Twenty minutes later, we found ourselves in the council room once more. This time, however, we were all fully fed and substantially more awake. Lord Jesu gave our presentation as the rest of us stood at the base of the table near him. As predicted by Duchess Amber earlier, it was eventually decided that there was simply nothing more we could do but wait for Father to return home. In the meantime, the four regional Dukes and Duchesses would walk the nobles of their region through what had already been done to prepare for the drought. By the end of it all, my body felt hollow and helpless, and a bottomless pit filled my stomach as I stood and found out that I could do nothing to help anyone during this process.

"Well that's all we can do for now," Mother sighed. "We still need to meet for the Unajo festivities this evening, and to congratulate Queen Anora on the birth of Princess Genevieve of course. So, I will see you all later this evening." Mother rose and dismissed the council.

"Ava," Mama called, still sitting in her spot by Mother's side. "Wait here a moment, won't you?" I nodded and maneuvered my way over to her and mother as the other council members filtered out of the room. As the last of the nobles left, and the door to the council room swung closed, Mama grabbed me by the waist and pulled me onto her lap.

"Mama!" I cried out in shock. "I think I might be a bit too old to sit in your lap." My body felt awkward and a little too tall and too heavy even against Mama's overwhelming height and strength.

"Nonsense," Mother said, sitting back down at the head of the table. She reached a dark hand over and soothed errant strands of my braided hair, "One can never be too old for a Mother's care." I wanted to argue that I had met several people who should definitely be out of their Mother's care, but Mama's palm was running soothing circles along my back and Mother's tender fingers were still running along my hair. I just couldn't find it in me to reject the warmth they projected between them.

"First, we want to tell you how proud of you we are. You handled a very stressful situation extremely well. It can't have been easy delivering Anora's baby like that, but you kept a level head and helped Anora and the baby pull through safely," Mama's voice rumbled through my body as she held me.

"I yelled at the King, his counsel, and the Agremerrian delegation to get out of the tent," I recalled suddenly. "And, I yelled at Queen Anora to take care of herself!"

Mother burst out laughing, and Mama soon joined in. "Wonderful," Mother chuckled, "it's probably a good thing you did. It was likely just what that crowd needed."

"Plus, it's good to use your voice when required, especially against those who may be more powerful than you. It keeps them in check and ensures that your own power doesn't get lost," Mama added. There was silence for a long moment, in which Mother and Mama shared a lingering glance. Finally, Mother sighed and reached out to grab my hand. "Ava," she spoke, her voice soft but loud in the quiet room, "What we really want to know is if you and your brothers are okay? We had hoped to tell you all about the drought before we informed the nobles and the public. We thought we would have more time to do so, and maybe even had a solution by the time we informed you. I am sorry you had to find out this way," Mother said, sincerity filling each syllable as she spoke.

"I just don't understand, why didn't you tell us? None of us knew, none of us! When all of those nobles came up to us at the banquet, they all looked to us for answers, and, not only did we not have answers, we didn't even know there was a problem." I cried out, my voice rising with every word. Tears threatened to fall down my face, as I paused for a moment to wipe my eyes with the back of my hand. "Why didn't you tell us?" my voice broke as I looked into Mother's almost black eyes. "Did you not think we could handle it?" my voice fell to a whisper as I said my deepest fear aloud. "Are we just not good enough to help the kingdom? To sit on the throne? Is everything Lord Nicholas said true? Am I just not good enough?"

"Avalynn, look at me," Mama said, her voice frighteningly stern as she shifted me and her lap, so I could see her clear blue eyes. "Don't you ever, ever think of yourself as anything less than capable and confident. I know it's easy for someone else to say, but you must believe it yourself. You are a brilliant, compassionate, and innovative young woman, and I know you can handle anything that comes your way. I know this, your Mother knows this, your Father knows this. Gods be damned, I'd wager anyone who's spoken to you for more than 15 minutes knows this. And, if you ever doubt this, I want you to repeat my words for however long it takes until you believe it. Whether that takes minutes or years, don't you ever believe yourself to be anything less than enough."

Mother nodded her head vigorously before adding, "We have never thought of you or your brothers as incapable or unable to handle the drought. In fact it was quite the opposite.

All of you have worked so hard ever since you were children to help the country, and of course that's important, but for Diana and me, who had never grown up as royalty, we couldn't help but feel like you were all growing up too quickly. All of you were constantly studying and training, inventing new taxes and brushing up on foreign policy or war tactics. The last time I saw my children play was nearly eight years ago. At some point each one of you became so focused on becoming a ruler, you forgot you were all just children.

Edgar would tell us that these sacrifices were all a part of living as a Prince or Princess. Elizabeth would tell us that she watched the same thing happen to Octavian and Edgar's childhood. She said that it never gets easier, and she would tell us about how grateful she was that Olivia decided to opt out of succession very early on. That Olivia, at least, had a childhood of privilege without the burden of responsibility. However, for us, all of our children want the throne, and, at the end of the day, only one of you can be on it.

When we first learned about the drought, we knew exactly what would happen if we told you all. It would be the same thing that happened every other time there was a crisis. All of you would get so serious and spend all day working to find solutions to help the people. Only this time the crisis would last at least a year, and none of you have the ability to control the weather. Not to mention that we and the council are extremely capable people. We were able to create appropriate countermeasures on our own. You would eventually have to know, but we wanted to let you have a fun and carefree, to the extent that any of you can be carefree, summer.

Of course, this went somewhat out the window when Lord Nicholas came and wanted to be King. You all got so serious once more, well except Azar, but Lord Azcarth made a very compelling case which was supported by Lord Heathcliff -"

"Lord Azcarth supported Lord Nicholas in becoming King?" I gasped. Lord Azcarth was the council's noble representative. He'd been a member of the council since my grandfather was on the throne. It was concerning, to say the least, to think that Lord Azcarth, and by extension the other nobles, were backing Lord Nicholas for King.

"Not exactly," Mother replied with a somewhat sad smile, "I'd recommend that you talk to Lord Azcarth about it. I suspect you'll be quite surprised by what he has to say. Now, let me finish." I shut my mouth and nodded for Mother to continue. "When Lord Nicholas came, we thought about telling you about the drought. It seemed like Lord Nicholas had already caused the reaction we'd hoped to avoid, so why hide anything from you now. It was actually Edgar who stopped us this time. The drought-aid jobs we provided for you had each of you start to develop a life away from the throne, and Edgar believed the knowledge of the drought may hinder that. Again you were already doing all you could, so we wanted you to have some fun. And, even with Lord Nicholas, it seemed like you were having fun.

Al was spending more time with nobles his age, Azar was getting closer with the knights, you, Ava, had friends your own age that you actually spent time with!" I briefly thought that she didn't have to sound so surprised, but even I had to recognize the truth to her words. "Even Ari grew closer with Lady Milfred and Duke Austin. So, we let you continue to live in ignorance, for as long as we could. Knowing how things turned out, it was likely not the best decision. From a ruler's perspective, it was definitely a mistake, but from a parent's perspective, I must admit that I cannot regret our decision. Still, I'm sorry that we've caused you pain."

An interesting sort of empty warmth filled my chest. The kind you get after you've just finished crying. Obviously, the problem that made you cry hasn't gone away, but you've now run out of tears. And, the act of doing something futile still brought a sense of relief. Despite only letting out a few tears, it was this feeling that filled my body as Mother finished speaking. I was enough. The drought was still around and I still couldn't fix it. But, I could still keep trying to help and keep trying to be Queen. "Okay," I said simply leaning into my Mama's chest. "Okay." We stayed like that for a bit longer before Mother and Mama went to find my brothers. They would have the same conversation with each of them, and we would all move forward from there.

I found myself back in the gardens, retracing the path I'd walked with Abel less than 24 hours before. After so many weeks of having every minute filled with study and training and the hospital, I was dazed by the simple thought that I had nothing to do. But, there was nothing I could do. It was perhaps due to this strange and new emptiness that I did not notice Lord Nicholas until I ran right into him. I blinked at his presence, a neutrality filling me as I looked at him. He no longer was the biggest problem in my life, and his previous venom was no longer piercing my skin and corrupting my blood. He was simply there, and I did not have the energy to care about what he may or may not do in the future. My new-found neutrality, however, was not matched by the man in question, and, as I opened my mouth to apologize for bumping into him, I was met with a harsh glare. "Are you here to rub it in?" he spat before I had the chance to speak. "Fine then, you were right! Are you happy? You are damned right, but that still doesn't mean I like any of you!" Lord Nicholas stormed past me and off down further into the garden.

I stood there, blinking next to the white roses with my mouth still open ready to apologize. I had the overwhelming feeling that I was missing some crucial element in our last interaction. His words were no help in solving the mystery, nor was reviewing our previous altercations, I believed I was always right, so I couldn't hazard a guess as to what we'd finally agreed on. Still unsure of what exactly to do, and still very confused about what Lord Nicholas was going on about, I decided to just simply lie down in the garden path. I looked up at the tragically cloudless sky, and felt the sun beat uncomfortably down on my skin. Rocks and sticks poked at my back, my head, and my legs, and I still did not move. The stifling heat clung to my black top and pressed down on my trousers, and still I did not move. I just laid there as the world crashed around me and time kept pressing determinedly on, as if my life and all the lives of the people in this country, in this world, meant nothing to time. As if all we'd ever done with time was give it a name we could use to explain it to each other and that didn't affect time one jot. As if time were a fixed object and all we'd done was build our lives around it. As I lay there watching both everything and nothing change around me, I supposed that it was true, time was wholly indifferent to those who chose to live around it.

It was with this thought that I finally pushed myself back up. Time may have the luxury of indifference, but I had the choice to care. Mother had lamented what she believed to be our stolen childhood, but I had never begrudged the life I chose. Even if endless hours of reading dry, academic text made my head hurt and my eyes water, the smiles on the faces of those we were able to help filled me with a greater sense of joy and accomplishment than could ever be negated by boring books. It was selfishness, really, my desire to absorb myself in the feeling of having done something to benefit another. I was going to pursue that feeling until someone told me I couldn't any longer and even then I'd find another way. So, until the time I could do something about the drought, if that time ever came, I would simply be with those who were worried or struggling and hope that I could help in any way. I brushed the dirt off me and made my way towards the palace. Just before heading inside, I caught sight of Azar sitting by the training grounds fiddling with a mace in his hands.

"What are you doing?" I asked plopping down beside him. His musing location, I noticed, was far less painful than my own. Azar was sitting on a large wooden bench that was slightly covered by a tree.

"Not many people out today," Azar commented in reply. I glanced around the desolate training ground. It appeared that Azar and I were the only people there.

"No, there are not many people," I agreed.

"I tried to take myself out of the line of succession today," Azar said casually.

"What?! Why?" I jumped up at his words, astonished by his admission. Azar just raised an eyebrow at me, and patted the space I just abandoned. I quietly sat down once more, waiting for him to continue.

"I'm not ready to be King. Not the way I act now anyways," Azar said lightly, tilting his head up towards the sky. "I realized that last night, not because I didn't know about the drought.

Mother and Mama talked to me, and I realized that sometimes you just can't know things unless someone tells you. I'm not a farmer or a weatherman. I know what a drought will mean for our crops, but I don't have the knowledge to predict the weather or to know how much rain each region has gotten. Not without help, at least.

No, what showed me last night that I was not ready to be King was what happened when the news of the drought broke. The chaos and panic that took over the nobles, and when they surrounded us demanding answers, I had none to give. In that moment, I felt fear and panic take over me, too, and I couldn't control it. I could not stop my own anxieties from taking over. Fighting in the tournament, Mama warned me that there would be moments where swords would be pointed at me and stronger foes would look like they could hurt me. She said in these moments my first instinct would be to freeze or run away, but if I could control my emotions and think, I could find another solution. She was right, and, in the tournament, I was able to do that. When those nobles came rushing up to me last night, I was not able to do that.

In the face of a crisis, I was not able to keep calm and keep a level head. I was only calm once I heard Mother speak, and by the end of her speech I was relieved. Relieved that I wouldn't have to do anything, relieved that no one could blame me for not aiding in the drought relief even though I didn't know that was what I was doing at the time. As the night progressed and we waited for more information, I realized two things: I lack the maturity necessary for calming the emotions of others and I place a higher value on the opinions of others than I do on do-ing what I think is right. I think both of these traits I lack are vital to being a good King, so I tried to take myself out of the line of succession. Mother said no though. See, the thing is I still want to be King. I'm not sure I'm the best candidate, but I still want the job. I think... I think I can help people, and I want to do that. So, Mother told me that she wouldn't take me out of succession just yet. She told me to take the time to try to fix the faults I saw in myself in the seven years before Ari turns 21. I decided to do the work and try to grow, but I wonder if I should take myself out of succession all the same.

We were always told that the decision on the successor happens when the youngest sibling reaches the age of majority because then we would have all had enough time to learn and grow. I'm 21 now, and I think I'm nowhere near done growing. How is it fair to judge me, who in seven years will have hopefully done the work required to fix my failures, to a 21 year old Ari who might just be learning of his faults?" Azar finished, turning to look towards me.

"Whether you become King now or never, you would still have to address your own shortcomings and I suspect that even after seven years you will find more. We all will. I don't think we ever finish growing. There will always be something more about ourselves that we can learn. I think the question the council is looking to answer for each of us is whether or not we will do the work necessary to grow and become a happier and stronger person and a better ruler. That's a question that can be answered by a 21-year-old. I think it's probably less about how far you progressed and more about whether or not you chose to grow," I said. "I think you could be a really good King, Azar. I don't think you should just give up, if it's something you want to do." Azar smiled at me.

"Perhaps you're right. I think I will step back from all the competition for a moment though, work on myself a bit. It's possibly the only way for me to beat you after all," Azar smiled back at me. I put my head on his shoulder.

"I wonder what will become of us all in the future," I mused.

"I don't know," Azar responded, "Seven years is an awfully long time after all."

Chapter 23

The Return of King Edgar

Later that evening, I met up with my entire family as we walked towards the border tent. It felt rather odd that we still had to dress up and celebrate the Unajo festival with all that was going on, but it was still an important celebration. Although I had yet to go down to Nera to see it, Nera and Pantheo (Agremerre's capital) were having large combined markets that filled the main streets of each city. There were also dances, plays, and concerts planned throughout each country. No matter the disaster both countries may be facing, it was still a vital ceremony that showed the strength of our relationship with Agremerre. So, we would continue to go to the festival all week, and we would hope that no one would learn that Agremerre technically declared war yesterday.

The festivities were already in full swing when we arrived. Agremerrian and Nevremerrian nobles and judges were laughing and chatting casually as they moved between tents. Servers weaved between the mingling guests carrying trays filled with various delicacies from both countries. Oddly enough, the drought seemed not to affect the spirits of the nobles who were so relaxed in their posture and mannerisms, you would never be able to tell that they were recently so panicked that they'd swarmed the Queens. As we moved past, nobles from both countries stopped and bowed. It seemed like their gazes lasted longer than usual. I had the distinct impression that we would be the center of each of their conversations once we were out of earshot. After all, even if they may appear carefree, every noble here, from both countries, knew the crisis we were in. I unconsciously smoothed the non-existent wrinkles out of the short light blue dress I'd chosen for this event, and tried to keep my pace steady.

When we entered the main tent we were told that Queen Anora had set up camp and one of the smaller tents towards the back of our encampment. Mother loudly excused our-selves, stating that we would greet Queen Anora. Gratefully, we hurried out of the main tent in the direction of Anora's oasis. When we finally moved past the curious stares of two countries' worth of nobles, knights, and judges, my brothers and I gave audible sighs of relief upon discovering the tent would only be filled with royalty or godparents of Genevieve.

"Much quieter in here isn't it?" Anora said by way of greet-ing. She was propped up by a fountain of pillows that made a colorful halo around her tan skin and ebony hair. "At the time, I thought that Troublemaker had decided on the absolute worst time to be born," she continued, smiling at the bundle in her arms. "But, now that everything has happened, she couldn't have been born at a better time! No greater excuse than a newborn to hide away from prying eyes. Now, it may be cowardly to run away, but-"

"No," Mother firmly interjected before collapsing onto another mountain of pillows, "No, in this case, a strategic retreat is exactly what is required."

"Well that settles it then," Anora smiled, "If the great General Elenore thinks so, then we can't be doing anything wrong."

"How are you feeling?" I asked Anora, while the rest of my family found their way to their own section of pillows.

"Just fine, dear," Anora said, "the healers checked me over this morning and declared me all healthy, and Genevieve too. Apparently, you did a wonderful job Avalynn, thank you."

"You should also know that we are ensuring she is carried everywhere for at least a week," spoke a deep baritone voice I recognized as Head Judge Michael. In Agremerrian culture, the majority of legislative decisions occurred through the High Court, whereas the Queen or King takes care of all foreign policy, war tactics, and has some veto power over the High Judges' decisions. To become a High Judge of Agremerre, one must pass a series of rigorous exams, and get at least a 60% support rate from the Agremerrian people. Once on the High Court, the High Judges would elect among themselves a Head Judge. Head Judges have 5-year election cycles, and, in that time, the Head Judge of Agremerre is only just shy of royalty. Michael was a young Head Judge, only just elected three years prior, when Aziarthia retired after 55 years of service as Head Judge. Thus Head Judge Michael's introduction to us occurred with quite a lot of fanfare.

"I'm so glad! Thank you for your help," I smiled into his blue eyes.

"I think I should be saying that to you," he responded with a quick wink before his face quickly bounced back to being serious.

"Can we see the little Princess now?" Mama cooed at the bundle Anora had in her arms. The room then descended into "oohs" and "aahs", as my goddaughter was presented to my family members. Genevieve's little sleeping figure was gently passed around, as she unknowingly brought unconditional joy to every person in a room of stressed and worried people. Quiet laughter filled the tent and smiles were present on everyone's face. As Genevieve found her way into my arms, I observed the faces of those around me. The tension that we all carried had, while not disappearing completely, significantly reduced. Mother, Mama, and Anora had huddled together as they swapped stories of childbirth and newborns. Al and Azar were getting along remarkably well as Kazi whispered stories of the Agremerrian knights. Michael was captivating Ari with a local fairy tale. Here, in a room where nothing was expected of us, I found the sense of calm that I'd been desperately missing since last night. Even if my day had been emptier than I'd experienced in months, I had consistently felt the pressure of the Kingdom's crisis upon my nerves, pinpointing every pressure point and needling its way into my mind. Only now, in a room full of people who experienced the very same needling (and one who was ignorant of it all), I found the pins pulled away. Without even realizing it, I let the calm wash over me, and fell into a deep sleep with Genevieve still cradled in my arms.

The next week passed in an anxious quiet. I spent my days in the hospital, Mother's words about keeping the public as healthy as possible ringing in my ears. So, even though placements were officially over, I went to Matron Terrella and volunteered my services. Unsurprisingly, I was sent to maternity calls, as "birthing season" began in earnest. To be honest, I was grateful for the distraction that it brought. Running around a hospital caring for patients made it difficult to think about much else, and, after delivering Genevieve, I was more confident in my abilities.

When I wasn't in a delivery room or doing prenatal care, I spent the rest of my time with Murphy. His presence was remarkably soothing. He filled my mind with herbs and medical procedures, his passion for research bleeding into my life. It gave my desperate brain something to grab onto, and there was a wonderful joy that came from talking with someone who had no idea about the drought. The palace, during this time, had a tension that filled its halls. Laughter seemed less frequent, and every noble I came across seemed in a rush to get somewhere else. If not going somewhere, they were desperate to talk to me. "Have you heard anything more?" "When will His Majesty return?" "Have you thought of any other options yet?" These questions peppered my time at the palace, and each time they were spoken, I had no answer to give. I simply responded, "We are doing everything we can until His Majesty returns; once His Majesty comes back we will update you with what we can expect to come next." This response always felt weak to my ears, but I tried to say it in a confident and soothing voice. Still, I reflected as Murphy rolled around prepping his latest experiment, perhaps there was a bit of selfish escapism occurring with the time I spent at the hospital.

"Right, so I was talking with Cozon," Murphy said, talking about the Agremerrian researcher who'd come by on the first day of the festival, and had dominated Murphy's conversation ever since. "And they were saying that in one of the coastal towns of Agremerre, they started using this certain type of eel after a patient goes into cardiac arrest, that gives off a shock!

Apparently that shock is enough to restart the patient's heart! Now obviously," Murphy continued as he tried to extract oil out of a big round hard plant that some along the coastal region swore could help prevent infections and improve memory, "the researchers in Agremerre haven't tested this claim, yet, but can you imagine what could happen if it turns out to be true? Maybe we'd have to keep eels in the hospital! I wonder if the shock could help any other organs or -"

"Princess!" I jumped at the voice, and felt my heart rise into my chest as I turned around. There, breathing heavily, stood Cameron, one of the palace pages. My, still wildly beating, heart soared at her presence.

"What is it? Is Fath- His Majesty back?" I asked, every fiber of my being trying to will her to answer in the affirmative, but Cameron just shook her head no.

"It's The Dowager Queen, she's just arrived at the palace. I was told to collect you at once."

"Oh..." I responded, and I felt my body deflate just a little. Not that I hadn't missed Nana, but her presence seemed a bit diminished compared to the idea of Father coming home. "Wait, why is she here? I thought we wouldn't see her until after the court leaves Nera."

"I don't know, Princess. I was just told to bring you back to the palace."

"A Princess' work is never done," Murphy said with interest as he appraised the situation. "Will I see you tomorrow?"

"I don't know," I replied moving towards the door, "I would assume so, but it depends on what the Dowager Queen needs me for."

"All right, see you around then," Murphy nodded.

Cameron had picked me up on horseback, so I joined her on the horse and we raced back to the palace. Upon arrival, I was hurriedly directed towards the small drawing room near the main entrance. I walked into the room to find my mothers and brothers already surrounding the white-haired figure of Nana. Despite the fact that everyone except Ari and I had reached the age of majority, the whole room looked like children as they sprawled around the chair Nana was sitting in. Al and Ari had taken up residence on either side of her. They sat on the floor resting against the legs of Nana's chair as her wiry hands moved gently through their hair. Azar sat on the floor in front of her, lazily leaning against the coffee table behind him. Mama sat in the chair to Nana's left, holding Mother in her lap and using her feet to gently nudge Al's outstretched legs towards the opposite direction. There was no other being in the room, and I couldn't help but be thankful as we all looked anything but regal.

"Hello my Songbird," Nana's gentle voice breezed towards me. Her voice broke through my being, hitting my soul and drawing me towards her.

"Nana," my voice called back, filled with emotions I'd struggled to name. I moved towards her, and I gave her a hug from behind to avoid disturbing my brothers. I hung my body over her shoulders and soaked in the safety that radiated around her. "I missed you," I whispered into her shoulder, and it suddenly hit me how true those words were. As if saying them had pulled the emotions from the darkest parts of my heart. I had missed her, so much, and I hadn't really known it until I'd seen her again. A childish part of me wanted to yell "Where were you? Why haven't you been here for all the turmoil that I've experienced this past summer?" Another part of me wanted to beg, "Please, please never leave me alone again." Instead, I just squeezed a little tighter. "I love you, Nana," I whispered to her.

"And I love you, Songbird," she replied, bringing the hand in Ari's hair up to my arm and patting it twice before reaching down to Ari once more. I squeezed her tightly before pulling away and moving to where Azar was sitting; I joined him on the floor facing Nana. The whole room sat in silence for a moment, basking in the clarity and warmth Nana exuded. "I'm sorry to have disturbed you, Ava," Nana finally spoke. "I'm afraid the servants read more into my presence than was truly warranted.

"Can you blame them, Elizabeth," Mama smiled, pulling Mother closer to her chest, "With Edgar gone on a mysterious trip, and then you showed up out of nowhere! It's of course going to cause a stir."

"Hmm, I suppose so," Nana acknowledged, "but, I do believe Edgar will be back soon."

"Have you had a vision?" Mother popped up suddenly.

"My dear, the spirituality of time is not one that can be interpreted so lightly. Any visions of the future are always far more vague and far more subject to change than the people realize. That's why all visions go through the clarity checks before being released to the public," Nana lectured lightly.

"Yes, but so many of your visions make it through anyways," Mother protested, but she pulled herself back up against Mama.

Nana smiled, "Well, you're not wrong, but, my confidence in my statement comes not from any vision, but knowledge of my son. Edgar would never leave you for longer than he has to." She reached over and squeezed Mother's leg that had been swung over the side of the chair. "No, I came here because I could feel all of your upset and stressed energies from across Nevremerre. I'm only sorry it took me so long to get here, but I'll help you all in any way I can now that I've arrived. I suspect that big changes are coming for us all in the coming days." Nana's eyes met my own for a brief moment before she shifted back in her chair and changed the conversation to what our summer had been like. I sat back and reveled in the brightness she brought into our drawing room. I thought her words were obvious, of course change would be coming. We have to prepare for a drought for one. At the time, I'd never have been able to guess the level of change that awaited me.

I did go and see Murphy the next day. He was starting his trials on the oil he had prepared the day before. I spent the day as a research assistant writing down notes about each participant as Murphy gave them detailed instructions about when and where to apply the oil. Whether it was Nana's return or finally getting used to the current situation, I found myself feeling lighter than I had all week. Murphy and I spent the whole day laughing about patients who came into the hospital for ridiculous reasons, and how the Matron had essentially strongarmed Murphy into taking some time off. It was hilarious to watch Murphy grumble over the mandatory vacation which was scheduled to start tomorrow as he passed his preliminary results to Healer Autumn. Healer Autumn insisted that this was a cause to celebrate, and they dragged us both out of the hospital an hour early to get pies from the bakery across the square. The whole affair was filled with Murphy's complaints of having to leave the hospital early, however, his protest did nothing to stop Healer Autumn from putting a pie in his hands and demanding he "shut up and eat."

"How much longer will you be in Nera, Princess?" Healer Autumn asked me, biting into their cherry pie.

"Well, normally we would leave in about a week, but it's a little bit up in the air until His Majesty returns from his diplomatic mission."

"Will you work in the hospital again next summer?" Murphy asked.

I thought about this for a moment before I responded, "I'd like to, if I have the time. I did enjoy my work there, although I doubt I'd work every other day like I did the summer."

"You should come back and work." Murphy declared, "If you can't be Queen, you'd make an excellent researcher."

"That's some high praise coming from you, Murphy," Healer Autumn responded. "I think the Princess would make an excellent Queen though. If you wanted to be, that is."

I smiled at both of them. "Thank you for those kind sentiments. I'm sure whoever is selected to rule will be the right choice. Although, if that person is not me, I don't believe my next choice will be a researcher. Sorry Murphy."

"Your loss," Murphy shrugs, finishing off his pie, "Research is the best job there is."

"Yes, well just make sure you stop and say goodbye before you leave, Princess," Healer Autumn laughed as we parted ways and I headed back up to the palace.

Despite the Unajo festival having ended two days before, the nobles had yet to leave the capital. In light of recent events, it was decided that they would all remain in the palace until Father returned from Dolma. While I understood the need for the intrusion, I couldn't help my resentment towards the living arrangements, especially as it took almost three times longer than normal just to get to my own room. I resigned myself to the journey as I walked through the main hall and saw Count Raiger, a count in one of the Mariposa provinces, move toward me. A loud bang rang through the hall, pulling my attention to the side door.

"The knights from the King's trip are coming! His Majesty has returned!" yelled someone who I believed was Countess Vivian, but I couldn't tell for sure as she was instantly surrounded by loitering nobles. I ran in the opposite direction towards the nearest footman.

"Go find the Queens and the Princes and inform them the King has returned." I said quickly, as the man scurried off into the palace. My attention jumped back to the pandemonium that surrounded the side door as nobles tried to force their way through and see where the King was coming from. The cries grew louder as another figure stepped through the door. With the start I realized I should probably try to stop the chaos in front of me, and I moved towards the crowd.

"Silence!" a voice I recognized as Mateo's called out, although I'd never heard his voice that loud. "The King has returned," he spoke over the now silent crowd "However, before he can discuss the results of the delegation, he has to relay what transpired with Queen Anora. I also need to find Princess Avalynn. Once they have come to a decision, King Edgar will inform all of you."

"Queen Anora can't be having another baby. Why is the Princess needed?" a voice called out.

"Don't be an idiot," called out another, "She's probably needed for childcare or something." The statement was followed by murmurs of agreement as quick chatter buzzed through the crowd. I pushed forward.

"Sir Mateo," I called out, and relief filled his honey brown eyes as he moved towards me.

"Princess," he called out. His face went stern once more, his mouth forming a firm line, "We must see His Majesty at once." With that he lightly grabbed my wrist and pulled me through the now parted crowd. I let him pull me out into the garden, feeling the watching eyes of the nobles follow us into the forest. I waited until we had made it further along the trail towards the Dormian coast, before speaking to Mateo.

"What happened in Dolma? Did we get the aid we need?" I asked my voice just above a whisper as I was still wary of lurking nobles. Mateo's hurried pace broke for a moment before he replied.

"It's best to hear what His Majesty has to say first," his grip on my wrist tightened slightly as he continued at his previous pace. I watched him lead me in silence towards the big tent we set up for the Unajo festival and the only tent we'd left standing as the festival closed. As we approached the tents, I noticed a wagon full of food parked nearby, guarded by two knights who had accompanied the delegation. They nodded at Mateo and me as we rushed past. Soon, Mateo was raising the tent flap and I moved inside. Standing around a wooden table was High Judge Miraz, Father, and Head Judge Michael. Queen Anora was seated across from them in a cushioned chair. Ricardo and Galileo stood a bit away from the table with an Agremerrian knight whose name I couldn't remember.

"Ava!" Father called, rushing towards me. He put his arms around me and pulled me into a large consuming hug. I moved to put my arms around him, but he pulled back too quickly. His eyes moved over me, filled with worry. "Mateo, Galileo, go to the Nevremerre side of the campground and make sure nobody gets in. Ricardo, get Oberon and do the same thing for the Agremerrian side," Father ordered. His emerald eyes were still fixed on me as the knights moved around us.

"Father," I whispered, "is everything all right?" Father just looked at me, his eyes mapping my face as he stared in silence.

"Would it make it easier if I asked?" queried High Judge Miraz, as I continued to stand around confused.

"No, no, I'll do it," Father finally said, tearing his eyes off me and moving across the tent. He walked and sat down with the table between us, and for some reason, I was reminded of that day nearly eight years ago when I asked my father what it meant to be King. Then, Father had sat proudly and pulled me close and told me the burdens and joys of ruling. Now, Father sat slouched at the table, bags visible under his eyes and white hairs peppered in against his red hair and beard. Here we were over a table-length apart, and I wondered if this was what he meant when he spoke of those burdens.

"Ava," Father looked at me. His voice was clear and steady, and his eyes fixed on mine. The worry that they'd held previously having all but disappeared. This, I thought, this was not a Father speaking to his daughter, but a King talking to a citizen. "Let me tell you about Dolma."

Chapter 24

The Choice of a Princess

The tent was quiet as Father spoke. "It was a three days' journey to Dolma from here. Now, we were rushing a bit due to the need for resources quickly, but it's still a long ride. During that entire trip, Judge Miraz was telling me about the culture and traditions of Dolma, but that whole trip wasn't nearly enough to prepare me for the country I was about to enter. Anora was not understating it when she said that Dolma was not like us. Nevertheless, we had a job to do.

In many ways, we were fortunate. Dolma, like Nevremerre and Agremerre, borders Calvine. However, unlike our two countries, Dolma does not have a strong military. We've been informed that Dolma fears that Calvine might attack and that they lack the military power to fight back. Dolma, also, did not face a drought this past year, in fact, they predict that this year will be one of the best harvests in recent history. With all that, Dolma proposed this trade: in exchange for supplementing one year of food for both Agremerre and Nevremerre, Dolma will have the benefit of both armies the next time they go to war.

Agremerre will also increase the amount of armor and weapons they sell to Dolma by 5% for the next five years.

Having spoken with High Judge Miraz, we believed these to be acceptable terms and Dolma sent us back with food as a gesture of goodwill as we finalized the deal with Queen Anora. However, Dolma also included one final condition. Now, before I go into the details of their final condition, I need to clarify a few things. First, this deal has not been officially signed. We lose nothing by backing out now. Second, while we have no proof of this, we are suspicious of Dolma's claim that Calvine may attack them. While it would not be out of character for Calvine to do so, we also believe it possible that Dolma may be considering attacking Calvine. If that is the case, signing this proposal would mean war with Calvine is definite. However, we have no proof of this and Dolma may only be concerned with a potential attack. If that is true, war may never come." Father looked at me once more and took a deep breath. "The final condition of the proposal with Dolma is that you marry their Crown Prince."

"What?" I blinked. Surely I'd misheard something.

"Honestly, it's ridiculous," Miraz stood up and began angrily pacing around the room, "I mean she's not even the age of majority! And, who uses their children as political tools!"

"Miraz, you have to remember that Dolma is a different place with different rules. Not to mention, in Dolma the age of majority is 16 for women and 20 for men," Anora sighed.

"That's still very odd," Michael pointed out, "16 is far too young, and why is it different for the men?"

"It's not our place to judge," Anora scolded. "This is exactly why we don't leave judges to deal with foreign affairs," she mumbled. "Nevertheless, in Dolma most noblewomen are married by 18, so it's not unreasonable for them to see Avalynn married at 19."

"Maybe not, but it is unreasonable for them to demand that she marry a man she's never even met to ensure that we get the aid we need! Plus, it's not like they'd let her take a lover, which means any thoughts of her finding love are utterly ruined. And, they want her to leave her home and permanently move to a foreign country where she knows no one, and will be treated like an outsider, possibly forever!" Father roared, his voice growing with each word.

"What?" I said, hardly processing the words around me. My brain felt heavy and confused. My mind didn't even know where to start forming a coherent thought. Astonishment and shock just took over my mind. The heads of everyone else in the room snapped toward me. Father's eyes were once again filled with worry as they met mine.

"Avalynn," he said gently, "you- ". A loud shout came through the tent breaking up Father's words.

"Your Majesty, please," the deep voice of Galileo called out. "the King specifically said- ".

"Oh, nevermind that! I know where I'm needed, and where I'm needed is right here!" Nana punctuated her sentence by walking into the tent, Galileo close on her heels.

"I'm sorry Your Majesty-" Galileo began, only to be cut off by Father's hand.

"It's all right, Sir Galileo, just go back to your post." Galileo nodded and sheepishly walked back out.

"Queen Elizabeth," Michael acknowledged, as he and the other Agremerrians all stood and entered into a deep bow.

Father, on the other hand, just sighed and remained seated. "Hello, mother. Should we be expecting any other interruptions?" he said, eyeing the tent's entrance cautiously.

"No, no, just me," Nana said cheerfully, waving at the Agremerrians to sit back down. "I've made sure all the others know to stay put, but, my dear, you certainly know how to draw an anxious crowd. There are nobles in the palace garden as far as the eye can see, not to mention all of your own family."

"We're trying to decide what to do now, so you don't have to-"

"Update me on the situation then," Nana interrupted.

"What?" Father gaped.

"Update me," Nana insisted once more. "It's obvious that whatever you're discussing involves Ava, and she looks so shocked a leaf might topple her! So, give her a moment to process everything and tell me what transpired in Dolma. And, for the Universe's sake, Songbird, sit down before you collapse," Nana finished, turning towards me. This seemed like a very good idea, and a command that I could follow. So, I sat, right where I was standing on the cold tent floor. "Gods above, Edgar, what did you say to that child," I heard Nana say. She turned back to Father, and prodded him to start to tell his tale once more.

I tuned out his words, and tried to focus on the buzzing that had consumed my mind. I was fairly sure that, by this point, Father was not joking when he said that Dolma wanted me to marry their Crown Prince. I also wondered if I would now be facing another week-long crisis, having only just gotten through the last one. Would I be forced to go to Dolma? To marry a mystery man without love? Admittedly, I hadn't really thought much about marriage. I'd been too focused on the battle for the throne. Not to mention, I still had two more years before I legally could get married, at least, as Anora had pointed out earlier, in Nevremerre's culture. However, even if marriage had not always been on the forefront of my mind, I had always looked at my parent's marriage and assumed I'd marry for love. I'd never even considered anything else. I mean what else was there besides love? Political gain and duty to help the people I was trying to serve, as it turned out.

"Have you come back to your senses now, Songbird," Nana's voice broke through to me, her tone gentle once more.

"Yes," I nodded. "I'm better now." It was only a little bit of a lie, as I picked myself off the tent floor.

"Why can't Al or Azar go?" I asked. My question felt childish to my ears, but they were both at least of age in both cultures.

"Dolma doesn't allow marriages between those of the same sex," Anora responded.

"That makes no sense," my mouth responded before my brain could catch up.

"I tend to agree with you, but there's not much I can do about it," Anora shrugged.

"Okay, so I have to marry the Crown Prince."

"You don't have to," Father said sternly, "We could just go to war with Dolma and simply take the supplies we need. Remember, war might be imminent either way, if Dolma is really planning to attack Calvine and not the other way around. If we fight now, at least we won't also have to give up you."

"But we don't know that war is Dolma's plan," I parried his words. "It's just as likely that they want our aid as insurance against a possible attack. With Nevremerre and Agremerre backing Dolma, Calvine is unlikely to attack. Just the threat of having to fight Nevremerre again would be more than enough to hold off any military action. Not to mention that if I do become Crown Princess of Dolma, and, if they do want to attack Calvine, I might be able to change their minds, or at least make them think about it more."

"If this were any other country, I might agree with you," Anora said, "but this is Dolma. Avalynn, if you go there it's very possible that you won't have any power at all, even as a Crown Princess."

"That makes no sense," I parroted my words from earlier. "I'd be the future Queen, how could I have no power?" Anora just shrugged in response.

"The point is, Ava, that you don't have to do this!" Father explained, "If you say no, then this ends right here. We will go to war with Dolma. It will be an easy victory with our two countries against only them. No one will even have to know we had another option. You could continue to grow up safe and healthy here."

"However," Michael's sage voice broke through, "it would be best if we could get the aid we need without war." Father glared at him. Michael was right though, how could I possibly ask three whole countries to go to war just because I would rather marry for love? Of course I would have to accept.

"No," Nana's voice was stern once more as her words shot through me. "You are not a passive participant in your life, Avalynn." Her deep blue eyes held onto me daring me to contradict her.

"I'm not?" I responded unable to tear my gaze away from her. I was not quite sure what her words meant, but her presence refused to be ignored. Despite her small frame, her body seemed to fill the tent, blocking out everything that wasn't her. I felt as though the rest of the world had disappeared and she and I stood in the milky blue void of the Universe utterly alone, her violet aura surrounding me, demanding and soothing me at the exact same time as her eyes bore into mine.

"Avalynn," she said, her voice quiet but fierce as it flowed through my ears and seeped into my brain, "I will not allow you to leave this room thinking that you are nothing more than a victim in these circumstances, and a martyr for the kingdom. That you had to comply with another country's invasive demands. This is your life, Avalynn! You have a choice. You decide the path on which your life will take. It is your decision what comes next. So what do you want, Avalynn? Setting aside everything and everyone else, what do you want?"

"I want to help people," I responded instantly. The words crashing into me like waves pounding upon the shore. "I want to help people," I repeated in awe. That's right, I thought. What have I been trying to do since I learned of the drought? What did I think about all those years ago when I sat with Nana under that big oak tree and decided to be Queen. I wanted to help people. I felt so stuck, so useless since Father went to Dolma. I was unable to do anything to help, and now, here was a way to help! I could do something now! Something I wanted to do because it would help so many people. I felt almost giddy at the thought, like a large weight had been blown off my shoulders, and my body shook with excitement.

I broke out of the odd bubble Nana's presence had created. Turning towards Father and the Agremerrians. I set my shoulders back, and lifted my head. Looking each of them in the eye, I spoke, my voice clear and steady overflowing with passion and authority. "There will be no need for war. I choose to go to Dolma, and I will marry their Crown Prince," I announced.

"Very good, my Songbird," Nana whispered to me. "Our greatest power comes from exercising our own free will and the ability to choose." I smiled slightly at her words. Anora let out a long breath.

"As a person," she said, "I want to tell you to change your mind. To just continue to live your life here, but, as a Queen, I know you are making the best choice for the people of all countries involved. Rest assured, you will have all the support Agremerre can give you."

"Agreed," nodded Michael, "Just say the word, and we will give you everything you need." All eyes in the room turned towards Father. He sat hunched over his chair, his face pressed into the palms of his hands. With a long-suffering sigh, he pushed himself back up.

"My gift, my treasure, my darling, darling girl, are you absolutely sure? This is not the life I would have wanted for you," he said, his eyes pleading with me.

I smiled back at him, filled with love for the man who would go to war for my happiness. "It's okay, Father. I want to do this. This is my choice, and I am happy with it."

Emerald eyes met emerald eyes, and Father slowly nodded. "Okay, okay my gift, you will go to Dolma." There were audible breaths of relief from around the table.

"Sit down, Princess and Queen Elizabeth," Michael called. "We should discuss the preparations before we inform the nobles of what is to come."

"Hm..." Anora said, folding her hands and looking at me. "Avalynn, do you want us to tell the nobles about this right away? Obviously, we will want to tell them that a deal has been made, but we don't have to tell them the details immediately."

My first instinct was to tell Anora that of course we should tell the nobles of the details of the agreement. Why wouldn't we let them know immediately, but something stopped me from responding. I pondered her words, turning them over in my head as I realized what Anora was offering. Once the news of my marriage got out, my life would change. I'd have to prepare for my move, and face the stares and the emotions that others would be forced upon me. I didn't even want to think about how my mothers or brothers would react. Would Mama be in tears? What would Al think after spending his childhood trying to defend me from a crown and a throne? I couldn't even begin to picture the reactions of Mother, Azar, or Ari. What if today was my last normal day of my youth?

"We can't delay for long," Father interjected, "Dolma gave us 12 days to accept and send over Avalynn. She shouldn't rush over like we did, which means she will have to set off for Dolma in a week's time."

"A week!" I turned towards Father in shock. I had less time than I imagined. Anora and Michael snapped towards Father as well.

"That doesn't give us much time to prepare," Anora frowned, "Still, we can still spare some time before informing others about the details." Everyone's heads turned to me once more.

"24-hours," I finally said, "Just give me 24 hours where no one else knows. That includes Mother, Mama, and my brothers," I said, focusing on Father.

He hesitated for a moment before nodding, "As you wish."

"Alright then," Anora smiled, "tomorrow evening we shall have a joint gathering of Agremerrian and Nevremerrian nobles to explain the official details of the treaty. We will have to meet tomorrow morning, Edgar, to prepare what we will say."

Father nodded, "And we will both need to prepare public statements for the people of our kingdoms," he added.

"Agreed. Michael, we will also need to send a runner to Dolma to inform them that we accept their proposal and that

Princess Avalynn will arrive in 12 days time with a party of-"
Anora paused. "How many people will the Princess be taking?"
There was a silence that filled the tent.

"Do I have to take any one?" I asked. "I don't want to have to
displace people who don't want to go."

"You'll need guards, my gift," Father shook his head, "It's
not like Nevremerre. Anora was right to have me bring at least
six."

"You will also need to bring your own personal maids,"
Anora added, "and maybe even a lady-in-waiting."

"A what?" I asked.

"It's a concept they have in Dolma. The way I see it, it's kind
of like a paid friend," Anora responded.

"Why would I want to pay someone to be friends with me?"

"I don't know, but you will certainly get some more while in
Dolma. It's required for women in the royal family."

"And I have to pay them?"

"I think so, they all kept talking about receiving a salary
when I was there last. Either way you might want to consider
bringing one or two people from Nevremerre or Agremerre, so
you have more people you can trust and rely on."

"I can't just take people away from Nevremerre because I
might get lonely," I exclaimed, reading between the lines of

Anora's words. "Besides, where exactly am I going to receive the money to pay these ladies-in-waiting?"

"Oh," Miraz chimed in, "Dolma did answer this one! They said that if you agreed, you would receive the standard Crown Princesses salary."

"I get a salary as Crown Princess?" I said, growing more and more confused.

"That's probably something similar to the treasury's discretionary funds, right?" Nana said, looking at the Agremerrians. There was a collective shrug in response.

"To be honest," Anora explained, "Agremerre tends to avoid communication with Dolma. We meet in Dolma every three to five years to reaffirm our peace treaty, but we never stay more than a week, and the King and Queen of Dolma have only visited Agremerre once in the past 300 years. Not for lack of us asking, but they've always insisted we come to them. I do know they have a lot of social rules that we will try to teach them all to you and whoever goes with you before you go."

I had a brief moment of panic as the phrase what in the Gods' names have I gotten myself into flashed through my mind. I took a deep breath to center myself before pushing on in the conversation. "Okay, so upon my arrival to Dolma, there will be a steep learning curve. I'm a good student, so teach me what you know and I'll be able to pick up the rest when I get there," I decided.

"Alright, but we still haven't figured out how many people will accompany you," Michael pointed out.

"Tell Dolma that nine people will accompany the Princess," Nana said definitively. "Six knights, two maids, and one lady-in-waiting. Then, tomorrow when you tell the nobles about the treaty, you can also ask for volunteers to go with the Princess. There, no doubt, will be applicants and we can select the people we want to go."

"All right then," Michael said, as the rest of the room unquestioningly followed Nana's words. "We will open this up to Agremerrian knights, nobles, and maids as well, to give you more options and show our support."

"We will have to be careful who you select, Avalynn. The rules we set up for the knights who joined your father will have to apply twofold now. It's vital for the safety of you and those who want to join your party."

"Right," I said, feeling a bit overwhelmed by the time frame and the amount of work I'd have to do to prepare.

"Don't mind that now," Nana said as if reading my mind, "Your 24 hours off comes first. Then we will make the announcement and open applications with a questionnaire Queen Anora or the High Judges can write. We'll close the applications a day later, and select your team the following day, with interviews as needed. You and your party will still have four days to learn Dolma's manners and customs while the rest of both kingdoms will pack and create all your team may need."

"Right," Father said, and the rest of the table blindly followed Nana once more.

"Okay," I murmured, taken aback by her definitive response.

"Good, good. Now Edgar, Queen Anora, you will go and tell the waiting nobles that we received the aid we need from Dolma through the treaty we have signed with them. The details of this treaty will be revealed at a joint celebration tomorrow evening, which we encourage all knights and nobles to attend. Head Judge Michael, you will send a runner to Dolma with the signed treaty, and the date of Princess Avalynn's arrival with her party of nine. High Judge Miraz, you will gather the knights taken to Dolma, and inform them that we are accepting all aspects of Dolma's treaty, but that they are to keep all details of the treaty a secret until the announcement tomorrow night. Be sure to remind the Nevremerrian knights that this silence is to include Her Majesties and Their Highnesses as well." The tent full of the highest officials in two different countries nodded in the affirmative as they obeyed Nana's orders. "And you," Nana said, rounding on me, "Are going to escape with me!" With that she grabbed my arm and pulled me out of the tent.

Chapter 25

The Way to Say Goodbye

Nana marched me along towards the Nevremerrian side of the camp. However, she did not take us towards the snaking path that would bring us back to the Dormian cliff and, eventually, the palace gardens. Instead, she led us right through some completely unmarked trees right into the middle of the forest. "When I was a young girl," Nana explained, her voice whistling through the trees as she moved adeptly through the roots and bushes that crowded the forest floor. She was completely unhindered by the diminishing light of the setting sun, which cast the sky in lavender as we moved. "I manifested my first spirituality early, as can happen with the first three spiritualities. Even though childhood manifestations are not terribly uncommon, my father, who was a temporary Count in the Utei region, thought he could use me to gain more power while my aunt, the actual Count, was away in the war.

So, my father pushed me into court at just eight years old, under the guise of being a spiritual master. Now, I've told you all a million times how my father's greed caused his downfall and how I came to live with my aunt. But, before all that, I still had to attend boring formal court events for several years. It was during this time that I began to play a little game. My first spirituality was Nature, so I liked to see, at each event, how far I could go into nature without anyone noticing. It was terribly difficult, for at all of the palace dinners, there was often no one to whom a child could talk. However, at big events like the Unajo festival, there were many more people, and even other children allowed to attend. The noise and the crowd in these events made it much easier to slip away.

I'd use my Nature spirituality to take me into the woods and lead me to wherever I wanted to go. It was doing this when I first met your grandfather. He was only 14, and his brother, Houston, had been named the war-time Crown Prince. He was ever so arrogant, a right bastard, really," Nana said, fondly. "He was convinced he would go ride off into war by Houston's side. Of course, he was still a child, so that was ridiculous. Oh, did he hate it when I told him that. He threw a fit entirely unbefitting of a Prince and of a 14 year-old, but it was ever so entertaining. I came back to the spot where I met him for all seven days of the Unajo festival, much to his displeasure. I memorized the route through the trees. Even though there was no set path, I still noted every turn and memorized every funky-looking tree and shrub just to find him again. I did it again the following year at the next Unajo festival, it was different then, though. Houston had died and your grandfather was now the war-time Crown Prince at just 15. I went back to that spot every day of the festival that year, but he never showed. I did it again the year after that with no success. Then Father's crimes were exposed, and I was sent to my aunt and later to a temple. I didn't see your grandfather for another ten years, by which point I'd already mastered two spiritualities, Nature and Wisdom, and was working on my third, Time.

You'll have heard our love story from there, but, what you may not know is that every Unajo festival we'd both slip away and follow the path back to where we first met. And, let me tell you, if you are looking to avoid nosy nobles, but still make it back to the palace, it is the perfect route." Nana tugged my hand a bit more, and pulled me past a final row of trees, beyond which, were the completely empty training grounds. "I present to you, the spot where I first met your grandfather!" Nana declared, triumphantly.

I laughed at her exuberance. "I'm more impressed that you were able to memorize the path. I don't think I could even begin to figure it out," I commented, trying and failing to recall even one turn we'd made to get here. Thinking back, I'm not sure I could even recall where the entrance to Nana's secret route began, nor, between which trees we had exited for that matter.

"You've only been through it once, in the dark, being pulled along by me. Of course you wouldn't be able to memorize it!" Nana laughed. "Come along now, we must go hide away in your room before anyone spots us." Nana grabbed my arm again, dragging me through a side door usually used by the staff, and gestured for me to keep quiet as we slid through the palace halls. I had to hold in my laughter as we hid behind walls or ducked behind furniture to hide from passing people. I felt like a child playing games with my brothers as we chased each other through the palace. When we eventually stepped into my room, I burst into a fit of uncontrollable giggles that bounced their way through my body and reverberated through the room.

I must have startled Charlotte and Ana who were already there, looking at me with curious but kind eyes. "Thank you for your service, ladies," Nana smiled at them, "But, why don't you take the night off and let this grandmother take care of her granddaughter this evening."

"Yes, Your Majesty," Ana and Charlotte smiled, wishing me a good night before exiting the room. I tried to bid them good-night through the occasional giggle that still pushed its way through me. Soon, Nana and I were left alone in the comforting silence of my room.

"Come and sit, my songbird, let me brush out your hair." Nana directed me towards the chair by my vanity. She sat me down facing the mirror, and gently moved the braid my hair had been in towards her. She carefully began picking out the leaves that had gotten caught while we moved through the forest. Her wiry fingers placed each leaf onto the table before she began unwinding my braid. "You've chosen a challenging path, songbird. Many will ask if you are sure, but I will not. I watched your energy fall into place as you made your choice. You spoke your truth and were confident in your answer. I know you have made the decision with your own will and freedom and I am so proud of you for it." She moved to pick up my brush, and began to brush my hair.

"Now, let me be very clear here, I am not proud of you because of which choice you made. I couldn't care less which option you chose because, in reality, you can never be truly certain about what will happen in the future. No, I am proud of you for making a choice based not on the pitfalls of victimhood, but in the power of your own free will. At times, it may seem like the freedom of choice is nothing more than an illusion. People may look at a choice like yours and insist that you had no other option but to go. However, there is a great strength in knowing that there was another option, even if that option was something as severe as death, you can still know that you made the choice. To face the things in life we can't control and say I can at least control myself-- be it your thoughts, your body, or your actions-- is the most powerful thing you can do. You can think of it like battling the Universe and coming out on top.

Still, this path will be filled with challenges. Not to say that other paths won't have their fair share of problems to solve, but this path will likely present some more unique ones than what you have faced in your life thus far. I know you are set on your path, so I will offer you this piece of wisdom," she paused, weaving her fingers through my now soft hair. Her eyes met mine as they reflected into the mirror in front of us, and she continued, "When we tell stories, they always center around grand moments of swift and sudden change, and, as we grow, we may come to believe that, like in the stories, our lives will center around these moments. However, the truth of the matter is that one's life is not built from these grand moments, but rather, life is painstakingly crafted from the banality of the everyday.

It is in the banality that our character grows and our life becomes satisfactory, abundant, and joyful, or where it can become dull, repetitive, and scarce. You see, we cannot always control the grand surprising moments where our lives are forced to change, but the banality of your own life is something you forge all on your own, through the choices you make and the priorities you set. I don't need to tell you of the trials you will face when you leave our country, as I don't know exactly what they will be. And, even if I did, I would be unable to adequately describe what you will feel as you experience them.

Over the coming week, you will no doubt hear the fears and worries of many others, and you will undoubtedly feel a pain at having to leave this place. I cannot protect you from these feelings of sadness, or even taking on the worries of others as your own. So, instead, I will ask of you only this: when you leave this place, do whatever you can to create a banality that brings you joy. Remember, anything you create can always be changed if you decide it no longer serves you."

"I will, Nana," I said. A piercing sensation flying through my chest with the realization that I would soon be leaving her hugs and wisdom behind. Her deep blue eyes were slightly watery as she kissed my forehead and turned me towards her.

"I remember when you were just a little girl," she said, kneeling down in front of me and placing a warm hand on my cheek. "I asked you what you wanted to be when you grew up." I smiled as she spoke, even though she'd told this story many times before. "You told me that you wanted to be a bird and fly in the sky. You knew nothing of the laws of nature that kept humans firmly planted on the ground, and yet, you said it so assuredly that I was convinced that you'd manage it. I still believe it to this day, songbird. If you ever wished to fly, I am positive you will be able to do it. Though I cannot physically be with you for all that is to come, my spirit will always be with you and my soul will always watch over you. The unconditional love I hold for you in my heart transcends all time and distance and will be carried within you forever. From this life to all your lives to come, you will hold my love, Avalynn."

Tears rolled down my cheeks, the hot weight of them burning at my skin. I threw my arms around her, burying my face into her neck and toppling my chair over in the process. I didn't even care if my knees smacked the floor a little harder than I'd anticipated, as long as I never had to release her from my grip. "I love you Nana," I sobbed into her neck, "I am going to miss you." Nana just pulled me close, rubbing soothing circles across my back. Her scent of sage and lavender enveloping me.

"And I, you, my songbird, more than words can say," Nana whispered into my hair. She held me until my tears dried into her neck. "I will come and visit you when I can," Nana decided, "And, of course, we will all be there for your wedding!" I smiled against her.

"My wedding!" I exclaimed suddenly, tearing myself out of Nana's hug. "I forgot to ask Father! His name, I don't know his name, the Crown Prince of Dolma, my betrothed! I don't even know his name!" I stared at Nana for a moment, my eyes wide with shock. A moment later we both collapsed into laughter.

"Oh- oh, I'm sorry, Ava," Nana said breathily, "I'm afraid I don't know his name either!" Giggles took over me again.

"It's all rather ridiculous," I laughed, "I mean who puts arranged marriages into treaties anyways!"

"Well, you're about to find out," Nana replied.

I grinned back, "I suppose so." I slowly stood up, and helped Nana to her feet.

"Take the night off," Nana spoke as she stood. "I'll get the kitchen to make you some food you can eat up here. Go read a book you enjoy, not one to study, but something you actually enjoy. A good romance novel or something like it. Just relax and be, and tomorrow, don't follow any schedule, simply do whatever you wish to."

"Alright, Nana," I smiled.

"There's my girl," she responded back before leaving the room. Not long after, a servant came up with a delicious pasta and chicken dish with a slice of warm bread and today's second apple pie. He also brought a few romance novels, courtesy of my Nana, which caused me to laugh once more. I changed into my night clothes, ate my food, and started one of the books, but I soon found myself staring at the dark sky instead.

Above me a crescent moon hung next to the endless scattering of hundreds of thousands of stars. It felt surreal to me. My life had been so different just this morning. Only a little over a week before my life had experienced another life shattering event. I did note that unlike learning about the drought, the surreal energy that surrounded me now didn't feel lost or hopeless. Instead, I was filled with a calm and confidence that had evaded me before. After all, I thought, I know I am making the best decision for me and everyone else. I can help Nevremerre and Agremerre, and I will work to be the best possible Queen of Dolma. In the quiet of my room, I could admit that I was also a little excited for this new adventure. Of course, I would miss my family and my home terribly, but I couldn't deny the small thrill I got at the idea of exploring somewhere new, with new ideas, and a completely novel culture. There was still a fear of all the new changes, but it blended in with a general excitement about all the new possibilities making it hard to distinguish between the two emotions. Yes, I thought, as I finally turned back to my book, no matter the challenges Dolma would bring, I would find happiness in this new life. I would also make sure I would serve the people of Dolma with all of the grace, wisdom, and love that I had.

Chapter 26

The Last Normal Day

I woke up the next morning to the sound of Ana's voice and Charlotte's gentle prodding as they told me it was time for breakfast. "Good morning, Princess," Ana teased as I finally sat up after a good ten minutes of trying to bury myself into my pillow. "It's unusual for you to sleep in."

"True," I yawned, "but it's very nice!"

"It certainly is!" Charlotte agreed. I languidly moved from my bed. For someone who had just decided to marry a stranger and move to another country, I felt oddly happy as the morning's sunlight peered through my window. My body felt light and free as Charlotte and Ana dressed me in a short green dress and pulled my hair into some sort of half up, half down arrangement. They teased me about my giggles the night before, and I dramatically recounted Nana and my escape from the nobles. Our laughter mixed into the sweet summer air that helped cascade the room in a golden glow.

A whole day with nothing to do but enjoy all of my favorite places in Nera. I felt a quick hit of sadness against my chest as I realized that some of my favorite places in Nevremerre I had already visited for potentially the last time. The mountains of Ninita and the beautiful beaches of Hallea, there would be no time to visit them now. I retained hope that I would see these sights again one day, even if it may not be for a while. I shook off my brief malaise and let my earlier cheer fill me once more as I bounced down to breakfast.

The table was already full as I entered; our usual family meals were still graced by Lord Nicholas and Sir Abel, but I no longer found Lord Nicholas' presence as grating as I once did. Sir Abel's presence, of course, was never really a bother. "Good morning!" I called out with a smile. I moved towards the head of the table where Father sat, and bent down to kiss his cheek.

"Good morning, my gift," Father said, his voice quiet, but heavy with emotion. He reached out and grabbed my hand to kiss it before smiling at me. His eyes were filled with both warmth and sorrow as he continued to hold my hand. I gently pushed my hand out of his grasp before taking a seat between Sir Abel and Al. I ignored the curious looks given to me by the rest of the table.

"So, what do you plan to do today, Songbird?" Nana asked, nonchalantly buttering her toast.

"I haven't decided," I answered honestly, "I know I want to go for a ride, and I'd like to go into town for a bit. Other than that though, I have no solid plans."

"You're not going to train today?" asked Azar as Al simultaneously questioned, "Will you be working at the hospital?"

I pondered each question as I started eating my eggs. "No," I eventually decided. "I'm not sure I'll have the time to train or to work at the hospital. I would go up to the research library, but Murphy has the day off."

"Do you want company?" Nana asked.

"Not at the moment," I decided, "But, I'll let you know if that changes." Nana nodded, and we both continued our meals.

"You're in a good mood," Al said, his voice making his words sound more like a question than a statement.

"I think today will be a good day," I responded simply, giving him a smile.

"After breakfast, Ava, I hope you can spare me a moment. I won't take up too much of your time, but I do have something I'd like to run by you," Father said.

"Of course," I responded. My brothers each gave me an odd look before returning to their own meals.

"Will you have to go to Agremerre today?" Mother asked, looking towards Father.

"Yes, I have a meeting with Queen Anora in the afternoon. We have a few things we must prepare together before we announce the details of the treaty this evening. Ah - but I would like it if the royal family would all enter tonight's event together," he replied with a glance towards me and my brothers.

"Yes, Your Majesty," we all dutifully replied.

"Can we really not know any of the details about the treaty until tonight?" asked Al.

"Yes, I confess, I am also rather curious as to the nature of the treaty," Mother agreed.

"All will be revealed tonight," Father replied. I felt a twitch of sympathy at having made him keep this secret from our family, especially Mother and Mama, but Father continued, apparently unfazed. "If it makes you feel better, the council won't know anything until tonight either, and neither will the High Judges of Agremerre."

"Actually," Mama chimed in, "that does make me feel a little bit better."

"Everyone is being so tight-lipped about it," Azar grumbled. "I mean we got the aid we needed and we are obviously not going to war. So, why all the secrecy? Even the knights who went are tight-lipped about it! Carlos and I grilled Sir Mateo about it for an hour last night and he wouldn't say a thing!"

"Azar!" I cried, "That's terribly rude! Why would you do that to Sir Mateo?"

Azar gave me a sheepish shrug, "We were just curious. We didn't realize there would be so much secrecy around it. Sir Mateo was so closed off about it, he wouldn't even tell us about Dolma."

"Did you learn anything while babysitting Princess Genevieve, Ava?" Ari asked.

"Babies can't talk, Ari," I pointed out. Trying to avoid mentioning that I wasn't actually babysitting my goddaughter last night.

"I know, I know, I just thought you might have overheard something," Ari protested.

"You will all find out the treaty details tonight," Father insisted, "And, don't pester the knights for information until after the announcement. They are acting under my orders to keep the details a secret, so don't give them any grief about it," Father finished sternly.

"Yes, Your Majesty," came Azar's sullen reply.

"I'm not criticizing, Azar," Father's voice softened, "I'm just letting you know for the future. The same rules apply to the rest of you as well."

"Yes, Your Majesty," we all replied.

"Ava, have you finished eating?" Father said, moving to get up.

"Yes, Your Majesty," I replied automatically. Looking down at my food, I decided that even if my reply was unintentional, I had actually finished my food, so I got up to join him as we walked out of the breakfast hall. I followed Father through the palace floors until we got to his office on the third floor. Father quickly ushered me in, closing the door behind him. I walked past the rows of bookshelves toward his large wooden desk. Here sat a large cushioned chair with emerald green fabric turned out to face away from the wall sized window behind him. I looked questioningly at Father, who nodded, before I jumped up to sit on his desk. Father pulled out his chair and turned it to face me.

"I don't want to waste your day off before madness descends, so I'll get straight to the point. I'd like to tell your mothers and brothers about the treaty prior to the event tonight." Dread filled my heart, sinking into my core like an anchor in water.

"No," I said instantly.

"My gift," Father said, "I don't want to blindside them with this tonight. They will have more questions that will be answered by Anora and me in our speeches. I already had to shock you and your siblings about the drought. I don't wish to have to shock them again."

Intellectually, I knew he was right. I remembered the heartbreak and shock I felt when I learned about the drought for the first time. I did not wish that experience for my brothers again or for my mothers a first time. Emotionally, I couldn't bare the thought of having their gazes change as they heard. To have to go through a noble event where they wouldn't be my comrades in arms, but rather another set of staring eyes upon me. I wanted the comfort that came from being one of four children of the King instead of the solitude that would come from being the Princess that was bartered off to another land. I knew that going to Dolma was my choice, but many would still likely view me as a martyr or a victim, and although they may respond differently, I couldn't stand the thought that my brothers or mothers would think that. As such, I was loathe to give up even a minute of my previous normalcy on something so uncertain.

"Mother and Mama pick me up before most big events; they comment on my outfit and tell me I look pretty. Ari's the first person I go to at any gathering. I check in on him and ask him how he's doing. He'll usually make an insightful comment or two about the surrounding nobles. Azar will come find me next. He'll direct me towards a friendly face or just try to make me laugh, just to make sure I am doing okay. Every five minutes, Al looks around the space we are in, and he won't stop looking until he spots each of us, and, if we ever look uncomfortable, he comes to us right away. He thinks we don't notice, but he's been doing it ever since we've entered society. At some point it gets pretty hard to miss.

We all know that everyone else can handle noble gatherings on their own, but we do all this anyway. I think we do all this because we get comfort in having people in the room that we do not have to work to impress and that have no expectations for us. I don't know what everyone will do when they learn that I'll be leaving, but I know it won't be the same. They will seek me out not because they find comfort in my presence, but rather, I think that they will worry about me on my own. I know it would be kinder to tell them, but I find I want to be selfish for just a bit longer. And be a comforting presence for those I love."

"Oh, my gift," Father sighed, grabbing my hands as his eyes filled again with tears. "The Universe gave me such a precious treasure in giving me you. This is, of course, your choice, and we will do what you want. However, I will say, the people of this family only wish to provide you with the same comfort that you seek to give us."

"But I don't need comfort, Father! I've made my decision, and I am satisfied with it," I exclaimed.

"I know, my gift, and I understand the point you're making. So, what do you want to do?"

I thought for a moment. "Before we exit the palace together," I began, "tell our family that the details of the treaty will be surprising, but, after the announcement, we will have a family meeting where everyone can ask questions and discuss the future. Do you think that will work?" I concluded.

Father sat quietly before responding, "Yes. That should work. They will still be shocked, but they will at least know to expect that. We will need to stay to address noble concerns, but if we stay an hour after the announcement, that should be enough. You'll have an hour at the event before we give our announcement. After we make the announcement, I won't ask you to stay at the event if you do not want to. You can plan to meet us in the small drawing room, if you wish."

"No," I shook my head. "I'll stay after the announcement. I won't run away."

Father beamed at me. "Alright, come up toward Anora and me when we take questions then. It'd be best to have you stand by us."

"It will be okay, Father," I said, "After all, we're protecting all of Nevremerre and Agremerre from hunger this year."

Father pulled me to his chest, crushing me into a large hug. "I love you ever so much, my gift." We stayed like that for several minutes, my head cradled in his broad chest before he finally pulled back. "I likely won't see you until tonight, so I will wish you luck, courage, and happiness throughout this day. I will also tell you just one more thing: whatever the reactions of our family, just remember that everything they do or say is out of love for you.

"I'll remember, Father."

"Alright, go have fun, my gift, I will see you tonight." I said goodbye and left Father's office making my way down to the stables. I'd just passed the rose garden when a voice called out, "Princess!" I turned to see Mateo running behind me. He was out of his knights uniform, wearing a simple green tunic with brown trousers instead. His black hair was pulled back into his usual ponytail, but pieces of it looked to be falling out, and sweat trickled down his tan skin.

"Mateo, is something wrong?" I asked.

"Ah-no, not really," Mateo looked around before stepping closer to me. Despite his sweat, a rather non-offensive scent of fresh soil and sword polish clouded me as he entered my space. "His Majesty told us yesterday that you agreed to Dolma's terms," he rushed out. "He also told us that you would be taking a delegation with you when you leave. I want you to know that I volunteered for that delegation last night. I would like you to accept my application and let me move to Dolma with you as your knight."

I stood in shock at Mateo's proclamation. I searched his face for any sign that he was joking, but his honey colored eyes held nothing but sincerity. "But Mateo, what about your family or Nevremerre? This place is your home," I finally breathed out.

Mateo smiled at me, "I'm quite confident that you will allow me to come visit my family every so often and I'm usually away from them most of the year anyways. We've gotten used to communicating through letters, and, honestly, Princess, I believe you will be a wonderful ruler, no matter the country. Dolma is a strange and somewhat scary place. I wish to support you through your life there. As a knight, it is the greatest honor to serve a great ruler, and I know that is you. I want to serve you in whatever country you end up."

I stared at him as he spoke, sincerity and passion ringing through every word, and soon, I felt something wet slide down my cheeks. "Princess!" Mateo exclaimed, worry marring his features. I quickly wiped at my tears, although they still continued to fall.

"I'm sorry," I said, dabbing at my face. "It's just that, I thought I'd be alone, and I was okay with that, this was my choice after all. But, now you want to come with me, and I'm just so relieved and happy." I beamed up at him through my tears, and threw my arms around his neck, pulling him into a hug. "Thank you. Thank you so much for coming with me, for wanting to come with me. I would be honored to have you by my side."

I pulled away, and Mateo caught my hand. Kneeling down, he said, "I will happily serve you, Princess Avalynn, until the day I die."

I laughed, overflowing with relief and joy, "Mateo, let's go to Dolma together." After that, Mateo joined me on my ride, and we spoke in hushed tones of all that Dolma might bring.

"It was a weird place," Mateo admitted, "We were really only there for a day and a half, but you could tell that we weren't really welcome, or, at the very least, they were judging us harshly. And, even though everyone was smiling, the air felt heavy, like the whole room was struggling to breathe. No one did anything to us, of course, but I was constantly on edge. I think we all were, really. Hopefully it will be better when you come as Crown Princess, but even if it isn't, I'm still very happy to serve you," Mateo smiled at me.

"Thank you," I replied before jumping in my saddle and turning towards him. "Oh, I almost forgot! You can tell me his name. What's the Crown Prince's name? The one I am going to marry."

Mateo stared at me blankly for a moment. "It's very weird to be asked by someone what their betrothed name is," he decided. "But, the answer is Thomas. In Dolma, people have multiple names. I think he has three or four, but all the nobles called him "His Highness, Crown Prince Thomas."

"Thomas," I said, turning the name over in my mouth, "There are worse names," I said.

When we finished our ride, I excused Mateo and headed into town. My mood stayed high as I decided to just walk around the city. It was a hot afternoon, which, I supposed, made sense for mid-day in the summer of a drought. Still, it was enjoyable to be in town. The cheerful shouts of children playing in the shaded areas filled the streets and restaurants buzzed with activity. There was a happy and lazy energy that swirled around, touching all who wandered through. Drawn in by the sunshine haze and the people's smiles, I spent the next few hours simply walking the streets, stopping by various food stands to purchase iced teas and juices, along with various snacks. I then sat in a nearby park watching all manner of people and animals pass by. It was peaceful, and I relished every second of it. I soaked up the sun and the pleasant calm the city had granted. All too soon it was time to head back, and I took a pay-to-ride carriage back to the palace.

Dread filled me as the carriage rolled closer to the palace. Nerves knotted in my stomach and screamed that I was not ready for the world to know of my engagement. When my feelings could not be swayed by my rational brain pointing out that people would have to find out eventually, I switched to repeating the mantra "the announcement hasn't happened yet." This was accompanied by an incessant focus on the houses passing in the carriage window, and violently listening to the sound of wheels on the cobbled stone and the horses clicking along ahead. This was more successful, but still could not completely quench the nervousness bubbling inside me. I walked through the palace, and nodded at the eager nobles milling around, hoping my nerves wouldn't show.

Finally, I reached my room, and pulled open my wardrobe as I waited for Ana and Charlotte. I put more thought into my outfit tonight than I'd ever put into any other outfit in my life. I needed something that would radiate authority when I stood next to Father and Anora, but would not be too noticeably different from my siblings. Eventually, I decided on a slim fitting purple dress with a slit that ran up my left leg. I'd wear the jewelry set that matched my crown, and I'd raise my head high when Father made his announcement. "It will all be okay," I whispered to myself.

Chapter 27

The Announcement

After a bath and various lotions and creams being slathered onto my face and body. I slid into my dress, and let Charlotte put my hair into some sort of elaborate updo. Mother and Mama came in as Charlotte and Ana filled in the final touches. "Oh how lovely!" Mama bounced in. Her joy brought a smile to my face. Her own gown was a stunning red to match her hair.

"The purple is a good choice," Mother smiled approvingly, taking my crown and placing it gently upon my head. "It's an excellent way to show your support for the country." I noted that Mother's own gown was gold with purple embroidery coating the skirt.

"Thank you," I beamed, looking at each of them.

"Shall we go then?" Mama asked, grabbing my hand excitedly. "I'm ever so curious about what the terms of the treaty are!" she exclaimed. I felt my heart drop a little at her words, but followed her out nonetheless.

"Patience, Diana," Mother said soothingly, linking her arm with Mama's. "We will know soon enough. How was your day, Ava?" I launched into a glowing review of my work-free day, eager to change the subject as we walked into the smallest drawing room where we would meet up with the rest of our family. Surprisingly, or perhaps not when one knew the situation, Father and Nana were already waiting as we entered the room.

"My, my Edgar," Mother teased, "It's not like you to be early."

"I'm not completely useless, Elenore," Father joked. "Besides, I have something to tell you all once the boys arrive."

"What is it?" Mama asked, sitting down on the nearby couch.

"I think the idea is to wait until the whole family is here, darling," Mother smiled, sitting down next to her. I perched myself on the couch's arm rest as we waited for my brothers to trickle in. When Ari walked in last, Father stood and turned towards the rest of us. My stomach fluttered with nerves as he spoke.

"Before we go tonight. I want you all to know that the details of this treaty are likely going to be a big shock," he raised his hand to silence the mouths that had been opened in response. "I have agreed," he continued when the threat of interruption had passed, "to keep the details of the treaty a secret from everyone until the announcement this evening. However, once the announcement has been made, you are all likely to have questions and/or opinions that will not be answered as we address the general public. Therefore, we will all meet back here an hour after my announcement to discuss the treaty as a family. I would also like to add that none of you are required to stay at the gathering after the announcement is made, and if you wish to leave immediately and wait back here for an hour, I will completely support you. Now, does anyone have any questions that I can answer?" A pregnant silence filled the room. "No? Good. Then let's head out!" Father said, and we all stood to follow him out.

We moved out in groups of two, the eyes of any remaining nobles fixed upon us as they hurried behind us. Ari was next to me as we moved through the woods. "I wonder what the terms of the treaty are," he said curiously as we walked. "Maybe the terms aren't favorable, and that's the shock."

"I don't know about that. I doubt Father would accept unfavorable terms," I said vaguely. I was trying not to think about the announcement too much, but I guess it would be expected that my family would talk about it. "I wouldn't worry about it too much," I implored, "We won't be able to know for sure until Father's announcement anyways."

"I guess so," Ari acknowledged. "With this much secrecy though, I'm not sure the details can be good."

"Just wait for Father's announcement," I practically pleaded before switching the subject, "What did you do today?" Ari dove into telling me about his new goal to spend more time mastering the longsword and trying to socialize with the knights.

"It's difficult because they are all very nice, but I'm not sure how to approach them in a friendly manner. I don't know what else to talk about other than fighting," Ari lamented. I opened my mouth to try and offer some advice before I suddenly realized that I had made all my friends because they had worked around me for an extended period of time.

"It is difficult to talk to people, isn't it?" I responded instead. "Maybe you should try asking Azar?" Ari quickly agreed that this was the best solution as we finally reached the border. All tents had, at last, been taken down, and the area was filled with trays of drinks and small snacks. Lanterns were strung up between trees. They were all unlit now, as the early evening sun was still present, but no doubt they would paint the forest a fiery orange soon enough.

There was already a huge crowd of nobles and knights from both countries present when we arrived, and Ari and I were soon surrounded by nobles clamoring for our attention. I gave Ari a quick supportive smile before facing the crowd of nobles in front of me. I made small talk with the nobles, including a group of Agremerrians who thanked me for delivering Princess Genevieve. It still wasn't my favorite task, but I greatly appreciated the normality in my interactions with everyone. I still found myself exceptionally grateful, however, when Mateo pulled me away.

"When will the King make his announcement?" he whispered in my ear.

"In about 30 minutes," I replied, my heart sinking at the little time I had left. Mateo just nodded.

"I will be at your side when the announcement is made," he declared softly. I squeezed his arm before replying, "Thank you." Once again, I was exceptionally grateful to this man.

"Has he told you anything about Dolma yet?" Carlos' voice startled me slightly as he came over with Azar by his side.

"I will tell you all about it, once His Majesty makes his speech," Mateo replied, dutifully.

"Don't pester him, Carlos," Azar scolded, "He is following His Majesty's orders."

"Yes, yes, but he is also our friend and should be able to tell us something," Carlos insisted.

"Carlos," Azar said seriously, "he is following the instructions of our King, and we will give him no more grief for doing so."

"Thank you, Your Highness," Mateo bowed.

"I'm sorry," Carlos conceded. "Is everyone excited to leave Nera? Rumor is we will be back to traveling around Nevremerre in a week or two!"

"I'm looking forward to it," Azar agreed cheerfully. "I always enjoy seeing the different regions of Nevremerre and getting to meet with people from all over the country. All of them have such different and interesting stories." We continued to talk about traveling through Nevremerre for a while, and I basked in the fuzzy comfort that could be found in the idle chatter of the people I loved and trusted. Soon enough, we moved on, having to fulfill our duties as Prince and Princess and speak to the nobility. I caught Al looking over at me as I moved across the forest to speak with some other nobles. A sense of completion filled me as Al quickly turned away. I still didn't know if I was ready to have everyone else learn of my upcoming marriage, but, at the very least, I had experienced one last normal day in my home.

I was talking with Marchioness Eliza about her son once more when Mateo moved to be by my side. With a quick glance at him, I knew the moment of truth was nearly upon us. My ability to process the Marchioness' words halted as I looked about the crowd to find my father. He wasn't too far away, standing with Anora and mixed into a crowd of people who appeared to be made up mostly of council members and High Judges. As if he could feel my gaze, Father looked up in my direction. Our eyes met, and he gave me a quick nod before whispering to Anora and they excused themselves from the crowd.

A quick bump from Mateo brought me back to my own conversation where Marchioness Eliza was staring at me pointedly. "Ah, forgive me Marchioness," I managed to say, "Only I believe His Majesty and Queen Anora are ready to make their announcement." I said pointing at Father who was helping Anora onto a wooden platform that must have been set up at some point during the last hour.

"Oh, how right you are, Princess. Well we must try to get closer," Marchioness Eliza exclaimed, before hurrying off towards the platform. I, however, stayed behind with Mateo.

"Are you all right, Princess?" Mateo asked.

"I'm well enough," I responded, "I just don't feel the need to rush towards hearing information I already know."

"Ladies, gentlemen, and the ungendered," Father's voice boomed across the clearing. "If you could please gather around, Queen Anora and I will now disclose the details of our new treaty with Dolma." The eager crowd shuffled towards them. I hung back with Mateo, taking up space at the edge of the crowd. I focused diligently on Father and Anora, and I tried to avoid spotting the rest of my family in the crowd. "We ask," Father continued, "that everyone remain silent while we explain the details of the treaty. Due to the size of the crowd we have here today, if people were to make their own comments while we are speaking, it would likely result in several people missing important details." Father paused, looking around the crowd before nodding.

"After the announcement," Anora spoke this time, "we will have a question and answer session, so please save your questions and comments until then." There was another pause before Anora spoke once more. "As you know, just nine days ago, King Edgar of Nevremerre went to the country of Dolma to negotiate a deal for drought aid for both Nevremerre and Agremerre. As we told you yesterday, we have succeeded in receiving that aid."

"In return, Nevremerre and Agremerre have agreed to support Dolma if they go to war with Calvine. We are confident that with both Nevremerre and Agremerre's support, Calvine is unlikely to lead an attack," Father continued.

"Beyond the promise of military support, Agremerre will also increase weapons and armor sales to Dolma by five percent for the next five years. This, we believe, will boost Agremerre's economy while the drought occurs, but still make it difficult for Dolma to create a military as strong as ours."

"Overall," Father said, slipping in so seamlessly to Anora's section that I felt sure they must have practiced this earlier in the afternoon, "we believe this to be a very beneficial deal for all countries involved. However, Dolma did have one final request." Father's eyes met mine as he spoke. "This request was not something that Queen Anora and I were expecting, and it is not anything that would even be considered in our cultures. However, Dolma made it a requirement in order for us to sign the treaty. It is the Universe's greatest blessing that I have a daughter who is compassionate and understanding, and agreed to the final condition for the good of the people of Nevremerre and Agremerre. The final condition being that Princess Avalynn moves to Dolma and marries their Crown Prince."

Chaos fell swiftly, descending on the waiting crowd like a summer storm. Cries of shock and outrage filled the air.

"What?"

"But she's only 19!"

"How could they even ask that?"

"Has she ever even been to Dolma?" All around me the voices of hundreds of people swirled. Their calls whistling around me like a tornado trying to sweep me up in their wind.

I had an instinctual desire to run away, to hide out in the forest where nobody could find me. I briefly entertained the notion of subsisting on mushrooms and herbs living in a tree somewhere before I pushed the thought out of my mind. Instead, I held my head up high and called out, "Excuse me." I didn't scream the command. I simply said it towards the crowd in front of me, and yet, somehow it worked, perhaps because most were looking at me anyways. My voice was able to cut through the storm, calm the hurricane, and bring the thundering voices to a low rumble. I moved towards the stage where

Father and Anora stood. Nobles parted like the trees on a forest path as I moved steadily forward. I worked to ignore the eyes following me as I made my way up towards the platform. Once there, I turned and faced the waiting crowd. Nowhere in the original plan was there mention of me making any sort of speech, but I felt that I couldn't leave things as they were.

"Thank you everyone," I began, "for the concern you are showing me right now. I understand the confusion you are feeling about the situation, as I believe everyone on this platform has felt the same way when we heard the condition. However, I want to assure you that the terms of this treaty are perfectly acceptable in Dolma's culture where I am well above the female age of majority. And, the decision to go to Dolma to marry the Crown Prince was, and is, my own. I was told all of the terms of this treaty, and I made the choice that I believe best for everyone involved, including myself. All I've ever wanted to do as a Princess of Nevremerre, and as a person, is to help people. I have no ability to stop or even prevent natural disasters like this drought. However, through this treaty, I've been granted the ability to help millions of people in Nevremerre, Agremerre, and even in Dolma as their Crown Princess and future Queen. I am very happy about the opportunity to help so many, so I would like to ask you all to please support me and my decision. Now, having said that, I believe His Majesty King Edgar, and Her Majesty Queen Anora have more to say." I took a deep breath and stepped back. Trying to keep the nervousness out of my eyes as I look back at the now silent crowd.

"Thank you, Princess Avalynn," Father smiled at me, pride glowing through his emerald eyes. Anora grabbed my hand and gave it a tight squeeze as Father spoke once more, "We've agreed to all aspects of the treaty, and both Nevremerre and Agremerre will be receiving enough food to feed both nations."

"That encapsulates the details of the treaty, however, we would also like to discuss some positions available in relation to Princess Avalynn's move," Queen Anora continued. "In accordance with Dolma's traditions, and for the safety and security of Princess Avalynn, we are asking for volunteers to move with the Princess. We will not force anyone to go, if no one wishes to volunteer, but, if anyone is willing, we are looking for six knights, two maids, and one daughter of a noble family who will fill a Dolmanian position called a "lady in waiting". We want to encourage people from both Nevremerre and Agremerre to apply, and we want to stress that, for all who apply, your allegiance will no longer live with Nevremerre or Agremerre or Dolma. If you choose to volunteer, your allegiance must lie solely with Princess Avalynn.

To apply for a position, you must answer the questions posted on the notice boards in both Agremerre and Nevremerre. Due to the vastly different culture and laws in Dolma, the application will contain very personal questions. I wish to make it perfectly clear that these questions are for your own safety and so it is vital that they be answered honestly and completely."

"Due to the hastened timescale brought on by a need for supplies, these applications will be due by tomorrow at six in the evening. Interviews will be conducted the following day, and final decisions will be made directly after that," Father took over. "Those chosen will be expected to attend classes on Dolmanian etiquette for the four days immediately after their selection. Then, six days from today, Princess Avalynn and her delegation will leave for Dolma." There was a slight gasp at the date of my departure, but the crowd seemed unwilling to break the ordered silence from their two rulers again.

"We will now be taking any questions from the crowd. We ask that you raise your hands to ask questions, and we will call on you," Anora concluded.

"We also ask that you please continue to remain silent unless we call on you to ask a question. You are, of course, free to leave at any point, but we ask that if you do so you try to keep quiet for those who are choosing to stay. Now, we will give you a minute to talk amongst yourselves before we begin the question-and-answer session." Father finished speaking and turned his back towards the crowd. This motion effectively blocked me from the crowd's view. "Well done, my gift," Father said to me as a hum of voices broke out behind him. "I'll admit, I was not expecting as large of a reaction as we got, but you handled the crowd beautifully and I couldn't be prouder."

"Nor I," Anora agreed, also turning towards me.

"Thank you both," I said. "Also," I rushed on, "I accepted Sir Mateo to be one of my knights. He said he applied last night, and I figured, as a part of Father's initial delegation, he would be all right. Was that okay?"

"Of course, darling," Anora said, patting my hair affectionately. "He's actually not the only knight in your Father's party that volunteered, according to Miraz," Anora continued to my deep surprise, "I was actually going to recommend you take at least a few of them as they have some experience in Dolma."

"I must say, I am rather relieved at you having Sir Mateo by your side. I am completely confident he will serve you well. Do you think it's time to start answering questions now?" Father said, looking towards Anora.

"Now's as good of a time as any," Anora shrugged. "Avalynn, if there are any questions you wish to answer, just let us know and you may do so." With one big breath, Father and Anora turned back towards the crowd, exposing me to their stares once more. Father held up a pointless hand for silence, as the crowd had hushed itself when Anora and Father turned around.

"It is now time for the question and answer session," Father said.

"Before we begin, I would like to update you that Princess Avalynn has already accepted a knight who was preapproved for the job, having visited Dolma with His Majesty King Edgar on his mission. As such, only five knights will be needed for the delegation." Anora jumped in. I was astonished by the smooth transition that I knew they had not practiced.

"And, with that knowledge, we will now begin the question and answer session," Father said, without missing a beat.

"Please raise your hand if you have a question." A sea of hands shot up into the air. The sight of so many almost made me take a step back, but I controlled myself before I could do so. Father pointed to someone in the crowd.

"Thank you. May I ask how the Princess is to marry someone when she hasn't even reached the age of majority? Is she not only 19?"

Anora was the one to answer stating, "In Dolma, the age of majority of women is 16, so while the Princess is still young in our culture, it is perfectly acceptable in Dolma." Anora moved to pick a new person.

"When will the Princess's wedding take place?" That, it struck me, was probably something I should know.

"The wedding date will be decided upon Princess Avalynn's arrival in Dolma " Father responded, calling on another noble.

"Where should we turn in applications for Princess Avalynn's party?" My head turned quickly towards the newest voice. A strong-looking man, probably in his early thirties, was waiting expectantly for a response. My heart leapt into my chest and I quickly smiled at him. In truth, I didn't really believe that there would be those who wanted to join me in Dolma. Just having Mateo join me felt like a huge sacrifice on his part, and so, I was immensely grateful to all who might volunteer.

"Agremerrians should drop off applications with the High Judges, while Nevremerrians should submit their applications to the council," Anora responded. One by one the crowd's questions were answered. With the exception of one question about when the food relief would be delivered, all the questions were related to my upcoming marriage. I learned, frankly, a slightly disturbing amount about my own wedding, and I had to internally curse myself for not asking more questions. Not that the answers would have in any way changed my mind, but I probably should have learned more of what I was about to do before this meeting.

The full name of my betrothed was, apparently, Thomas Rayforth Ecardio Davenforth Carleon, Crown Prince of Dolma. My family and Anora would attend the wedding, but whether or not other nobles could attend would depend on Dolma. I would still be a candidate in Nevremerre's succession competition, and I could still, potentially, be selected for Nevremerre's throne. This last one came as a major shock, especially after learning I couldn't even remove myself from consideration for another two years! Beyond this, there were also several questions about Dolmanian culture that no one had an answer for. After about 45 minutes, all questions had been answered, and Father closed the official portion of tonight's events. He and Anora invited everyone to enjoy the food and drinks provided before excusing himself and me from the rest of the evening. Taking my hand, Father led me away from the crowd and back towards the palace.

"I know I've already said it, but you did amazing today, my gift," Father said as we walked arm in arm back towards the palace. "It takes a lot of courage to speak confidently in front of a crowd filled with turmoil."

"Thank you, Father," I replied.

"Are you ready to talk with our family?" Father asked.

"I'm not really sure," I admitted, "on the one hand, I want them to know everything there is to know about my decision, so that they can all help me prepare to leave and to support me. On the other hand, I'm worried that they might be angry at me for not telling them sooner, or worse, they will somehow blame themselves for me having to leave."

Father sighed, "I can understand their feelings, if they do. I have been having a hard time not blaming myself for the decision you had to make."

"It's not like you can control the weather, Father, and you had no way of knowing Dolma would ask for an arranged marriage as a treaty condition. Besides, at the end of the day, it was my decision to make. I was not lying when I said that I was happy with my choice."

"That's what your Nana said," Father sighed once more. "She gave me what was essentially a two-hour transitioning session disguised as a 'friendly chat' this morning."

I laughed, "That sounds like Nana," I agreed. We walked in silence for a bit, steadily approaching the palace. "I couldn't look at them," I confessed in our shared silence. "Mother, Mama, and the boys. I couldn't look at them as we made the announcement. I couldn't even look at them as we did the question and answer session, I looked over the crowd instead. I was too afraid to see their reactions."

"I believe your Mother left before the question and answer session, your Mama went shortly after. Nana left before the announcement so that she could be there for all who left early. All of your brothers were still there when we left. There will, undoubtedly, be some anger, but please remember, Avalynn, any anger that is directed at you or me comes from a place of hurt. We are hurt that you'll be moving so far away, we're hurt that your life will be so different from any sort of happy ending known to us, and, most likely, they will be hurt that you didn't tell them sooner. Unfortunately, we lack the ability to heal all the hurt they may be feeling, but we will try our best to soothe whatever we can and respect their right to the feelings we cannot heal." I nodded and we continued along the forest path.

Chapter 28

The Thoughts of
Those I Love

Not long after we made it into the castle, from there it was only a matter of moments until we reached the small drawing room. We stopped momentarily in front of a large wooden door before I nodded at Father and we walked inside. We were instantly greeted by the rushed sight of Mama's fiery hair as she stormed towards us. She had just opened her mouth to say something, when a loud, furious voice boomed over us.

"Edgar, how dare you sell my daughter," Mother's voice spat. This effectively shut Mama up as she turned towards where Mother was standing across the room. Mother looks positively ethereal glaring down at Father. Her voice radiated authority as her words shot at Father with the precision of several thousand knives. Her back was straight and her head held high as her eyes peeled Father open, demanding a response. Her golden dress reflected upon her golden crown which glowed around her black skin. The dignity and righteous fury that encompassed every fiber of her being rolled out with such thunder, one could easily mistake her for a goddess or something even more powerful, if such a creature existed.

"Elenore," Father gasped, struck speechless for a moment in trying to respond. "She- I- they," Father struggled, any semblance of composure lost to him. "She's - she's my daughter too," he finally replied, his shoulders sagging heavily around him. This softened Mother's face for a moment, but it now gave Mama a chance to jump in instead.

"She is not!" Mama yelled angrily at Father, "Real parents do not sell their children! Until further notice she's my and Elenore's child!" A loud bang filled the room as the door slammed open and Al, Azar, and Ari entered the room.

Azar rushed in first, clearly responsible for the earlier noise. He bulldozed his way towards me and clasped both of my arms and physically carried me towards the center of the room. "What in the Gods' names were you thinking?!" He screamed at me. I flinched at the volume of his voice so close to my ears.

"She can't possibly be expected to go marry this stranger," Al said, turning towards Father, "If someone must go, I will marry him instead. I, at least, am the age of majority."

"That's right! How could you do this, Edgar! She's only 19!" Mama said.

"If nothing else," I commented dryly, still stuck in Azar's grasp, "this whole ordeal has at least proven that the whole country is very aware of my age."

"Don't joke," snapped Mama, "This is your life we're talking about."

"I think if anyone has the right to joke about my life, it's me," I responded back.

"Stop being so flippant about this!" Azar yelled again, "I also volunteer, Father, I will also go to Dolma to marry the Prince."

"None of you are going to be sold off like cattle to some foreign Prince!" Mama exclaimed.

"I'm not cattle!" I cried out.

"I know, that's what I'm trying to say!" Mama yelled back.

I took a deep breath, "I'm not being sold, Mama. This was my choice. Father would have gone to war if I said no. No one's sold me. I simply chose the option that I believed would be best, and that will make me the happiest. I get to save thousands of people from death and hundreds of thousands of people from starvation simply by marrying this guy. It's not exactly a bad deal."

"The point is, Avalynn," Al glared at me, "you shouldn't have to marry him."

"But, this is how it's done in Dolma. There's no use denying that my options are to marry the Crown Prince or go to war. My choice is far less bloody."

"That's why Al or I should go!" Azar explained. "Why does it have to be you?"

"You're not going to go to Dolma, Azar," I replied, a little frustrated. "For starters, you're not even attracted to men. How could we possibly ask you to marry one."

"Some guys can be good looking. I could make it work!" Azar insisted, as I looked at him skeptically. "I could!" he tried once more. "I could just close my eyes or something."

"For your whole marriage, which could last the rest of your life? Azar that's the stupidest thing I've ever heard," Al said condescendingly. "This is why I should go. I'm of age and I'm attracted to men."

"Neither of you can go," Father said sternly. "Dolma does not allow same-sex marriages, and don't ask me why, I do not know. Avalynn Is the only one who can go, and she has chosen to do so. This is no longer up for debate, now is the time to ask questions and support Ava as she prepares to leave." Al and Azar moved to speak, but were stopped by Mother as she strode from her spot across the room towards me. Her previous energy still lingered, silencing the rest of us without even saying a word.

She stopped in front of me, placing a gentle hand on my cheek before tilting my eyes up towards hers. "Avalynn, my dear,". Even though she spoke quietly, her voice echoed across the room, "Are you sure?" she asked me.

"Yes," I said confidently, filling the still air her words had left behind. "Yes, I am sure."

"Okay," she said simply. Pulling away from me and breaking the spell she'd cast on us all.

"Okay? How can you be okay with this, Elenore?" Mama exclaimed.

"Because she is sure, and it is her choice. There was a reason we decided on the age of maturity at 21, but that doesn't mean that people younger can't make big decisions about their lives. I was just 18 when I decided I wanted to marry Edgar. It was a big decision that I made not just about love, but about being a ruler of a country. I can honestly say I was completely unprepared for what was to come, but it was still my choice and I've never once regretted it. Ava was given a choice, and made her decision. I know she has made the decision she thinks is best, for all involved, and I will support her in it." I threw my arms around her.

"Thank you, Mother," I said into her chest.

"You are not just your father's precious gift, my darling." she whispered to me, "I will support you however I can."

"I will go with her!" Al and Azar said simultaneously before exchanging glares at each other.

"You can't all go!" Ari said suddenly. I turned to look at my youngest brother. His face was red with tears as he looked helplessly at us all.

"Oh Ari," Father, Mother, and Mama all moved determinedly towards him. Each trying to awkwardly hold him as he cried.

"If they go, I have to go too!" he cried.

"Don't worry," Father soothed, "they won't all go."

"Why not?" Azar protested. "Ava got a choice, shouldn't we get one too!"

"Someone has to rule Nevremerre," I scolded, "We can't just all leave the country because I'm leaving. I'm going to be okay, you don't have to come and protect me."

"Besides," Father chimed in, "I don't think either of you would meet Anora's requirements for joining Avalynn's party. Al because same sex relationships are banned in Dolma and –"

"All the more reason to have one of us join Ava in such a weird and backwards place!" exclaimed Azar.

"And Azar because he would be unable to keep his mouth shut and may cause a diplomatic incident," Father continued looking pointedly at Azar.

"Okay, that's fair, but it's still a backwards place," Azar conceded.

"Your sister doesn't need your protection anyways," Mama said, finally coming around.

"I know that!" protested Al, "I just don't want her to be alone."

"She won't be," Father said, pulling him into a hug. "We will all support her with all we have from here, and she will have a whole delegation of people to be by her side. Including, the already appointed, Sir Mateo."

"I suppose that's better than nothing," Azar grumbled.

"So you're really going?" Ari asked, still being held between Mother and Mama.

"Yes, I am," I nodded.

"But I'll miss you," he said quietly, and I felt my heart shatter just a little bit as I looked back at him.

"I'll miss you too," my voice broke as I responded back. Large arms moved around me, and soon I was surrounded by the arms of my family as we moved into a group hug. I let myself fall into the embrace of those who loved me, and I felt quiet tears fall down my cheeks. I was so very blessed to be loved this much, I thought as we all finally pulled away, not a dry eye among us.

"All better now?" Nana asked from a chair in the corner causing me to jump. I'd completely forgotten she was meant to be here.

"Yes," Father replied, "although I thought you were meant to help soothe us all." he scrutinized Nana with his eyes.

"Emotions are not meant to be hidden, or even soothed. They should simply be allowed to be," Nana said sagely. "It was far more beneficial to all of you to let things play out as they did. I was simply here to ensure that all of your feelings were heard and understood by everyone in the room, and you all did that quite marvelously without me."

"Okay, Mom," Father said, only a little bit of exasperation leaking through his tone.

"So what happens now?" Ari hiccuped.

"We will all have to help Ava prepare to leave," Mother said. "You'll likely need a whole new wardrobe, do we know what the weather is like in Dolma?"

"Should we also have her design her wedding dress?" Mama asked excitedly.

"Oh yes!" Mother turned towards me, "I don't know what Dolma's wedding traditions will be, but you should make sure that they also incorporate some of Nevremerre's traditions as well. Even if you aren't marrying for love, a wedding can be a very fun event, so it's important that you get your fair say in the proceedings. I will need to teach you debating and negotiation tactics."

"You taught me that when I was fifteen," I pointed out.

"Well you'll need a refresher!"

"I'm already going to have to take etiquette lessons with Anora. When exactly am I going to have time to take a refresher course on negotiation tactics?!" I said, more than a bit overwhelmed.

Mother thought for a moment, "Tomorrow," she decided.

"No, she can't tomorrow," Father chimed in, "I'm sure Dolma will have their own methods of preparing their future Queen, but I want her to do some of the Nevremerre Queen preparation tasks as well." My heart raced at the thought of doing ruling prep work. Everyone knew that Nevermerre had a very specific training program for its Crown Prince or Princess before they could take the throne, but the exact process is a secret for all those who don't go through it. When we were younger, my brothers and I had spent several hours discussing what might occur, ranging from Ari's "It's probably just more lessons," to Azar's "They probably take you on a super special quest to fight all the kingdom's monsters!" In Azar's defense, he was only twelve at the time.

"Calm down, both of you," Nana intervened, "while it's true that we have a lot to teach Avalynn before she goes, we cannot take all of her time. She does need a bit of time to enjoy her last week in Nevremerre."

"Oh don't say that!" Mama cried. "It's so sad," she said, pulling me into a hug. "My baby is leaving."

"I thought I was the baby," Ari said, a bit confused.

"Just an expression, darling," Mother said, running a hand through his hair, "you're still our baby."

"Okay," Father said, clapping his hands together, "here's the plan: each of us will take on the logistical details for Avalynn's departure. We will do all the packing, prepare the needed horses and carriages, prepare the funds and food she might need, and ensure that she finds the best possible delegation. Ava, will of course have the final say in staffing choice, but we can do preliminary interviews. That way, the only thing Ava will have to focus on is her studies with Anora and the brief lessons Elenore and I will give her. Sound good?"

"Yes!" rang out a chorus of my family's voices.

"Right, Ava, you'll have a two-hour revision session with your Mother on foreign diplomacy and negotiation tomorrow morning, and then you are free until the afternoon where I will take over to go over some rulers training!" Father declared, "Now, I'm going to assign tasks for everyone else, and, remember, Anora and Agremerre have agreed to provide support as well, so please coordinate with them!" I watched a little in awe as my family took over the logistics of my move. The next hour was spent trying to sort out basic details. Eventually, we all went to bed.

When I woke up the next morning, I found Ana and Charlotte already waiting. They each wore matching pensive looks as they hovered by my closet. "Good morning," I said, sitting up.

"Is it true?" Ana asked, looking at me worriedly, "Are you really leaving Nevremerre?"

"The paper this morning said you were leaving to fix the drought or something," Charlotte chimed in.

"Ah," I replied, "Well, I guess broken down to the barest of essentials, yes, that is true. I leave in just six days to go to Dolma and marry their Crown Prince." Charlotte burst into tears.

"I'm coming with you!" she decided through her tears.

"Me too," announced Ana, "They said they were accepting applications for two servants, and we will apply!"

"I'm touched by the thought, and I would love to have you both with me, but it's not that simple. For starters, Charlotte, in Dolma same sex marriages aren't allowed. Plus, they seem to have some issue with the misgendered that I can't quite understand. I don't want you to have to be in any danger, and I don't want you to have to leave Dame Elise," I continued. "And Ana, your goal is to become this palace's housekeeper, I don't want to ruin your dreams."

"Charlotte, it's okay, we all know you love living in Nera, so it's okay to stay here," Ana soothed a tearful Charlotte in her no nonsense manner. "However, as for me, Princess, I will be applying to be your maid in Dolma, and I am extremely confident in my credentials. I believe I will be picked to tend to you again, whether or not you approve. Besides, there are housekeepers in Dolma too. I'm confident I can work to be a housekeeper there as well. In fact, I have a stronger chance at getting the position as the former maid of the future Queen," she finished defiantly.

I quickly rose out of bed and threw my arms around the two of them. "Thank you both so much, you'll never know how much this means to me," I smiled at them.

"I swear I will cheer you on from here, Princess!" Charlotte exclaimed, "And just send whomever you hire for your hair to me, I will get them into shape in no time at all! They will be able to do all the best styles, and know all the best skin care routines!" I laughed at her exuberance.

"And you will accept my application?" Ana asked, staring me down.

"Absolutely!" I smiled. "Thank you both. I am very grateful to have the two of you in my life."

"Oh, don't say that! I've only just stopped crying!" Charlotte wailed. We all hugged once more before pulling apart once more. I informed them about what the days ahead might look like, and told them how Mama and Mother would be taking over packing my clothes, jewelry, and other essentials for my departure.

"I'll go to them after dropping off my application," Ana nodded. "I have some ideas for the colors and styles we should use in your wardrobe."

"I'll go too," Charlotte chimed in, "I can make sure they don't forget any essential items." Now dressed and with everyone's day decided, we all parted ways to accomplish our separate tasks.

I ate a comfortable breakfast with just my family. Lord Nicholas was blissfully absent for some reason, and Sir Abel had something else to do. Then, I spent two hours frantically scribbling notes as Mother gave me the fastest lecture I'd ever heard. By the end, my hand was cramping and my brain felt incapable of constructing a single human thought. In light of this, I elected to spend the next few hours wandering the garden where no one could ask me to think.

Meandering past an iris strewn flower bed, I found myself stopped by the looming figure of Lord Nicholas. Before I could turn around and sneak off to another area in the garden, he looked at me and smiled. "Good morning, Princess," he said, his voice light and friendly. I eyed him warily before responding back.

"Good morning, Lord Nicholas." My voice was a little curt as I tried to stroll by.

"I've given up my spot for the throne," he said casually. I gaped at him. My mind, already battered by this morning's lecture, took a final blow as I lost any hint of composure and simply stared at him, mouth open and eyes wide. I was probably eerily reminiscent of a dead fish with the blank space that filled my mind; however, Lord Nicholas didn't seem to care. He expounded, "I told the council this morning that I no longer wish to be King. Don't think that means I will be going away, however," he smirked at me. "I've accepted a position as Lord Azcarth's apprentice. He seems to believe that I would make a good noble representative on the King's council. So, I'll still be traveling around the country with the royal family for several years to come. Of course, you'll be gone by then... will you walk with me, Princess?"

It was probably the first time I'd ever really willingly accepted his request, as I closed my mouth, put my eyeballs back inside my head, and took his proffered arm. I let him lead me around the gardens in silence for a while, taking the time to recollect myself before I finally asked, "Why did you change your mind?"

"Well, a lot of reasons, really. For starters, I learned that there are other strong positions of power I can have. Perhaps not the same level of executive control, but still powerful positions nonetheless. I also, as much as I hate to admit it, realized that you were right. When we learned of the drought, I had to acknowledge that the drought was not something I could control," I suddenly remembered our last conversation, or rather the time Lord Nicholas screamed at me in this very garden. "Sir Abel actually helped talk me through it. You see, my plan was just to convince everyone to like me, amass a large fortune and spend it however I pleased, and, every now and then, make sure things were functioning just enough to make it easy for everyone to keep liking me. It was, honestly, a very simple task," Lord Nicholas admitted, shockingly open about the whole thing. "However, as I said before, I could not control the weather. I would not be willing to make the sacrifices and choices that King Edgar, and now you, have made. In the end, people would die. I enjoy wealth, power, and the comfort that they can provide, but I'm not willing to cost people their lives to get it."

"Just their economic security?" I cut in, unimpressed.

"Well now, Princess, nobody said that I was perfect," Lord Nicholas smiled at me. "The truth of the matter, Princess, is that both you and your brothers would likely all make good rulers. You all have flaws, but none of them insurmountable."

"Then why are you so adamant that we weren't fit rulers all those days ago!" I explained.

"Ah, well I was mostly hoping to get a reaction out of you that I could exploit. Didn't work the way I had hoped, but it hardly matters now." I glared at him. "Anyways, I must admit that what really helped were my sessions with Sir Abel. I was not expecting transitioning sessions to be as useful as they are. Someone with his skills would really be an excellent asset, if you could retain his loyalty."

"People are not assets!" I frowned at him, "I can't believe they are even letting you stay with the council and royal family."

Lord Nicholas just laughed, much to my chagrin. "You'll have to take that up with Lord Azcarth," he said.

"I most certainly will," I mumbled.

"Do you remember, Princess, when I asked if you knew the rumors that were spoken about you?" Lord Nicholas said, effectively changing the subject. "Well, you should really hear them now. When I first asked, I really hadn't heard anything bad. The general public consensus is that, if you got the position, you'd be a gentle and wise Queen. No doubt the gentle part would have changed once you had fought in the Open Tournament," he mused, sidetracking himself momentarily. He shook his head briefly before continuing on, "Mostly, the public had determined that any one of the King's children would make a good ruler. That all changed this morning. With the story about your move to Dolma, you have become the talk of all of Nera, and, as the story gets a chance to travel, all of Nevremerre.

The dedicated Princess, who would give up her future for the sake of her people. They've painted you as quite the martyr. Now, we both know that's utter bullshit. You're too damned righteous to ever really be a martyr. You probably see it as a great opportunity to help people and are "very happy" about all of this," he said, with a touch of disgust. I scowled at him. Something in his tone made it incredibly hard to admit he had nailed down my feelings exactly. "The point is," Lord Nicholas moved on, "the public is clamoring for you now. They think you'd be the best Queen for the people of Nevremerre. You have quite the following."

"The story has been out to the public for less than six hours, how could you possibly know that?" I said skeptically.

"Because I keep my ear to the ground," Lord Nicholas said, with a touch of irritation laced into his voice. "Plus, that's what the servants are saying, and a fair few of the knights and nobles, but you and your brothers constantly flip between the support of different nobles. So, their thoughts matter less. The servants, on the other hand, are the best representation of the general public we have in the palace, and you're all they're talking about. I'll go down to the city just in case, but it'll be the same there as well."

"Hmm," I replied noncommittally.

"Don't worry, I'm sure even you will realize the extent of the turbulence you've caused soon enough," Lord Nicholas said with a condescending tone.

"You make it sound like I am going to cause Nevremerre some sort of turmoil," I huffed.

"Excuse me, I believe this will cause great turmoil to my peace of mind! Everywhere I go, I'll have to constantly hear about you," Lord Nicholas exclaimed.

I fought the urge to giggle. I still didn't like the man, but now that he wasn't trying to claim the throne, his presence had become a lot more tolerable. "I don't know, I think hearing about me would do you good. Now, if you'll excuse me, I have lunch with the royal family."

Lord Nicholas smirked and bowed. "Until next time, Princess," he said as I walked away.

The first lunch after Lord Nicholas was removed from the fight for succession was less loud and rambunctious than I had hoped. Al and Azar were in Agremerre, discussing details about my transportation and staff with Anora and the High Judges, so the table was significantly reduced. It was still a nice meal though, as Mother, Mama, and I got to discuss fashion and style. We even forced Ari to join the conversation. Father reminded him that all people should take care of how they look, especially if they want to be King, when he tried to complain. Overall, it was an enjoyable time, and I had high hopes for dinner when Al, Azar, and Nana would join us around the table and we could eat with just our family again.

Chapter 29

The Wisdom of
Those Long Gone

Once we'd finished eating, Father took me up to his office on the third floor. I followed him through his office to a secret door I had never known existed behind his bookcase. "I was surprised by it too," Father said, as he moved through the hidden door. "I'd been to my father's office for years and never even known that there was a secret passageway. It's just for future rulers though, so keep this a secret, my gift."

"Yes, Father," I replied, as we moved down the passageway.

"The day after I became the official Crown Prince, my father took me down to this chamber. He told me what his father told him, which is what his mother told him, which was what her mother told her, and so on. This wisdom has been passed down from generation to generation of Nevremerre rulers, and now I shall tell it to you.

You have been selected to rule a kingdom. You will be given the power to shape hundreds of thousands of lives, but, at the end of the day, you are just one person. You will make mistakes and feel overwhelmed, and, some days, it will be tough to keep your head high. You will also face triumph you've never known and feel joy you'd never known possible. The job you've been hired for has many highs and lows, and it's likely that I will not be there to help guide you through these trials. However, I want you to know, you will never be alone," Father walked a bit faster towards an approaching door. He threw the door open and we entered a large chamber filled with bookcases and a wooden desk and chair sitting right in the center. Up at the top of the room there was a large glass window Illuminating the desk.

"This room," Father continued, as I looked at the room in awe, "contains the private journals of every King and Queen of Nevremerre since King Dormian. Let me show you around! This side of the room contains all the books you can access. All journals have to be rewritten every 100 years, so it's the job of every ruler to make sure all transcriptions are done. I, myself, had to transcribe the journals of Queen Estelle's final years before her abdication and the first half of Queen Magnolia's reign. Along with re-transcribing the previous transcriptions of Queen Tillian, Queen Amara, King Tobin, and a few others," Father said proudly.

"On this side," he continued, "there are all the original journals. Some are quite old, and should only be touched with gloves if you absolutely have to access them, but again, we have workable copies right on the other side. We also have old translations on the top shelves, but you need to use the ladder to access those. The shelves are organized by year, and King Archion in the mid 1200s placed a handy list of each ruler and their dates of rule in the corner there. Each new ruler updates it with the ruler who came before them upon their ascension to the throne.

Right now, you don't have the time to read all of them, so I pulled out a few that may be important to you. This one," he said, moving towards the desk and picking up a journal. "This is King Karl, your great-grandfather's journal about the war with Calvine. He only wrote two journals, this one about the beginning of the war and another about selecting your grandfather as the Crown Prince and the end of the war.

I also think you should read this one," he said, holding up another journal. "Queen Estelle wrote many journals throughout her 42 year reign, but this is her first one. The one she wrote after the council begged her to succeed her father despite having previously removed herself from the line of succession. I think you'll find it very interesting. You can read any other book you'd like however. I'll leave you here until dinner, if you'd like."

I smiled at him, "Thank you Father."

"Anything for you, my gift," Father said as he left the room. I looked around a bit more before settling down to read the first journal father and talked about.

King Karl's messy scribbles filled the pages. Even though it was a more rushed sprawl than I was used to seeing, the writing was still fairly legible. I ran my hand on the page, thinking with a certain amount of reverence that these were the words of my great-grandfather, and just 19 years after penning these words, he died. I was reading the words of someone long dead, and as they told me their story, they'd come alive once more. I began to read.

For twenty years I've sat on this cursed throne, and for 20 years I didn't write any of these Gods-be-damned journals. They are fucking waste of time. Now, of course, in my true hypocritical form, I have frequently used and found wisdom in the other journals. But, writing my own is a chore and I have seven fucking kids to tend to and try and raise. Best of luck to any future leader who has boys, and late apologies to my mother. Of course, I love the damn bastards, but they don't leave much time for writing.

Now, excusing my above rant, I will move on to why I am writing this journal now. Yesterday we declared war with Calvine, and today we declared Houston the Crown Prince. And, I really want to say from the bottom of my heart for all generations to hear: FUCK. FUCK. FUCK. FUCKITY FUCK FUCK FUCK.

FUCK

The kid is eight-fucking-teen. And you know what he said to me today? After he'd been crowned, he came up to me and said, "Thank you, Father. I'm ready to fight for our people. I'm ready to help lead Nevremerre to Victory. I'm grateful for the opportunity to protect this country." Fuck it all!! Fuck it all so damn much. He's just a fucking baby! I wanted to scream at him "No! Just say no, be selfish, don't fight." He's not even legally eligible to fight, and yet, because he's the Crown Prince, he will. And I can't stop him.

The worst part is that a part of me is proud that I'd managed to raise a child to be so brave and so noble, who at 18 is already showing fantastic promise as a future King. He's so strong he doesn't even flinch at the thought of riding into battle with me, and it fills me with pride. That pride rapidly slides into disgust with myself that I'm forcing him to do this. That I'm creating the situation that is causing my son, and so many other sons and daughters, to go to war.

And, yet, there was no better option. We tried negotiation, but were shot down, then Calvine's soldiers started raiding our borders. We tried peace again, the next time they killed and raped people. We then tried to reinforce our borders, and essentially put the knights into a series of mini-battles without the extra support that comes from calling it a war. I can't leave my people out to die. I simply can't, not without doing all I can to protect those who cannot fight and providing the knights and armies with all the support allowed. I'll be damned if I let any other citizen of Nevremerre die without doing everything in my power to save them. So, I have declared war. We will load up on supplies and weaponry, and I will lead my armies, my knights, and my second oldest son into battle.

Harrison also wishes to go to war, but even if he is a year older than Houston, I will not risk any more of my children's lives while they are still under age. If I could prevent it, I damn well wouldn't let Houston go either. I will carry the guilt of sending a child, my child, to war with me for the rest of my life. May the Gods be with him as he fights, and, one day, may his soul forgive me for asking this of him.

Before I finish, I would like to give a very biased review of Calvine. I'm aware that due to the Both Sides of History Act of 1056, future generations will be presented with Calvine's perspective of the war which will likely try to paint themselves in a better light, Nevremerre being the one to officially attack first after all. But, it's important for me to let all who are reading this know that Calvine is full of a bunch of fucking bastards. They are a country of war hungry nobles who had a few tastes of vic-

tory in other places, and now those cocky ass bastards think they can win against us. Well they fucking can't and I will crush them with my shoe.

The journal ended there. I could see why Father had asked me to read it. No doubt it reflected some of his thoughts about me leaving, and it also highlighted the duality of being a ruler. The contradiction between what you want to do and what is best for the country. However, coming from the perspective of the child who had been asked to make a difficult choice, I never blamed my father once for the position I was in. I knew, after all, that this was my decision and my choice, and I also knew it was the best for the people. Even though Houston died one year later, and therefore never got to write a journal, I'm quite sure he felt the same way I did. So, I moved on to Queen Estelle's journal and began reading.

Well, it's finally happened, Father is dead. I am now Queen. It's actually a little underwhelming. I suppose I just assumed that something inside of me would change, that I'd stand up taller, speak with more dignity, or just generally become a more imposing figure, but no such luck. I'm still the same person, but now with a dead Father and a bunch of angry siblings banging at my door wanting to know why I became Queen. Apparently, saying it was because they were all entitled assholes was not a good enough explanation.

Still, I can understand their feelings. They were given no reason to think that the love child of the King and a one-night stand who had already taken herself out of consideration could be brought back in and instated as Queen. I wonder if this will finally teach them that they can't be rude and selfish and just expect that it will fly. After a life half-spent in my mother's little cottage by the sea, and half in the great palace of Nera being bullied by children 10+ years my senior, I can't say I ever really expected to rule all of Nevremerre. I'd never even considered it.

I was so thrilled when I took myself out of succession four years ago. I was finally free of the palace and it's politics. I'd simply be a teacher and stay with my mother longer. Perhaps my error lay in successfully coordinating the relief plan for the bad storm three years back, or when I raised more than enough funds to help rebuild the neighboring town when the fire came rampaging last summer. Although, I'm not sure I could ever consider helping people to be an error. Whether those instances contributed to my current situation or not doesn't really matter, I suppose, as just ten days ago the entire council came knocking at my door begging me to be Queen.

Is it normal to still be wondering if I made the right decision? I know my siblings are predominantly spoiled brats, with the exception of us "love children" that is. But, Kiron is about as smart as a brick, and you couldn't tear Chiriony away from a piano for anything. Cassie is still too young, being only sixteen. I suppose I can see why I was our country's one and only option. What really tipped me over the edge was Father, on his deathbed, begging me to take his place.

Just to be very clear to all those who read this, it was not the dying wish of a man I only saw for half a year that convinced me to take the job. Rather, it was the confidence of a man who was so focused on his job that he neglected everything and everyone else, of someone who, if nothing else, was a great King, who thought that I, too, would be a great leader. Father, who neglected his wife and took several lovers. Father, who ignored his children and allowed them to fight and bully each other in the hopes of gaining his love. Father, who would never do anything to hurt the people of Nevremerre, whose life revolved not around

*us, but our country, believed me to be our best chance for suc-
cess. And, if I get to help the people, how can I say no?*

*I want to help this country stay strong, healthy, and peaceful.
But, I still wonder, will that be enough to keep me happy in
this job? Especially considering the immediate backlash from
the three children of the now Dowager Queen and father. I wonder if I can find comfort and stability in this job, and I wonder if
it will bring me the joy I found teaching children in the cottage
by the sea.*

Queen Estelle's first journal entry had stopped there, but at
the bottom of the page an extra paragraph had been added.

*An addendum: Today I am 67 years old, and today, I am ab-
dicating the throne. Before I left, I wanted to read this, my first
journal, and, having done so, I wish to answer the oh so pressing questions I had at 25. The answer is yes. I have found in my
years as Queen so much more joy than I had ever known possible in caring for this country and the family I have created. And,
to my darling Magnolia who will be taking this title later today, I
know it will bring you the same joy. I send my love to all future
leaders, and especially to those who may have been unwilling at
first. I look forward to new adventures in my retirement in a big
house by the sea (room was required for the children and grand-
children I have accumulated and who are still arriving). May the
Gods bless you all.*

I closed Queen Estelle's journal. Even though she was my
great-great-great-grandmother, I had no idea her childhood
had been so disjointed. Nor that her siblings were in any way
cruel. Queen Estelle was always exalted as one of the greatest
rulers in Nevremerre, her name forever linked with names like
King Dormian, The Founder, King Kazon, The Justice Bringer,

and Queen Amara, The Warrior Queen. Queen Estelle brought an era of unparalleled prosperity, and several of her policies have stayed in place to this day. It was so strange to think that she was once just a 25 year old who wasn't convinced she even wanted to rule. It was all so delightful to see her postscript, especially knowing that she lived 35 years past her abdication, and actually watched her grandson, King Karl, be crowned.

I wondered what my life would look like. 67. Would I fit in in Dolma? Would I come back often to Nevremerre? Would I have a family and grandkids around me? Would all my trials fade away like Queen Estelle's had? I hoped so, but the only way to find out was to live through all the years that came first. I decided that I too, would keep a journal, perhaps I could bring this tradition to Dolma.

I continued to read until Father collected me for dinner, and we excitedly exchanged thoughts on the memories in journeys of our ancestors. At dinner, I received a letter from Murphy, Healer Autumn, and the Matron. I read it happily upon returning to my room. The letter was filled with happy wishes for the future (Healer Autumn), reminders that I could always run away and become a healer (Murphy), and a shockingly lovely review of my character that finished by lamenting that Dolma was getting someone who could have been a "phenomenal Queen of Nevremerre" (the Matron). The letter closed with everyone's contact information, and requests to be invited to the wedding (all). I went to bed feeling happy and loved, having been so cared for by my friends and family and having learned so much. I laid down, holding a bit of excitement at the thought that tomorrow I would know who, beyond Ana and Mateo, would join me as I moved to Dolma. My last thought before I went to sleep was that I'd hoped we'd all get along well.

Chapter 30

The Plan of Lord Azcarth

The next morning I had time off, so I went down to the stables to enjoy a ride on Kolasi before the day really began. Walking back from my ride, I ran into the exact person I'd been meaning to talk to: Lord Azcarth, Nevremerre's noble representative. Lord Azcarth was just a bit older than Father, with black and silver hair and a slight frame. He was always very polite, but he did exude a kind of slippery aura that always made me a little uneasy. However, it was always very clear that he was loyal to my father, so I didn't think about it too much. Looking at it now, I realize that he reminded me of Lord Nicholas in a lot of ways.

"Lord Azcarth," I smiled, walking towards him, "good morning!"

"Good morning, Princess," Lord Azcarth said. "I was told you might have some questions for me. I hope I can answer them to your satisfaction."

"Yes, I do," I frowned at him, "Why did you advocate for Lord Nicholas' addition to the succession, and why did you want him to become your apprentice once he took himself out of the succession?"

"Ah, well you see, Princess, the answer to those questions are one in the same, since my goal from the beginning was to get Lord Nicholas to become my apprentice."

I blinked at him. "That is a very convoluted way to get someone to be your apprentice," I finally decided.

Lord Azcarth laughed. "Forgive me, Princess, but that is a very expected response from you. Let me explain," he said quickly as I opened my mouth again. "As you know, the Nevremerre system is designed to weed out corruption and give the people the best rulers. This system has evolved for millennia to get where we are today. And, while we believe today's system to be the best we've ever had, it is vital that we keep looking for its flaws.

While we have now spent several centuries dealing swiftly and efficiently with corruption, we are very cognizant that there is no cure for the true depth and capacity for human greed. Most of us live our lives hoping to overcome that greed. Our society has been built on morals that tell us that such greed at the expense of others is unconscionable. In reality, the morals we've created are, truthfully, neither good nor bad, and the "sin" of greed is simply just another aspect of human life. Our morals are entirely self-imposed and not a true reflection of nature.

However, if we just let greed and corruption run free, society would collapse, as it has throughout history, although not always instantly and not always in the ways one might expect. The truth is that corruption cannot be sustained forever, so we have to fight it swiftly and efficiently wherever we can find it. Of course, it can be difficult for those who are more honest and straightforward to see what might be exploited. Ideally, one needs people cunning and just a touch selfish, to expose these flaws, but not exploit them. And that is where people like Lord Nicholas come in.

Since the succession rights are technically available to anyone, there have been many attempts over the centuries of other people trying to add themselves to the line of succession. In the late 1000s and early 1100, there was a trend in which hundreds of people tried to add themselves to the succession competition. Many would drop out once they realized how much work was actually required, but there was still quite a sizable candidate pool. However, this trend faded after The Warrior Queen Amara took the throne and the general public realized that the ruler would be expected to fight in wars, no matter age or size.

Ever since then, adding yourself to the succession has become a bit taboo, especially if the Princes and Princesses hold promise as potential leaders. But, each time the succession drew near, there were always a few people who ignored the taboo and tried to add themselves anyways. We now have a thorough vetting process before we agree to a candidate. However, and in every succession since Queen Amara, we've always let one person through that meets a specific set of criteria. Essentially, we are looking for a new and cunning person to try to exploit the system. The council knows of this person, so it's already agreed that they won't become the ruler. However, they are closely monitored to see what loopholes they can find.

In the end, one of two things happen: either they eventually fail and move back to their previous life, or they learn and grow and become loyal to the crown. It also has the added benefit of pushing the actual candidates to work harder. I was the added corruption candidate in your father's day."

"What?" I jumped.

"Oh, yes," Lord Azcarth smiled. "But in the end, I realized that my own goals weren't appropriately fulfilled by the job as King. And, that my plans could hurt a lot of people. Now, I have, really, a much better life. I have a schedule that I design. Access to all the best foods and homes in the country, a great salary, and I get to spend my days spotting corrupt nobles and trying to think of unlawful ways to overthrow the King. And, His Majesty pays me for that!" Lord Azcarth said, looking positively delighted. "I don't even have to do any of the work to actually overthrow him. It's really the ideal job," he sighed, happily. "Lord Nicholas could be a promising replacement for me," Lord Azcarth pushed himself back on topic. "He will still need to be closely monitored, but he at least now realizes the ruling position is not one he could have. I'm excited to see how he progresses.

Now, Princess, I hope you will allow me to give you some advice for your new life in Dolma." I nodded and he continued, "You, Princess, are not very cunning. I don't mean this is an insult, and it doesn't necessarily prevent you from being a good leader. A cunning ruler can go far, but an honest one is easy to follow. His Majesty is not a cunning man, but is a fine King. Before His Majesty, former King Carsien was most definitely a cunning man and a very scary one too, but he was also a great King. The key to each of their success is to have people around them who can make up for what they lack. His Majesty has me and Her Majesty Queen Elenore, and some others to be cunning for him.

When this was still a battle between you and your siblings, one of the things the council was looking for was whether or not you, Prince Azar, or Prince Ari would make any cunning and dependable allies. Prince Al is already cunning, but there are other concerns with his candidacy. We were also watching to see if you, and your brothers could be taken in by unscrupulous characters. Fortunately, you don't have that for a shortcoming. So now we come to my advice for you as the future queen of Dolma. When you choose your staff this afternoon, choose a few cunning people who will be loyal to you. You will need them to help you transition to life in Dolma, and as you rule. And, also, trust your judgments about the people you meet. You, over your brothers, have had an extremely good track record with identifying those you can trust and those you should be wary of, so, even when you are far away, and the cultures and traditions are very different, trust your own initial judgment. It will serve you well.

I believe you will make an excellent Queen, Princess. I would want to wait and see your own thoughts about Dolma, but I would not be opposed to combining our two countries under your rule. Now, if you'll excuse me, Princess, I wish you good health and good mind for the rest of your day." I nodded Lord Azcarth off and took in his words.

Although I personally dislike the idea of being cunning, it was clear to see that cunning was an important trait whenever one looked at a history book. There was no use denying Lord Azcarth's words, I was not cunning. I wasn't even sure where to begin to try to become cunning. It seemed Lord Azcarth was right, I needed to find some cunning people to be on my side. With that in mind, I went towards the large drawing room where Azar, Father, Mateo, Anora, Head Judge Michael, and Miraz had taken it upon themselves to sort through the applications for my delegation.

When I entered the room I was amazed to find six haggard-looking people, each with their own large stack of papers, occasionally throwing papers into a discombobulated pile in the middle of the floor. " What on Earth?" I asked as I moved through the room.

"Avalynn!" Anora exclaimed, "Good, come here and hold little Genevieve for a bit won't you?" I noticed a small bundle in Anora's arms that I'd missed before and moved to hold my god-daughter.

"No fair," Miraz whined, "you won't let any of us hold her."

"That is my daughter and your Princess! No one but me, her godmothers, and her nurses will hold her until she's at least two," Anora responded.

"I'm a good father," Father said, with puppy dog eyes. "I have four children and I've never dropped any of them. I can be trusted!"

"You stole a baby from a boat, Edgar, I won't allow you to try to steal Genevieve," Anora shot back with a raised eyebrow. Azar and I burst out laughing.

"I didn't steal her! She was just there for the taking. We did look for her biological parents!"

I laughed once more as Anora said, "Doesn't matter, there will be no holding of Genevieve unless I say so."

"You still haven't told me what's going on here," I said, as I bounced Genevieve's sleeping form.

"What do you think?" Azar asked, throwing another sheet onto the center pile, "We're going through all your applications."

"There are this many?" I said in shock.

"You've become a bit of a national hero," Mateo said. "Everyone is clamoring for a job to serve you."

"In Agremerre too," Michael chimed in. "It seems you're rather popular." I looked once more at the flood of applications a little taken aback by it all. I aided in their search, mostly by holding Genevieve and making everyone's piles neater, but it still took us the rest of the morning and through lunch to sort out the preliminary round of applications. We then called applicants in for interviews, which took up the better part of the afternoon. We all had dinner together before finally coming up with my official delegation. Other than Mateo and Ana, the easiest choice was my lady-in-waiting. Lady Lucy was the Agremerrian niece of Duchess Amber, and the granddaughter of King Carsien's oldest brother, Prince Harrison. She was wildly clever and had actually been preparing for Agremerre's High Judge exam before she decided she'd rather work for me. She also, I believe, would perfectly fill my gap in cunning.

Next, we hired another Agremerrian, Miri, who, I was told, was not in fact a hairdresser, but a former Agremerrian spy. Father and Anora insisted I needed at least one, and Charlotte could always teach her how to do hair. She did seem nice enough, if a bit quiet, but I suppose there's not much friendly chatter that goes on in an interview. Other than that, I did note that she was quite a bit older than me as her hair was already fully gray. Finally, We hired six new knights. Mateo, Galileo, and Oberon from Father's original delegation were all accepted to go with me. Father and Azar heavily pushed Galileo as the second place champion in the tournament this year. There were several other good reasons for him to be chosen, but I think Father and Azar both breathed easier when he was selected. We also added Sir Leonard, Sir Challa, and Sir Hugo.

It felt strange to have six knights and none of them be female, but then, I suppose everything was going to be strange in Dolma. As everyone exited to inform the selected about tomorrow's lessons, I was left alone with the room full of completed applications. My heart was filled with both love and doubt as I stared at the papers in front of me. On the one hand, I was honored by the flow of love and support that was so obvious in the applications. On the other hand, I couldn't get Mateo's comment about being a "national hero", Michael's belief that I was a "hero" in Agremerre as well, and Lord Nicholas' thoughts regarding my "supporters" throughout the kingdom out of my head. I didn't feel like a hero. I mean, honestly, all I was doing was moving and getting married. I even was becoming a Crown Princess in the process. I hardly thought of myself as worthy of such praise.

"Quite the array of supporters you've amassed here, Princess," the rolling baritone of Sir Abel washed over me.

"I'm not sure if I deserve it," I responded, still looking at the pile.

"It doesn't matter if you deserve it," Abel responded, startling me as I gazed into his dark eyes. "This was the only possible response, really. You are already a beloved Princess, and now, from their point of view, you're sacrificing your life and future for them. They won't ever know your reasonings and feelings about this, they will only see one aspect of this decision, which is that you are helping them. The obvious reaction is to support you. There's nothing you can do about it. They simply will turn you into a heroic figure. It's completely out of your control."

"You say the weirdest things to make me feel better," I said.

"I say the truth," Abel shrugged, "Sometimes it works, sometimes it doesn't. I came in here to inform you of a development in your delegation."

"Oh?" I responded curiously, "What's that?"

"With your presence in Dolma, it has been decided that Nevremerre should have an ambassador there. After speaking with the council today, and confirming it with His Majesty just now, it has been decided that I will be that Ambassador."

"You?" I said, startled.

"Yes. I have a plethora of diplomatic skills. As a spiritual transitioner, we are trained to read people, and understand their thoughts and emotions. We can even predict their behaviors in some cases. These are useful tools as a diplomat and making new deals, and as an ambassador for reporting back possible attacks on Nevremerre. I hope I can also serve you as well, while I am there, Princess," Abel bowed.

"I know you aren't going for me, but thank you. Thank you so much," I said, going up to him and throwing my arms around him.

"On the contrary, Avalynn, you are most certainly a factor in my decision," Abel responded, hugging me back. "Well then, I will see you tomorrow as we learn the manners of Dolma."

Chapter 31

The End of The Beginning

So that was it. The next few days were incredibly frantic for everyone in both palaces. My delegation and I spent each day in Agremerre as Anora, one of her diplomats, Dame Zoe, and her historian, Sir Walter, took us over each facet of known Dolmanian manners. It seemed like the Dolmanians had an etiquette rule about everything. The gruelling memorization left little time to get to know more about those who were to accompany me, so I supposed that would have to wait for the journey ahead. All too quickly, my bags were packed, Dolmanian etiquette was slammed into me, and it was time to go.

The last night before my departure there was a big party. Nobles and knights from all over Nevremerre and Agremerre showed up to greet me. I even got to say in-person goodbyes to Murphy, Healer Autumn, and the Matron, although those ended up being rather brief as so many other people were trying to talk to me. I had never before been so popular. By the middle of the event there was an actual line of people waiting to talk to me. I nearly cried with relief when Father announced that the royal family would now be leaving to have a private farewell, and Al came to get me safely away from the flurry of nobles surrounding me.

Hidden away in the dining room, my family had our last family dinner. It was bittersweet, as we told stories that had us bursting with laughter and we also watched everyone try to hold back tears. In the end, our efforts failed, and the whole group of us wound up in tears. I blamed Father as his tears broke first. Although, as usually comes with a good cry, I did feel better afterwards. We then all moved to a drawing room just to chat some more. We talked like that for hours before Mother had to insist that we all get some sleep before tomorrow. However, even she held me in an extra long hug before sending me off to bed. I wondered if I'd actually be able to sleep, leaving tomorrow to go to a brand new country and all. However, the tears and the exhaustion of the past few days must have gotten to me, as soon enough, I was fast asleep.

It was quiet in the morning as Ana and Charlotte got me ready to go. The usual chatter and laughter seemed all but lost today, as Charlotte's occasional sniffles pierce the room. Normally, I would try to soothe her and try to lighten the mood on my own, but today this tense silence seemed to perfectly encapsulate the nerves that ran through my body. It felt like something was eating away at me, while simultaneously an excited energy longed to jump out. My mouth felt a little dry, and I could not bring myself to speak.

All too soon, I found myself in a pair of black riding pants and a short purple tunic, my hair was intricately woven into an updo on the base of my head, and gold jewelry adorned my neck and wrists, completing the Nevremerre colors. I was waiting for my silver crown when Ana pushed me towards the door, "It's time to go now, Princess." I moved to follow her in a bit of a daze, my nerves shooting up to my throat. We moved through the palace halls, my boots making an eerie clicking noise along the way. I found myself wondering if they had ever done that before. It seemed like all the times I've come down these halls ready to ride there had never been a clicking of shoes before. I vaguely wondered what else I might have missed in the palace I'd spent every summer in for 19 years. I gave Charlotte a good-bye hug and exited the palace.

It felt like the whole world was waiting as I walked outside. A large crowd of Nevremerrians and Agremerrians swarmed the exit. I tried to project confidence as I moved forward, and every eye turned towards me. I felt a little relieved when I saw the rest of my delegation at the front. Next to them were two large carriages filled with all of our luggage. There was also an empty carriage that would carry me, Sir Abel, and Ana. Everyone else would either be driving one of the other carriages or riding along next to us. I found Mateo sitting on the top of the second carriage, and he gave me a reassuring nod.

I walked towards the final row of waiting people where my family stood along with Queen Anora, Genevieve, and Carlos. Although Carlos appeared to be mostly hovering over Azar's shoulder as he technically wasn't meant to be in this row. I didn't mind at all though since it would allow me, and probably Mateo, to give him a proper goodbye. I turned towards my parents.

"It has come time to say goodbye to my daughter, the Princess of Nevremerre," Father said to the crowd, in a very official tone of voice, "The countries of Nevremerre and Agremerre thank her for aiding us in this way during our time of need. And, as a father, I am very proud. I will also miss her...

very much," Father's eyes became wet, and he had to blink a few times before he could finish his speech and turned towards me. "You are now to be a Crown Princess, and, according to Nevremerre tradition, that means you will require this," Father pulled out a beautiful golden crown, and I couldn't hold back a gasp of surprise.

The thin crown was made with intricate metal work that caused the crown to look like it was made of three intertwining golden flowers. I identified the flowers as sage, thyme, and salvia. It was beautiful, and I felt tears come into my own eyes as Father placed it ever so gently on the top of my head. "You leave us today to make new memories, and to have adventures of your own. As you leave, always remember this: no matter what you do and where you go, this family will always love you, and you will always be welcome here." Father's arms enveloped me in a warm hug, that made me feel effortlessly safe and loved. When we broke apart, he gave me a cheery smile and I began to move down the line of my family.

"We will see you soon, Ava," Mama trembled, "We will come and visit as often as we can. You simply won't be able to get rid of us." I knew that would never be possible, at least not unless Father abdicated, but the sentiment made me feel warm and full nonetheless.

"Remember all I taught you, and try to learn as much about their culture and history as possible," Mother advised. She then pulled me into a fierce hug and added, "and you must write as often as possible. I wouldn't mind if you wrote five times a day, as long as I can hear from you."

Al came next, as he hugged me goodbye he said this, "It was not long ago when I wanted to protect you from all of this, but, now, even I can see that you are no longer that eleven year old girl, and you never really needed my protection. You are a strong and compassionate person; I'm sure you will do well over there."

In lieu of words, Azar simply tackled me into an all-consuming hug, and refused to let go until Father yelled at him to put me down. "I'll miss you, Ava," he smiled.

Ari stood at the end of the line of immediate family members, and he looked down at me with pleading eyes as I gave his arm a tight squeeze. "Don't worry," I soothed, "You heard Mama, we'll see each other very soon. Dolma it's not so far away that you cannot visit."

"I'll miss you." Ari said bluntly.

"And I you," I replied, fighting tears.

Nana said her goodbyes next, giving me one more bit of wisdom before sending me off. "Whenever things get down and hope seems lost, just look at the sunlight shining through the trees and remember that you can always find joy in the little things until bigger joys come back around." I held onto her extra tightly before backing away.

I quickly pulled Carlos out from behind Azar to give him a hug goodbye. "Look after them, please, all of them," I begged quietly in his ear.

"It would give me no greater pleasure, Princess," he said, squeezing me back.

Finally, there was only one goodbye left, and I turned towards Anora. "I don't know how you will be received upon your arrival in Dolma," repeating the warning she'd given us all last week. "But, I will give you this piece of advice: don't let anyone tell you or treat you like you are anything less than the Crown Princess. If there is any trouble, write to me. I will be able to understand in a way your Father cannot." She gave me an awkward half-hug as she was still holding Genevieve, and I kissed Genevieve's forehead goodbye.

Then I had to leave. I waved toward my family and the ever-present crowd one last time before getting into the carriage where Sir Abel and Ana we're already waiting. Galileo, as the most senior knight, gave the signal, and the party lurched forward. I watched the tear-stained, but smiling faces of my family wave me off as I rolled onwards. As we cleared the palace, I watched as the sun streaked canopy guided me to the future unknown.

Princess Avalynn's journey continues in Book 2, "The Kingdom We Don't". Expected release in Spring 2022!

Acknowledgements

A big thank you to everyone who helped me create this book. The cover was designed by the amazing and talented Jen Leong. Check out more of her incredible art at www.jern-inc.com. The maps and family tree were the work of my wonderful mother, Julie Nelson. Thank you also to my editors, Julie Nelson, Tim Nelson, and Diane Peterson Mathis. Finally, I am immensely grateful to all of you who have read and enjoyed this book. You have helped me bring my dream to life--literally--this story came to me in a dream!

About the Author

Halle Clark grew up in Phoenix, Arizona. She moved to Scotland to attend the University of St. Andrews and graduated in 2020 with a degree in Honours Biology. She currently lives on a 36-acre ranch in Pagosa Springs, Colorado, where she working on her next book, the second book in this Trilogy. She also works part time at a local animal hospital. Her hobbies include reading, playing with her dog, and flying through the air as much as possible.

CPSIA information can be obtained
at www.ICGtesting.com
Printed in the USA
LVHW020320050921
696998LV00011B/1095